Praise for the novels of
MARC CAMERON

Open Carry: An Arliss Cutter Thriller

"A double-barreled blast of action, narrative, and
impossible-to-fake authenticity with a great sense of
place and a terrific protagonist. I'm looking forward
to many more Arliss Cutter thrillers."
—**C. J. Box,**
#1 *New York Times* bestselling author
of *The Disappeared*

"Cameron's books are riveting page-turners."
—**Mark Greaney,**
#1 *New York Times* bestselling author

"Terrific series launch . . . Cameron creates sympathetic
heroes, depraved villains, and nail-biting action. Readers
will eagerly await his next."
—*Publishers Weekly* **(starred review)**

"A terrific new series . . . *Open Carry* reads like a cross
between Lee Child's *The Killing Floor* and
C. J. Box's *Blood Trail* . . . and is perfect for fans
of both. Cameron, a natural storyteller,
brings the Alaskan wilderness to life."
—*The Real Book Spy*

"Cameron effectively combines investigation and
straight-ahead action, and he has fashioned a
compelling, never-give-an-inch hero who will appeal to
Jack Reacher fans. Jump in now for what looks to be a
series that thriller fans will follow closely."
—*Booklist*

MARC CAMERON

STONE CROSS

AN ARLISS CUTTER NOVEL

PINNACLE BOOKS
Kensington Publishing Corp.
www.kensingtonbooks.com

PINNACLE BOOKS are published by

Kensington Publishing Corp.
119 West 40th Street
New York, NY 10018

All Kensington titles, imprints, and distributed lines are available at special quantity discounts for bulk purchases for sales promotions, premiums, fund-raising, educational, or institutional use. Special book excerpts or customized printings can also be created to fit specific needs. For details, write or phone the office of the Kensington sales manager: Kensington Publishing Corp., 119 West 40th Street, New York, NY 10018, attn: Sales Department; phone 1-800-221-2647.

This book is a work of fiction. Names, characters, businesses, organizations, places, events, and incidents either are the product of the author's imagination or are used fictitiously. Any resemblance to actual persons, living or dead, events, or locales is entirely coincidental.

PINNACLE BOOKS and the Pinnacle logo are Reg. U.S. Pat. & TM Off.

First Kensington hardcover printing: April 2020
First Pinnacle printing: December 2020

10 9 8 7 6 5 4 3 2 1

ISBN-13: 978-0-7860-4271-5
ISBN-10: 0-7860-4271-0

Printed in the United States of America

Electronic edition:

ISBN-13: 978-0-7860-4272-2 (e-book)
ISBN-10: 0-7860-4272-9 (e-book)

For
Anchorage Police Department K9 Midas;
his partner, Officer Brandon Otts,
and the K9 teams at APD

"There are three things all wise men fear: the sea in a storm, a night with no moon, and the anger of a gentle man."

—Patrick Rothfuss, *The Wise Man's Fear*

Characters

Arliss Cutter—Supervisory Deputy US Marshal, Alaska
Mim Cutter—Arliss's widowed sister-in-law
Michael Cutter—Arliss's nephew
Matthew Cutter—Arliss's nephew
Constance Cutter—Arliss's niece
Lola Teariki—Deputy US Marshal, Alaska Fugitive Task Force
Nicky Ranucci—heroin addict and Cutter's informant
Sean Blodgett—Deputy US Marshal, Alaska Fugitive Task Force
Nancy Alvarez—Anchorage PD Officer on Alaska Fugitive Task Force
Scott Keen—Judicial Security Inspector, US Marshals Service
Jill Phillips—Chief Deputy US Marshal/AK
J. Anthony Markham—US District Judge, Alaska
Gayle Jackson—Markham's administrative assistant
Brett Grinder—Markham's law clerk
Kenneth Ewing—Native corporation attorney
Tina Paisley—attorney for the village of Stone Cross
Sarah and David Mead—caretakers at Chaga Lodge
Rolf Hagen—Chaga Lodge handyman
Tim Warr—Lieutenant, Alaska State Troopers, Bethel Post
Earl Battles—Alaska State Trooper, pilot

Ned Jasper—Village Public Safety Officer, Stone Cross, AK

Lillian Jasper—Stone Cross school counselor

Daisy Aguthluk—Stone Cross resident

Cecilia Aguthluk—former Stone Cross resident

Bertha "Birdie" Pingayak—principal, Stone Cross K-12 school

Jolene Pingayak—Birdie's teenage daughter

Marlene Swanson—Rolf Hagen's girlfriend in Stone Cross

James Johnny—Marlene's ex-boyfriend

Vitus Paul—Stone Cross K-12 maintenance man

Sascha Green—Jolene Pingayak's biological father

Natalie Beck—Stone Cross special ed teacher

Abe Richards—Stone Cross shop teacher

Aften Brooks—Stone Cross science/math teacher

Bobby Brooks—Stone Cross language arts teacher

Donna Taylor—third grade teacher, substitute

Rick Halcomb—man in the woods

Morgan Kilgore—man in the woods

Prologue

Sarah Mead pictured her husband's face on the log she was about to split. She wasn't the murderous sort, not really, but the spot between his vaporous eyes made the perfect target for her axe.

She was mid-swing when the terrible cry suddenly rose again from across the river. It had plagued her all afternoon, but was louder now, and caused her concentration to wobble. Out of habit, her axe fell true, splitting the upright log perfectly in half. She scanned the dark line of spruce trees across the river, ignoring the newly split pieces of wood as they clattered, marimba-like, to the pile at her feet. The cry made the tiny hairs on her arms stand up. At first, she thought it might be a wolf—low and long, and so incredibly sad.

The sun had just dropped into the muskeg to the west, leaving the gurgle and slurp of the freezing river sounding even colder than it had just moments before. It would be dark soon. Dusk didn't stick around long this time of year. Vapor blossomed around Sarah's oval face with each panting breath, but it was quickly ripped away by the wind. Apart from a few pockets of trees, there was little but open tundra and a few caribou to stop the bitter blow that was kicking up out on the Bering Sea—a scant hundred and fifty miles away.

Her eyes were still glued to the trees; her brain worked in overdrive trying to pinpoint where the mournful sound was coming from. She'd grown up in Alaska, but in all her twenty-seven years had never even seen a wolf except in the Anchorage zoo, not until she came out here. They were big things, wolves, monsters really. No, that wasn't right. If Sarah had learned anything in the month she and her husband had been at the lodge, it was that wolves were neither good nor bad. Internet memes notwithstanding, they did not possess human emotions. They were beautiful and efficient, but they were not monsters any more than they were angels. They were just wolves doing what wolves did without thinking about it. They ran and raised their young and hunted and killed— sometimes even each other.

Sarah told herself she was being stupid for fixating on some phantom noise. She placed a new log on the stump and raised the axe over her head. As if on cue, another baleful moan, thick, almost visible against the gathering darkness, rose from the trees across the churning river. The noise made her flinch, causing the axe to ping off the upright spruce log. She prided herself on her aim, her uniform pieces. It was a Zen-like practice, splitting stove wood—at least it could be without this god-awful sound.

No. That was definitely not a wolf. At this point, a wolf would have been welcome.

Whatever this was, it was less than a hundred yards away. Thankfully, most of that hundred yards was across a river. Silver ice laced the rocks along the shore. The whole thing would soon freeze up completely. It offered Sarah no small measure of calm that for now at least, the water was too cold and deep to cross without a boat.

A tiny drop of moisture hung at the tip of her red nose. She dabbed at it with the forearm of her long sleeve T-shirt, still holding the axe with both hands. It was getting too dark to see anyway. The screened meat-shack was already little more than a black blob just a few dozen yards from the main lodge to her right. Below her, two aluminum skiffs lay tilted on the bank. The river was freezing too fast to leave them tied up in the water for even one more day.

Sarah toed the split wood to one side with her rubber boot, making a path to the main lodge behind her in case she had to run. Running. That was a joke. The stuff that killed you out here only killed you more quickly if you ran. The rational portion of her brain told her she was being foolish, but it was easy to be foolish when you were alone in a place like this.

The last paying fishermen had gone back downriver a week before. That left Sarah, her husband, and the handyman, Rolf Hagen, the only human beings for miles. Nighttime temperatures dipped into the teens now. Each morning there was more ice on the river, inching out farther and farther from the bank. They were losing five minutes of light each day. Winter was still a couple of months away according to the calendar, but the ice on the river said it would blow in any day.

Sarah looked—and some would say acted—older than she was. She was attractive enough, but she habitually slouched broad shoulders to mitigate the fact that at six feet she was two inches taller than her husband. Biggish ears peeked out from beneath a head of mousy hair. Her sophomore year at the University of Alaska in Anchorage, she'd overheard three guys in her sociology class describe her as the most desirable of her female classmates to take to a desert island. She was, they said, not exactly ugly, and would probably be a "solid six" after a few weeks on the island if there was no one else to look at. Her best quality, according to the boys, was her "big bones." She'd prove handy, they said, for chores like chopping wood.

The observation had been asinine and sexist; however, it had been honest, and if Sarah's mother—also a big-boned woman—had taught her anything, it was the value of honesty. And here she was, ready to spend four months alone with her new husband— the only man who'd ever gotten serious with her—but instead of a sunny desert island, she got a winter smack in the middle of the Alaska bush.

And she was chopping wood.

She preferred the axe over the heavier splitting maul, but even swinging the axe raised a sweat, and Sarah had hung her ratty green fleece jacket on a sawhorse while she worked. She'd bought the fleece new from Sportsman's Warehouse off Old Seward Highway in Anchorage just six weeks before. A month of constant contact with fish guts, spruce resin, and river silt made it look like something she'd found in a dumpster. She wore it like a badge of honor.

The moan in the treeline started up again, louder now. That was enough. Sarah sank the blade of her axe into the stump and shrugged on the fleece while she kept one eye across the river.

A load of split wood in her arms, she turned toward the log lodge, almost, but not quite, running up the hill. David was inside, hopefully putting the finishing touches on some caribou stew.

Sarah had made it clear as soon as they signed on as winter caretakers, that there would be no "pink and blue" division of labor. David still mildly bitched about it, even after a month, but tonight was his turn to cook—and anyway, she was better with the axe.

Her arms full, Sarah kicked at the varnished pine door with the toe of her Muck boot, rattling the wooden sign bearing the image of birch—and the name of the lodge, Chaga, after the medicinal fungus that grew on the nearby trees.

The door swung open to reveal her husband of seven months wearing a pair of running shorts and a T-shirt. A blast of warm air rolled out around him, hitting her in the face. All the lights were off and he was silhouetted against the fire in the open woodstove, a flashlight shining up under his chin like a schoolboy telling a ghost story.

"Bwhahahaha!"

She glared at him. "David, please move. I'm about to drop this on your feet."

"Bwahahahah," he said again, flashlight casting a ghoulish shadow over his red beard. "The Hairy Man comes from across the river!"

The Hairy Man was a local bigfoot creature Yup'ik Natives in western Alaska apparently saw all over the place. Even the pilot who flew gear and mail out to the lodge—an otherwise rational human being—claimed to have observed the creature from the air many times.

David craned an ear toward the river. "Arulataq! He Who Makes a Bellowing Sound!"

"You need to shut up."

"I heard some hunters from Stone Cross spotted one three miles upriver just last week." Firelight gave more depth to his beard, making it seem longer and fuller than it was. His green eyes sparkled, full of mischief—and a hint of cruelty. Sarah's mother had warned her about that look, but she'd never noticed until after they were married.

"I'm telling you, David." Sarah let the armload of wood clatter to the tile floor beside the stove. "If you ever want to see me naked again . . ."

David flipped on the living room lights immediately at that and lowered the flashlight. He gave a nonchalant shrug. "It was probably just the wind."

"Probably," she said, hands to the fire, soaking up the heat. "It sounds just awful though."

"Could be a brown bear," David said, "going for the caribou shoulder in the meat shed. Whatever it was, you should stick close to me tonight."

The idea of marauding grizzly bears didn't calm Sarah much more than a lurking Hairy Man.

She glared at David, seized with a sudden thought.

"What caribou shoulder? All the meat I know of is in the freezer. Since when do we have caribou in the shed?"

"Bobby stopped by this afternoon on his way back downriver." This was a gut-punch. "Where was I?"

David shrugged. "Beats me . . ."

Sarah hit him in the shoulder. "Was Aften with him?"

Bobby and Aften Brooks were from outside Chicago. They taught high school in Stone Cross, a Yup'ik village eight miles downriver. Eight miles might as well have been fifty out here on the marshy tundra, so they didn't get together often. Still, Aften was about Sarah's age and was the closest thing she had to a friend for five hundred miles.

A mixture of anger and despair clogged her throat. "I can't . . . I can't believe you didn't tell me."

"Relax," David scoffed. That spark of cruelty flickered in his eyes again. "It was just Bobby and one of his teacher buddies. They only stayed a minute. Bobby left us a fresh shoulder and I gave him some salmon."

Sarah shot a look at her husband as she picked up the poker from beside the stove, wondering how deep into the winter it would be before she smashed him in the face with it. For now she used it to stir the coals, making room for a couple more pieces of spruce. Resin popped like gunshots. Flames curled out the open door, throwing more light on the varnished log walls. But more light brought more shadows.

Another croaking moan pulled David's attention to the large picture window that faced the river. His own scary stories about bigfoot and bears had gotten the better of him. He sat back on the overstuffed couch in the center of the great room.

"It really is just the wind, you know," he said, trying to convince himself. "Branches rubbing together."

Sarah sank into the cushions beside him, still holding the iron poker. The couch was old and soft, but in relatively good shape as far as bush furniture went. There were no roads here, so everything had to be brought in by boat or aircraft, which meant things got used until they were completely worn out. This couch smelled just a little bit like old fishing gear, which provided the lodge with good ambience.

Sitting there on the fishy-smelling couch, she leaned back, letting her head fall sideways as she gave David a halfhearted smile. He was handsome enough, in a vaporous way, but no one would have described him as solid. Sarah's mother said he was either conniving or vapid, depending on her mood. Sarah's older brother called him a "popped-collar Thad" and said he looked like he should be back East at a prep school instead of living in Chugiak, Alaska.

When Sarah had let it slip that she and David got a gig managing a remote lodge in the Alaska bush for the winter, her mother had mistakenly thought she was asking permission. They'd fought, the way they always did, sullenly. There was no yelling, not even a raised voice. Sarah's mother was an expert at flaying skin with quiet words. Looking back, the only reason she'd married David at all was because her mother had been against it.

Another moan came in on a gust of wind, this one lower, a plaintive croaking that rattled the windows.

Sarah shot to her feet and clomped quickly across the room. She was still in her Muck boots—verboten when clients were there—but she'd clean up the bits of mud in the morning. She double-checked the dead bolt on the front door—as if that little piece of metal would stop anything. There were just too many other ways inside. The main room was not very big as lodges went, just over twenty feet square, but it was high, with floor-to-ceiling windows that made her feel cold and exposed. No one had to defeat a lock. There were a million rocks along the river to smash through the glass. David had joked when they got there that at least she'd hear whatever it was that killed her. She'd nearly strangled him then. She returned to her spot in front of the fire, staring into the flames, trying to settle her thoughts, defiantly turning her back to the windows and her husband.

David reached out with the toe of his slipper and touched the back of her thigh, causing her to jump.

"Sorry," he said. "How about we have a shower? Then I can paint your nails for you."

His customary glibness had returned.

She looked over her shoulder at him, incredulous. "Do you want a girl who splits firewood and caulks logs or one who dolls herself up with nail polish? 'Cause I don't see how you can have both for the next couple of months."

"Jeez," David said, lips pooched out like he was wounded. "I'm just saying you don't have to let yourself go because we're living in the bush."

"Keep it up," Sarah said. "That's the way to talk me into the shower."

"Really?"

She scoffed. "I'm not about to take my clothes off so I can be murdered with soap in my eyes—not with that awful noise out there."

"I'll be in the shower with you," David said, raising his eyebrows up and down the way he did when he wanted sex. He was pretty much a giant human gland, so his eyebrows were moving all the time.

She ignored the suggestion and stared into the fire, trying not to imagine four months of this.

"You should have told me when Bobby stopped by."

His dismissive chuckle galled her enough to chase away some of the chill.

"I'm sorry," he said, not meaning it at all. He patted the couch cushion beside him. "At least sit—"

Every light in and around the lodge went out at the same time, leaving them bathed in the orange glow of the fire—and the shadows. Lots of shadows. The ever-present hum of the generator was gone. They turned it off every night to save on fuel, but the lights ran on backup batteries. They should have stayed on for a while. Voles or squirrels must have gotten into the wiring.

The hissing sound of the river seemed louder now, closer, more invasive. David didn't appear to notice. He slumped in defeat, slowly beating the back of his head against the couch. No generator, no shower—even if he by some miracle managed to convince Sarah it wasn't a stupid idea.

The sudden blast of a car horn outside caused Sarah to jump.

David bolted to his feet.

The racket of Rolf's makeshift alarm was grossly out of place against the sounds of the wilderness. The handyman had rigged the contraption using a boat battery, weighted milk jugs, and fishing line to warn him if bears tried to break into the meat shed.

"Hmmm." David stepped into a pair of insulated Xtratuf rubber boots, the toe of each decorated with a smiley face drawn on with a Sharpie. He threw a wool jacket over his shoulders before scooping up the rifle beside the front door. Sarah didn't know what was more ridiculous: the sight of David in his shorts and calf-high rubber boots, or the sight of him holding a gun. It was astounding that she'd not noticed what a child he was before she'd married him. He'd grown up in Alaska, but as far as she knew, he'd never shot a gun until they came to Chaga.

The noise of the horn was deafening, but at least it obscured the moan across the river.

David opened the door and peeked out, aiming his rifle downhill toward the meat shed. "Maybe it really is bears. You wait here and I'll go check."

"Not a chance." Sarah grabbed the shotgun from the corner by the door. It was only loaded with birdshot, but was better than her fingernails—which were chewed down to the quick anyway. "I'm coming with you."

He nodded. "Probably a good idea." "Don't shoot Rolf," she said.

"Another good idea," David said, dripping with condescension.

There was no moon. The wind blew harder now, coming off the freezing river and adding a sinister layer to the darkness. Lengths of split spruce reflected like bleached bones in the harsh beam of David's headlamp as he took tentative, creeping steps down the hill. Sarah stayed close behind him, playing her flashlight back and forth. She carried the shotgun down by her waist, her hand wrapped around the action. Rolf was out there somewhere, and it was beyond dangerous to go aiming into the darkness without knowing where he was—even if there were bears.

The meat shed was a relatively flimsy affair, its screened sides held in place with scrap two-by-fours and weathered plywood. It did little to protect meat from bears, but that wasn't the point. The shed was meant to allow air to flow freely around hanging meat while keeping flies at bay.

David flipped the toggle switch to turn off the alarm and then lowered the rifle.

"Good," he said. "No bears."

Sarah frowned, though David didn't see it in the dark. "Isn't there supposed to be a caribou shoulder in there?"

"Son of a bitch!" David stomped a rubber boot, making a dull thump on the frozen ground. "Rolf must have taken it for himself."

"An entire shoulder?" Sarah wasn't buying it. "Why would he do that?"

"Beats the hell outta me," David said. "I think he's been

out here by himself so many years he's lost it. Why do you think they hired us?"

Sarah moved her light across the concrete floor, catching her breath at what she saw.

David gave a low whistle. "Well, that's creepy as hell."

A perfect, circular design about a foot in diameter, like a maze or a miniature crop circle, had been drawn in blood on the concrete.

Sarah forced herself not to stare too long, looking up to make sure that whoever had drawn the strange pattern and stolen their meat wasn't lurking anywhere nearby.

"Almost looks like that Aztec calendar," she said. "Or some kind of code."

"I guess." David gave a grim chuckle and then kicked an empty plastic R&R whiskey bottle that was just inside the door. "It's code for *Rolf's drunk again and trying to screw with our heads.*"

Sarah relaxed a notch at the simple explanation. They'd been warned that Rolf liked to tip a few back now and then after the guests had gone—and even when they hadn't. It was weird that he'd taken the caribou shoulder, but hey, guys did a lot of odd things in the name of practical jokes.

"You go start the generator," David said. "I'm going to kick the shit out of Rolf." He obviously didn't realize how stupid that sounded with his bony legs sticking out of gym shorts, and rubber boots with smiley faces on the toes. Rolf Hagen was built like a Viking.

Sarah stopped cold, pointing her flashlight at the rusted tin generator shed. Even following her brainless husband was preferable to going out there by herself. "I . . . I don't think we need the generator tonight."

"I want a shower," David said. "Even if you are gonna

abandon me in my time of need. Just start the damned generator."

He marched into the night before Sarah could argue.

Sarah sniffed, shining the light over the frozen mud. She'd walked the section of land between the river and the lodge hundreds of times over the last few weeks but there always seemed to be some new rock or ice clod to send her sprawling. The cold made her nose run. She started to wipe it with the wrist of her fleece but stopped, chuckling to herself despite her fear. She'd heard one of the elders in Stone Cross joke that he and his friends had been called The Silver Sleeve Gang when they were children, because of all the frozen snot on their parkas.

The river hissed in the darkness to her left. For the time being, the current was stronger than the cold, but that would soon change, probably overnight. Even now, she could hear the telltale gurgle of air bubbles trapped under newly formed ice. The wind lulled, leaving the trees beyond the far bank strangely silent. Sarah picked up her pace, wanting to get back to the lodge before the awful moan started again.

The interior of the shed smelled of diesel fuel and grease. Spare parts and tools overflowed the wooden shelves along both side walls. The engine had only been out for a few minutes and was still warm. Sarah checked the fuel, made sure the switch that controlled power to the lodge was turned to the off position, before turning the ignition key. The engine sputtered, coughed like it was going to start, and then fell silent. She tried again with the same result—one-handed because she didn't want to give up the shotgun. A gust of wind popped the tin siding, making her jump. She turned the key to the off position and stepped back.

"Screw this," she whispered, already moving to the door. "He doesn't need a shower that bad."

She hustled back up the hill toward the lodge, stumbling twice on the frozen mud, cursing, but catching herself before she rammed the shotgun into the dirt. She expected David to step out of the darkness at any moment, berating her for not trying hard enough to get the generator started. The thought galled her, and she found herself looking forward to the confrontation. She'd tell him what he could do with his stupid shower, and this lonely shithole of a lodge for that matter.

The beam of a headlamp flashed around the corner. Spoiling for a fight, she turned and strode toward the light. It would feel good to get some things off her chest. For one thing, David had better never forget to tell her when company came by again.

The sudden boom of a rifle carried through the cold air. The sound was so sudden, so out of place, that it stopped her in her tracks as surely as if she'd been the one to get shot.

The light still came from around the corner of the lodge. David must have seen a bear.

"Hey!" she said. "Where did you go? David! Where are you?" Maybe it was Rolf.

She kept walking, madder than scared now. Shooting into the darkness was dangerous. She'd almost reached the steps when she saw it. Someone was sprawled out on the ground around the corner with one stockinged foot visible around the wall.

"David!" she screamed.

The horrible moan picked up again across the river, closer now.

A scuff in the gravel behind her sent a shudder down her back. Her legs were heavy, posts set in the frozen mud. But she still had the shotgun. "David!" she said again, more of a squeak this time, through clenched teeth.

Before she could turn, something heavy slammed into the side of her neck. She stumbled forward, sinking to her knees. The shotgun slipped from her grasp. She tried to call David, but could manage nothing more than a pitiful croak.

A second blow sent her reeling, this one to the back of her head. The night closed in around her, and the moan across the river faded away.

DAY ONE

Chapter 1

Anchorage, Alaska

In addition to being a heroin addict, Nicky Ranucci was also an extremely talented chef. Unfortunately, the thirty-year-old junkie could never remember to turn off the stove, and his mother's four-plex burned down around what was probably the best bucatini carbonara anyone in Alaska would have ever tasted.

Worse than that, Ranucci found himself in jail and in desperate need of a fix—which meant he ended up in the back seat of a government SUV with tinted windows, sitting next to a mountain of a deputy US marshal who frowned like someone had just fed him a spider.

Fortunately for Ranucci, he had something to trade. And it was good stuff too. With any luck, it would be enough to get him out. Feeding a six-hundred-dollar-a-week heroin habit put Ranucci in constant contact with the worst of humanity, the kind of dudes who prayed to their patron saint one minute, then preyed on some hooker's addiction the next. Ranucci was a small fry, a user. The cops wanted the big fish and he intended to give them one in trade for his freedom. In this case, the big fish was Twig Ripley, a dealer and leg-breaker who was wanted for selling black tar heroin in Nevada. Lucky for Ranucci, Twig had burned every bridge he had from Vegas to Northern Cali and had come to hide out with his cousin Sam, who owned a used-car lot in Anchorage.

The lady marshal behind the steering wheel drove past a sign that said HONEST SAM'S HONEST CARS. She was hot, if a little scary looking. Hawaiian or something like that.

Ranucci's gut churned. Snitching could get him killed. Someday. But he had to think about the here and now, the shit that was staring him dead in the eye at this very moment. Turning rat was better than the alternative. *Getting sick*. That's what they called it. What a joke. *Sick* was nothing compared to coming off heroin. *Sick* was puking up your lunch. Withdrawal was having your skull opened with a chisel while someone scraped out your brain with a spoon. Overdosing was what killed you, and they had Narcan for that. Getting clean sure as hell felt like dying. The jail doc had given him methadone, but not nearly enough, and it just made him thirsty.

People kept telling Ranucci he was lucky to be alive. But he didn't feel lucky.

He'd escaped the fire with the clothes on his back and a Crown Royal bag that contained a burned spoon, a well-used insulin syringe with a bent needle, and a gram of black tar. None of the junkies he knew ever had any luck, and the kit had fallen out of his shirt when the firefighters were helping him to safety. Some cop, who should have been minding his own business on the fire perimeter, saw the whole thing. Everyone knew the purple whiskey bags were the worst possible place to stash drug paraphernalia, but they were just so damned convenient. Nicky's mom had never used anything stronger than aspirin, but she did love her Crown Royal and had collected enough of the bags over the years to make a couple of quilts, a Christmas-tree skirt, and a big curtain for the missing door to her spare bedroom—all of which Nicky had just torched along with the carbonara.

Now, a day after the fire, he found himself handcuffed in the back seat of a Ford Expedition dying of thirst—an aftereffect of the damned methadone. The big, blond deputy sat in the back seat too, hands folded quietly in his lap. Gray clouds hung low over the squat, earth-tone buildings, spitting rain on midtown Anchorage. The side streets off Arctic Avenue were paved—contrary to what people in the lower forty-eight believed about Alaska roads—but a layer of gravel from last year's winter maintenance caused the tires to crackle and pop as the SUV rolled slowly south. Ranucci wished the pretty Polynesian lady in the driver's seat would speed up. The dark Expedition was obvious enough. Rolling slowly through this kind of neighborhood left no doubt in anybody's mind that this cop car was hunting.

Ranucci strained against the metal chain that secured the handcuffs to his waist. He pushed the bologna sandwich toward his mouth with the tips of his fingers, craning his neck down in an effort to reach it. This jailhouse lunch was a far cry from bucatini carbonara, but it was food, and anyway, it was nice to eat it somewhere that didn't smell like farts. The marshals would probably have him out past evening chow too—which was okay. The jail would just hold another sandwich for him if he missed whatever slop they happened to be serving that night.

The big marshal looked over at him across the back

seat, sun-bleached hair mussed like a surfer who'd been chillin' on the beach. His name was Cutter, and if his stony expression held anything, it was the remnants of a disappointed sigh, like when you let your grandma know college wasn't in your cards—or told your mom that you'd just burned down her house. Deputy Cutter said nothing, but his disgust was apparent in his narrowed eyes.

Nobody liked a snitch, not even the cops.

Alaska state court judges were notoriously soft with their conditions of release, but Ranucci's record was "deep, wide, and continuous" enough that he didn't qualify to bond out on his own recognizance. That was kind of a joke anyway: nobody but a judge was ignorant enough to believe that a tweaker who'd rip off his own mother for a score could be trusted to show up for breakfast, let alone a court appearance. In the end, the judge had set a five-hundred-dollar cash bond. It was low enough to elicit an eye roll from the arresting officer, but, considering the fact that the forty-three dollars Ranucci did have went up in flames with his mother's Crown Royal curtains, bond may as well have been set at a million. He'd been forced to turn to the only coin he had to trade when it came to dealing with "the man." It was good information, the stuff he was offering about Twig, but Deputy Cutter didn't seem all that happy to get it. Maybe he just wasn't a happy guy. Ranucci didn't care, so long as they let him out once he'd cooperated.

The muscle under his right eye began to twitch. He rattled the restraints, softly; some cops took it real personal when you made noise with the chains.

"Any chance I get you to take these cuffs off so I can get a drink?" He shrugged, but it came off as a sort of spastic twitch. "Seeing as I'm helping and all. That jungle juice they have me take at the jail gives me a powerful thirst. Know what I mean?"

The lady marshal behind the wheel glanced in the rearview mirror, catching his eye. Ranucci had heard the others call her Lola. She wore her black hair pulled back in a tight bun, which made her look a little stark for Ranucci's taste. She couldn't be over twenty-five, and even in his present circumstances, he couldn't help but imagine her shaking out the bun and letting her hair down. *Nicky, sweetie, how about you and me . . .*

"Jungle juice?" she asked. "Methadone," the big marshal grunted.

The pretty Polynesian nodded slowly, adding another term to her lexicon of street slang, and returned her focus to the wet street.

Ranucci set the sandwich in his lap, exchanging it for a paper cup and straw he held between his knees. He'd already drained it twice.

Cutter poured him some more water from a plastic bottle. Nicky drank it all immediately. The water gave him a little courage.

"Ma'am," he said, earning himself a side-eye from the big deputy beside him.

Deputy Lola looked in the rearview mirror. "Yes?"

"Can I ask what you are?"

Her eyes were stones in the mirror, unreadable. "What I am? I'm a deputy US marshal."

"No," Nicky said. "I mean, I was just wondering if you were Samoan or Hawaiian or what."

She made a buzzer noise. "Wrong," she said. "None of the above. Cook Island Maori."

"Maori," Nicky said, giving a little nod like he understood, though he did not. Then it dawned on him. "Like the New Zealand guys with those scary tattoos, who do that dance."

"Very good," Deputy Lola said.

"I read they were savages until the eighteen hundreds, when the missionaries came."

"Savages?" Lola chuckled.

"That's what I read," Nicky said. "I read they were cannibals."

"You know," Deputy Lola said, staring at him in the rearview mirror. "Those are my people you're talking about. I'm one of those savages."

Nicky gave a nervous chuckle. "But you're not a cannibal."

Deputy Lola's eyes grew wide as saucers in the mirror, showing their whites. At the same time, she drew her lips back in a horrifying grimace that nearly made him piss his pants.

"I could be," she said.

Ranucci looked away, then gave the chains another rattle.

"How about it, Marshal? What do you say about the cuffs?"

Cutter looked him in the eye long enough to make him uncomfortable—which didn't take very long—and then gave an almost imperceptible shake of his head, less than Mount Rushmore moved in the wind. "You're doin' great."

Lola spoke over her shoulder again. "Sure you don't want a burger?"

Yeah, she was hot all right. She looked like she could kick his ass, but it would almost be worth it for the physical contact . . .

Deputy Lola snapped her fingers to bring him out of his stupor. "A Big Mac or something? Jailhouse bologna can't be very tasty."

"I'm good." Ranucci used the shoulder of his tan scrubs to wipe mustard off the corner of his mouth. "Guys in my cellblock would smell it on my breath and beat my ass. Snitches get stitches. Know what I mean? They'd figure I did something to earn the reward."

Ranucci's mouth watered at the idea of an actual hamburger.

He closed his eyes and tried not to imagine food beyond what he got in Cook Inlet Pretrial. Life inside was hard enough for a wigged-out junkie. It would be impossible for a snitch with a burger on his breath. He groaned, and craned his neck again to reach the last of his sandwich, since he wasn't about to get any help with the chains.

Deputy Cutter was obviously the boss, but for some reason the big guy had opted to sit in the back of the SUV with the prisoner and let the pretty Hawaiian drive. Maybe the two of them had something going. Ranucci had enough experience with cops to know that the senior guy rarely took a seat next to a junkie. Hell, Nicky Ranucci wouldn't have sat next to himself if he could have avoided it. And there was the whole partner thing, friends, confidants, badges with benefits . . . He'd heard about the PD's *no booty on duty* policy. Policies like that didn't happen without a reason.

Deputy Lola shrugged, working something out in that beautiful head of hers as she made the block.

"So," she said, "Twig's cousin owns that car lot?"

"As I understand it," Ranucci said. "They're not close or anything. Fact is, Twig don't trust him. You know—"

The big guy cut him off. "Does Sam deal heroin?"

Ranucci chuckled. "Nah. He just has the poor luck to be related to an asshole like Twig. I never even saw the guy until a couple of days ago. Twig was trying to score some black tar from my dealer for resale, earn a little money to live on. Know what I mean? My dealer thought he might be a cop, so we followed him to Sam's . . . you know, to establish his bona fides."

Cutter raised an eyebrow. "And they trust you enough to let you come along?"

"I needed a ride to midtown," Ranucci said. "APD put my Nissan in car jail after my last DUI. They get you every which way. Know what I mean?"

Lola slowed, swerving around one of Anchorage's numerous car-eating potholes. "You sure Twig's still with him?"

"I think so," Nicky said, forehead knitting in concern that his information might not buy his freedom. "He was before I got arrested. Twig makes sure they're attached at the hip so Sam don't rat him out. You find one, you find the other, but you better do it quick. My dealer says Sam's wife wants Twig gone, so he'll be moving on any day now."

"Tell me more about Sam," Cutter said.

"Twig is big, but Sam's bigger. Know what I mean?"

"You mean fat?" Lola said.

"Kind of," Nicky said. "Sure, Sam's got some weight on him, but he's got the muscle to carry it around. He seems harmless enough. Twig, on the other hand, I once saw him bite the head off a guy's pet lizard. For the sport of it. Know what I mean?"

"That's stuffed up," Lola said under her breath. There

was a hint of Kiwi there, which made Ranucci catch his breath a little, even with the scary faces she made.

She took a painfully slow right off Arctic beside the car lot. "Looks like the shop is locked up tight," she said. There were a half dozen cars on the lot, dusty, rained on, unkempt, like all the other cars in Anchorage at this snotty time of the year. "Maybe this place is just a front. You know, money laundering or something."

Ranucci wolfed down the last of his sandwich.

The big deputy's phone buzzed. He checked it, then looked out the window at the dealership. At length, he raised a handheld radio, keeping it low enough that casual passersby couldn't see it from the street.

"Hello, Sean."

The radio broke squelch. "Go ahead, boss."

"That hearing in front of Judge Markham is still going strong."

"I just saw," the other deputy said.

Cutter spoke again. "We're taking our guest back to the courthouse so he can catch the late jail run. You two keep an eye on this place while we're gone."

"Copy."

Ranucci began to bounce in his seat, twitching at the prospect of going back into lockup. His words came out whinier than he'd intended. "Hold up, now . . . I thought we had an arrangement."

"We do," Cutter said. "I'll call your probation officer and tell her you helped us as soon as we get Twig in cuffs."

"What if you don't?" Ranucci felt tears welling up at the prospect of spending another night in lockup. "I did my part by showing you where Sam works."

"That you did," Cutter said. "If things pan out, you could get out by tonight."

"Tonight?" Nicky nodded. "Tonight would be good."

Cutter poured him another cupful of water, which he sucked down immediately.

"But things have to pan out," Cutter said. "Know what I mean?"

Chapter 2

Along with a Colt Python revolver engraved with the seal of the Florida Marine Patrol, Supervisory Deputy US Marshal Arliss Cutter inherited his grandfather's natural aversion to smiling. Arliss had not been able to say "grandpa" when he was a boy, and had instead called his grandfather "Grumpy." The name so fit the elder Cutter's personality that it stuck at once. He became "Grumpy" to everyone who knew him, friend and foe alike—and he had plenty of each. Neither Arliss nor his grandfather seemed to be in possession of the facial muscles that allowed normal people to grin without looking slightly dyspeptic. Arliss would have inherited the name as well, but his older brother, Ethan, had rightly observed that though there were two grumpy Cutters, there could only be one Grumpy Cutter.

Arliss's grandmother died before he was born; judging from the photo albums, she was one of the few people on earth who could make Grumpy smile. Everyone who knew her described Nana Cutter as a patient Christian woman who practiced what she preached, and gently chastised her husband for being so judgmental in the way he went about his law enforcement duties. Grumpy often told stories about his bride, as he called her, when he had the boys out on his boat. Hate the sin, love the sinner was her motto. Can't argue with the Good Book, Grumpy would say. Damnedest thing, though. I put the sin in jail, the sinner always hitches a ride.

Cutter smiled inside at the thought, but his face remained passive.

It was completely dark by the time they dropped Nicholas Ranucci at the Marshals cellblock in the James M. Fitzgerald US Courthouse and Federal Building, and returned to Honest Sam's Honest Cars off Arctic Avenue. Cutter was in the front seat now. His partner on the Alaska Fugitive Task Force, Lola Teariki—Fontaine until her recent divorce—remained at the wheel. Her father was Maori and had grown up in the Cook Islands in the South Pacific near Tahiti and Fiji and a whole load of other places Cutter wanted to visit someday. Lola's mother, a handsome woman of Japanese heritage, had met Mr. Teariki when she'd stopped in Rarotonga on her way to spend a gap year tramping around New Zealand. She made it no farther, instead staying in the mysteriously beautiful Cooks long enough to get Lola's father to fall in love with her so she could lure him back to California. As it turned out, his mother was originally from Nebraska, so immigration wasn't a problem. Lola spent nearly all of her summers growing up on her father's island—Raro, they called it. They spoke English there, with a beautiful Kiwi accent that had, more or less, rubbed off on Lola over the years. She used phrases like "right as," meaning right as rain or good to go, "yis" instead of yes, and referred to bad situations as "stuffed up" instead of more colorful words. Although Cutter never admitted it, the accent made him enjoy hearing Deputy Lola speak—most of the time.

Her cell phone sat on the center console. Deputy Alfredo

Hernandez from the District of Nevada was on speaker. He and Lola had gone through Basic at the US Marshals Academy at the Federal Law Enforcement Training Center in Brunswick, Georgia. Hernandez seemed particularly interested that Lola was now Teariki and not Fontaine, as he'd known her in training. Cutter sensed he might have a little crush on his former classmate. After going through the obligatory pleasantries of people who'd sweated through the rope runs and other hellish tortures the training cadre dreamed up for five long months, they got down to the business of discussing Twig Ripley.

"Okay, Smurf," Lola said. "Tell me what you got on this guy."

Cutter had no idea what had earned Hernandez the nickname of Smurf and resolved not to ask—though he was certain Lola would tell him anyway milliseconds after she ended the call.

"I been looking for Twig Ripley for nearly a year," Smurf Hernandez said. "This lead of yours, you think it's solid?"

"We've got some info on his cousin," Lola said. "But our informant says your guy will be on the move anytime now."

She rolled to a stop along the grimy curb across the street from a municipal park, half a block farther away from Honest Sam's. Idling in front of a park didn't draw quite as much attention as sitting at a car lot.

Cutter spoke next. "Have you dealt with Twig personally?"

"I've arrested him twice," Hernandez said. "Had him in court a half dozen times or more."

"He ever fight?" Cutter asked. "Cause you problems?"

"No and no," Hernandez said. "He's got crazy eyes

though. Always looks like he's a split second away from going apeshit."

Rain spattered on the windshield, falling harder by the moment. A sudden wind buffeted the SUV, driving the downpour and making it seem as if they were in a car wash.

"How about weapons?" Lola asked.

"No again," Hernandez said. "Like I said, he's never fought me, or any cop as far as I know, but he's kicked the crap outta assorted baby mamas. Las Vegas Metro is pretty sure he smashed his ex-wife's hand with a hammer, but she says she shut it in a car door, so he skated on that one."

"Sounds like a peach," Cutter said.

"Hope you can scoop him up," Hernandez said. "Give me a call later, Lola. Fill me in. It'll be good to catch up."

"Oh, we'll get him," Lola said. "Be safe."

She ended the call, made certain the screen was locked so she didn't accidentally butt dial Hernandez back, and dropped the phone in her vest pocket.

"He seems like a good guy," Cutter said.

She laughed under her breath. "He is. Kind of goofy sometimes, but who isn't, right?" She shook her head, remembering. Here it came. Cutter sat back to listen to the story, thankful he'd at least be able to hear it with a bit of Kiwi accent.

"So," she said. "Hernandez bought this bright blue shirt at a Brunswick mall. Then he wore it to a party one weekend at Pam's. You've been there, right?"

Cutter nodded. Pam's was a local watering hole that catered to FLETC students. Everyone went to Pam's at least once, if only for a class graduation party.

"Well," Lola continued. "The dye in the stupid shirt turned his whole torso blue. Everybody had knocked a few back already and a bunch of 'em started yelling at him to strip—"

"I get the picture," Cutter said.

Lola gave a mock shudder. "I'm sure you don't . . . Anyway, he is a good dude. I imagine you did some wild stuff in the academy."

Cutter just stared at her.

"Okay, boss, I get it," she said. "No need to curse me with your eyes."

Cutter zipped the neck of his fleece vest a little higher and then reached down to retrieve a dark blue Helly Hansen raincoat from beside his feet. Originally from Florida, he still wasn't quite used to the chill of Alaska. Summer had been lush and green, if a little rainy for his tastes. Alaskans tended to go on and on about their long days in the summer, but Cutter wasn't quite sold on that either. He was a man who felt guilty if he wasn't up and doing something with the sun. Short nights wore him out. October had gotten back to a more reasonable cycle, but now the days were getting shorter fast, so that wasn't going to last.

"I've been here for almost four years," she said, "and I'm still not used to it."

"Used to what?"

She nodded at his coat. "The cold. Seems like Alaska has two seasons. Winter and July. I love the work but I wouldn't mind a little longer summer. I'm a warm-weather girl. My mom says I'm like a *paina*—one of those Cook pines."

"How's that?" Cutter asked, knowing Lola would tell him anyway.

"They're not really a pine, I guess, but from some islands near Australia. Anyway, they're all over now, even in

California. In the south they bend to the north. In the north, they lean south—like they're always looking for someplace a little warmer." She turned toward him and grinned, showing her teeth. "Just like me."

"I know what you mean," Cutter said honestly. Alaska was great, but he missed the warm-water beaches of Florida. "Still, this is a beautiful place."

"True enough." Lola's brow furrowed, the way it did when she was deep in thought. She pushed the sleeve of her jacket up enough to check her watch. "I can't believe Markham held court so late."

Cutter shrugged. He made it a point to listen to his deputies when they bitched, just in case there was a bona fide complaint, but he rarely joined in. He had to admit that Judge J. Anthony Markham was a piece of work though.

"I walked past the chief's office this morning," Lola said. "Scott Keen was in there talking about some kind of threat. He shut the door when I walked by. All very hush-hush. He likes to make everything double top secret."

"Must be," Cutter said. "Because it's news to me."

Being out of the loop might have bothered another supervisor, but Cutter didn't care to know every little thing going on in the district. That was the chief's job. There was plenty to worry about in his own wheelhouse. His own "swim-lane," the bigwigs in DC called it. Protective investigations were all well and good, but he'd leave those to the judicial security inspector and spend his energy hunting fugitives.

"Mark my words, boss," Lola said. "If we don't get Twig tonight, we'll be yanked away to work some protection detail." She threw her head back against the seat and stared up at the headliner like she was in agony. "Let's get this show on the road. You know we have our FIT test next week. I was supposed to run tonight."

"I thought you ran this morning," Cutter said. He enjoyed a good workout, but when it came to fitness, Lola Teariki was beyond maniacal.

"I did three miles," she said. "But like you said, I am putting in for SOG this next go around. You know how hard they look at your shooting and FIT scores."

SOG—the Special Operations Group—was the Marshals Service's version of SWAT.

Cutter almost smiled. "You want exercise? Then let's get some exercise." He keyed the radio. "Lola and I are going to do one more drive-by." He let off the mic so he was just talking to Lola. "And then we'll go for a walk."

"In this crap?" Lola peered across the seat in the dim glow of the dash lights. Her brows were raised, eyes wide and slightly crossed, like she was staring at the tip of her nose. Her top lip curled in the grimace of her Maori ancestors' haka war dance.

"Hold on to that face," Cutter said. "We may need it if this works out."

"You mean if it doesn't work out," she corrected.

"Nope," Cutter said. "I mean if it does." He nodded down the street. "But first the drive-by. When you get in front of the car lot, I want you to punch it so you peel out."

Lola threw the Expedition into gear. "Peel out?"

Cutter shrugged. "When I tell you, I want you to hit the gas like you're fleeing the scene."

Lola did as instructed, stomping on the accelerator to send up a rooster tail of gravel and sludge in front of Honest Sam's.

Cutter pointed a half a block down with an open hand. "Pull up there and then flip a U-turn."

The Expedition's headlights reflected silver-black off the rain-soaked asphalt. Wipers thwacked back and forth against a back-drop of hissing rain and crunching gravel.

Cutter shrugged on the raincoat and opened his door to a gust of wind.

"I was thinking," he said a minute later as they trudged side by side through the rain toward the lot. "You can't do any better than a hundred percent on your FIT test."

"Not true, boss," Lola said. "SOG looks at times, not max points. I'm competing against other applicants, not the standard."

Cutter thought on that. In his forties, he could still run a sub-ten mile-and-a-half, bench press his body weight fifteen times, and pump out seventy pushups without any trouble—but contemplating Lola Teariki's workouts made his bones ache.

They paused two hundred feet from the shop, scanning for security cameras. Cutter found two—one facing outward from the front door, and another that pointed toward the lot. The side of the building next to the roll-up garage doors appeared to be a blind spot. Sean Blodgett and Anchorage PD Task Force Officer Nancy Alvarez were parked around the corner in another SUV, giving them a view of the front and side doors as well as the driveway onto the lot, but not the garage.

"Keep your hood pulled up around your face," Cutter said to Lola. "In case we missed a camera."

She adjusted her jacket around the thick bun of hair on top of her head. "Okay. But I'm still not sure what we're doing."

"Ranucci says Twig is on the move," Cutter said. "So time is of the essence. We have a cell number for Sam, but I don't want to burn it if we don't have to."

Lola's shrug was almost lost in the oversized rain jacket. "Agreed."

"Sam is our only real lead, but APD says there's no one at his address of record."

"Right . . ." Lola said, still not tracking. "So how do we get in touch with Honest Sam if we don't want to call the only number we have?"

Cutter squatted to the ground, as if he'd dropped something. "You brought your binoculars with you?"

She patted the chest of her raincoat.

Cutter wiped the rain out of his eyes, pointing at the shop with an open hand. "Take a look at that sign in the shop window and tell me what you see."

Lola fished out the binoculars and raised them. "'Warning: Facility Protected by All Guard Security.'" She gave Cutter a wary side-eye, then looked back through the binoculars. "I get it," she said, finally tracking.

Cutter picked up a rock the size of a golf ball and stood, hurling it through the four-by-four window next to the garage doors. "Exactly. We'll get his alarm company to call him."

Chapter 3

Blodgett and Alvarez didn't have eyes on the broken window, but Cutter was fairly sure they knew what was going on when the alarm siren wailed.

Officer Alvarez came over the radio.

"I'll let Dispatch know it was us."

"Stand by on that," Cutter said. "We don't have a three-sixty view of the building. Owner should still respond."

There was radio silence for a beat before Alvarez broke squelch again. "Copy that," she said. She'd not seen Cutter throw the rock, and though she surely had her suspicions, didn't quiz him for any details. She let APD know the US Marshals were already on the scene, and requested a single marked unit to keep Honest Sam honest when he arrived to check on his dealership. The rest of them would stay in the shadows until he left, following him back to wherever he was staying, hopefully with Twig.

Anchorage was Alaska's largest city, but the law enforcement community was small enough that Cutter had worked with many of the same APD officers on multiple occasions over the months since he'd transferred in from Florida. Officer Leon Cho rolled up in his SUV two minutes later. Cho had what Nancy called swing-shift hair—full and expertly cut, unlike the buzz cuts of her cohorts on mid-shift, where she'd worked before coming to the fugitive task force. His Ken-doll do notwithstanding, Cho was no pretty boy. He was a sniper with APD SWAT and was built like a sprinter, a welcome trait when hunting fugitives.

Nancy Alvarez's boyfriend, Theron Jensen, was in the area, knew Nancy was there, and dropped by with K9 Zeus when he heard the call. Jensen was a muscular thirty-something who'd served with Army Special Forces before joining APD. Easy to like. It was difficult to tell who was more devoted to whom, Zeus to Jensen, or vice versa. Cutter had watched the agile Belgian Malinois work before, and was more than happy to see the dark face and amber eyes peering out the side window of Jensen's patrol car.

Everyone met on the side street next to Honest Sam's lot. The rain had slowed to a cold spit. Vapor filled the night air each time anyone spoke.

Cho canted his head in disbelief at the shattered window.

"So you guys just happened to be here when the window broke?"

"No," Cutter said, nodding to the tire tracks in muddy gravel where Lola had spun out. "It's a hundred percent our fault. The Marshals Service will pay for the damages." He would not have actually said the tires had thrown the rocks, but he didn't mind implying it. Thankfully, Cho didn't press any further, whether he made the inference or not.

"This is what broken window policing has come to . . ." Cho shook his head smugly and said, "That's convenient."

"So," Officer Jensen said, "you got no paper on Sam Ripley, just his cousin, Trig?"

"It's Twig," Nancy said, giving Jensen a mock punch in the arm. Alvarez was a compact woman, reaching just below Jensen's shoulders. He outweighed her by at least eighty pounds. But that didn't matter. Zeus saw her as a threat and went berserk in Jensen's back seat, ears pointed forward like targeting radar.

Lola grinned. "I think somebody's jealous."

"Tell me about it," Alvarez said. "That dog's batshit crazy . . . in a good way. He'd do anything for Theron, so you gotta love him."

Cutter tapped the powder-blue warrant folder in Lola's hand to get things moving. She folded back the face sheet and showed Twig Ripley's Nevada driver's license photo to both Cho and Jensen.

"Seriously?" Jensen scanned the folder. "This guy's actual name is Twig Ripley?"

"Seems so," Alvarez said. She touched him on the arm, inciting another round of frenzied barks and growls from Zeus.

Jensen chuckled. "Don't worry about it," he said. "I'll let you throw the Kong for him tonight and he'll be your bestie."

APD dispatch advised over the radio that the owner of Honest Sam's was en route, ETA ten minutes.

Everyone pulled well back from the building, except Cho, who waited out front as the officer responding to the alarm.

Six minutes later, they'd just taken up their previous positions when Sam Ripley skidded a white late-model Dodge crew-cab to a stop in front of Cho's police car—and he wasn't alone.

"Boss . . ." Lola's voice buzzed against her hands as she peered through her binoculars. "That big dude in the passenger seat look like Twig to you?"

"Yep," Cutter said, looking through his own binoculars.

Honest Sam got out and strode quickly toward the door of his business. He swung a lanyard full of keys as he walked. The passenger stayed put in the Dodge.

Cutter keyed his radio. "Let's let Cho get Sam away from the truck." He called out a play by play of what he knew the others would do. None of them needed the direction, but it helped to keep everyone on the same page as the situation progressed. "Nancy, Sean, go ahead and roll up. Lola and I will come in from the east."

"I'll approach from the south," Officer Jensen confirmed over the radio, mixed with Zeus's excited barks. "We'll box him in."

"Good deal," Cutter said.

Half a block away, Nancy Alvarez started her engine and pulled into the street—evidently a little too slowly for Twig Ripley.

Fugitives didn't get to stay fugitives for long unless they were endowed with a healthy dose of paranoia. Paranoia had been Twig's daily companion since he'd jumped bond almost eleven months prior. His head snapped up as soon as Alvarez pulled the SUV onto the street. He jumped behind the wheel of the white Dodge before she could close the gap. Instead of running, Twig threw the pickup into reverse and stomped on the gas, slamming into the oncoming SUV with enough force to deploy both airbags, stunning both Blodgett and Alvarez.

Sam Ripley spun at the noise of the crash, saw what was happening, and decided to take up for his cousin. He growled and ran directly for Leon Cho, who sidestepped deftly and stomped on the back of the big man's heel as he went by, following him to the ground to wrap him.

Cutter pounded on the dash. "Get him stopped!"

"On it," Lola said, speeding down the street to plow into

the pickup's left rear wheel with the push bumper. The Dodge spun, folding up the side of the Expedition to slam driver's door to driver's door, so Twig and Lola were looking directly at each other. The outlaw mouthed something unintelligible and then lay down in the seat, disappearing from view. The passenger door flew open before they'd even stopped moving and he hit the ground at a dead run.

Officer Cho had Honest Sam well in hand. Alvarez and Blodgett were obscured from view by their air bags, still inside the idling SUV.

"You check on Sean and Nancy," Cutter yelled over his shoulder to Lola as he flung open his door. "I'll back up Jensen and the dog."

Along with luck and paranoia, Twig Ripley had incredible speed for a man of his hulking size. He'd made it almost to the end of the block by the time Jensen released K9 Zeus. Target in sight, the dog tore down the street like a growling missile, claws clicking on the wet pavement. Twig had disappeared, but the dog veered left, cutting through the parking lot behind a Korean church.

Cutter sprinted to keep up with Officer Jensen, staying a half step behind so he didn't risk getting in between handler and dog—a surefire way to get bitten.

Frenzied barking echoed through the darkness ahead, bouncing off the walls of the church.

The K9 officer called out encouragement to his dog as he ran. "Get him, Zeus! Hold him, Zeus!"

Jensen and Cutter homed in on the riot of threatening shouts and growls. Uncomfortable with the dog out of his sight, Jensen picked up his pace, still shouting. "Hold him, Zeus. I'm coming, bud. Twig Ripley! Do not move!"

The outlaw screamed something unintelligible. Cutter heard banging, like a trashcan or metal building. They were close now. Then the dog broke into a series of frustrated, high-pitched barks.

"He's climbed up high," Jensen said as he ran. "Zeus is trying to get to him."

Cutter and Jensen were shoulder to shoulder when they rounded the corner of the church. Fifty meters away, Twig Ripley stood on top of a large metal dumpster alongside an eight-foot chain link fence, just out of reach of the dog.

Zeus was incredibly athletic, able to scale ten-foot walls if he had a running start, but the sides of the dumpster were angled outward and a fraction too tall to get a toe hold. He bounced up and down, growling and whining in frustration.

Cutter scanned for other routes, hoping to find a way around and make up some time. Twig put both hands on the fence as if to vault, and then he stopped, grabbing something that was hanging on the chain link. It took Cutter a half second too long to realize it was a crowbar. Instead of running, Twig turned and stepped to the edge of the dumpster to peer down at the dog.

Jensen attempted to call Zeus off, his voice tight with worry, nearly as high pitched as the dog's whines.

"Stop!" Cutter yelled.

Twig ignored him, stooping slightly, holding the crowbar like a golf club. He waited, timing his movements with the Malinois's bounce, and then swung hard, directly to the side of the dog's head with a sullen thud. The powerful K9 yelped pitifully at the horrific impact, and fell to the grimy pavement like a sack of sand.

Jensen let loose a guttural yowl.

Twig dropped the crowbar, seemingly aware that holding it gave the officers cause to shoot him. Then he turned and made for the fence, teetering there a moment, nearly losing his balance on the dumpster.

Zeus lay still at the base of the dumpster, looking much smaller than he had only a moment before. Enraged, Cutter shot Jensen a quick glance as he ran. "See to your partner. I've got this guy."

Twig's attack on Zeus slowed him enough that he was still in the process of climbing down the other side of the fence when Cutter reached the dumpster. Instead of climbing up, Cutter ran straight past, slamming with all two hundred and twenty pounds into the loose chain link as if he intended to run straight through it. His shoulder impacted Twig Ripley's groin, sending the outlaw flying like a billiard ball backward onto the filthy pavement.

Cutter was prepared for the sudden impact and used the rebound to scramble onto the dumpster and over the fence. His boots hit the ground on the other side at the same time Twig clambered to his feet.

"U.S. Marshals!" Cutter boomed. "On the ground!"

Ripley spun, squaring off, ready to fight. He had three inches and at least a fifty-pound advantage, both of which made it look much less like Cutter was kicking his ass for no reason. This guy had chosen to stop running and viciously attack a police dog. Cutter didn't concern himself with the niceties of de-escalation. Filled with rage, Cutter plowed straight, letting a sloppy hay-maker from Twig slide off his shoulder. Moving close, he delivered a staggering head butt, nearly peeling Twig's nose down the front of his face. The outlaw doubled over but kept his feet.

Cutter snapped in a lightning-fast jab, followed by a right uppercut, intent on hitting the man until he got heavy. The outlaw fell backward, turning over to push himself up on all fours, and receiving a boot to the ribs for his trouble.

A piercing whistle cut the chilly night air as Cutter reared back for another blow.

Cutter planted another boot, feeling ribs crack and separate.

"Arliss! You good?" It was Lola. "Hang on. I got your back."

Cutter blinked, then looked down at the moaning Twig Ripley, who had curled up on the wet asphalt like a dead spider.

"Let's have those hands," Cutter barked. He rolled the outlaw over, and, pressing a knee none too gently in the small of the man's back, ratcheted on the handcuffs.

Twig groaned, spitting out a mouthful of gravel. "What's . . . your problem?"

"You had to hit that dog?" Cutter hauled Twig up by his elbow.

Twig shrugged, wincing from the pain in his ribs. "It would have just kept coming after me. Anyhow, you didn't have to beat the hell out of me. It was just a damned dog—"

Lola swooped in and took control just in time. "I got him, boss." She leaned in. "Word to the wise, Mr. Ripley. Keep your mouth shut around Officer Jensen. You're lucky it was my partner and not Jensen who got to you first."

Twig groaned. "I don't feel lucky."

Cutter glared at him. "How about that."

Nancy Alvarez and Sean Blodgett met them as Cutter and Lola came around the corner with the prisoner.

Blodgett nodded at Twig. "You want us to take him, boss?"

"I catch 'em, I'll clean 'em," Cutter said. He looked at Nancy. "What's the news about Zeus?"

"Theron took him to the twenty-four-hour animal hospital," she whispered. To the prisoner, she said, "You're lucky the marshals got to you before he did."

"People keep tellin' me that," Twig groaned.

Cutter gave him a more thorough pat-down before putting him in the back seat and buckling him in. The Expedition had no cage, so Cutter secured his pistols in a lockbox in the rear hatch.

Lola put a hand on his arm as he got ready to open the door and climb in the back seat with the prisoner. "You okay?"

He gave her a curt nod. "Why wouldn't I be?"

She glanced at his skinned knuckles, and then touched her own face to signal he had a bit of Twig's blood on his cheek. "You are aware that the Marshals Service issues pepper spray and Tasers now?"

"It was handled."

"Yeah," she said. "I saw that. Good thing for Twig I came along when I did. It looked to me like you were about to handle his teeth in."

"Arrests can be dynamic." Cutter shrugged. "Sometimes things aren't what they seem."

Lola folded her arms across her chest and stood hipshot, looking at him for a long moment. Rain moistened her high cheekbones and made them shine under the streetlight. "And sometimes, they are exactly what they seem." She winked. "Fortunately, you have yourself a Polynesian Jiminy Cricket."

Chapter 4

"This is death," Sarah Mead thought, fighting the urge to vomit. She panted, gulped for air, then panted some more, trying to focus on her surroundings to take her mind off the pulsing agony in her head. Summoning her last ounce of courage, she choked back the sobs and forced herself to take long, slow breaths. Her skull felt like it would explode any moment. Something was tied over her eyes, but the acid pain in the center of her brain brought with it a blue light, throbbing with each beat of her racing heart.

Her arms were pulled behind her, her hands tied. Whoever had done it obviously didn't care if her hands eventually fell off and had cinched them so tight that they'd gone completely numb. She could hear voices, but they were muffled and unintelligible. She lay on her stomach, left hip pressed against something hard and cool—a log wall maybe. Was she still in the lodge? That wasn't likely. Chaga had a slight mothball stench that she'd hated when she first arrived. She'd gotten used to it, somewhat, but it had never gone away completely. This place smelled like old socks and urine—and something else she couldn't quite place. She heard more voices, still garbled. The left side of her face was warmer than the right, as if there was a fireplace or a stove on that side.

She replayed everything she could remember in her mind. Someone had hit her. Twice. She knew she was fortunate to be alive. Blows to the head could be deadly. Whoever had hit her used enough force to knock her out, or even kill her. That could only mean they didn't care whether she lived or died. Then why was she bound and blindfolded? And where was David? She remembered now. There was a body. Without thinking, she tried to scream.

"David!" But it came out garbled, like she had a broken jaw or a mouth full of rocks.

More muffled sounds, closer now, as if someone was trying to get her attention.

She cried out again with the same gibbering result.

Unable to see, or hear, or scream, she could at least feel. She could smell. Someone was close to her, inches from her face. A man? He smelled awful, like sewage and wood smoke—an out-house on fire. She froze. What was he going to do? Her breath came in ragged, terrified gasps. She was helpless to do anything but wait and wonder. Her heart beat faster, pushing the pain deep in her skull to an agonizing crescendo. Bright lights flashed behind her eyes like an oncoming car at night, and then faded as she slipped from pain into unconsciousness.

DAY TWO

Chapter 5

"You let them play with knives and fire, Uncle Arliss," Constance Cutter said, turning up her nose at the mess her twin seven-year-old brothers were making in the kitchen. "That's the only reason they get up so early to help you with breakfast."

The heavy bass beat spilling out of the white buds in her ears made it clear that the prickly fifteen-year-old was making an observation, not conversation. Mousy brown hair was parted in the middle, hanging to her shoulders and forming curtains over her eyes, which allowed her to shut out the rest of the world. For most teenage girls, the straight hair, ripped jeans, and loose sweatshirts were all carefully executed to make it look as though they didn't care about their appearance. Constance truly didn't—which made her probably the most authentic sophomore in the Anchorage school system. She had her mother's natural beauty and her father's athleticism, which allowed her to pull off the look, where someone with less confidence might come off like a female Napoleon Dynamite. She threw her backpack—pink and covered with a pattern of tiny white skulls—on one of the heavy Amish chairs at the dining room table, and grabbed a cup of yogurt from the fridge. Arliss remembered a time when she was all

bubbles and brightness—but the death of her father had
knocked the happiness right out of her. She cultivated all
the coziness of an aggravated porcupine, forcing everyone
else in the house to get out of her way or suffer the consequences.

Arliss's brother had been gone for over a year. Bedtime
was still difficult—when the house grew quiet enough for
little boys' hearts to run wild with emotion. But the twins
had rebounded, for the most part. Cutter's sister-in-law,
Mim, was still struggling, emotionally and financially.
She'd not only lost her husband, but the engineering firm
that sent him to the Kuparuk River oil fields on the North
Slope blamed him for a design flaw that caused the explo-
sion that killed him. The court battle over any insurance
money was stomping her into the mud. Cutter fantasized
about meeting some of the suit-and-tie shitheads responsible for her misery, in a dark alley. He often dreamed of
demonstrating to them that losing someone you love was
a lot like having a couple of teeth knocked out. Cutter
knew all too well. In the end, neither worry over losing his
job or consequences of the law kept him from bludgeoning
the executives into a greasy smear. He simply cared too
much for Mim. Violent action on his part would trouble
her—and she had enough trouble.

Arliss poured some buttermilk into a glass measuring
cup and gave his grouchy niece a rare smile, even if she
didn't want one.

Michael, the older of the two boys by twelve minutes,
sifted flour, salt, and other dry ingredients into a glass
bowl. He had honey-colored hair and the natural sobriety
of his father. Matthew, the younger twin, inherited his
great-grandpa Grumpy's flaxen blond hair and blue eyes,
as well as the natural tendency toward a mean mug at an

early age. He looked and acted much like Arliss had when he was seven. It wasn't at all uncommon that people in the grocery store commented on how much Arliss's "son" looked like him.

"We're making Grumpy pancakes," Cutter said to his niece. "We'll make extra."

Constance peeked around a flap of hair with a sulky side-eye that would have terrified a lesser man. "Pancakes go straight to my ass."

The twins looked at each other and giggled. Michael pursed his lips.

Matthew put a hand over his mouth. "Constance said ass."

"Well," Cutter said, "Grumpy had a man-rule about that."

Both boys threw back their heads and crowed in unison. "Grumpy Man-Rule five: No rough language in front of ladies!"

Matthew took the measuring cup full of buttermilk from Cutter and poured the liquid into the dry ingredients. "Constance is a sister, not a lady."

Michael nodded in agreement, then dipped his finger into the batter, tasted it, then grimaced. "More like *pan* than *cake*," he said, sounding an awful lot like his father.

Mim came down the hallway at that moment, head beautifully tilted, putting in an earring as she walked. Her damp hair was pulled back in a thick ponytail with a purple scrunchy that matched her hospital scrubs. Cutter caught his breath when he saw her, glancing away for a moment to steady himself so she wouldn't see the look in his eyes. She wore very little makeup, but the morning shower had pinked her peaches-and-cream complexion, making her look flushed, like she'd been exercising. Cutter suspected she'd likely gone to sleep crying and then woken up the same way. He wanted to comfort her. To tell her that he was there for her. But she was his sister-in-law. That made it feel weird. It didn't matter that he'd met her first, when they were only sixteen, in Manasota Key. That he'd been about to ask her out when his older and much cooler brother had swooped in and swept her off her feet with his smile and charm. Ethan had won her and that was that. He'd gotten the girl, had the beautiful kids, and then he'd died. Arliss chided himself for the pity party. He'd come to Alaska to take care of Mim and the kids, not kindle some unrequited romance from his youth.

She finished with the earring and took a deep breath. "Is that bacon I smell?"

"Yep!" Matthew said.

Michael gave a flourish with his drippy spatula. "Bacon and Grumpy pancakes."

"Smells great," Mim said. "What's this about Constance not being a lady?"

Constance looked at Cutter, waiting.

"Nothing to worry about." He shook his head. "Just some sibling rivalry."

"No, it's not," Matthew said. "Constance cursed."

Michael gave another of his smug nods. "She said the pancakes would go to her ass."

Mim heaved an exhausted sigh. It was too early in the morning for a fight. "*Ass* isn't really a curse word. But it isn't polite, for a sister or a lady."

"Sorry," Constance said, obviously not sorry at all.

"It bothers me more that you're worried about getting fat," Mim said. "If anything, you could use a few more calories."

"I just don't want pancakes, okay?"

Mim decided not to press the issue, turning instead to Cutter. "Are you teaching them your famous flip?"

"They're watching this time," Cutter said. He looked at his watch. "Okay. The batter's made and we've waited a couple of minutes for the magic-y science stuff to happen with the buttermilk and baking soda. This way they'll be nice and fluffy."

Matthew poured a quarter cup of batter into the hot frying pan. Mim checked the time on her cell phone, then looked up at the boys and smiled, clearly appreciating what Cutter was doing. "Now you just wait for the little holes to app—"

Matthew raised his hands like a traffic cop. "We know how to cook it, Mom. Uncle Arliss let us cut the bacon into pieces and weave it into squares."

"Cool," Mim said. "I'm starved. Where is this bacon you speak of?" "In the oven," Michael said, still waving the batter-covered spatula. He quoted something Arliss had told them at least a dozen times over the past few months since he'd arrived from Florida to help out. "Grumpy was bakin' bacon before anyone knew it was a thing."

"Holes!" Matthew sounded the alarm, pointing at the pan. "Time to flip it!"

Cutter drew a chorus of oohs and aahs with his pan-cake-flipping skills. Even Constance looked on, but side-ways, as if it was the most boring thing she'd ever seen.

It took the boys less than fifteen minutes to eat, wash the syrup and bacon grease off their faces, and help pile their dishes in the sink. They fled out the front door at the first sound of the school bus. Constance had gone well before the boys, taking her yogurt on the fly. Cutter saw her snitch a piece of bacon and fold it in a pancake, but pretended he didn't.

Mim set her coffee on the table and checked her phone again when she and Cutter were alone. "I'm late," she said. "I'll do the dishes when I get home."

"I got it," Cutter said. "Grumpy's pancakes are light as a feather, but the batter turns to indestructible concrete in an hour."

"Thank you, Arliss," Mim said.

He gave her a rare grin—the dangerous kind, the kind with dimples that had gotten him married four times. "It's okay. I like doing dishes."

"No, you don't," she said. "You hate doing the dishes. In fact, I'm not a hundred percent sure that's not what caused your second divorce."

"I can confirm or deny nothing."

"You know what I mean," she said. "Thank you for everything. Those boys were crushed when Ethan died. I didn't think Michael was ever going to come out of it. Now you have them leaving the house each morning trailing pancakes and confidence."

"They're good kids," Cutter said. "Constance will come around eventually." He changed the subject quickly so she didn't have to dwell on how long that might take. "How about cowboy chili pie for dinner?"

He stood to clear the table, wincing at a new pain in his back.

Mim raised an eyebrow. "Need some ice?"

"I'm good," Arliss said, carrying the dishes around the bar to the sink. He'd probably overextended a tendon in his hip kicking the shit out of Twig Ripley, but that wasn't something he wanted to talk about with Mim.

"I heard you come in late," she said. "Rough night?"

"We got our guy."

"Grumpy Man-Rule twenty." Mim nodded. "Let no guilty man go free."

Cutter rinsed the plates. "Yeah, well, I got to this one a little slow. He beat the crap out of a police dog."

"Is he okay?" Mim asked. "The dog, I mean?"

"I don't know," Cutter said. "But it was bad . . . Anyway, sorry to start your day on a downer."

"Oh," Mim said, "I can do that without any help from you . . . What were we talking about before?"

"Cowboy chili pie," Cutter said.

"Right. That sounds outstanding."

"Good," Cutter said. "Because I promised the boys they could cut up onions."

"They don't even like onions."

"I didn't either when I was a kid." Cutter shrugged. "Grumpy had a rule about that too . . . well, an axiom really. 'It's more about the knife than the onion.'"

"Touché." Mim sat with both hands resting in her lap. "It's supposed to rain all day," she said. "Want to go to the Dome and run if you get home in time?"

"Works for me," Cutter said, drying his hands.

"Good, because, you know, pancakes and cowboy chili pie in the same day. Constance thinks only she has a problem." Mim put a hand on her hip and winked. "For some of us, the struggle is real."

Cutter started to say something that bordered on flirtatious, thought better of it, and made do with an awkward hug goodbye.

Chapter 6

Cutter parked his government vehicle—colloquially called a G-ride—beneath the James M. Fitzgerald US Courthouse and Federal Building. His parking space put his driver's-side door against a thick concrete support pillar so he had to suck in his gut to get out. He'd learned from Grumpy that a boss should always take the oldest car in the fleet and leave the best assigned parking to the troops. He grabbed his war bag from the passenger seat and took the elevator to the ground floor.

The Alaska Fugitive Task Force offices were down the hall and around the corner from a bank that rented space in the federal building, in a separate location from the rest of the Marshals Service. Cutter had just punched his access code into the scramble pad beside the door to the task force suite when Lola stepped out from the USMS gym across the hall. As usual, her bronze skin was slightly flushed from a recent workout—Cutter doubted she ever went more than a few hours without some form of exercise. She wore a pair of black jeans, loose enough she could fight in them, but tight enough to look stylish. A dark blue pocket T-shirt with the short sleeves rolled up past her biceps revealed the border of a Polynesian tattoo on her shoulder. The hallway was a dead end and generally out of view of the public, so she carried her brown leather jacket, leaving the Glock on her belt exposed. The silver circle-star of a deputy United States marshal was clipped to a round black leather case just forward of the pistol. Two spare magazines and a flashlight rested over her left hip. Her handcuffs rode over her left kidney. A CZ folding knife nested in her right pocket slightly back from the leather holster. There was room for a Taser too, but not much, so she customarily left it in her desk while she was in the office.

"Morning, boss."

Cutter pushed open the door, stepping to the side so Lola could go in ahead. "Have a good workout?"

"Leg day," she said. Anyone who'd ever experienced leg day wouldn't need an explanation and anyone who hadn't wouldn't understand anyway.

Cutter walked into his small office, which was barely big enough for his desk and a couple of side chairs, and dropped his war bag before sitting down. Lola followed him in, standing there like something was on her mind.

"What is it?" he asked.

"It's Zeus," she said, looking glum.

"That was going to be my first call," Cutter said. "What are you hearing?"

Lola sat in one of the two chairs in front of Cutter's desk. The other was piled high with blue warrant folders. Both hands in her lap, she fidgeted, uncharacteristically nervous.

"Nancy says it's bad. Theron took him straight to the animal emergency hospital off Tudor last night. It sounds like he's got swelling on the brain. The vet put him in a drug-induced coma. He has to be on a respirator. I didn't even know that was a thing for dogs."

Cutter sighed. "Thanks for letting me know. Is Nancy coming in?"

"I don't think so," Lola said. "She's with Theron right now."

The phone rang. Cutter looked at the number and then picked it up. "Morning, Chief."

Lola mouthed, "Want me to leave?" He waved an open hand, motioning for her to keep her seat.

He listened a moment, and then hung up.

"Chief wants to see us."

Lola raised a wary brow. "Both of us? Did she say why?"

"Something about Judge Markham."

"What did I tell you?" Lola threw back her head and stared at the ceiling. "I really don't like that guy. Did she say what she wants from us? Scott Keen handles judicial security. We stay plenty busy hunting bad guys, thank you very much."

"Keen's in the chief's office now. For some reason, Jill wants to talk to us too."

Cutter felt the familiar tickle on his neck that said something unpleasant was about to go down. Federal judges could be funny animals. Grumpy often said that the difference between God and a federal judge was that God didn't believe he was a federal judge.

"Markham . . ." Teariki said, her voice taking on an uncharacteristic whine.

"Do you two have some kind of history I need to know about?"

"He chastised me once for yawning during a trial," Lola groused.

"In open court?"

"Well," Lola said, "he didn't really chastise out loud.

But he glared at me so everyone could see. The prisoner thought it was all pretty hilarious. I think Markham's dad was a judge in New York. Not a real judge, but a parking-ticket judge kind of deal. I think he's outdone Daddy and has gone and turned all purple with his terrible cosmic power of the federal bench. You'll see what I mean."

"We've met," Cutter said.

"Then you already know." Lola closed her eyes and gave a mock shudder. "We are soooo stuffed."

Jill Phillips, the chief deputy US marshal for the judicial district of Alaska, sat poring over a stack of photographs at her cherry-veneer desk. It was a nice enough piece of furniture, but still held the slightly chintzy look of government-issue. Large windows ran the length of the wall to her right, giving her a view of Eighth Avenue. During the summer, vendors sold reindeer hotdogs from umbrella pushcarts along the quiet street that ran between the federal building and the social security annex. In winter, the occasional moose stopped by to rest on the bark mulch beneath landscaped birch and spruce. The southern exposure lit various marksmanship trophies, challenge coins, and photographs—mementos of the chief's career and her personal love of horses. An eight-by-ten photograph of her husband and new baby got center stage.

Scott Keen, the judicial security inspector, or JSI, stood at the end of her desk, examining each photograph. He was on the back side of his forties, having been promoted to the rank of senior inspector later in his career. A quiet man, Inspector Keen was an expert at dealing with judicial whims while still maintaining a high level of security. He had the thinning silver hair of a grandfather—though his own kids were still in middle school—and, like many deputies in Alaska, the callused hands of an avid outdoorsman. As a supervisor, Cutter and he shared the same rank, though Cutter ran a task force of people while Inspector Keen oversaw the judicial security program. Keen liked the JSI gig—managing a program instead of subordinates. He was good at it, and would likely stay there until he retired.

Chief Phillips flicked her hand at the two lavender paisley chairs in front of her desk without looking up, and then chuckled, turning the photographs on her desk so Cutter and Teariki could take a look. Her brunette hair was longer than when he'd first met her, as if the new baby made it too difficult to find time to cut or style. She was about Cutter's age, freckled, which he found attractive but would never say out loud since she was his boss. He suspected she was the only person in the district who could routinely outshoot him. Her Kentucky accent was pleasant, reminding him of folks he knew from rural Florida. More important, she was a damned good boss.

Where the position of United States Marshal is filled by presidential appointment, changing with the tides of whichever political party is in the White House, the chief deputy is the top career boss in each district, protected from the vagaries of political change by civil service rules. Cutter had worked under several different US Marshals. Most were seasoned law enforcement professionals, but a couple were businessmen who got the gig because of their political connections. Gaining the rank of chief deputy was different. Climbing up the career ladder didn't make all chiefs perfect—Cutter had worked for some real winners—but at least they knew the culture and had enough contacts at headquarters to provide top cover for the deputies in their respective districts if they wanted to. It was often said (though rarely within earshot of the Marshal) that the gold badge was given; the silver badge was earned.

Jill Phillips had certainly earned her promotion. More leader than manager, she proved to be the type of straight-shooting boss that the A-type souls who were likely to become deputy marshals craved—even if they didn't care to admit it. If you screwed up, her tune-ups were excruciatingly direct, but done privately and face to face. When you did well, the whole district—and maybe the entire Marshals Service—heard the praise. She was famous throughout the agency for being an incredible mentor, the kind who helped her direct reports become chiefs themselves—which was the last thing Cutter aspired to do. He spent too much time at his desk as it was. Being chained to a chief deputy's office would be the lowest circle of Hell.

Phillips tapped the eraser of a gray Blackwing 602 pencil against the photograph. "What does this look like to you?"

Lola studied it for a moment and then looked up, frowning as if her time was being wasted. "It looks like some teenage boy drew a dick pic on a dusty tailgate."

The chief gave a low chuckle. "That is exactly what I said."

"The problem," Keen said, "is that this particular dusty tailgate belongs to Judge Markham's Suburban. His grandkids saw it too, which has him ready to hold everyone in contempt."

"Okay," Cutter said, leaning back in his chair. "I doubt a juvenile drawing rises even to the level of criminal mischief."

"All true enough," Phillips said. "But I didn't call you

over to discuss lewd artwork. According to my contact in the Central Violations Bureau, there's a guy with a warrant, living near the village of Stone Cross."

The Central Violations Bureau, or CVB, was the repository for citations issued by various government entities in national parks or other federal lands. Generally unpaid tickets for offenses against regulations dreamed up by some bureaucrat behind a desk rather than laws set forth by Congress, CVB warrants were not in the bottom of the pile for a deputy's enforcement priorities. They were in an entirely different pile, in the bottom of a forgotten drawer, under a bunch of other things that no one wanted to do. Ever.

"What's this CVB warrant for?" Cutter asked.

Phillips gave a conspiratorial wink. "Public urination within three hundred feet of an outhouse in a national park."

"Guess we really are the action service," Lola scoffed. "You're sending us five hundred miles to arrest a guy for peeing in the woods?"

"No," Phillips said. "I'm sending you five hundred miles to protect a federal judge."

Chapter 7

There was no escaping an edict from the chief, but Cutter tried anyway. "Excuse me, ma'am, but a protective detail because someone drew a penis on the judge's car?"

"There's a little more to it than that, Big Iron." Phillips rarely missed the opportunity to tease him about the fact that he carried his grandfather's revolver—an anachronism in this era of high-capacity semi-automatic pistols that Cutter thought of as combat Tupperware. The chief envied him, so she teased him.

She nodded to Inspector Keen, giving him the floor.

"Three days ago," Keen said, "Judge Markham received this letter, postmarked from Bethel." Keen opened a manila folder and took out a plastic sleeve containing a single sheet of paper. He passed it to Lola, who scanned it, then gave it to Cutter. This was a photocopy, but the original looked to have been handwritten on a sheet torn from a spiral notebook, the frayed edges still attached. Printed in all capitals, the writing was neat and meticulous, as if the author had taken a great amount of time on each individual letter. There were a few misspellings and some kind of stain on the bottom corner, but it was impossible to tell what it was on the copy.

Cutter read it aloud.

TO: THE DISHONORABLE JUDGE
MARKHAM.
FINDING: WE WILL MEET ONE DAY. VERY
SOON AS A FACT.
JUGMENT: VERY GUIOLTY SENTENCE:
SHALL BE TAKEN AWAY. NO ONE CAN
EVERY FIND YOU. MY HAPPINESS IS TO
HOLD YOUR BEATING HEART IN MY HAND.
YOU WILL NEVER SEE ME COMING BUT
YOU WILL KNOW JUGMENT.

"Jug-ment," Lola said, reaching over to tap the misspelled word. "That sounds interesting. Maybe the letter-writer is a porn star with an axe to grind."

"Yeah," Keen said. "Because you have to be able to spell to be a threat."

Lola rolled her eyes. "I'm joking, Scott."

"Okay," Cutter said. "We'll be happy to head to Bethel and arrest whoever you want us to arrest."

"Nice try," Phillips said. "We don't have any suspects."

"Not yet," Keen added. "But the way the letter is written suggests someone who had a case before the judge."

Phillips put a hand flat on her desk and leaned back slightly in her chair. "Our problem is this. Judge Markham is on his way to a Yup'ik village called Stone Cross tomorrow, where he will preside over arbitration in a land dispute. He'll have to fly to Bethel, where he'll take a boat or small plane upriver to Stone Cross. He won't be in Bethel long, but the arbitration in Stone Cross has been in the news for a couple of weeks."

Keen took the letter and slipped it back in his file.

"How about the Bureau?" Lola asked. "Are they sending anyone out?"

Though the two agencies worked in tandem after a threat to a federal judge, the FBI customarily handled the criminal investigation, while the Marshals Service focused on the protective intelligence that might or might not be used in a prosecution.

"They have the original letter," Phillips said. "And they've already interviewed Markham."

"The case agent and I are supposed to meet this afternoon to share any intel we each have. I don't think Markham likes the FBI much. They have a tendency to spin him up."

"I hate to defend the Feebs," Lola said, "but spinning up this judge is not all that difficult."

"Scott already suggested a protective detail," Phillips said. "But Judge Markham is having none of it."

"Okay then." Lola threw up her hands. "I say that's great news. We can't protect him if he doesn't want us to."

"That's where you two come in," Phillips said. "The CVB warrant gives us an excuse to go to Stone Cross."

Keen spoke next. "Markham seems to think a protective detail would make him appear weak. He's not a bad guy, really. Just used to everyone telling him yes all the time and laughing at all his jokes."

"Due respect, Chief," Cutter said. "But I may not be the right guy for this."

Phillips waved off the notion. "Because of that deal with Gayle during the fire alarm? You briefed me about that when it happened. It won't be a problem."

Cutter nodded, still sounding unsure. "Okay . . ."

Lola cocked her head. "What deal with Gayle? I never heard about any deal."

"Don't worry about it," Cutter said.

"Exactly," Phillips said. "Don't worry about it. I doubt he even remembers."

Cutter closed his eyes and groaned. J. Anthony Markham didn't strike him as the type to forget much of anything, least of all a perceived slight in front of his administrative assistant.

"You've not had the pleasure of spending a night out in a bush village yet, have you?" Phillips asked.

"I have not," Cutter said, already thinking through how this was going to play out. He was accustomed to workarounds. One of the things he'd always loved about the Marshals Service was the unpredictability of coming to work. He'd learned early in his career that he might show up thinking he was going to spend a day hooking and hauling prisoners from jail to court, only to have the chief send him on an assignment to seize a horse ranch, or hunt down a bunch of escaped convicts in the Caribbean after a hurricane blew down their prison.

Phillips slid the single sheet of paper with the CVB warrant across the desk to Lola. It didn't even rate a warrant file. "I haven't run this guy yet, but you never know. Make sure you do a workup on him."

Teariki gave her a dyspeptic thumbs-up and tucked the paper in her pocket.

Cutter's eyes narrowed and he looked directly at the chief. "So Markham has agreed to let us shadow him so long as we're there on other business?"

"He doesn't know yet." The chief pushed away from her desk and stood. "We're about to go tell him."

The elevator from the US Marshals cellblock exited into the secure hallway on the second floor, allowing deputies to escort prisoners into court through a back door without passing through any public areas. The arrangement gave USMS personnel direct access to judges where other law enforcement agents and employees of the US Attorney's office were required to make an appointment. Still, judges were notoriously aloof, so few besides the brass and the judicial security inspector ventured into the no-man's-land of the hall where their paths might cross with anyone in a black robe.

Chief Phillips led the way down the narrow hall, mumbling quietly that she was a nursing mother and this appointment with Markham was cutting into the time when she needed to pump. Cutter had gotten used to the chief's lack of a filter. There was nothing sneaky about her. No guile, no hidden agenda. She said what was on her mind, making it easy for her subordinates to know where they stood. Like any large government organization, the Marshals had its share of bosses who liked to pit staff against one another, if only to see who was the most loyal. Phillips mentored everyone, even the misfits—which meant even the few who didn't like her, still trusted her. Grumpy always said that there were damned few people worth emulating. But Cutter was certain his grandfather would have liked Jill Phillips.

"What's the news on Zeus?" she asked as she walked.

"Not good, I'm afraid," Cutter said. "Brain swelling. He's in a drug-induced coma."

"Dammit!" Phillips made no secret of the fact that she liked animals more than she liked most people. "Keep me posted."

She paused at the end of the hall beside a varnished wood plaque that read: J. ANTHONY MARKHAM, UNITED STATES DISTRICT JUDGE.

"The action service," Lola whispered again.

"Remember," Phillips said. "You signed up for this." She took a deep breath, then pushed open the door.

The attractive redhead at a desk behind the reception counter brightened visibly when she saw Cutter. "Hi, Arliss," she said. "Hey, Jill."

"Hey, Gayle." Phillips nodded toward the back of the office. "He's expecting us."

"I'll see if he's ready for you," Gayle Jackson said. She was Markham's administrative assistant. Forty-something, with short, Tinkerbell hair, she wore a forest-green wool suit that perfectly accented her porcelain complexion.

Phillips nodded at Jackson's perfectly manicured nails. "I like." Jackson held her hand out for Phillips—and probably for Cutter as well. "It's called Big Apple."

"I'll make a note," Phillips said, smiling as Jackson disappeared around the corner to Markham's chambers.

Lola leaned in closer to Cutter and whispered, "That woman is a knockout. I'm surprised she passed the Mrs. Markham test. I heard His Honor's better half is the jealous type."

Cutter didn't respond, though, in truth, he'd been thinking the same thing.

Lola pressed. "You have to tell me about this deal that happened with Gayle."

Phillips gave her a quiet glare and pantomimed zipping her lips.

The outer chambers were spacious, but sparsely furnished. Other than Gayle Jackson's desk and two floor-to-ceiling cases full of the tan, red, and black volumes of the *North Western Reporter* that seemed obligatory for any judge's office, there was a Fred Machetanz print of a polar bear on the pack ice and a whalebone carving of an Iñupiat

Eskimo dancer. To the right of the door, just beyond the counter, two harried law clerks slouched behind their respective computers, looking like something from a modern version of a Dickens novel, surrounded by stacks of folders and yellow legal pads. Their cubby offices were so small that Cutter wondered how they ever got the desks inside.

Jackson came back around the corner. "Go on in," she said, absent the condescension some got when they worked for powerful people and felt they were powerful too, by extension. She beamed at Cutter, but said nothing.

"Come on, boss," Lola pleaded. "I gots to know." Cutter ignored her.

The trademark bow tie made Judge Markham a difficult man to miss. Today's tie was gold and navy blue, like something from a New England prep school. A dark blue suit jacket, tailored and surely as expensive as all Cutter's suits put together, hung on a hanger on a wooden coat-tree behind an expansive oak desk. The sleeves of Markham's starched white shirt were rolled halfway up his forearms, which were surprisingly well muscled. A set of ebony cuff links sat in a molded leather tray that looked like it was there expressly for that purpose, suggesting the judge made a habit of rolling up his sleeves at work. If anything, the inner office was even more sparsely furnished than the outer one, the main décor being books, all neatly arranged, even the open ones. There was nothing else on the desk but a yellow legal pad and an open laptop computer.

The judge came around his desk to shake hands with Phillips—a move Grumpy would have approved of—and motioned Teariki and Keen to sit on the couch. The chief and Cutter got the chairs in front of his desk.

If Markham remembered the fire alarm incident, he didn't mention it.

He leaned back in his leather chair, hands steepled at his chest, looking professorial, while Phillips went over her plan. She explained that the Marshals Service took all threats seriously, and Cutter and Teariki would be in the area should he need assistance.

"That won't be necessary," Markham said. "I'm sorry you wasted any time planning this operation."

Jill Phillips had too much experience with people who actually wanted to kill her to be intimidated by the curt dismissal. "Your Honor," she said, "I don't waste time. My deputies are going to Stone Cross when you do. It is our job to protect you, and we will do our job."

Markham gave a thoughtful nod, pooching out his bottom lip. "I've no desire to be obstreperous. That said, I do expect the wishes regarding my privacy to be heeded. I know very well what a protective detail is like, and I do not want to have deputy marshals underfoot while I'm doing my job."

"Understood, sir," Phillips said. "This will not be a formal detail. As you are no doubt aware, Stone Cross is a long way from the road system. They have no armed police force, no ambulance, no hospital, no emergency services should anything go wrong. My deputies will simply be nearby in the event they are needed. They will not be underfoot."

Markham leaned forward, resting his elbows on the desk blotter. "What do you think of this, Deputy Cutter?"

"I agree with Chief Phillips."

"You would." Markham gave him a narrow look. "I've been on the bench long enough to read people."

Cutter waited for the rest of it, but Markham seemed to

decide against whatever it was he was going to say. Instead, he stood and offered his hand. "Very well," he said. "I suppose I'll see you in Stone Cross, then."

"They're probably flying out on the same plane you are," Phillips said.

Markham gave a slow nod, and then sat back down at his desk to resume his reading, glasses perched on the end of his nose. "I see. Not underfoot then?"

"That wasn't so bad," Scott Keen said when they were back in the secure hall, walking toward the Marshals' elevator.

"You think?" Phillips glanced at Cutter. "You read it the way I did?"

"Yep," Cutter said. "He's not putting up much of a fight because he knows I'm not happy about this whole arrangement. I'm thinking he's going along with it to spite me."

"If that's what it takes, Big Iron," the chief said.

Lola tugged on Cutter's arm. "Seriously, boss. You gotta tell me about this incident."

Chapter 8

Birdie Pingayak's chin tattoo sewed her to her past.

In her great-grandmother's time the indigo lines would have been accomplished with a bone needle and a length of sinew from a bowhead whale. Back then, the ink would have been made from urine mixed with the soot of a seal-oil lamp. Things were different for Birdie. Bone was too porous to sterilize and autoclaves turned sinew to mush. Seal-oil lamps had given way to electricity. And urine . . . well, there were probably better antiseptics out there. Modern methods called for a stainless-steel needle through the skin, pulling a length of sterile floss dipped in commercial tattoo ink.

Telltale dots in the lines beneath Birdie's bottom lip said her marks were skin-stitched. *Tavlugun* in her maternal greatgrandmother's native Iñupiaq, Birdie's chin tattoo was comprised of three pencil-thin lines that ran from the base of her lower lip to the tip of her chin. Parallel, they were spaced a quarter inch apart—the width of the nail on the tattooist's little finger. The center line was slightly wider than the outer two. It was applied with a technique called hand-poking, which was just what the name implied. Birdie preferred the skin-stitch, but that was just her.

Birdie's father, and his father before him, were Yup'ik from right there in Stone Cross, but her maternal great-grandmother was Iñupiat from Wainwright, clear up on the Chukchi Sea. The whites called them Eskimos. In some parts of the world, the term was offensive, but here in Alaska they used the term themselves. Birdie never met her great-grandmother, Bertha Sovok Flannigan, but she knew her namesake had been highly regarded for great wisdom and common sense. And Bertha had the same tattoo, and others as well. The stories said she had ornate designs tattooed on the inside of her thighs, so her babies would have something beautiful to look at when they were born. She was a fine woman to emulate, Birdie's mother had said.

There weren't many tattoos today, not traditional ones anyway, and not given in the traditional way. But they were common in the old times, before the 1890s when missionaries came to Alaska. The Moravians who arrived in Bethel translated the Bible into Yup'ik, but virtually all the other religions forbade the speaking of Native languages altogether. They banned traditional dancing and drumming—and, instead of the old stories, they preached the Bible, especially Leviticus 19:28. By 1910 almost every indigenous person from Point Barrow to the tip of the Aleutians was Christianized. The old ways shriveled with each successive generation until they were good and dead.

Great-grandmothers had tattoos, grandmothers had rosaries.

Birdie Pingayak saw things differently. In her mind, preaching Leviticus 19:28 was cherry-picking. The same chapter that condemned tattoos talked about animal sacrifice and how a man should cut his beard. The elders who hired her as a teacher didn't mind the tattoo, or, more likely, they'd grown numb to the sight of it by the time she finished college and applied for the job.

At thirty-one, she was awfully young to be the principal of Stone Cross K–12, or any school for that matter. The two men and four of the five women who sat with her at the folding table in the gym were village elders, none of them under sixty years old. Ethyl Kipnuk sat to Birdie's right with her head bowed in prayer. She was in her early fifties.

All eight rows of bleachers were filled, from the edge of the basketball court to the cinderblock wall. Stenciled lettering said the Stone Cross girls' basketball team had been regional champions four years running—two of those years with Birdie's daughter, Jolene, playing forward. Birdie peeked through a half-open eye, scanning the crowd for the fifteen-year-old, who had apparently defied her mom and skipped out on the meeting.

Birdie pressed back the urge to panic. She'd seen *Sascha* that morning, walking through the snow in the dark. He'd been out of state for a while after he got out of prison. She didn't know where he'd gone, but that didn't matter as long he wasn't here. But now he was back. The court said he could come through town to visit family, but Birdie knew full well he came just to torment her—and see Jolene. So far, he'd never been stupid enough to come to the school. One of these days she was going to have to shoot him, but until then, she wanted to keep Jolene under her wing.

Like the other women at the table, Birdie wore a traditional parka-like blouse of thin cotton called a *kuspuk* that hung to midthigh. Birdie's was light blue with darker blue forget-me-nots, worn over a pair of not so traditional khaki slacks. Many of the others in the gym, both women and men, had on sweat pants. The loose *kuspuk* hid Birdie's slender figure—a change from the norm of many Alaska Natives, male and female alike, ever since sugary pop and starchy foods had found their way into the bush diet of meat and fat. Birdie stuck to traditional foods—salmon, whitefish, caribou, moose, beaver tail, and wild berries. She had a teenage daughter to think about. It was hard enough raising a kid in the village without worrying about the problems brought on by a steady diet of cookies and cola. And anyway, a gallon of milk was fifteen bucks. The good candy bars were three dollars each. It didn't take long to eat up a teacher's salary if you didn't supplement it with hunting and fishing.

Birdie kept her head bowed, but opened her eyes a little wider. Where was that kid?

As a rule, children ran wild in the village, considering all adults to be their aunties or uncles. Rubber boots, a T-shirt, maybe a hoodie when it got super cold, a basketball to play with—or a rusted bicycle if they were lucky—kids played outside in everything but a blizzard. Chronic coughs, snotty noses, runaway eczema, it didn't matter. Tundra tough, they called it.

She didn't want that for her daughter. She wanted her here, where it was safe. Birdie knew all too well that fifteen was plenty old enough to get herself into life-altering trouble. Jolene had come home from her basketball game with two new hickeys on her throat. You had to stand still for someone to give you a hickey, and if a girl stood still long enough around some of these boys . . . Birdie didn't want to think about that. The love bites weren't the worst of it. Just last week, Sylvia Red Fox had looped the fiber-glass band from a pallet of canned peaches around her neck, then put the other end over a door handle on the loading dock and sat down on the cold concrete to hang herself. Sylvia Red Fox had been fifteen. She'd seemed like such a happy girl, with a hickey or two on her neck—just like Jolene, who was not where she was supposed to be right now.

Flutters of panic began to push their way into Birdie's chest. Birdie raised her head now, joining the clandestine group of others in the gym who had their eyes open during the prayer, checking Facebook or sending texts. At last, Birdie located her daughter, sitting on the top row, her back to the mural of the school mascot, a howling timber wolf. She too surfed on her phone when she should have been praying. The schizophrenic emotions of wanting to bite her toes off or give her a hug ebbed and flowed in Birdie's chest. She willed herself to relax with each breath. Sascha was nowhere to be seen. Jolene was okay, for now.

The door prizes were good enough this time they'd had to set up two rows of plastic chairs in front of the bleachers to hold everybody. The village council offered three chances to win: ten gallons of gasoline, fifteen gallons of fuel oil, or a fifty-dollar credit at the village store. Many in the audience attempted to cool themselves with cardboard fans, made from the navy-blue boxes of Sailor Boy Pilot Bread. They put up with the stuffy auditorium air and uncomfortable seating in hopes of winning the gas for their ATVs or snow machines. At over seven dollars a gallon, it was by far the best of the three prizes. The fuel oil was second, and the store credit was nothing to sneeze at. Fifty bucks didn't go far in bush Alaska. A jar of peanut butter was twenty-two dollars. But free food was free food, even if you could carry fifty bucks' worth home under one arm.

Her panic gradually subsiding, Birdie glanced at the others sitting with her before she closed her eyes again. She'd known them all since she was a child and called them auntie or uncle.

Martin Jimmy was on his feet behind a microphone at the end of the table, engaged in one of his notoriously long prayers in the Yup'ik language. Even the people with their eyes open pretended they were pious enough to enjoy it, but Birdie could hear the shuffling in the bleachers as people began to wish he would wind it down. The twelve teachers at Stone Cross school sat in chairs to the side of the gym under the basketball hoop. They were part of the community, so Birdie wanted them at the meeting. None of them spoke Yup'ik, so this was five minutes of phlegmy, wetmouthed gibberish to their ears. Too bad, Birdie thought. It was actually a pretty good prayer.

Martin Jimmy's voice finally reached the crescendo that was his customary sign-off to the Holy Trinity.

The city secretary, Ethyl Kipnuk, scooted back her plastic chair and stood to brief the attendees about the upcoming visit of a federal judge. He was to help them decide a dispute over who owned a spit of land out by the airport— the residents of the city, which included everyone under the age of fifty, or the Native nonprofit shareholders who were alive in 1971 when the Alaska Native Claims Settlement Act was passed. The land's location made it worth a great deal of money and the disagreement over who owned it was no small cause for concern, even among individual families.

Several people wanted to make their cases in this forum. Kipnuk listened respectfully, for that was the Yup'ik way, but when the opportunity arose, she reminded everyone that the judge was coming for that purpose. Some groused about him coming to the village at all. Birdie couldn't help but agree.

Representatives of the federal government didn't have a great reputation for looking after the best interests of bush Alaska. Mistrust of *gussaks*—white people—in general ran deep in the Native community. Most of the teachers were *gussaks*. Newbies were not trusted. The priest, Father Nicolai, was white. He was married to a Yup'ik woman and they'd been in Stone Cross since Birdie was a child. Though not exactly revered, he was more than tolerated. The ones like Aften and Bobby Brooks, who'd returned to teach for three years running, even after experiencing firsthand the difficulties of life in a bush village, they fell somewhere in between.

The city secretary reminded everyone that they were just a week away from the forty-day memorial service for Lyle Skinner, a sweet seventeen-year-old boy, as bright as Birdie had ever seen, who had shot himself over a girl from downriver. Like most in Stone Cross, the Skinners were Eastern Orthodox. Forty days from his death, his spirit could finally quit wandering. His family could lock their house if they wanted to—though few did out here—and turn off the light in Lyle Skinner's room. They would take down the spruce branches they'd placed over the door so the departed could more easily find his way home if he wanted to stop by. They could now decorate his grave. They could stop mourning; though, from the look of his poor mother, Birdie doubted if that would be the case after four hundred days, let alone forty. The gym fell silent. Nervous coughs echoed through the bleachers. Everyone shuffled in their seats. The village was still raw from the recent death of Sylvia Red Fox. Birdie didn't want to think about that one for too long.

"I hear there was a Hairy Man sighting upriver," a man on the front row said, changing the subject. A murmur of relief at the new subject rippled up and down seats like a wave. "Lots of folks out hunting this time of year," another man said. "Everybody should remember and be watchful."

Even Birdie found herself nodding. She'd spent her college years at UAF in Fairbanks, away from village sentimentality and superstition. Her roommates had made fun of her when she told them about the Hairy Man or any of the numerous otherworldly beings that seemed as real as the nose on her face in the loneliness of the bush. Birdie was an educated woman, and still, she didn't know what to believe. Was the thought of a hairy man wandering over the tundra any more incredible than Lyle Skinner's spirit needing some spruce branches over the door to find his way back to his house?

Stories about the Hairy Man went on for a full five minutes. Again, Ethyl Kipnuk listened quietly until she saw an opportunity to speak without interrupting. Birdie had concluded long ago that these meetings would have been half as long had a white person been running them—and twice as long if any Eskimo besides Ethyl Kipnuk had been in charge. It just wasn't in Yup'ik nature to butt in while someone else was speaking.

Kipnuk reminded everyone of the potluck the following evening to welcome Judge Markham, urging them to bring traditional Native foods. Eyes wandered, Sailor Boy fans flapped, some people dozed, until she mentioned that it was time for door prizes. Birdie was ineligible to win—a rule she'd made herself—so she drew the names out of a woven grass basket. Ethyl won the groceries. That pissed some people off, but not as bad as if she'd won the gasoline.

People began to clear out once the door prizes were awarded, chatting with each other about the Hairy Man, or the visiting judge, or where the caribou were hiding this week. All of them ignored the rows of chairs on the gym floor as they walked past. Vitus Paul, the school handyman, would stack them. That's what he got paid for. He was on the lazy side, and Birdie thought she might have to remind him, but he got right to it. The teachers pitched in too. Birdie nodded to several sets of parents and went to find Jolene so she didn't slip out with the crowd. Birdie might not ask anyone else, but her own daughter was going to help.

Two women in their fifties stood at the end of the bleachers chatting while they watched the chairs being stacked. Birdie knew them—she knew everyone in the village. These women were not bad people, but they were probably no more likely to help stack chairs than their grandkids.

Birdie spied Jolene standing at the end of the bleachers, talking to Charlene Ayuluk. Charlene was a good girl. Never in trouble. Had her eyes on the Air Force after graduation. Jolene had trouble making friends sometimes, so Birdie decided to let her talk a minute. She caught the end of the women's conversation while she stacked chairs.

". . . they used to have bigger parties when we were kids," one of the women said. "They used to do up a big deal at Christmas."

"Those were good times," said the second woman.

"I know. Right?" the first woman said. "And remember, they used to plan a parade through the village. I wonder why they don't do that anymore."

The second woman thought for a minute. "I guess we are *they*. Maybe we should plan something."

The first woman shrugged. "Maybe so." She looked up at the clock on the cinderblock wall behind the basketball hoop. "Listen. I got *The Big Bang Theory* recorded. I gotta run and watch it before I have to cook dinner."

Both women waved sweetly as Birdie passed them, pushing a stack of seven chairs toward the storage closet. It would have been easy to blame village culture, but Birdie had seen the same behavior in Fairbanks. Stone Cross was just keeping up with the times.

Jolene came by just then from the other direction, pushing her own stack of chairs along the gym floor. She didn't speak to her mother, barely even looked at her, but she'd pitched in to help. Maybe Birdie wasn't doing such a bad job after all.

Vitus pushed a row of chairs past, causing a small group of milling people to open up and give way, giving Birdie an unobstructed view of Sascha Green's face as he peered around the bleachers by the back door. He just stood there, staring at Jolene.

Birdie had to clutch the chairs to keep from falling. She had to remind herself to breathe. He wasn't supposed to have contact with Jolene. Ever. It was court ordered. She would have laughed at that had she not been so scared, so angry. He'd never come to the school before. Which meant he was getting bolder. The Troopers would never get here in time when he did decide to make a move. The village public safety officer was new. He was a hard worker, but he was too diplomatic, too kind. He had no idea what kind of person he was dealing with. It would take more than a Taser to deal with this problem.

Sascha turned without acknowledging her, which made sense since she'd nearly killed him once before. He'd be back. Someday soon, she was going to have to finish the job.

Chapter 9

Aften Brooks walked straight to the kitchen as soon as she walked in the door. For the past hour and a half, she'd been trapped in the community meeting, unable to think of anything but calling Sarah Mead on the VHF radio. Attendance was mandatory and excruciating. Birdie decreed it. It was the right thing to do, Aften knew that, but like her granddad always said, it took a mighty fine meeting to beat no meeting at all. These village get-togethers were just so long, mostly because Yup'ik people were just so damned polite. Everyone who wanted to talk got the floor for as long as they wanted, and there were always those who wanted to talk . . . on and on and on. Aften usually loved it—or at least she didn't mind. The way these people switched so naturally back and forth between English and their back-of-the-throat, wetmouthed Native language was pleasant to her ears. She understood a few words, and spoke fewer still without bringing giggles from her students, but loved the way it sounded.

She hadn't heard much of anything today. Her mind was too busy worrying about her friend.

There was nothing but static on the VHF, so Aften hung the mic on the clip attached to her cupboard. Groaning with pent-up frustration, she leaned both hands on the lip of her sink. Snow whirled and looped in the wind outside the kitchen window, already piling up in drifts along the weathered siding of the neighboring duplex—more teacher housing—thirty feet away. A frozen caribou hide hung across the porch rail like an old and matted rug, flapping in the wind, rapidly covering with snow. The decapitated head from the same caribou stared back at her from under the porch.

Aften looked at the radio again. Sarah hadn't answered her all day. She couldn't reach David or Rolf either. Everyone at Chaga had gone radio silent. The lodge had a satellite phone, but it was a handheld unit that had to be powered up with the antenna oriented in order to receive a call. Bush Alaska could be an awfully lonesome place and Sarah was new. Aften made it a point to talk to her every day, if only to say hello, to let her hear another feminine voice.

Living in the bush gave you a sense of the flow of things. Disruptions to that flow seemed much starker than they did when you had more resources, more safety nets. Something was wrong. Aften could feel it.

She was tall, slender, athletic. A streak of silver ran from her temple through dark, shoulder-length hair. It was a beauty mark she'd acquired in childhood when she'd fallen out of an apple tree and landed on her head. At twenty-seven, she already had three years teaching high school in Stone Cross under her belt. To her, teaching was more of a calling than a job. In the bush it was doubly so. She loved her students, the raw challenge of living in such a remote spot—but she had to admit it would probably account for more gray hair. The recruiter for the school district had found her at a job fair. He'd made it sound like a grand adventure—come north, teach some math, coach some basketball, discover yourself. Bobby was an outdoorsman to the bone. He hadn't been too hard to convince. So they shipped a few household goods—mostly Bobby's hunting stuff—and moved to Alaska as a package deal. Aften taught math and science, Bobby taught English and social studies, and they made this little village off the Kuskokwim their home.

"I'm going upriver," she said. A decree really, but her husband was used to that.

Bobby Brooks glanced up from a pair of insulated pants he was mending at the small Formica table. He'd torn a gash in them hunting caribou two days before. "You can't go upriver."

She dipped her head, glaring over the top of her big, blackframed glasses. "What do you mean *can't*?"

He returned to his mending, ever calm. "This isn't me exercising unrighteous dominion, darlin'. The river is the one saying no. Abe's boat was sucking up ice crystals all the way home yesterday."

Abe Richards was the shop teacher in Stone Cross. He and Bobby had taken two days off to hunt caribou upriver. Richards was a little on the weird side, but Birdie gave them the time without complaint because they provided meat for several elders who were too old to go hunting.

"Everything was all right when you stopped by the lodge?"

Bobby nodded. "I didn't see Sarah, but we left a caribou shoulder with David." He set down the pants, carefully sticking the heavy-duty needle in the fabric so he didn't lose it. Like most things in the village, you couldn't just run to the store and get another one.

He wrapped his arms around her waist, hugging her from behind. "Look, hon, I think David is kind of a putz, but Sarah's a tough lady. They're probably so busy getting everything ready for freeze-up she hasn't had time to call."

"I already talked to Melvin," Aften said. "He told me he would try and take me up in his boat."

"He did?" Bobby said. "That doesn't sound like him."

"He tried to talk me out of it."

"Smart guy, Melvin," Bobby said. "I heard Vitus say he's taking the day off for subsistence hunting. He plans to take his ATV out tonight and try to catch a moose. Maybe he'd give you a ride if you asked. That new substitute, Donna, said she's been taking out Mr. Gordon's dog team for short training runs, pulling the four-wheeler to keep 'em in shape. You could probably talk either one of them into letting you tag along."

Vitus Paul, the school's maintenance man, was just nineteen years old. He had a massive crush on Aften, which would make riding behind him on an ATV beyond awkward. Plus, he was taking subsistence time and she doubted Ms. Pingayak would allow her to miss a day to go hunting, since she'd already let Bobby go.

Donna Taylor was new to the school, having taken over Colby Gordon's combined second- and third-grade class when Gordon went in for emergency knee surgery. Unlike the rest of the teachers who lived in district-owned duplexes next to the school, Mr. Gordon rented a small cabin at the edge of town with twenty-six Alaska huskies. One quarter Yup'ik, he was something of a local celebrity and planned to run the Kuskokwim 300 sled-dog race in January if his knee healed up in time. Donna Taylor had not only agreed to teach his class, but to exercise his dog team as well during his absence. There wasn't enough snow to run a sled yet, so she made do by hitching a team to the front of Gordon's fourwheeler and waiting until after dark when the trails froze solid enough they didn't bog down.

"Donna's probably the best bet," Aften said.

"Or," Bobby whispered into her ear, "you could wait a day or two. It's supposed to warm up tonight and things'll only get worse. We're not going to do anyone any good if we're buried up to our necks in mud. Fog's supposed to roll in sometime in the morning. We might run aground on a sandbar or two, but the river should be a little better for a few hours."

"We?"

"I'm not staying home while my wife runs off and has all the adventure."

Aften wheeled suddenly. "I'm thinking about this all wrong."

"That's a first," Bobby said. "Not the being wrong part. Just you admitting it."

Aften ignored him. "I don't have to be the one to go in person," she said. "Sarah told me she's seen a couple of good moose in that little drainage south of the lodge. If Vitus is going out tonight, I can ask him to check on her while he's hunting."

Bobby nodded. "You know I love it out here, but this nasty little period of time when the ground is too mucky to drive on and the river is too slushy to use a boat really sucks. If that fog moves in like the weather-guesser says, we'll all be stuck wherever we're at."

"I know," Aften said. "And so will Sarah."

Chapter 10

Cutter rarely jogged. When he wasn't walking, he ran. Hard.

It was a Grumpy thing. The old man believed that if you were going to take the time to exercise, you may as well focus on the *work* part of the workout. "Outlaws don't trot away from you," he'd say. "They haul ass, so you can't afford to screw around." As far as Cutter knew, Grumpy never did anything halfway. He was still running a solid eight-minute mile the week before his aorta exploded and he dropped dead on his boat. It was a hell of a way to go out. He couldn't even bring himself to half-ass being sick.

It was spitting sleet outside, *coldy-cat-cold* the twins called it. Cutter would have rather run outside, even in the snotty weather, but Mim looked like she needed to talk, so they all loaded in her Toyota minivan and went to the Dome. Cutter drove, listening to the twins jabber about their day, while he alternately glanced between the image of Constance bent over her smartphone in the rearview mirror, and Mim looking content in the passenger seat. Cutter couldn't imagine a circumstance where he'd admit it, but he'd pictured just such a scene when he was sixteen, the moment he first met Mim at the shop where she worked in Manasota Key.

No, he wasn't ever going to admit that one.

The Dome was just what its name implied, a massive inflatable bubble, located off Dowling Road in south Anchorage. Arched, stark white walls made the artificial turf fields in the center of a 400-meter track appear so green it looked like real grass. The shape, the lights, the sheer size of the place gave it an other-worldly feel, like an explorer base on Mars or some far-flung star system in the stories Grumpy read to Cutter and his brother when they were kids.

Bad weather made the Dome a happening place in the evenings. High school and college athletes alike used the track and field to stay in shape. Business folk too ran off steam after work, doing CrossFit in the corners, playing Spikeball, soccer, or football on the field. Tonight, the Cutters shared the track with a couple dozen others, and it was sure to get busier. The twins tossed a football at the end of the turf. Mim walked, keeping to the outside, leaving the inside lanes for runners. She wore a blue Alaska Grown sweatshirt and a pair of black nylon running shorts that threatened to slow Cutter down every time he passed her. Constance had come too, self-conscious enough about her body to want to run off the pancakes she'd refused to eat that morning.

Cutter worked through each of the Marshals Service Fitness-in-Total, commonly known by the acronym FIT, events in the order he would complete the actual test: a minute each for sit-ups and push-ups, a straight-leg sit-and-reach test for flexibility, and a mile-and-a-half run. Passing the test wasn't difficult unless you were a Deputy Donut. Sadly, Cutter knew a few of those. But he wanted to do better than pass. As a line supervisor, he felt it was important to set the standard for the PODs—the plain old deputies, the line troops, the backbone of the Marshals Service. Lola Teariki didn't need motivation when it came to working out, but she was an anomaly. Setting an example for the rest of the deputies meant not just running with them, but excelling as an "old guy." Cutter was relatively new to the district. He wanted his people to trust that he could catch the bad guys when they took off. A good reputation only lasted until your first screwup. You could swagger around the office and tell all the war stories you wanted, but there was no faking it on the street. If a twenty-something pothead took off at a sprint, you better be capable of running him down, or it got around the squad room pretty damned quickly. That was another reason he ran instead of jogged.

He was on his fifth of six laps, digging in to make sure he kept the run under ten minutes. A lanky college-age kid in green racing shorts burned past, chuffing like a steam engine. Green Shorts sprinted the straights, ducking in and out of lanes as he passed other runners like he owned the place. He got a little close for Cutter's taste, almost but not quite touching shoulders. Cutter chalked it up to immaturity and ignored him. The kid was probably just showing off for the three college-age ladies who'd come in at the same time.

Putting Green Shorts out of his mind, Cutter focused on his own run, and ticked down a list of things he needed for his upcoming trip.

He kept a go-bag ready to travel for fugitive work, so it didn't take him long to pack for the trip out west. In some parts of the country, the winter and summer kits might be different, but in Alaska, where rain and freezing temperatures might happen any month of the year, the things he took with him remained substantially the same, just adding a heavier parka and winter boots.

Most rural villages had no restaurants or hotels. Visitors brought their own sleeping bags and food, which usually consisted of Meals Ready to Eat. Cutter had eaten enough MREs in the military that he could just about identify each entrée by feeling the weight of the pouch. He'd picked out his favorites from the task force storage closet—chili mac and three-cheese tortellini (that one came with Skittles)—and done his civic duty by steering Lola away from the veggie burger and beef enchilada. They'd bring assorted granola bars and other snacks as well, along with a water filter, iodine tablets, and some powdered drink mix to mask the taste of the iodine. Cutter had a strong gut, but one of his military instructors in Basic had pointed out that for every soldier who died in battle during the US war with Mexico, seven had died from dysentery. He had eaten enough half-cooked goat and drunk enough cloudy water—and suffered the consequences— to last him ten lifetimes.

They'd each bring a .40 caliber semiautomatic pistol; Lola's was the larger Glock 22 issued by the USMS, Cutter's was a smaller Glock 27 that he carried over his right kidney to comport with US Marshals policy. He considered his grandfather's Colt Python, worn over his hip, the primary weapon. Since Stone Cross was a long way from anywhere, each deputy took three extra magazines rather than the customary two. Cutter had a speed loader for the revolver in his coat pocket and a plastic "speed strip" with six additional rounds in the breast pocket of his vest. The semiauto was certainly faster to reload, but the Colt had character—and a long history. In truth, in the bush the .357 revolver made a heck of a lot more sense than the Glock. But USMS headquarters firearms policy didn't often make sense regarding Alaska. For one thing, it didn't take big bears into account.

Lola would bring her long gun, a Colt M4 with an Aimpoint Patrol holographic sight. Each would also carry a small day pack with basic survival and first-aid gear for self-care as well as extra in case they had to treat any wounds the judge might receive. The chances that Markham would need a Band-Aid or cold medicine were much greater than them having to fight their way out of a confrontation. Still, they wanted to be prepared for anything.

Cutter kicked up his pace on the last straightaway. He checked his watch when he crossed the finish, slowed to a walk as he rounded the curve, catching his breath. Nine forty-one. Not too shabby. Out of habit, he'd kept something back. Running after a fugitive wasn't like a track meet. You couldn't leave it all at the finish line. You had to have enough steam left to fight the guy after you caught up with him.

Mim was ahead of him now, halfway down the straight, still in lane five, second from the outside. Cutter liked to walk a few laps after he ran, so he jogged to catch up. They could walk together while he cooled down. Green Shorts chuffed past again, still weaving in and out, veering outside so he very nearly ran over Mim.

Cutter picked up his pace, catching Mim in a few easy strides.

"Well, he's kind of a jerk," she said, nodding to Green Shorts.

"I noticed that."

"How was your run?"

"Good."

"You don't seem tired," she said. "You must recover fast."

He smiled. "I got a big heart."

She walked in silence for a moment. "That you do, Arliss Cutter. That you do."

"You look deep in thought," Cutter said, consciously slowing his breathing.

She smiled. "I was thinking about how much you look like Grumpy."

"Old and grizzled?"

She snorted. "Not quite yet. I found a photo the other day while I was going through some of Ethan's books. It's a good one of Grumpy and you on the beach, but your first wife is in it too so I've never put it out."

"Yeah." Cutter groaned. "Grumpy warned me about her."

Mim looked sideways, smirking. "To say the least. Grumpy told Ethan she asked him to pay for a boob job."

"Rita had no filter," Cutter said. "Or good sense. I'd just headed out on my second tour to Afghanistan, making buck-sergeant wages, and she decided she needed . . . well, you know."

"Grumpy didn't pay, did he?"

"Not a chance," Cutter said. "But that didn't stop Rita. She put it on a credit card and then went begging to my aunt Linda for the money when the bill came due." He shook his head. "Aunt Linda has never let me forget that she paid for a boob job that neither of us ever saw any benefit from. She also never lets me forget that I have a certain type."

"Like you said, you have a big heart. I think your type is a damsel in distress." Luckily, Mim decided to move the subject away from his former wives. "I don't want to give you a big head or anything, but the twins are grouchy that you have to go away tomorrow."

"I'm not too happy about that myself," Cutter said. He had to concentrate to keep from swaying too close as they walked.

Mim changed the subject again. "I feel like I should run too. It would help offset all the cowboy chili pie I plan to eat when we get home. You know, Ethan used to make that at least once a month. He'd always let the kids eat it off metal pie pans like they were on a trail drive or something."

Cutter chuckled, remembering. "Grumpy used to let Ethan and me do that. I was always more excited about the pie pans than I was about the pie."

Mim stared down at the rubberized surface of the track as she walked. "Thank you."

"I like cowboy chili pie too," Cutter said. "You don't have to—"

"I mean for coming to Alaska," Mim said, quieter now. "After Ethan died. You have your own life to deal with—"

Cutter chuckled. "Yeah, and I've done a great job of screwing that up. You guys help me more than I help you."

"Nope," Mim said. "If you hadn't come to help, the kids would be eating hot dogs five nights a week. With you, they get to use knives."

They walked together in silence for a time, Cutter enjoying the closeness. Green Shorts shot by again, brushing Mim's shoulder and nearly knocking her down.

"Hey!" Cutter yelled. "Watch it!"

"You watch it, gramps," the kid yelled over his shoulder. "The track's for running, not camping out."

Mim held out her hand, palm down. "I'm fine," she said. "Don't worry about it."

Cutter watched as Green Shorts moved up behind Constance, jockeying for position as if he were trying to set a record for most annoying idiot in the Dome. Constance was the smallest in the knot of people rounding the curve ahead of him, making her the spot he chose to go through instead of around. She tripped as he hip-checked her, skidding face-first into the rubberized track. Green Shorts half turned, yelled something over his shoulder to Constance that Cutter couldn't quite make out, then kept running. Whatever he said, it didn't look like an apology.

Cutter and Mim both broke into a run. Cutter reached Constance about the time she got back on her feet, with Mim just a few steps behind. Embarrassed and flustered, Constance promised she was okay, waving them off to continue her lap with her head down, limping a little as she picked up speed.

Cutter found himself running again before he knew it. Mim called out to him, but he chose not to hear. He caught up with his quarry at the far side of the next curve.

Green Shorts glanced over his shoulder, surely expecting something like this. He scoffed when he saw Cutter, twice his age, sweating through his T-shirt, surely exhausted from his run. Cutter lengthened his stride, picturing his fallen niece as he poured on speed. The kid looked up again, a sudden flash of panic crossing his face this time. His arms pumped faster as he wrung out his last drop of speed, a gazelle in a last desperate attempt to shake a closing lion. Normally, he would have been faster than Cutter, but righteous anger gave a little added boost for the scant few yards Cutter needed to pull ahead half a stride, and then crowd in, stepping directly in front of the other man's lead foot. Cutter slowed immediately, turning in time to watch Green Shorts do a Superman dive, arms outstretched to catch himself as he fell.

Cutter forced a grin, reaching to help the startled young man to his feet. Stunned, Green Shorts took the offered hand. Cutter held nothing back, and almost yanked the kid's arm out of the socket helping him to his feet. He didn't need words to get his point across. *I am more than capable of running you down and beating you to death with your own arm.*

Green Shorts started to protest, but Cutter stopped him with another slightly maniacal grin.

"Sorry about that," he said for the benefit of other runners who filed past. "These old legs get away from me sometimes." He gushed like they were buds. "Man, you're fast. Another ten strides and I think you would've pulled away from me."

Green Shorts cursed under his breath, rubbing his shoulder as he limped to the edge of the field where the three college girls waited for him. Two of them smiled at Cutter, which seemed to irk the kid more than the stumble.

The twins were engrossed in an argument over their football and had missed it all. Constance stared straight ahead as she jogged past.

Mim trotted up, panting, giving Cutter a wary side-eye. She wasn't overweight, but she wasn't used to running, or dealing with the stress of watching her brother-in-law pull the neck off a careless turd.

"You're gonna put someone's eye out with that pointy moral compass of yours," she said. "Ethan warned me you could be a hothead."

"Is that right?"

They started walking again. "So did Grumpy."

Cutter followed, giving an honest laugh. "That's rich, considering Grumpy had more scars on his knuckles than most people have knuckles."

Mim put a hand on his elbow as they walked. "You've been in Alaska, what, ten months?"

"About."

"And in that time, you've done nothing but listen to our problems. That's a lot of sin-eating, if you know what I mean."

"I'm fine," Cutter said.

"Not so sure about that," Mim said. "I'm a mom, re-member. Ethan said you used to get so angry as a kid you would forget to breathe."

"I grew out of that."

"Did you, Arliss? I've known you since we were sixteen years old. You went off to Afghanistan a tough but basi-cally happy guy. Ever since you came back, you've been this ticking bomb."

"Honestly, Mim," he said, "I am fine. I just don't put up with bullshit."

She glanced up. The sadness in her eyes should have crushed her, but it didn't. "There's always going to be bull-shit, Arliss. The earth is basically just one big spinning ball of it. It's all around us. You have got to let it roll off. The way I see it, we have two more laps to give you time to cool down. We can walk in silence, or you can trust that I care about you the way you care about me."

Cutter doubted she felt the same way he did. Not by a long shot. If there was anyone he wanted to tell, it was Mim.

"There was someone I should have saved," he said, his throat so tight he had to swallow hard to force the words out, ". . . and I didn't. I won't let that happen again—"

The twins ran up from the sidelines, tugging on the tail of Cutter's sweatshirt.

"Uncle Arliss," they said in unison.

Matthew shouldered a little closer than his brother. "Will there be some more stuff to cut for the cowboy chili pie?"

"Matt and me want to use the knives again."

"Knives?" Cutter said, grateful for the interruption. He glanced at Mim and then back at the boys. "I guess you can cut up some onions if you're game for that kind of work."

"Let us be men!" the boys said.

"You bet," Cutter said, coughing a little to regain his composure. "There's always stuff that needs to be cut."

DAY THREE

Chapter 11

Vitus Paul came across the tracks in the snow when he was five minutes from the lodge. He was soaked and chilled to the bone from spending three hours digging his Honda out of a tundra bog. At first he thought his mind was playing tricks on him.

The terrain was in that middle time between liquid and solid. He'd been out all night bouncing his Honda over frozen hummocks before his luck ran out and he got stuck. Digging out the ATV kept him warm for a time, along with munching on some salmon strips, but it wasn't good to be wet and cold. He'd flooded his bunny boots, then simply dumped out the water and put them back on. The oversize things some people called Mickey Mouse boots looked goofy, but they were essential out here in the winter. His feet were now the only thing on him that was warm. He kept to the river after he got himself unstuck, riding just inside the spruce and cottonwood forest beside the bank. There was always a good trail along the water, well-worn by thousands of years of animals and the hunters that had gone before.

Vitus had seen no game yet on his journey, but he had come across a ton of caribou and moose tracks. There were lots of scrapes, where the big bulls had ripped up vegetation and peeled the bark on birch trees higher than Vitus's head. He saw wolf sign too, lots of it. Paw prints as big as his hand overlaying the spade-like moose tracks or the more circular prints like two half-moons left by caribou. Yellow snow showed where the wolves had left messages to mark their territory. Vitus estimated eight or nine adults and a couple of teenagers. Where there were caribou and moose, there was always something to eat them, be it man or bear or wolf. It was the way of things. Being food was their job.

Vitus could tell the cold was robbing him of his wits. If he did not stand in front of a hot fire soon, he would end up being food for *tulukaruq*—the raven. The lodge was close. They would have a fire going there. Lucky for him, Ms. Aften had asked him to stop in and check on her friend. Visitors were few and far between out here, so most didn't need a reason to drop by for a visit. Vitus was glad he had one though. He'd never given anyone cause so far as he knew, but a lot of people didn't trust him. Not because of anything he'd ever done, but because of his cousin. Vitus could kind of understand. He didn't like the guy either. But, hey, you couldn't pick who God gave you as a cousin.

His mind wandered back down to the tracks and his eyes followed. Getting warm could wait for a minute or two. First, he wanted to study the ground.

Some *gussuks*—especially the new teachers—were scared shitless of wolves. Vitus had been around wolves his whole life. He respected them, knew they were capable of killing a grown man if they were sick, or brave, or hungry enough. If it got really cold before the snow got deep, the caribou and moose found it easier to get away. That's when wolves got dangerous, not so much to people, but they would damn sure sneak into the village and snatch a dog, sometimes right off the chain. His people hunted wolves. That made them wary of humans, which meant Vitus didn't have to be scared.

Wolves weren't the problem here. Not today.

Shivering and covered with mud, he got off the Honda to get a better look. These tracks did not belong to anything he'd seen before. Half covered in driven snow, they looked human, only much, much larger. Vitus shot a glance behind him, suddenly feeling more like prey than predator. The wind moaned in the trees. Birds chirped. Red squirrels chattered. If there was anything out there, they would have let him know. Lots of people in the village were talking about Arulataq—He Who Makes a Bellowing Cry. The name was scary enough. Vitus had never seen the Hairy Man, but he'd sat by the stove lots of nights, eating frozen fish dipped in seal oil, listening to his father's stories. Much like the yeti or bigfoot, Western Alaska's Arulataq was over nine feet tall, with arms that dragged the ground, thick fur, and a stench you could smell for miles. Vitus's father had come across the Hairy Man years before when he was out hunting. Twice. And he still went back out by himself, which proved how brave he was.

Low clouds left the early morning light flat and gray, like the skin of a long-dead salmon. Vitus got back on the Honda and backed it up so the headlight cast shadows across the best tracks, highlighting the ridges and lines to help him get a complete story. He unslung his rifle and dismounted again, squatting in the trail to take a picture with his phone. His hands shook so badly with cold he had to brace the phone against his leg to keep it still. Careful not to disturb the snow, he put his own boot beside the best track to offer some scale. This one was twice as wide and half again as long as his size ten bunny boot, which was already huge. He used a mitten to gently fan away the snow like his father had taught him—his breath would have melted it if he'd tried to blow it away. Tiny crystals of hoarfrost covered the interior of the track. Taking the recent weather into account, Vitus guessed it was maybe two days old. That made him feel a little better. Whoever . . . or whatever had made these tracks was long gone . . . Probably . . . He glanced behind him again. The prints headed north, toward some rocky hills, the kind of place where the Hairy Man was supposed to live. That was just fine with Vitus. *Go home, Arulataq. Be happy, so long as you aren't here, standing in your tracks. I have no wish to see you.*

Vitus snugged the soggy army surplus coat tighter around his neck and climbed back aboard his Honda. It would be fully light soon. Chaga Lodge was just ahead, a good thing too because he was getting seriously cold. Maybe they would give him some hot grub to warm his stomach.

He didn't know if he was more frightened or relieved when the mysterious tracks vanished at the edge of the river. The ice was too thin to support a snowshoe hare, let alone a Hairy Man. Vitus rode on, relaxed in the knowledge that the Arulataq had gone into the water a day or two before, when there had been no ice.

It was well after ten in the morning by the time he reached the lodge. The grounds were dead quiet. No tracks in the fresh dusting of snow. That was odd. Everyone should have been up, working on all the things that needed to get done before freeze-up. Vitus switched off the Honda and sat there shivering, the rifle still across his lap, listening for signs of life. It wasn't polite to go around yelling at someone else's house—or yelling anywhere for that matter—but he was lapsing into hypothermia. He needed a fire. He needed warm food. Bad.

He passed the meat shed on the way to the lodge. The idiots had left the screen door wide open, banging in the breeze. He trudged by on stiff, cold-soaked legs, hoping the white lady might have heard him approach. Maybe she was getting up right now to make him some hot soup.

He moved to shut the screen door. No point in leaving it—

Blood. A lot of blood.

His mind was thick, foggy from the chill, and it took him a moment to make sense of the design on the floor. Concentric circles, drawn in blood. What the hell? The young Eskimo backpedaled, tripping over his own feet as he scrambled up the hill to pound on the lodge door. The giant tracks had spooked him, no joke. The cold was playing tricks on his brain. He needed to talk to another human being, hear someone tell him he wasn't going crazy—even if they were mad at him for waking them up—but there didn't seem to be anyone at home.

Chapter 12

Alaska Airlines flight 43 approached Bethel from the south in buffeting winds and spitting snow. It was a little before noon. The lights of the city of Bethel—"Paris on the Kuskokwim," according to the Michael Faubion song—shone anemically through the fog and snow on haphazard streets along the meandering left bank of an oxbow slough. Small tributaries wormed their way off the main river. Countless lakes pocked the landscape. Since he was new to Alaska in general and the bush in particular, Cutter spent the one-hour flight reading articles about the area on his phone.

With just north of six thousand residents and seventy taxis, Bethel, the ninth largest city in Alaska, was large enough to serve as bush hub for fifty-six much smaller surrounding villages. It reminded Cutter of a frontier town in the old Western movies he used to watch with Ethan and Grumpy. Dusty, on the verge of becoming something, but still a long way from anywhere.

Bethel boasted a hospital, a high school, multiple churches, and numerous restaurants that sold everything you could want to eat so long as you wanted Korean, Korean/Chinese, Korean/Japanese—or Subway. There were two decent-sized grocery stores (though not enough competition to drive down grocery prices) and a people's learning center called the Yuut Elitnaurviat, where adult students earned certifications to be commercial truck drivers, dental assistants, or village health aides. It also had a prison. The sale of alcohol was illegal, so there were no bars. Mouthwash and Nyquil were kept behind the counter at the grocery stores. Drunks, however, were not exactly unheard of. People who wanted to drink could usually find a way.

Markham rode in first class with his law clerk, an earnest-looking young man named Brett Grinder, with a buzz cut and goatee. Cutter and Teariki had seats in economy, along with an attorney named Ken Ewing, who represented the Native corporation, and a young woman named Tina Paisley, who looked fresh out of law school. She represented the city of Stone Cross in the arbitration.

Passengers disembarked down a set of air stairs exposed to the weather. In this case, a miserable mix of snow and rain. Lola called it "snain."

"My Polynesian blood will never get used to this crap," she said, lugging her heavy pack down the metal air stairs behind Cutter.

"You keep saying that," Cutter observed. "Maybe Alaska wasn't the best choice of offices."

"Now, boss." Lola gave him a wink. "You trying to get rid of your Jiminy Cricket? Because considering our mission, I'm thinking I'll have to step in and save you at least twenty times in the next two days."

Cutter spun his hand around the top of his head and then made a fist, indicating that he was now in a cone of silence and Lola wasn't allowed to speak to him.

She ignored it, and he didn't care. It was as close as he came to being playful.

The Alaska Airlines terminal was packed shoulder to shoulder with people greeting loved ones and visitors. Outbound passengers lined up along the back wall, filing through the single security checkpoint to board the flight. A state plane was supposed to take Cutter and the rest of the group on the short flight upriver to Stone Cross. He'd expected a state trooper to meet them for transport to the hangar. Markham didn't want the marshals underfoot, but he sure didn't mind when Cutter made a call to the Alaska State Troopers post to make sure everything was on track. The clerk said the lieutenant had gotten tied up but was on his way.

"That's the way it is in the bush," the attorney named Ewing said. "I've spent the better part of an hour sitting on my bag at some lonely airstrip waiting because my contact had snow-machine trouble. Still, I just love it. Come out here every time I get a chance." He turned to his female opponent. "How about you, Ms. Presley?"

"Paisley," she said. "Not Presley."

"I expect he knew that already," Cutter said, loud enough for everyone to hear. "A man as smart as Mr. Ewing surely has an entire oppo-file. He's just hoping to put you on your back foot early in the game."

Paisley canted her head, squinting slightly. "My back foot?"

"A fighting term," Lola said. "Means to put you on the defensive."

Ewing gave the deputies a sneering grin but turned back to Paisley. "So have you been out before?"

"Only once," she said. "But I'm eager to learn."

"Let me give you a little advice," Ewing said, as much for Cutter's benefit as Paisley's. "Things are different out here. It's important to know when to go along to get along.

I know an AST sergeant who gives each new trooper a long list of realities when they're assigned away from the road system. He calls it knocking the pavement out of their mouths."

"Sounds like a real charmer," Cutter said, eyeing Mr. Ewing like a piece of meat.

The attorney, accustomed to debate and verbal confrontation, plowed ahead with Ms. Paisley. "Have you ever heard the story of the eider duck?"

She shook her head.

Ewing clapped his hands. "It's my favorite story. Eider ducks play a significant role in the subsistence lifestyle for Alaska Natives in the Arctic. Duck meat, duck fat, duck feathers . . . Anyway, the government in its infinite wisdom decided that the eider duck should only be hunted during a specific season, not when the Iñupiat hunters traditionally caught them. A few years after Alaska gained statehood, a young Iñupiat man from a village way to the north on the Chukchi Sea killed an eider duck out of season and was promptly cited by the trooper on duty. The next day, the young man killed another duck. The trooper gave him a second citation, and warned him that he would be arrested if he repeated the offense. Of course, the young Iñupiat killed another eider duck and was promptly jailed to wait for the traveling judge."

Markham stood nearby, waiting for his bags, obviously listening, especially now that there was a fellow member of the bench in the story.

Ewing continued. "The day for the trial finally arrived. The trooper picked the judge up from the airstrip and took him to the school where the gymnasium would serve as the makeshift courtroom. The trial was big news in the village and every man, woman, and child lined up outside the school to either watch or serve on the jury. And as they filed inside, every last one of them left a dead eider duck in a pile beside the door."

Lola smirked. "What happened?"

"From what I hear," Ewing said, "the trooper took the judge home and fed him a piece of his wife's lemon pie before taking him back to his plane. The Iñupiat hunter was released. And bush justice was served, along with lots of fatty eider duck soup."

"Justice is justice," Markham said. "There is no 'bush justice.'"

"I'm sure that's true, Your Honor," Ewing said. "But I've always liked the story."

A tall man wearing a blue Stetson campaign hat and a dark Tuffy jacket over his blue Alaska State Troopers uniform came into the terminal. The hat was wet and dusted with snow. He caught Cutter's eye, waving a gloved hand. Cutter nodded and the trooper worked his way through the crowd.

"Lieutenant Tim Warr," he said, pulling off a glove to shake hands with Cutter. "I apologize for being late. Things got a little crazy this morning . . . Well, it's always crazy here."

"No worries," Lola said, shaking the lieutenant's hand after Cutter. She'd tried a long-distance relationship with a trooper stationed on Prince of Wales Island for a couple of months, and always looked a little starry-eyed at the sight of the blue Smokey Bear hat. "We don't even have our luggage yet."

"Outstanding," Warr said. "My AST pilot will meet us at the hangar. I have another trooper bringing the van over to grab your gear. It's only a nine-minute flight to Stone Cross once you're in the air, but I have to warn you, the weather is looking bum out there. To top that off, I need the plane. Earl has to do a turn-and-burn and leave to pick up a body in Nightmute right after he drops you off." The trooper pushed the flat brim of his Stetson back a little with a knuckle. "If this weather settles in like they say it's going to, he won't be able to come back and get you when you're ready to leave—which might be ten minutes after your boots hit the ground, to be honest. Bush villages can be a little daunting if you've never been to one. I've seen new teachers spread out at the aircraft door like a cat over a bathtub. They flat-out refuse to get off the plane when they get a good look at the place." He glanced at Cutter. "Speaking of that, the special education teacher from Stone Cross has been in the lower forty-eight for a couple of weeks on a family emergency. All but a handful of the teachers in the village are brand-new, but this will be her fourth year at Stone Cross. That makes Natalie Beck a friggin' maven of local knowledge. She's a good kid. Well respected. Anyway, she needs a ride out so I thought it might be good if you had someone to give you a quick brief—conditions on the ground, as it were." He grimaced, sucking air through his teeth. "I generally only see villages at their worst, but the hard truth is that it can be awfully bleak."

Markham pursed his lips, the let's-move-this-along look any deputy who'd worked in his courtroom recognized at once. "We'll be fine. What about the river? If it's only a nine-minute flight, surely it can't be that long a boat ride."

"You're the federal judge?"

Markham nodded. "I am."

"Well, Your Honor," Warr said, "normally, a boat ride would be no problem. Forty-five minutes, tops. But your trip happens to coincide with freeze-up. The Kuskokwim is covered in fresh ice that's too thick to run a boat through and too thin to drive on. An ATV might be able to do it along the bank, if it didn't get stuck in the mud or beat you to death during the half-day ride. Air travel is the only way right now. This happens quite a bit during this time of the year. When the river freezes solid enough to drive on, they flag it and call it a winter road."

Speaking over her shoulder, Ms. Paisley dragged a heavy canvas bag off the conveyor. "I read that Bethel has a hovercraft. Can't that negotiate thin ice?"

"It can when it's working," Lieutenant Warr said.

The handheld radio on the lieutenant's belt clicked twice.

"Your ride is here," he said.

Cutter looked out the terminal windows to see a female trooper in a Toyota minivan like Mim's. The trooper pulled up to the curb so the judge didn't have to walk too far in the blowing snow. His law clerk and the two attorneys reaped the benefit. Lowly protectors, the marshals had to hoof it across the road, carrying their guns and gear to Lieutenant Warr's unmarked Tahoe in one of three AST parking spots. Another SUV with the distinctive golden-bear badge of Alaska State Troopers was parked alongside the Tahoe. Cutter sat in the caged prisoner compartment, leaning forward a little so he could hear through the small sliding window in the partition.

Warr took off his Stetson to reveal a bald head. He slid the hat into a wire holder on the ceiling of the SUV.

Lola gave him a wary smile. "How'd you know Markham was the judge?"

"I've got a sense for people who believe themselves to be wise and all-knowing." The trooper laughed. "Seriously, your boss called my boss and let us know about the threat. They emailed me Markham's photo. That guy's got a celebration of hair. And how about that bow tie. He wears it wherever he goes?"

"Apparently," Lola said.

Warr ran a hand over his smooth scalp. "Any suspects?"

"Nope," Cutter said. "Unless you have a list of people in this area who hate federal judges."

"That's liable to be a long list," Warr said. "No offense, but the feds are only slightly more loved than Alaska Fish and Wildlife Troopers, which ain't much. Subsistence rights, steel versus lead shot, fishing limits. We're not lacking for hot-button topics in the bush. Anyway, the AST hangar's just up the road. Earl should have the Caravan ready to go. Sorry he has to dump you off and leave."

Warr looked capable enough, if a little tense around the edges, like someone who had far too many emergencies on his plate at the same time, but was managing to keep ahead of everything by sheer force of will. Cutter had seen the look before, on the faces of leaders who got their orders from a headquarters who had forgotten about the chaos in the field—if they'd ever known at all.

"We'll be fine," Cutter said. "I have a feeling we'll have to pry the judge out of there. And we're not leaving until he does. This body you have to pick up, is it a homicide?"

Warr gave a somber shake of his head. "Nope. Accidental drowning. Eleven-year-old boy fell out of a boat when he was fishing with his dad on the Kolavinarak. The body washed downriver and got caught up under some scrub willow leaning out over the water. Took us a couple of days to find it with all the slush ice. Sad deal all around."

"That's stuffed," Lola said, her father's Kiwi accent peeking through again.

"I wish I could say it wasn't common." Warr turned in at a gravel lot in front of a large metal hangar. "These rivers are so cold, a lot of bush kids never learn to swim. But water accidents aren't the half of it. We had a homicide three days ago in a village up on the Yukon, a double murder–suicide. The day before that, there was an ATV accident downriver that pretty well cut a poor lady in half on a utility guywire. The oversight trooper for that village had just taken an assault report from the same woman the day before he responded to the accident. Seeing her like that really shook him up. A lot to process for a twenty-four-year-old kid."

Lola stared at the window, releasing a long sigh. "I had no idea."

"Yeah, well," Warr said, "we don't get much play on the evening news. I think most folks in the big village of Anchorage would rather read about what's going on in New York or Hollywood than be reminded of the shitload of deaths and dismemberments that occur in their own state." He threw the Tahoe into park. "Sorry to get all gloomy on you."

"No worries," Lola said. "I'm sorry we had to show up on such a shitty day."

Warr retrieved his hat, checked the brim to make sure it was still straight, and then snugged it on his head. "This stuff happens *every* day. If I had any hair, it would be on fire most of the time." He nodded at the prisoner cage. "You'll have to let your partner out. Doors don't open from the inside."

* * *

Lieutenant Warr punched the code into a mechanical cypher lock on the door. Cutter couldn't help but notice the telltale numbers scratched into the dusty metal siding of the nondescript hangar in case someone forgot their code. The heavy steel door groaned in protest against the cold as Warr pushed it open, standing back so Cutter and Lola could carry in their bags.

Judge Markham and the others were already inside. Ms. Paisley stood near the nose of the state Cessna Caravan, chatting with a rosy-cheeked young woman who Cutter assumed to be Natalie Beck, the Stone Cross teacher who would be riding with them. Where everyone else in the room dressed in gear as if they'd outfitted themselves for a winter expedition at REI, Beck wore a serviceable combination of wool and fur. Military surplus pants were held up with suspenders and tucked into the top of insulated Muck boots. A black merino wool top, slightly frayed at the cuffs, hugged the curves of her torso. Two plastic Rubbermaid totes—quintessential bush-Alaska baggage— were secured with zip ties beside everyone else's gear on the rough concrete floor at the open rear cargo door. From what Cutter had seen, these highwing single-engine planes were the workhorses of Alaska. A Cessna 185 taildragger painted in the blue-and-white Troopers color scheme occupied the corner of the hangar to the Caravan's right. A smaller, flimsy-looking Piper Super Cub squatted on huge balloon tires in the shadows near a green portable toilet on the opposite side of the hangar. Wing covers, aircraft skis, survival gear, and assorted spare parts packed tall wooden shelves that ran along both side walls. Cutter was by no means a pilot, but he was a gearhead. Motor oil and rubber tires emitted comforting smells that reminded him of younger days working on project cars with Ethan and Grumpy.

Earl Battles, the trooper pilot, was a Yup'ik man in his late forties. He was built low to the ground with broad shoulders and a wide, canary-eating smile—the kind of guy who was always thinking of a good joke, even if he kept it to himself. Obviously in a hurry to get going, he was situating the bags in the back of the airplane. He glanced up and saw Lola's rifle case.

"Natalie's bringing food and necessaries for months, so I don't mind her plastic totes, but I appreciate you bringin' luggage in soft cases. Makes it a heck of a lot easier to stow."

Markham's eyes fell to his fat, hard-sided suitcase and gave a nobody-told-me scowl.

On his knees inside the plane, the pilot reached down from the cargo door and snapped his fingers at the judge. "Let's have that one next. It needs to go near the bottom."

The law clerk stifled a snicker.

Cutter turned away. It was refreshing to see someone who treated judges like everyone else.

Earl reached for Lola's rifle case, snapping again. "We'll have to Jenga this in with everything, but I'll make sure we don't screw up your sights."

After securing the wide nylon cargo net across the rear of the aircraft, Earl jumped down and shook hands with everyone. He was enthusiastic as he took each hand, like he was genuinely glad to meet them.

"So," he said, "Lieutenant Warr told you I have to leave as soon as I drop you off?"

"He did," Markham said.

"If the weather holds then I'll check in with you later tonight and see if you're ready to come back."

"Why does everyone think we're going to want to leave right after we get there?" Tina Paisley muttered. "It's starting to creep me out."

"Past experience," Earl said, completely sincere.

"We have a job to do," Markham said. "And we will get it done. I am told that the school principal . . . a Ms. Pingayak, has rooms for us at the school."

"Pin-GUY-akh," the pilot said, wet-mouthed, sounding like he was clearing his throat at the end. "You accented the last syllable. The stress should be on the second."

"Thank you," Markham said.

Lola leaned in to Cutter and whispered, "Earl better hope he never has a case in federal court."

"Just call her Birdie," Lieutenant Warr said. "Unless you were born out there, you'll never get the language right. She's a squared-away lady, so she'll take care of you. Runs her school like a ship—which can be terrifying. Can't it, Natalie?"

"She's amazing." Beck smiled, showing deep dimples. "You'll see."

Earl clapped his hands together. "Everyone has what they need? Sleeping bags, air mattresses, food, your last will and testament?"

"He's kidding." Warr glanced down at his phone. "But this is the last chance to change your minds. Arbitration can always happen next month when the river is solid and the ice road is passable and flagged."

"It's up to the pilot, of course," Markham said, "but I say we go ahead. All parties are present and ready to proceed. If we have to stay in Stone Cross for a few extra days, that's just how it is."

Markham's clerk stared up at the plane, shaking his head. "Maybe the trooper's right, Your Honor . . ."

"Brett . . ." The judge chided him like a dog that was getting into mischief.

Earl put his hand on Brett Grinder's shoulder. "You ride up front with me, son," he said. "I can tell you're the brains of the outfit. First time in a small plane?"

The law clerk nodded.

"Really?" Earl leaned in and whispered, sotto voce, "Mine too."

He tapped the grab handle and folding metal stepladder that Grinder would use to climb into the right front seat. "Seriously though. This weather sucks, but it's still doable. Not even a federal judge can get me to defy the laws of physics and fog. We should be fine. Besides, it's only a short flight. We'll know in a couple of minutes if we're all gonna die in a ball of flames."

Chapter 13

The acrid odor of something burning wormed its way inside the bag over Sarah Mead's head. She'd read somewhere that people smelled burned toast when they were having a stroke. She had no idea if the toast part was true, but the pain in her brain made it easy to believe there was some serious damage going on up there. She blinked, licking dry lips. Even that small movement brought wave after wave of nauseating agony. She tried to push herself into a seated position. It was impossible without the use of her hands. Where the hell were her hands? And what was over her eyes?

She coughed, a sickening ache yanking her back to the brutal reality of her situation. One big, fat mystery. How did she end up here, bound, facedown? She vaguely remembered getting hit. Twice. The blow must have done some serious damage because her head was on fire. She couldn't see, her hearing was toast, and her hands were so numb they could have very well been gone for all she knew. She couldn't even scream like a normal human being. And now something was burning. Maybe the lodge was on fire.

A sudden heaviness filled the space around her, as if someone was standing inches from her face. Shadows flickered across the blindfold. A familiar odor seeped in to replace the burned toast. She tried to speak. "David?" It came out slurred and unintelligible inside her head: "Dwoooid." Maybe her jaw was broken. She pressed her face downward, bringing more nausea. She swallowed the agony and used her tongue to check for damage. As she expected, she'd lost a couple of teeth. No wonder she could do nothing but babble.

Locked inside her world of pain, she flopped and squirmed like a landed fish when a hand suddenly pressed against her shoulder.

There were muffled words. Sarah couldn't tell if something was wrong with her hearing or the part of her brain that processed sound, but she couldn't understand what was being said. She didn't even know if it was being said to her. The hand seemed gentle enough, but it didn't untie her. She smelled the odor again. It was the scent of her husband—the coconut body wash he liked. He was here. She prayed he was okay. The hand pressed more firmly on her shoulder, like it wanted to get her attention. Shadows passed in front of the hood. The heaviness of another person in her space loomed over her as someone bent closer to her ear.

More words, still garbled, but she could make out some of them now. ". . . eat . . . want to hurt you . . . be afraid . . ."

She screamed in spite of her jaw. *Be afraid.* That was rich. What else could she be?

The hand slid from her shoulder to her elbow, lifting her to a seated position. It was surprisingly gentle for a kidnapper.

The voice spoke again, slower this time. "Please . . . eat soup."

The bag over her head lifted slightly, just a few inches,

giving her space to reach an offered straw with trembling lips. It was incredibly painful, but she was so thirsty she drew in as much of the warm soup as she could before the straw was taken away. It was salty and rich and seemed to go straight to her core.

"Waaer," she said.

The same straw came up under the hood again, now in a cup of cool water. She drank slowly, drawing out the process, looking down to see her own feet for the first time in recent memory. She had no idea how long she'd been here, but judging from her hunger, it had been a while. Her eyes slowly adjusted to the light. Things were still blurry, but she needed desperately to see, to get some sort of bearings or she would float away. More garbled words. ". . . get sick . . . if . . . eat too much . . ."

She shook her head, despite the electric pain. *No! Don't take it away! Not yet*.

Her eyes felt like they were set in her skull with hot sand. It took all her effort to glance down, at the feet of the person holding the cup.

She gagged when the image came into focus. Dizziness washed over her, pressing her back on the bed.

This couldn't be. It was wrong. All wrong.

On the ground, gawking back up at her, was a pair of Xtratuf boots, each brown toe bearing a ludicrous smiley face drawn in black permanent marker.

Vitus Paul banged on the lodge door with his fist. His teeth were chattering so hard he thought they would crack any minute. Water dripped from his sodden coat, making a puddle on the wooden porch. Much longer and his body wouldn't have the energy to warm itself. He'd seen hypothermia before—and it wasn't pretty. He shook now. He still felt the painful effects of deep, penetrating cold. His bones ached. His lungs felt heavy. His hands refused to do what he told them. Even more important to his survival, he was still scared to die. Soon, that would change. The chill would seep into his core and he'd begin to feel warm. His coat would feel much too hot and he'd shuck it. He might even abandon all his clothing. The shaking would stop. Fear and pain would take a back seat in his brain—though they would never leave altogether. He would simply go to sleep, probably naked and certainly alone—until ravens or wolverines or shrews found his body.

There was still enough warm blood flowing to his brain that the idea of being eaten by tiny shrews made him queasy. He banged on the door again, calling out. This was bush Alaska, where everyone had a couple of guns. Barging into somebody's house was a good way to find out quick what kind of a shot they were. Still no answer. He thought of kicking in the door. He'd wanted to ever since he was old enough to watch cop shows on TV. But this door was made of split timber and he could barely stand up.

And anyway, it turned out to be unlocked. No one locked their doors in the bush.

Vitus stuck his head in, still a little worried about getting shot.

"Hello!"

Nothing.

No fire in the stove. Odd.

He flipped the switch on the wall, then stuck his hands back under his armpits, hugging himself to stay warm. The wood stove was out. Stone cold. Dammit. It didn't matter where everyone had gone. He had to get a fire going, or they'd find him dead on their floor when they got back.

There was a good supply of kindling in a bucket beside the stove, along with a few brittle pieces of old spruce crown and some newspaper. Somebody here knew how to start a fire. The matches were in a small glass mayonnaise jar. He had to swing his arms for almost a full minute in order to get the blood flowing enough to twist off the lid and hold a match in his fingers. Even then, his hands were so wooden he dropped two matches before he could get the flame to the paper he'd crumpled inside the stove with his shaky hand. The small twigs in the spruce crown were filled with sap that went up like gasoline as soon as the burning paper ignited them. Vitus took his time, feeding the growing flames progressively larger pieces of kindling. He was still shivering like a jerky marionette by the time he could add actual logs. His hands were starting to ache, which was good. At least he could feel them again.

He wished he could crawl inside of the stove and warm up more quickly, but settled for squatting in front of the open door with his shirt open, letting the heat bounce off his exposed skin. It took five minutes for the shivering to abate enough for him to remember he was hungry. He was going to have to borrow some food before he returned home. The river had a lot of ice, but it was still flowing. Maybe he could borrow a boat too so he wouldn't have to ride through the bog again to get back to Stone Cross. It wasn't all that cold outside, so long as he wasn't soaking wet.

Vitus hung his coat on the back of a chair in front of the stove, stood for a moment to watch the steam begin to rise off the fabric. He thought about taking off his pants too, but he was too afraid someone would walk in on him.

That was probably a crime, he thought glumly—being naked in somebody else's house—even if you were freezing to death. Instead, he decided to see what there was in the pantry and then bring something back to eat in front of the fire so his pants could dry.

The lodge kitchen was set up for feeding a dozen people, with long stainless-steel counters, a six-burner gas stove, and a walk-in pantry that contained an overwhelming amount of canned and dried food. He'd just finished making himself a peanut butter sandwich when he heard the hollow, dripping-water sounds of a raven outside the window. Blue-black against the snow, the *tulukaruq* squawked and squabbled, hopping back and forth to peck at something in the snow. Ravens were tricksters, but when they made a fuss, there was usually something worth investigating. Vitus leaned forward, craning his head over the sink to get a good look.

His mouth fell open at what he saw. A pale blue hand, fingers curled into a frozen claw, stuck out from beneath a snowdrift. The ravens ignored the hand. They were interested in something else. Something more gruesome, something bright and red against the snow.

Chapter 14

Cutter sat on the left side of the airplane, directly behind the pilot. The stopover in Bethel hadn't taken long. The sun wouldn't set until seven, which gave Cutter time to get settled and scout the village before nightfall. He had a feeling that when it got dark out here, it would be really dark, especially in this weather. A green David Clark headset protected his hearing and connected him via intercom to everyone else onboard, while he watched the tiny droplets of water skid by on his window, vibrating from turbulence and prop wash. The fog was getting worse. High wings, mounted on the top of the plane, gave passengers an unobstructed view when there was anything to see but clouds. The Caravan was a nice ride, fairly new, but it was more farm truck than company car.

Earl had isolated the intercom so only he and Markham's law clerk in the right front seat were privy to their conversation. The two of them sat chatting away, while everyone else rode in silence for the first few minutes of the flight. Even Natalie Beck, who was surely used to the scenery after three years of teaching in the bush, appeared content to lean her forehead against the window and watch the wet and foggy earth pass beneath them.

Earl's voice suddenly crackled over the headset, causing Cutter to glance toward the cockpit.

"A couple of nice moose in the water off the left wing at about eight o'clock." He flipped the switch isolating him and Grinder again, leaving everyone else to look at scenery worthy of a *National Geographic* cover.

Less than a thousand feet below, Cutter could just make out the sweeping oxbows of the Kuskokwim, one of the two mighty rivers, along with the Yukon, that formed the southern and northern reaches of the YK Delta in Western Alaska. There were a few trees right out of Bethel, but not enough to call any one spot a forest. Tall cottonwoods grew along the banks of the river and its many smaller tributaries, towering over clumps of more stunted willow, alder, and birch. Gnarled spruce stuck up here and there, out of place, like patches someone had missed when shaving.

Thousands of lakes and ponds pocked the flat tundra below, some frozen enough to be covered with ice, others gaping black holes of open water against a background of patchy snow. They flew over several villages on the river north of Bethel, handfuls of weathered houses, short gravel airstrips, boats along the bank.

Lola's voice squelched in the headset. "Even the smallest villages look like they have a school."

"Yep," Natalie Beck said. "I think the minimum is something like fifteen kids. The school serves as the community center, library, gym, theater on movie night, art center, wood shop. Ours is the only building in Stone Cross big enough to hold everyone for a funeral."

"A lot of funerals?" Ms. Paisley asked.

"Too many," Natalie said, so quiet her voice cut out a little on the intercom. "We had one for a student right before I flew out."

"Are you from Alaska?" Lola asked, obviously trying to lighten the mood.

"Michigan," Natalie said. "Ann Arbor."

Ewing cleared his throat. "I'm a Buckeyes fan."

"Go Blue," Natalie said out of habit, still subdued.

Paisley laughed. "Ann Arbor is beautiful. Surprised you left it for bush Alaska."

"This place has its charms," Natalie said. "You fall in love with the people."

Lola spoke next. "New Zealand Maori have a saying: *It's the people, it's the people, it's the people*."

"I like that," Natalie said.

Ms. Paisley half turned in her seat. "My boss told me we shouldn't use the term Eskimo, but I've heard them call themselves that."

"They do indeed," Ewing said, one of his usual pronouncements of wisdom.

"The Canadians I've met don't like it much," Natalie said. "They seem to prefer Inuit. I just follow the lead of whoever I'm speaking with. The people I know in Stone Cross don't seem to mind Eskimo. If you're unsure, just call them Yup'ik . . . or, better yet, don't give them a label."

Cutter didn't know if this teacher was wise before she came to the bush, or if the bush made her so. Either way, she spoke with the maturity of someone with a lifetime of experience.

"Stone Cross is supposed to be a fairly grim place," Markham said. "At least according to Lieutenant Warr. Is that how you would describe it?"

Natalie continued to look out the window.

The mic picked up her soft groan. "I might not be the one to talk about those details. I'm still an outsider."

"You appear to be a bright woman," Mr. Ewing said

from the back of the plane. "There must be some positive things if you return for what, your fourth year?"

"Oh," the teacher said, turning, though she was talking over the intercom. "There are plenty of upsides. I've never seen anyone with more respect for their elders. And they have this intense relationship with the land and water . . . But honestly, I would be dishonest if I didn't tell you about the domestic violence, sexual assault, and the rampant poverty. More than a couple of the children in our school have been sexually abused, and it's not a very big school. The people voted in the local election to make it a dry village. Sale and even possession of alcohol is a crime. Some people bootleg—an eight-dollar plastic bottle of R&R whiskey can bring a couple of hundred bucks—but most don't have that kind of money. They get around that by making this nasty home brew in five-gallon paint buckets. Baker's yeast, sugar, and some kind of fruit juice."

"Like the pruno inmates make in prison," Lola offered.

"If pruno smells like old bread dough and an orange-juice can you dug out of the garbage."

Lola turned up her nose and gave an understanding nod. "That is exactly what pruno smells like."

Natalie beat the side of her head softly against the window while she spoke. "It's a real problem. I'd say most of the violent crime is directly related to home brew. And many of the students I deal with in SPED suffer from fetal alcohol syndrome."

"You make the whole village sound horrible," Paisley said.

"Oh, it's far from horrible," Natalie said. "But there are some horrible situations. Like I said, to leave out those issues would be dishonest."

"Aren't the troopers doing anything about the crime?" Paisley asked. "It's a little place. It can't be that difficult."

Natalie laughed derisively, then apologized. "People here are no different from people anywhere else. They are smart and vibrant and rich in culture. They get plenty of missionaries who think they need to be rescued."

"But they do need rescuing?" Markham said, a little too smugly for Cutter's way of thinking.

"Everyone needs rescuing, Judge," Natalie said. "Like all of us, though, they have to be the ones to rescue themselves."

"Do you think we're in danger?" Ms. Paisley said. "Of getting mugged, I mean."

"No," Natalie said. "At least not any more than you would be in Anchorage."

"Not saying much, these days," Lola said.

"Stone Cross has wonderful people," Natalie said. "And a handful of assholes, just like everywhere else in the world. Don't get me wrong though. I love it. I wouldn't be living in an apartment with a couch that smells like cat pee and a grime ring around the tub that looks like it was sand-blasted in, if I didn't . . ." Her voice trailed off and she sat up straighter in her seat, as if steeling herself for something. "We're about there."

Cutter pressed his forehead against the window. He saw nothing but fog.

"How do you know where we are?" Paisley asked. "The rest of us can't even see the ground."

"It sounds weird," Natalie said, "because I'm a science nerd, but you build up a sort of radar out here. You just know when you're getting close to home."

The village of Stone Cross ghosted into view just then, as if to illustrate her point. A dozen aluminum boats sat along the riverbank, looking sad and abandoned out of the water. They were tumped this way and that as if they'd been deposited by a receding flood. Rough clapboard houses ran along the river for about two hundred yards, then up five short, muddy side streets, like sparse and uneven teeth on an old comb. A gray-white church lay at the eastern point of the southernmost tooth. Stone Cross K-12 was at the opposite end of town, where the main street ran along the river. The school was easily the largest structure in town and had an outdoor basketball court as well as playground equipment.

The three-thousand-foot gravel runway was located almost a mile out, past the dump, farther from the bank of fog that ran along the river. A parade of ATVs was already heading out of town as they flew over. Some of them pulled plywood trailers.

"Welcoming committee," Earl said into his headset as he banked the airplane to the left on final approach. "Hondas should be there by the time we land."

"Those are green," Judge Markham said, face against the window. "I expect they're some model of a Polaris. Honda ATVs are usually red. That yellow one is probably a Can-Am."

Earl half turned, before focusing again on landing the aircraft. "Do a lot of four-wheeling, do we, Judge?"

"A fair amount with the grandchildren," Markham said, sounding pleasant enough.

"Well," Earl said, "in the bush, *Honda* is a generic for every kind of ATV. It's like when you order a Coke in Texas and it could be Dr Pepper or Sprite."

"Noted," Markham said, nodding slowly. If he was offended, he didn't show it.

The plane settled in, the discomforting blare of the

stall warning pouring through the cabin as the pilot used throttle and angle to bleed off the speed necessary to make the airplane stop flying. They glided just a few feet off the runway before touching down with little more than a bump. Clouds of snow blew by the windows. The stall warning horn fell silent. Earl rolled to a wide gravel apron at the very end, then gunned the throttle to turn the airplane around before taxiing back to the line of waiting ATVs. Cutter noticed that he turned again so he was facing slightly downhill, probably to keep from having to rev the engine to get moving when it was time to go. This gravel surely wreaked havoc on propellers.

The ATVs growled up to surround the plane as soon as Earl shut off the engine. He asked everyone to stay seated until he had a metal stand situated to keep the tail from squatting as the weight moved aft as they deplaned.

Cutter scanned the crowd through his window. It looked like the scene of some unwinnable scenario in protective training. Passive faces he didn't know, no clear avenue of escape, and virtually everyone had a rifle over their shoulder.

"Well, that's stuffed," Lola said, her forehead pressed against the window. "Want me to get out the rifle?"

"What I want to do is have Earl turn the plane around," Cutter said. "But I suspect we're going to have to get used to everyone having guns and knives."

Cutter walked ahead of the judge, his hands free, eyes playing across the crowd as he made his way down the folding stairs.

The bulk of the greeters stood by their ATVs and looked on in stony silence. It was difficult to tell if they were upset to have visitors or just indifferent. The first smile of the group came from a bear of a man beside the bottom step.

He wore the brown uniform and ballistic vest of a village public safety officer. Trained by the state, but paid by the nonprofit Native corporations, these VPSOs provided law enforcement, fire, and rescue response in rural villages where there weren't enough troopers. They worked alone. Dark bangs stuck out from the edges of a black wool beanie. He had the slightly Asian features of a Yup'ik Eskimo. The patch on his shoulder read: FIRST RESPONDERS IN THE LAST FRONTIER. His Sam Browne duty belt held handcuffs, pepper spray, and a Taser—but no sidearm. Hunching forward slightly, eyes half shut against the snow, he stepped forward when he saw Cutter.

"Are you the marshal?"

Cutter extended his hand. "Deputy Arliss Cutter."

"Ned Jasper," the VPSO said. "The L.T. told me about the threat to your judge." He tossed a nonchalant look over his shoulder. "Don't pay any attention to all the guns."

"Hard not to," Cutter said. "In our line of work."

"True enough," Jasper said. "But these guns aren't for you. We've had a couple of rabid foxes lately so everyone is a little bit on edge."

"Rabies . . ." Lola's hand drifted to the pistol on her belt. "That's a relief."

Ned Jasper shrugged. "It is what it is."

"It is at that," Lola muttered. She took a deep breath, as if bracing herself. "Step off the airplane into the food chain."

Cutter motioned her forward. "This is my partner, Deputy Lola Teariki."

"Welcome to Stone Cross." Jasper glanced back and forth from Cutter to Lola. "I never met a marshal before. To be honest, I've only heard stories about you guys."

Lola smiled. "About the marshals riding into town to get the outlaw?"

Ned studied her for a moment, then looked back at Cutter. "Something like that."

"Thanks for meeting us," Cutter said. "I'm assuming we load our gear in the trailers."

"Afraid so." Ned gave an embarrassed grin. "I was gonna pick you up in the school van, but it's got a dead battery. You can pick which Honda you wanta ride on and we'll take you to the school. It's a ways though, so if you got hats, you should definitely put them on."

A Native man with a round face and broad middle made a beeline for the judge. Thick salt-and-pepper hair was mussed in back like he'd just gotten out of bed to come meet the plane. His zippered sweatshirt was open to the chill and a tremendous belly pushed a thin T-shirt out away from his body so it hung like a skirt past his waist. One leg of his sweat pants was tucked into black rubber boots. The other, slightly too long, was sodden with snow.

"Melvin Red Fox," he said, offering a hand, squinting a little as if he'd forgotten his glasses. There was a sadness in his deep brown eyes that was unmistakable, as if he was on the verge of breaking into tears. "I'm the Stone Cross city manager."

Markham shook the offered hand, working hard not to react to the man's disheveled appearance. "Thank you for having me out to assist. I look forward to seeing more of your village."

"That won't take long," Melvin said, giving a forced smile. He reached to touch Markham on the elbow. "I joke. We are very proud of Stone Cross. We got a big potluck planned at the school tonight. Don't worry, both parties to the case are invited so no one will think you're playin' favorites before the arbitration." He hooked a finger over his shoulder at a green four-wheeler. "Come on, Judge, you can ride up front with me."

"I should probably ride—"

Red Fox ran a hand over his thick hair. "If you think I'm gonna try and talk to you about the arbitration while we ride, you ain't been on that many bush Hondas. I'm good as deaf anyhow."

The VPSO loaded the sleeping bags and other luggage into the nearest plywood trailer. "Here, Judge," he said. "I made you a seat out of sleeping bags if you'd rather ride in the back."

Markham gave a nod. "That would probably be best."

Red Fox shrugged. "Suit yourself," he said. "But there's only six hundred fifty-two people in the village. Everybody here's on one side of this thing or the other. You might as well relax and talk to folks."

Earl removed the tail stand from the rear of the Caravan and stowed it back in the belly pod as soon as everyone had their gear off the plane. Three minutes later, he was down at the end of the runway, opening up the throttle to barrel back toward the crowd. The cold air and slight headwind made the airplane leap off the gravel. It disappeared into the clouds before they had all the bags loaded in the trailers.

A chilly quiet settled in as soon as the Caravan was gone.

A few of the roughly two dozen people in the Stone Cross welcoming committee chatted with each other, but they did so in hushed tones, dampened even more by the soupy mist.

Lola turned a slow three-sixty and shuddered. "This is

creepy," she said. "Why is everyone whispering like we're in church?"

"We don't yell too much," Ned said. "Yelling's bad for you." He shrugged. "We may beat the crap outta each other if we get drunk, but we don't yell . . ."

Tina Paisley stood a few steps away from the group, hugging herself as she stared at the spot where the plane had disappeared. "Does anyone else feel like we've been dropped off on a faraway planet?"

The VPSO raised his hand. "I feel that way every time I go to Anchorage." He chuckled. "To be honest, I'm new here myself. My wife and I transferred from Tooksook Bay, over on the coast. These folks in Stone Cross are good people though. They'll take care of you. I promise."

Cutter had Lola ride on the back of Ned Jasper's four-wheeler, which would follow the trailer with the judge. Up to now, keeping Markham in sight had been straightforward, but he was sure to get more passive-aggressive now that they were in the village. The VPSO said he'd already been briefed on the threat by Lieutenant Warr and promised to be an extra set of eyes.

"How about you, Officer Jasper?" Lola asked when it was just she and Cutter with the VPSO. Everyone else was still getting situated and ready to ride. "Any idea if anyone from Stone Cross could have sent the threat to the judge?"

Ned Jasper threw a leg over his ATV, nodding nonchalantly to a group of three Native women at the end of the line, standing beside their own Hondas. Like everyone but the city manager, the women were dressed for a sloppy ride in the wet snow. "See the one in the middle? That's Daisy Aguthluk. I was going to talk to you about her as soon as we got back to the school."

Cutter shot a quick glance at the women, then let his

eyes travel over the rest of the crowd so as not to appear too interested in them. Everyone remained stone-faced. Thankfully, neither Aguthluk or the two women with her appeared to have a gun. "You think she's our threat?"

"Pretty sure," Jasper said.

"She hates Markham enough to threaten to kill him?"

"I would, if I was her," Jasper said. "I mean, I wouldn't threaten him, but I'd hate him if he did to me what he did to her family."

"Everybody ready to go?" Melvin Red Fox shouted over the engine noise of his ATV. Snow fell down the top of his rubber boot. His jacket remained unzipped. Either this guy was impervious to the cold, or he flat didn't care about much of anything. Cutter recognized him as the latter. He'd been there before himself.

Red Fox gunned the throttle, waving Cutter over. "You can get warm in the school."

Cutter raised his index finger, the universal sign to hold on a minute, before turning back to the VPSO. "What did Markham do to her family?"

Jasper gave a noncommittal shrug. "My wife and I are new to the village, but the way I understand it, he kidnapped Daisy's aunt."

Chapter 15

Red Fox gunned his engine again. From his nest among the bags in the back of the plywood trailer, the judge yelled for everyone to hurry.

"We need to talk about this some more," Cutter said to Ned Jasper. "You stay behind the trailer and make sure nobody gets close to the judge. I'll see if I can get Red Fox to help me keep an eye on Daisy Aguthluk."

Cutter climbed on behind the city manager, facing aft so he could hold on to each side of the luggage rack and watch his new suspect. This put the calves of his Fjällräven pants in the perfect position to catch a constant spray of mud and snow from the ATV's spinning tires.

The route in from the airport headed directly toward the river, bringing the procession into Stone Cross on one of the smaller gravel side streets. Junked ATVs and snowmobiles—called snow machines in Alaska—slumped forlornly in front of, beside, and behind almost every house. Here and there, black strips of meat hung drying under flat-topped sheds. Canadian jays flitted back and forth over the bloody remains of a caribou ribcage. Caribou hides were everywhere, hanging over sawhorses, draped over porch rails, or tacked against walls with the flesh side out. Heads and antlers lay strewn beside most of the weathered houses. Dogs sat in front of wooden boxes, some chained, some loose, all watching with mild disinterest as the procession of ATVs roared past.

Aguthluk and the two other women stayed with everyone else as far as the edge of town, then peeled off at a thick line of willows, disappearing to the south. The rest of the ATVs kept going up the side street. If Cutter had his bearings right, they'd turn to the left at the end when the road made a T, and head north toward the school. He toyed with the idea of asking Red Fox to follow her, but decided he'd better stay with the judge. The quicker they got him inside the school, the better.

A stub-legged village mutt that looked like a cross between a German shepherd and a Corgi stood and watched them pass, holding a caribou hoof in its mouth.

Ned Jasper rode up so he was shoulder to shoulder with Cutter, working the handlebars to keep his ATV out of the potholes and ruts. "Looks like that scene from *Yojimbo*— where the dog carries in that guy's arm . . . I love that movie."

"I know what you mean—"

Cutter paused. He'd heard something—a scream maybe. Red Fox slowed. As did Jasper. They must have heard it too. The noise came again, muffled, but out of place. Jasper used his chin to gesture toward a sun-bleached plywood house on the north side of the street that they'd driven past.

An instant later, a large window beside the front door shattered outward, and a woman launched through the opening as if she'd been shot from a cannon. She hit the ground facedown, skidding in the snow and gravel, before coming to rest in a stunned pile. Naked from the waist down, she wore nothing but a dingy gray T-shirt. Blood poured from a gash on her forearm. Even from thirty feet away, it was easy to see when she looked up that she'd been beaten badly enough that one of her eyes was swollen shut.

Cutter jumped off the back of Red Fox's ATV while it was still rolling, ducking to the side to avoid the attached plywood trailer that carried the judge and attorneys.

Lola dismounted as well, but Cutter pointed to the trailer, ordering her to stay with the judge. He waved Red Fox toward the school, leaving Cutter and Ned Jasper to deal with the girl.

The front door to the house flew open as Red Fox pulled away with the judge and a very unhappy Lola Teariki. A wiry man shot out the door but stopped on the porch, fists clenched, cursing at the top of his lungs at the woman. He wore saggy briefs and a pair of unlaced military boots. Long, black hair was mussed like he'd just gotten out of bed.

Neither looked to be over twenty-five. The woman scrambled to her feet to face him, screaming back. The man stood on his porch and ordered her back in the house. When she didn't move, he spat out an obscene threat and ran down the steps directly toward her, leaving no doubt as to his intentions.

The woman held up her hands, bracing herself to ward him off. Blood dripped from the point of her elbow, painting the snow. Her index finger bent unnaturally at a right angle from her hand.

Cutter was already running. This guy had thrown a woman out a window. He was, as Grumpy used to say, bought and paid for.

Cutter came in at an angle, reaching the shirtless kid just as he cleared the last step. Instead of trying to catch him before he got to the screaming woman, Cutter simply reached out and gave him a shove between the shoulder blades. Momentum and blind rage carried the guy's torso forward faster than his legs. He threw his hands out in front of him, still cursing as he surfed into the sloppy snow on his chest. His feet, wearing the weight of the heavy, ungainly leather boots, kept moving forward even after the rest of him stopped. His back arched, his legs bent at the knees, and the boots flew up, slamming into the back of his head like a scorpion stinging itself.

Cutter glanced up to see the woman pedal backward. Too drunk or high to know how much pain he was in, the young man scrambled to his feet, but Cutter came in from the side, grabbed a handful of hair. He pushed up and over, driving the kid back and down, as if he were spiking a ball. Grumpy always called long hair a murder-handle. It certainly made for a nifty handhold when there wasn't much of anything else to grab.

The shirtless man's chin shot skyward as his head followed Cutter's fist toward the snow. The image of the bleeding woman was burned into Cutter's mind, and it was all he could do to keep from following up with an elbow to the kid's face. Instead, he let the ground administer the beating.

The kid hit with a sickening *oomph*, the wind driven out of his lungs. Cutter had him rolled onto his belly and cuffed while he was still attempting to manage a croaking breath. The kid was in his twenties, no small fry, probably pushing five-ten and one eighty. Cutter still had him by five inches and fifty pounds, not to mention a lot more experience smacking people who were even bigger and stronger than he was.

A Native woman holding a baby peeked out the door of the neighboring house, looked at the scene, then glared at Cutter like he'd been the one to attack the half-naked woman. She ducked back inside without saying anything. A wizened old man carrying a plastic bag of groceries over the arm of a traditional parka slowed his ATV long enough to look from Cutter to the man in handcuffs, and then drive stoically on.

The kid cursed and jerked against the cuffs, trying to get his feet under him so he could stand. Cutter kept him in the snow with a knee in his back.

Two elderly women from across the muddy street brought out a blanket and covered the sobbing woman. Both appeared to ignore the handcuffed kid, instead giving Cutter the same accusatory stare and head shake before leading the sobbing woman through the fog, back inside the house with the broken window. She left a trail of bare-foot tracks and blood in the mud and snow.

The VPSO looked sheepishly at Cutter. "I guess some of us do yell."

"You've handled this guy before," Cutter said, once the women were out of earshot.

"Oh yeah," the VPSO said. "And I haven't been here all that long. This is Archie Stepanov. As you can see, he gets a bit mean when he hits the home brew." Jasper squatted next to the handcuffed man. "How are you doing, Archie?"

"I didn't know the Troopers were comin'," Stepanov said. "Tell him to let me stand up."

"Ready?" Cutter said to Jasper, ignoring Stepanov.

The VPSO gave a curt nod, and helped Cutter haul the kid to his feet.

"Where's your lockup?" Cutter asked.

"Across from the school," Jasper said. "But it's not really much of a lockup. More like a big dog kennel with a padlock on it. I'll need to hire someone to watch him until the Troopers can get here or I transport him out."

"I'll be out before that, genius," Stepanov said, staring daggers at Cutter. "My mom's on the village council and the nonprofit board. She has dinner with your colonel every time she goes to Anchorage. Soon as she tells him how you beat my ass, he'll have you hauled before a judge for police brutality."

"Doubtful," Cutter said quietly, fighting the urge to point out that if he beat someone's ass, they wouldn't have the ability to gripe about it for days.

"Come on," Stepanov said, going from belligerent to weepy drunk in a mercurial change of tactics. "Please. Can't you just let me go? I help you guys sometimes with my boat."

Cutter led him by the elbow toward Jasper's ATV. "Where do you want him?"

"Mind riding in the trailer with him?" Jasper asked. "The VPSO office is just up the road."

Stepanov wailed, pulling against Cutter's grip. "Somebody please call my mom. She'll straighten this out. It was all a big misunderstanding. Ask Doreen. We were just screwing around and she fell out the window. If she's hurt, that's what caused it."

"Hmmm," Cutter said. "We were right here. Saw the whole thing."

"She fell," Stepanov said, wide-eyed and shaking his head as if it was all so clear.

Cutter's voice grew more sinister. "How about you remain silent."

"Seriously, Trooper," Stepanov said, pleading now. "Come on, buddy. I'm telling you. I make some mistakes when I'm drinking, but you know me. We'll be laughing all this off by tomorrow. This is all a big misunder—"

"I'm not a trooper," Cutter said, reaching the back of the trailer. He pulled Stepanov close, looking down so they were eye to eye. "US Marshals, and I could not give a pinch of shit about who your mother knows. I am not your friend. I am not your buddy. Fact is, you see me anywhere besides the courtroom and you should do yourself a favor and keep walking."

Cutter set him down on a patch of bare plywood in the trailer, his back against a wall.

Stepanov shivered. "Can I get a blanket?"

"Fresh out of blankets," Cutter said.

"That was badass," Ned Jasper whispered before Cutter climbed into the trailer with the prisoner. "But I should probably let you know, his mother really does know the colonel."

"So do I," Cutter said. "And I happen to know he hates domestic violence. Anyway, that wouldn't matter."

Jasper sighed. "We usually have to play things a little calmer out here. Sort of a going-along-to-get-along type deal."

Cutter cocked his head, raising a brow. "You wouldn't have arrested him?"

"Oh yeah," Ned said. "I would have arrested him. But I woulda had to be nicer about it. You never know if Stepanov might be the guy to come by in his boat when you're stuck on a sandbar."

Cutter scoffed. "This guy beat the hell out of a girl half

his size. I'd rather spend the night on a sandbar than pull my punches with somebody like him."

Ned Jasper thought about that a moment, then shrugged, his broad face cracking a smile of approval. "Like I said, badass."

Chapter 16

Ned Jasper used his cell phone to call someone on his list to watch the prisoner while they were en route to the office. The jail guard must not have had far to walk, because he was waiting when they pulled up. He was young, maybe eighteen, and wore a hoodie with the Stone Cross Timberwolves basketball logo on the front. Jasper introduced Cutter as the visiting marshal. The kid nodded like he knew already and shook Cutter's hand.

"Fog's rolling in fast," the kid said to Jasper. "Might have to do a telephonic hearing if you can't get him to Bethel."

"Maybe so," the VPSO said. He looked up at Cutter. "Think your judge would want to do an arraignment?"

Cutter started to answer but Jasper cut him off.

"I joke. We'll get you settled and I'll call the court in Bethel. They'll probably let him out though . . ."

Booking someone wearing nothing but tighty whities didn't take long and they had Archie Stepanov locked up in less than five minutes. Ned Jasper was right. The holding cell wasn't much, just six eight-foot by eight-foot sections of dog kennel that formed a chain-link cube. A blue rubberized wrestling mat functioned as a floor and mattress while a five-gallon plastic bucket in the corner provided a latrine. Considering that many of the homes in Stone Cross still used the honey-bucket system, the arrangement couldn't really be viewed as cruel or unusual.

The school was just across the road.

The beige metal façade looked out of place compared to the faded, wind-bitten houses they'd passed on the way in from the airport. Ned Jasper's plywood trailer contained half the airplane passengers' luggage, so everyone including the judge came out to help unload when they rode up. Lola snickered when she saw the back of Cutter's pants as he was getting his bags from the trailer. "Looks like they dragged you here."

Melvin Red Fox gave a sheepish grimace. "Shoulda warned you, Deputy," he said.

"I think he got most of this when he took down Archie," Jasper said.

Red Fox groaned. "Figured it was probably Archie who threw Doreen out the window. I heard last night on the VHF somebody made a big batch of home brew. That boy ain't the only one who has problems when he's drinkin'. You're gonna be busy, Ned."

"Maybe they'll wait till after the potluck," the VPSO said. He nodded toward Cutter's muddy pants. "Just stomp a couple times to get the big chunks off and you'll be fine. School is still in session for a couple of hours, so you'll have to stage all your gear in the library until classes get out. Judge, I think they have you in the consumer and family science room—what we used to call home economics. You'll have your own toilet, but I'm afraid you'll have to shower in the locker room. I'm not sure where Birdie is putting the rest of you."

Jasper had a fair amount of mud on his own boots and did as he'd instructed Cutter, stomping them on the heavy metal grating that led up to the double set of glass doors. Cutter suspected they weren't the first to come to this school with muddy boots.

Markham stood at the top of the steps, bag in hand, looking a little stunned. "Is she all right? That girl who crashed out the window?"

"Who, Doreen?" Jasper shrugged. "I'll go and take some photos of her injuries in a few minutes. Sad deal, that one. I've been tellin' her to get away from Archie since I moved here two months ago."

Lola faced outbound without being told, keeping watch for Daisy Aguthluk or any other threat. Cutter put his body behind the judge, and gently cajoled everyone toward the front doors.

"I'd like to be kept apprised of her condition," Markham said.

"You bet, Judge," Cutter said. "We should get inside."

Ewing, the attorney for the nonprofit corporation, shuffled along with his bag, grousing under his breath. "Now everyone's in a hurry."

The school had two sets of doors, providing a dead air space or arctic entry, to conserve heat. Lola paused alongside Cutter at the outer set of doors.

"Reminded me of that old no-win scenario they tell us about in the academy."

"Weren't they all no-win?"

"True," Lola said. "Still, I'm surprised you peeled off from the detail to save the girl."

"Are you really?"

"No, boss." Lola laughed out loud. "Not one damned bit."

Cutter relaxed a notch once the judge returned to the school proper. It wasn't exactly a fortress, but any building was better than standing in the fog like sitting ducks.

There was a small lobby just inside the door with two long classroom wings running east and west from a center common area that served as the lunchroom. The main office was just inside the front doors. On the opposite side of the lobby was a set of restrooms labeled in what was presumably Yup'ik, written underneath the plaques that designated them BOYS and GIRLS. A piece of printer paper was taped to each door with a reminder about the water limits of the village. IF IT'S BROWN FLUSH IT DOWN. IF IT'S YELLOW LET IT MELLOW.

"Kind of in-your-face," Markham's law clerk said.

Jasper gave a shrug. "It is what it is. Pipes tend to freeze this time of year. There's a storage tank for water under the school, but a lot of houses still use five-gallon honey buckets to take care of business. Most kids wait until they get to school so they go through a lot of water . . ." He waved at two elementary-age girls coming down the hall toward them, on their way to the restrooms. Both stopped and giggled when they saw the group of strangers with their VPSO. Rosy cheeks, jet-black hair, fleece jackets. Cutter could not remember ever seeing more vibrant smiles.

"Whach you're doin' here?" one of the girls asked, staring at Lola.

The other one edged tentatively closer. "You got tattoos?"

Lola shot a sideways glance at Jasper, who chuckled. "She's not interested in any of your real ink," he said.

"Troopers sometimes bring the kids gum or temporary tattoos."

"And candy," the other girl said, covering her mouth to stifle a giggle. "I joke!"

The VPSO took on a serious tone. "Do you ladies have permission to be out of class?"

Both girls looked at him, eyebrows raised on high foreheads.

"Okay then," he said. "Hurry along with your business and then get back to class."

"Why didn't they answer you?" Markham's law clerk asked.

"They did." Jasper raised his own eyebrows, exaggerated to illustrate his point. "That means *yes*. Lots of talkin' goes on without words, if you know what I mean."

Jasper led them past two open classroom doors on the way to the library. Markham stopped at the second door, standing in the hall to listen, so everyone else stopped too.

A white woman wearing a lilac *kuspuk* and faded jeans was in the middle of a lecture to a class of ten or so high school students, most of them girls. She was tall, in her twenties, but with a silver streak in her dark hair.

". . . statistics and averages," the teacher said. "Both can be deceiving if we don't look at all the data. Let's suppose we have a group of one hundred caribou. Of this group, fifty are bulls and fifty are cows. That means that the total number of testicles in the group is . . . ?"

A couple of the girls giggled. The boys in the back of the classroom squirmed.

"One hundred," a girl on the front row said.

"Correct," the teacher said. "One hundred. One hundred caribou, one hundred testicles. A statistician who was only acquainted with math and not caribou biology might conclude with this limited information that each caribou had one testicle . . ."

Lola gave Cutter a nudge in the ribs. "Bet they remember this lecture."

Jasper grinned at the rest of the group, like he was proud. "My wife is the counselor here. She says Aften Brooks is a heck of a good teacher. She has a real connection with the students, knows what makes them tick."

The group picked up their bags and continued toward the library.

Cutter started to quiz the VPSO about Daisy Aguthluk some more, but Judge Markham picked up his pace to walk beside them.

"Mr. Jasper," he said. "You mentioned honey buckets earlier. I was under the impression that Stone Cross received a federal grant two years ago. Everyone should have running water and indoor plumbing now."

"That's right, Judge," the VPSO said. "Everyone should. But they don't. If you look at the grant paperwork, it clearly states that the toilets were all installed, one in each dwelling. The thing is, there's no place in that documentation to mention that half of those toilets are hooked up to a septic system that doesn't work unless the temperature is above freezing and we aren't getting any rain. The data clearly shows that the US government has helped us Natives out with brand-new toilets. The folks in DC and Anchorage get to feel better about themselves."

"Everybody gets one testicle," Lola said. "Even if it doesn't work."

Melvin Red Fox gave a sad chuckle. "Yep."

Judge Markham looked down at his shoes as they

walked, deep in thought. Cutter generally didn't much care for his royal attitude, but it was hard not to respect a guy who was so focused on his job. Depending on who oversaw the federal grant, all this information could have a direct bearing on the arbitration.

They dropped their bags with the librarian before retracing their steps back to the office to check in with the principal. Lola carried her rifle case over her shoulder rather than leaving it behind. The M4 had a short barrel and the triangular case resembled something that might hold a tennis racket rather than a weapon.

Birdie Pingayak was still in her office, seated beside her desk instead of behind it. Her hands were folded quietly in her lap as she addressed a bony little Yup'ik boy who Cutter guessed was maybe nine or ten years old. The boy's eyes were red and swollen. Every few seconds his little shoulders shuddered, remnants of a sobbing cry.

The protective operation briefing sheet said Birdie's real name was Bertha Pingayak, leading Cutter to expect someone older. He guessed this Birdie to be in her thirties. She was slim, with black shoulder-length hair, straight and parted in the middle. Cutter had never been a fan of face tattoos, on either gender, considering them job-stoppers. But the lines on Birdie Pingayak's chin were nothing short of breathtaking. She wore nice khaki slacks and a blue polo shirt with a Stone Cross timber wolf mascot on the left breast. Her office was sparse and neat, as if Marie Kondo herself had done the decorating.

She spoke to the boy in hushed tones, glancing up just long enough to tell everyone she needed another moment. She listened as much as she spoke, letting the boy have his say. Then she reached behind her desk to retrieve a canvas purse. She took out her wallet, handing the boy a twenty-dollar bill. He began to sob again. She touched him softly on the shoulder before sending him out of her office.

"*Waqaa*," he said as he ran past, still sniffing back tears.

Jasper whispered, "Clarence says hi."

The others all said hello back, but the boy was already out the door.

Birdie rested her hand on the door frame of her office, leaning toward the school secretary at the front counter. "Clarence is not allowed on school grounds for the rest of the day," she said.

"Okie dokie," the woman at the counter said, smiling. She'd seen the passing of the twenty dollars as well. "Good job, Ms. Pingayak."

Birdie shook hands with everyone in turn. "Sorry to keep you waiting. My friend there had himself a little anger issue right before you arrived. He threw a chair at his teacher, Ms. Donna."

Markham's eyebrows shot toward the ceiling in surprise. "Good Lord! A chair? Is she all right?"

"Miss Donna?" The principal gave him a sad smile. "She's fine. You saw Clarence. He's so scrawny he can barely pick up a chair, let alone toss it with any force. You're probably wondering why I gave him money."

"The question did cross my mind," Markham said.

Birdie motioned them all into her office with the flick of her hand. "I heard you met Archie Stepanov." She stood behind her desk, singled Cutter out of the group with her gaze, and gave him a quick once-over.

"Are you the marshal?"

"Why doesn't anyone ever ask if I'm the marshal?" Ewing groused.

Birdie swung her gaze to him. "Are you?"

"No," he said, incredulous.

"Right," Birdie said. "I'm guessing you're one of the lawyers." Cutter liked this woman already.

"Anyway," she continued, "if you've had the great pleasure of meeting Archie Stepanov, then you've seen the effects of our local home brew. Clarence's parents are good people, but this new batch of hooch is making the rounds in the village. Everybody suffers, but kids suffer the most. Clarence is the oldest of four, so he feels the brunt of the responsibility to take care of his siblings. It's a heavy load for a nine-year-old to carry. I gave him twenty bucks so he could buy some food."

"What's to keep him from buying candy with it?" Ewing asked.

"I'm guessing you've never looked at the eyes of a hungry sibling." She sighed. "No, Clarence is a handful, but he cares deeply about his brother and sisters."

Brett Grinder, Markham's clerk, frowned. "What about Child Protective Services?"

Birdie gave a scornful chuckle but said nothing.

"CPS tries," Jasper said. "But it is what it is—"

The cell phone in his vest pocket began to play a Bob Seger ringtone. "Sorry," he said. "I have to take this." He held the phone to his ear, listening intently. His expression grew darker with each passing moment.

Aften Brooks, the high school math teacher they'd listened to earlier, came running up the hall and into the outer office. She stopped short when she saw the crowd and began to wring her hands.

"I just heard from Vitus on his VHF," she said.

"Vitus Paul?" Birdie asked. "He took the day off to go hunting for the elders."

"He is," Aften said. "I asked him to check in at Chaga Lodge as a favor. I haven't been able to get in touch with Sarah or David since yesterday."

Ned Jasper ended his call. He breathed deeply, gathering his thoughts.

Birdie put both hands flat on her desk, looking from Aften to the VPSO. "What is it?"

"That was my office," Jasper said. "Patching me through to Vitus on his VHF. He said the radios at the lodge have been destroyed—and Rolf Hagen's body is lying out in the snow. Looks like somebody shot him."

Chapter 17

Everyone including Aften Brooks crowded into Birdie Pingayak's office and shut the door. Ned Jasper got through to Lieutenant Warr on his cell phone on the second try. He put the call on speaker, then gave a quick rundown on what he knew, which wasn't much. To his credit, Warr listened without peppering him with questions until the end.

Birdie spread a map of western Alaska across her desk blotter. The area between the Yukon to the north and the Kuskokwim to the south formed a delta as they flowed toward the Bering Sea. She pointed to the black star that represented Stone Cross and traced a line with her finger about eight miles upriver to Chaga Lodge.

"No sign of the caretakers?" Warr asked.

Aften spoke up. "This is Mrs. Brooks, a teacher here at Stone Cross. Sarah Mead is my friend. I haven't been able to contact her by radio since day before yesterday. My husband dropped off some caribou meat that same day, but as far as I know, that's the last time anyone has seen Sarah or her husband."

Ned Jasper said, "Vitus says the lodge looks abandoned. The generator's off. Stove was cold when he got there."

"Didn't Hagen have a girlfriend in Stone Cross?" Warr asked. "That Swanson girl?"

"Marlene," Birdie said. "And her old boyfriend, James Johnny, wasn't too happy about that."

"Ned," Warr said. "See if you can locate James. Don't approach him until we get there. Just find out where he is."

Red Fox held up his hand, like a student waiting to be called on.

Ned nodded.

"This is Melvin Red Fox, Lieutenant," he said, introducing himself, leaning toward the phone to make sure he was heard. "James Johnny left to go hunting yesterday afternoon. He usually stays gone a couple days unless he catches something, so nobody thinks anything of it. I can see if his uncle has heard from him."

"Okay," Warr said. "Check with him, but let's keep the details of this to ourselves."

"That leaves the body to recover," Ned said. "And the crime scene. Not to mention the missing caretakers."

Aften Brooks clenched her eyes shut, stifling a sob. "Somebody took them."

The line fell quiet for a time, with nothing but the ruffling of papers on Warr's end of the call. Cutter could picture him bent over a map of his own. "What's the weather look like out your way?" he asked.

Ned walked to the window.

"Pea soup fog," he said. "Twenty, thirty feet of visibility, maybe, and getting worse."

"That's what I thought," the lieutenant said. "We're looking at the same conditions. Earl's stuck in Nightmute on that body pickup. He's telling me this pattern is supposed to stick around for another day. Planes are grounded here. Even the Alaska Airlines flight tonight is on a weather hold. I'll see about a chopper from Anchorage, but they'd have to fly through the Lake Clark Pass in the fog at night, so

I'm not hopeful on that account. This damned river can't decide if it wants to be ice or water. It'll be dicey, but I'll work on getting a couple of troopers up to you by boat. In the meantime, Ned, do you think you've been in Stone Cross long enough to get familiar with the river?"

The VPSO grimaced. "I'll do my best, L.T."

"All I can ask," Warr said. "Secure the scene if you can make it out there. I'll check with the Aniak post, upriver. They might be able to get as far as the lodge, coming in from the north. Wait for them. I don't want you going after the Meads unarmed."

"I grew up here," Birdie Pingayak said. "I know the river. If you want, we can take you up in my boat."

Ned Jasper gave a sigh of relief. "That would be good."

Cutter said, "Anything we can do to help, just say the word."

"Honestly," Warr said, "the body isn't the problem. He'll still be dead when we get there. But if David and Sarah Mead are missing, they're either suspects or victims. I could use a few sets of eyes on scene if you don't mind trying to get out to the lodge with Jasper."

Cutter shot a glance at Lola, and then the judge. The threat was still a problem.

"One of us will go," Cutter said.

"Thank you," Warr said. "I need to call and brief the captain. Ned, check in with me at regular intervals."

"Copy that," the VPSO said, and ended the call.

Birdie Pingayak grabbed her coat and hat off the willow hook in the corner of her office. She reached below her desk and came up with a pair of brown rubber boots, holding the corner of the desk with one hand while she kicked off her Nike runners. "Ned," she said, pulling on the boots. "How long do you need to get your gear ready?"

"I'm always packed," the VPSO said. "Just need to stop by my house. I'll meet you at the river."

Pingayak looked at Cutter. "How about you guys?"

"Good to go," Cutter said. "We haven't had a chance to unpack."

Aften Brooks took a half step forward. "I'm coming too."

"I know you want to go," Birdie said. "But I need you to do me a favor and stay here and look after Jolene. We'll figure out what happened with Sarah. I promise."

Birdie turned to get a pair of glasses off the low credenza behind her desk.

Cutter turned to Lola. "We're going to have to split up."

Lola closed her eyes and gave a resigned sigh. "I saw this coming already. You want me to stay here and watch—"

Judge Markham gave an emphatic shake of his head. "And watch over me. That's not necessary. I'll be fine."

"I'm sorry, Your Honor," Cutter said. "But that won't work. There hasn't been time to discuss it with you, but after we landed, we received information about a person of interest in Stone Cross related to your threat."

"The woman at the airport who was looking at me so hard?"

Lola nodded, obviously impressed that the judge had noticed anything beyond the fact that the marshals were crowding him.

"Yes," Cutter said. "The point is, there are a lot of pieces of the situation to consider. Deputy Teariki will go over it all with you and come up with our next steps—"

"Let me get this straight," Markham said. "You think that woman on the four-wheeler wrote the letter threatening to hold my beating heart?"

"Makes sense, Your Honor," Lola said. "The letter came after your trip out here was publicized in the papers."

"I . . . I just suspected the threat was tied to the arbitration," Markham said. "A stunt to dissuade me from coming out."

Ned Jasper checked his watch, beginning to get antsy. "We should get on the river."

"Your Honor," Cutter said, "any other time, I'd suggest flying you out tonight." He paused, thinking over his options before turning to Lola. "Honestly, as much as I want to assist the Troopers, I should stay back here too."

"Nonsense," Judge Markham said. "Ms. Pingayak, how many people can fit in your boat?"

"It's rated for seven," she said. "But four is better if we have much gear." She looked over the top of her reading glasses. "And in this weather, skimping on gear can get you killed."

"Hang on, Judge," Cutter said. "You understand what's going on out there? It's a homicide scene. Somebody's been murdered and the killer is still at large. My job is to protect you, not lead you into a danger—"

Markham cut him off. "No, Deputy. I was present at the meeting with Chief Phillips. Your job is to follow me." He took a deep breath, his eyes playing around the room, brow furrowed, almost conciliatory. "And right now, I've decided it will make things easier if you follow me to the lodge." He shot a look at Birdie. "If it's all right with you, Ms. Pingayak." He pronounced it with the accent on the second syllable, like the pilot had taught him.

"Fine by me," Birdie said. "I'm only taking the VPSO. As far as I'm concerned it's up to him who else comes with us."

Ned Jasper raised his hands as if in surrender. "I'm glad for any help I can get."

"Okay then." Birdie checked the time on her phone, then looked out the window at the pea-soup fog. "We got a little less than five hours till dark. Meet me at the boat in twenty minutes. I'm gonna stop by my house and pick up a couple of things. Make sure you each got long underwear, good boots, and a warm coat. Go ahead and bring your sleeping bags too if you got 'em in waterproof bags. Ned, bring extra life jackets if you have them." She nodded at Lola. "And it wouldn't hurt my feelings if you bring that rifle you got hidden in your tennis racket bag."

Lola gave her a thumbs-up.

"So we should pack as if we might have to spend the night in the lodge," Markham said.

"No, Judge," Birdie said. "You should pack as if you're going to spend the night on the river."

"Very well." Markham addressed his law clerk, and then Cutter, as if he were making a formal decree from the bench. "Brett, you begin groundwork for the arbitration— meeting locations, things of that nature. Deputy, when we're on the boat, you can tell me why this woman wants me dead."

Cutter had all his gear in a rubberized dry-bag that had belonged to his brother. Rather than sort through everything, he simply took out the extra clothing he didn't think he'd need and left it on a chair in the library. Florida was warm, but Grumpy had taught both his grandsons to get in the habit of taking a vacuum-sealed set of dry underwear when they went into the woods, in case they went in the drink. Now that he was in Alaska, he'd exchanged the extra boxers for a set of merino-wool long johns and socks. Sealed in the same bag was a box of waterproof matches and a candle. Cutter wore both pistols, and a sheath knife Mim had given him, on his belt. In his pocket he had a folding knife, a lighter, and a small flashlight—the basics of everyday carry.

Lola would have a similar setup. She'd been in Alaska longer than he had. He considered asking to check the judge's gear, but thought better of it.

Cutter, Lola, and the judge all loaded their bags into the trailer behind the VPSO's Honda and then climbed in to sit on top of them. The snow had stopped, but fog had moved in with a vengeance, making it impossible to see past the ATV from the trailer. Melvin said wistfully and to nobody in particular that he hoped they could make it back in time for the potluck later that night, but that he understood they might be a while because somebody had died.

Ned made a quick stop at his house. It was just around the corner, one side of a duplex that Cutter guessed was teacher housing since Mrs. Jasper was the school counselor. He came out almost as soon as he went in, carrying a dry-bag similar to Cutter's over his shoulder. A scoped bolt-action rifle was in his left hand.

"I thought VPSOs weren't supposed to be armed," Markham said as Ned swung a leg over the four-wheeler.

"We're not supposed to hunt murderers either," Jasper said grimly. "I guess there's technically a way to get qualified, but that's a long and political road—way above my pay grade. Rules or no rules, I'm not going out there without my rifle. My wife would never let me hear the end of it if I got myself killed."

"Wise," Cutter said.

Jasper checked over his shoulder to make sure he had everyone, then rode into the fog toward the river.

Gray buildings ghosted by in the mist. Snow and sky and air melded together, making it impossible to tell which way was up, let alone see the road. It was easy to understand how pilots could become disoriented and auger into the ground in this kind of soup. Cutter couldn't see the water, but they must have arrived because Ned stopped his ATV and killed the engine, leaving nothing but the hiss of ice on the Kuskokwim and the telltale thump of Birdie Pingayak already moving around on her aluminum boat. The air was dead still, slightly warmer than it had been when they'd arrived—a bad sign when they needed the fog to lift.

Ned led the way past two aluminum skiffs pulled up on the mud, down to where Birdie's boat bobbed along the shore. The bow rope was tied off to a piece of old drill stem that had been hammered into the dirt. Pingayak was a misty apparition at the stern, barely visible though she was less than twenty feet away. Every few seconds, a large chunk of floating ice thudded against the side of the boat, reminding everyone that the river would not stay liquid much longer.

"Put your stuff up there in the front," Birdie said. "Two of you sit in the middle, but I need a couple of you to ride up front and be my eyes. Watch for trees, sandbars, thick ice. We have a little bit of a trip ahead of us and not much time till dark. We should hurry, but we won't do anybody any good if I run up on some pan ice and rip the lower unit off my motor."

"Sounds like a wise plan of action," Markham said.

Cutter was mildly surprised when the judge didn't make seating assignments himself, but took a position on the wooden bench amidships.

"I'll take the bow," Jasper said. "It will help me learn the river better."

"You have a preference, boss?" Lola asked, sloshing ankle deep on her rubber boots into the river. She stowed her bag over the side.

"You can ride up front if you want," Cutter said.

"Cool," Lola said. "I'll see if Ned needs help pushing us off."

Judge Markham carried a small dry-bag he'd presumably borrowed from someone at the school since he'd traveled from Anchorage with a hard suitcase. "Taking one for the team," he said.

Cutter pulled a black wool beanie out of his pocket and snugged it over his head. "How's that, sir?"

"Not forcing your partner to sit next to me," Markham said. He gave a sleepy half smile.

Cutter hated to admit it, but this guy was remarkably self-aware.

A professional boat driver with the Florida Marine Patrol, Grumpy would have been proud of the way Birdie Pingayak saw to her skiff. It was an open vessel that was exposed to the elements, but she kept it clean and uncluttered. A heavy wooden oar lay tucked under the starboard rail. A red plastic jug of extra fuel was bungeed up front to even out the weight. Birdie secured a bright orange dry-bag the size of a watermelon to a cleat at the stern, letting it hang inside the boat. She shot a glance at Cutter, then gave the orange bag a pat.

"First-aid and emergency gear," she said.

The outboard motor started without much coaxing. Jasper cast off the bow line and he and Lola pushed the skiff away before clambering over the side. Curtains of fog closed in quickly. The bank disappeared as Birdie backed up enough to catch the current and turned her little vessel to the north. She proved herself a capable skipper, navigating sandbars, sweeper trees, and meandering braids of the ice-choked Kuskokwim River. Each new obstacle appeared through the fog when they were almost on top of it, giving her little time to react.

The judge slid down low so he was sitting on the plywood deck, leaning his back against the bench. He pulled his wool cap down over his ears and stuffed his hands in the pocket of his coat, knees to his chest. His life jacket rode up around his neck, turtle-like.

"Let's have it," he said. "Why does that woman hate me so much that she wants to kill me?"

"Honestly, Judge," Cutter said, "I'd just learned about it when we landed in Stone Cross. Ned was about to brief me in detail when he got the call about the murder and kidnapping."

Markham glanced toward the bow. "Officer Jasper, might you shed some light on this matter?"

"I might, sir," Ned said. "The woman's name is Daisy Aguthluk." The last syllable of the name clicked in the back of his throat, like the call of a raven.

"And she was at the airstrip when we landed?"

"Yes, sir," Ned said. He kept his voice up to be heard over the whine of the outboard. "Does Aguthluk ring a bell?"

Markham shook his head. "No. I mean, I've heard the name before. It's not an uncommon name in rural Alaska."

Birdie stared sideways into the fog, as if to distance herself from the conversation.

Jasper kept his lookout for dangerous water, but spoke over his shoulder as he continued. "How about the name Cecilia Aguthluk?"

The judge shook his head.

"It makes sense, I guess," Jasper said. "It was a long time ago. Cecilia was Daisy Aguthluk's auntie. Her father's sister, if I understand it correctly. Like I said, I'm new in this village."

Markham drew back, incredulous. "And how am I supposed to know this woman?"

"I'll tell it," Birdie said. "Ned just found out anyway, so he might get the details wrong."

"Please," Jasper said, focusing on the river again.

Birdie slowed the boat slightly, quieting the motor just enough to make herself more easily heard. She kept her eyes glued to the current as she spoke. "In 1983, an itinerant nurse named Diane Patrick was forced to overnight in Stone Cross because of a summer storm. She was part of a program vaccinating children for measles or something. Anyway, the new school wasn't built yet but the church had a cot for visiting clergy. The elders made sure Miss Patrick was fed a good dinner, and then made her comfortable in the church. Cecilia Aguthluk was always a little . . . you know, handicapped. She was thirty-eight, but people describe her as being like a sweet little child. She was walking to pick up some blackfish from a neighbor by the church when she happened to have a seizure. The nurse, along with several others, came outside and helped her. It was common knowledge throughout the village that Cecilia had epilepsy. Everyone here made sure she was safe, and took care not to embarrass her after she had a seizure. The nurse went on her way and everyone thought that was the end of it."

Markham closed his eyes and began to shake his head, obviously remembering something.

"It took about a month," Birdie said, "but eventually, a

plane landed at the old airstrip. Two strangers in suits, *gussuks*—white men—got off the plane. Nobody ever wore suits in the village, so this stood out as an omen. Something bad was about to happen. Older folks still didn't speak much English in the eighties, but these men said they were deputy marshals, and they'd come for Cecilia. She wasn't hiding, just down by the river singing and cutting fish with her teenage niece, Daisy. She was scared, so she fought—and who wouldn't when they are being kidnapped. Anyway, the men in suits put her in handcuffs and took her away. They had a piece of paper, a document from the court, saying it was all completely legal. Cecilia Aguthluk needed to be arrested for her own safety. There was an affidavit attached to the court document, signed by an itinerant nurse named Diane Patrick, and a petition signed by Assistant Alaska Attorney General J. Anthony Markham."

"Dear Lord in Heaven," Markham gasped, slack jawed. "*I* would want to kill me."

"What happened to Cecilia?" Lola asked.

Birdie shrugged. "We think she went to a hospital in Oregon, then fell off the radar. Some official there told Daisy that she was transferred somewhere near Spokane, but the people in Washington had never heard of her. Somebody thought she might have contracted TB and been sent to a facility in Arizona for the drier climate. She'd be around seventy now. If she's not dead, then she's lost in the system."

"Due respect, Judge," Lola said, "but you were an assistant attorney general thirty-four years ago?"

"It sounds lofty," Markham said, still stunned. "But assistant AG is an entry-level position in Alaska. I'd just moved up from New York with a new law degree."

"That's what I don't get," Lola said. "If the writ came from the state system, why did the marshals pick her up?"

Birdie nudged the tiller slightly, steering around a raft of jagged ice twice the size of her boat. "Why are you doing a homicide investigation for the Troopers just now? This is the bush. You guys work together all the time."

"Yeah," Lola said. "But I can't see the Marshals Service flying in and kidnapping innocent people without letting their family know where we're taking them."

"Makes me sick," Cutter said, "but I've heard of this sort of thing before on Indian reservations in the Southwest."

"Exactly," Ned Jasper said. "You may already know this, but even today, a lot of our elders still refer to troopers and deputy marshals as *tegusta.*"

"*Tegusta,*" Cutter repeated. "What's that?"

Birdie stared into the fog. "*The one who takes people away.*"

Chapter 18

It took an hour and a half to make the eight miles to Chaga Lodge, fighting ice flow and current the entire way. Judge Markham sat locked in his own thoughts, uncharacteristically silent.

Birdie arced her boat through the fog toward a clump of scraggly willows that looked no different from all the others they'd seen since leaving Stone Cross.

"We got maybe two hours here," she warned. "I don't want to run this river in the dark."

"Understood," Jasper said, glancing at the shadows. "One of us may have to stay here until the Troopers arrive."

"Long as it's not me," Birdie said.

A slender Native man with sparse black whiskers on hollow cheeks was waiting on the bank as the bow bumped frozen mud below a small cluster of whitewashed outbuildings. The man didn't look long out of high school. A large log structure, presumably the main lodge, loomed up the hill, barely visible behind him.

The man introduced himself as Vitus Paul. He rocked back and forth from one foot to the other, looking like he was about to jump out of his skin as he helped secure the skiff to a concrete block that looked set up for that purpose. Birdie eyed him as if she didn't like the way he smelled. Cutter noticed a small dab of peanut butter on his chin.

"How long have you been here?" Cutter asked him.

Vitus looked up at the sky—such as it was in the fog—then gave a noncommittal shrug. "Since late morning. About sunup, maybe."

His head on a swivel, Cutter stood with his back to the river, trying to get some sense of direction. "No sign of anyone else?"

"Just the body," Vitus said. "Are you guys troopers?"

"US Marshals," Lola said. "We're here on another matter—"

Vitus's eyebrows shot up in realization. "Ahh," he said. "That federal judge thing with Daisy."

Markham hugged himself against the chill. "Seems as though the entire village is aware of this."

Cutter ignored that. "What was the lodge like when you got here?"

"There was nobody here, if that's what you mean. I'm the one who called you. Remember?"

"Nobody's accusing you," Lola said.

Cutter tried again. "Was it still warm inside?"

Vitus shook his head. "I wish. Had to start a fire in the stove to keep from freezing to death. The Meads must have been gone a while."

"Okay." Cutter shot a glance at Lola. There was something about this place that wasn't right—and she felt it too. Dark shapes—buildings, trees, stacks of wood—materialized and then disappeared intermittently in the drifting clouds of vapor. Birdie still moved around at her boat, perhaps two dozen yards down the bank at the river—and she was completely invisible. Threats could be everywhere, and very likely were. It took every ounce of self-control Cutter had to keep from grabbing Markham by the scruff of the neck and dragging him to the relative safety of the lodge.

"Judge," he said, "let's get you inside."

Markham dug in. "I'd like to see what's going on first."

"There is something in the meat shed you'll want to see," Vitus said.

Cutter could be just as stubborn as the judge. "Is it on the way to the lodge?"

"Yeah," Vitus said. "It's right over here." He led the way up the hill, to an eight-by-eight building made of weathered plywood and window screens. S-shaped metal hooks hung from two-by-four rafters under a sloping tin roof. Parachute cord ran through small eyebolts around the outside of the building, terminating at a toggle switch that led to a car horn and boat battery.

"The meat shed," Vitus said. "But get a load of this." He held back the door and pointed to a circular design on the concrete floor, apparently drawn in blood. "That's weird, huh?"

"Indeed," the judge said.

"Gives me the creeps," Lola said. "Some kind of symbol, you think, boss?" She tilted her head to get a different angle. "A target, maybe?"

"Take some photos," Cutter said. He stooped to study the ground in front of the door. There were several depressions in the half frozen path, but nothing in the most recent snow other than a single set of boot prints where Vitus Paul had initially gone in and scrambled away after he'd seen the bloody design.

Both Lola and Ned Jasper took several photographs with their phones, placing one of the VPSO's Bic pens beside the design for scale.

"Got any guesses as to what that crazy thing is?" Vitus asked as they walked toward the lodge.

"Guesses," Cutter said. He and Lola flanked the judge, but if anyone was out there with a rifle, that would offer precious little protection. "But only guesses."

Vitus stopped when he reached the wooden steps in front of the lodge, using his chin to gesture to the right. "Rolf's around the side. I was gonna check to see if he was still alive, but . . ." He swallowed hard. "Well, you'll see."

Cutter sniffed the air, catching the odor of wood smoke. "Judge, if you don't mind waiting inside for a few minutes."

"I'm not comfortable—"

"You're in charge here, Officer Jasper." Cutter ignored Markham's protests. He looked past the VPSO at the gray apparition of tree line to the east. "Where do you want us? The fewer people we have around the scene the better."

"You and your partner come help me," Jasper said. "If everyone else would please hang back until we take some photos . . ."

Markham licked his lips, looked like he might say something.

Instead, he turned and clomped angrily up the steps toward the lodge door.

Cutter gave Lola a subtle nod, then glanced at Birdie. "Deputy Teariki will go inside first and do a quick check of things."

Markham turned. "To make certain we don't mess up the crime scene?"

"No, sir," Cutter said matter-of-factly. "To make certain someone doesn't shoot you in the face."

Chapter 19

Every two weeks since her husband had died, no matter what else was going on in her life, Mim Cutter sat down with the kids' teachers for a face-to-face meeting. Looking after their well-being, or trying to at least, was the only way for her to stay relatively sane. She wanted to do something for Arliss too, but that was proving more difficult—so far, anyway.

She'd gotten off early from the hospital and spent the last half hour at Rabbit Creek Elementary visiting with Mrs. Herbert, the twins' second grade teacher. The boys had taken the bus to piano lessons after school—something they had fought tooth and nail until Arliss, wonderful Arliss, had nonchalantly mentioned that Grumpy Man-Rule twenty-two said that a man should know how to play at least two songs on the piano and two songs on the guitar. Mim smiled at the thought. Sneaky man, that Grumpy. Mim often wondered, whenever Ethan would bring up one of Grumpy's manrules, if the old man invented them as each problem raised its head, or if he actually had a list he'd been keeping for most of his adult life. She supposed it didn't matter. They were good rules, and made good men.

He'd raised Ethan and Arliss after their dad had died and their mom had run off. Arliss had been around the same age the twins were now. Ethan was a little older, but not old enough to understand why a mother would abandon her children. Grumpy's ways—and his rules for manhood—had been just what a couple of traumatized boys needed. Mim had never told her kids that little factoid about their grandmother. She didn't want them to know that moms did things like run off. Their situation was sucky enough as it was.

The meeting at Rabbit Creek Elementary had gone as she'd expected. Soft smiles and straight talk from Mrs. Herbert. A casual observer might suspect that Michael was having the roughest time since his father's death. He was the quieter of the two, but, according to the teacher, it was outspoken Matthew who was struggling the most with his emotions. He was, Mrs. Herbert said, a fixer—a person who saw a problem and wanted to solve it right then. Matt missed his daddy, but he understood death, as much as any seven-year-old could. He was adjusting to the loss. The real problem with Matt was that he saw his mom was sad. He couldn't abide the thought of not being able to cheer her up. A fixer. That reminded Mim of someone else she knew.

She left the elementary school feeling responsible, as usual, for all the things that made her children unhappy. It was a vicious cycle. It depressed her that they were upset. Her depression upset them all the more. And now she had to go pick up Constance the she wolf. Mim needed to talk to her teachers too, but not today. Thirty minutes of hearing what a crappy mom she'd become was plenty, thank you very much, no matter how veiled the terms. Besides, Constance blew a gasket every time she thought about Mim getting into her business at the school. No, today it was a simple pickup since she was in the area—and a sullen ride to get the twins at their lessons.

Mim headed east on De Armoun Road. Winter was right around the corner, but for the time being, it was still fall in Anchorage, with chilly temperatures, miles of golden birch, and buckets of cold rain. With any luck, she'd be home before rush hour. She was lucky. She'd made it across the city from the hospital before evening traffic got bad. The poor unfortunates who commuted on the one and only highway out to the valley had it rough. A single accident with a moose—and there were a couple hundred of those every year—could stop traffic for hours. One of the many quirky things about living and working in Anchor-town. There weren't too many places on earth where you had to worry about dodging moose on your way home from work, or watching out for bears at city parks.

Anchorage lay nestled between the Knik Arm and Turnagain Arm of the Cook Inlet, a larger arm off the Gulf of Alaska, and the Pacific Ocean. The Chugach Mountains towered above the city to the east. Ethan had taken the family to pick blueberries off the Glen Alps trailhead when they'd first moved to Anchorage. He'd looked for bears the entire time. The boys had found some poop, and a lot of berries, but no bears. It was a wild place up there above the city.

Home to glaciers and icefields year-round, many of the Chugach Mountains remained snowcapped all summer. Now, they were completely white, and had been since a few days after termination dust—the first mountain snow of the season—had fallen in mid-September. Mim had heard a story of a guy hiking on Flattop Mountain—not far from the berry-picking spot—who'd broken both legs.

He'd sat there, alone and unable to move, looking down at all the traffic on the Seward Highway just a couple thousand feet below. It was one of those stories that ended differently depending on who told it. Sometimes the guy was rescued; sometimes other hikers found his bones in the spring. The mountains looked even more deadly now that Ethan was gone, and Mim was inclined to believe the hiker ended up as bear poop.

Arliss talked about taking the family berry-picking this year. Luckily, he'd been too busy.

Mim hung a left on Elmore, through a manicured neighborhood of big, cedar-sided homes with spacious lots and gobs of plump blue spruce. She and Ethan had talked about moving here. She stayed on Elmore at the roundabout, then took the next left into South High School parking, steeling herself to face Constance. Maybe she was trying too hard. Maybe she needed to just relax and let time do its job, healing all wounds—or beating the shit out of her—whichever came first.

Constance waited in the lee of the front entry, out of the wind. Other students were waiting too, chatting in groups of three or four. Mim groaned when she saw her daughter. As per usual, the she wolf ran alone. Odd, that she wasn't wearing her backpack. Instead of going around the van to get in, Constance approached Mim's door. That was weird. She usually wanted nothing but to go home and go to her room.

Mim rolled down her window.

"What's up?" she said, catching her breath in the chilly air. The sweet odor of birch in the fall would have made her smile had she not been so terribly sad.

"Mr. Gee said I can make some extra money tutoring some kids in math."

"Tonight?"

"Right now," Constance said.

Hands on the steering wheel, Mim rolled her wrist so she could look at her watch. She didn't like last-minute changes, but anything that signified a thaw in Constance was more than welcome. "Okay," she said. "How long do you think?"

"I don't know yet," Constance said. "I'll catch a ride."

"With a friend?" Mim asked, sounding snarkier than she wanted to.

Constance wagged her head. "Yes, with a friend."

"Okay," Mim said again. "No later than seven—and call when you're on the way home."

"Of course," Constance said, as if she was clearly old enough not to be reminded of stupid details.

Mim rolled up her window, fighting the urge to play detective and dig deeper. She told herself this was good. This was progress. Still, she wished Arliss were here. He'd go all marshal-y and follow her or something. If Constance was meeting a boy, Arliss would do his job as an uncle and give the kid chronic diarrhea with a stone-cold glare from those blue eyes of his.

Mim turned left on De Armoun again to go pick up the boys, when her cell phone rang. At first she thought it might be Constance, changing her mind and wanting a ride home. She did that lately. But the caller ID was blocked. Mim tapped the hands-free button.

"Ms. Cutter?" the voice said. "Jill Phillips here."

Mim took a second to make the connections.

"Chief," she said. "Thanks for returning my call."

"No problem," Phillips said. "What can I do for you?"

Mim pulled onto a patch of gravel at 140th. Her heart was beating far too fast to drive and talk about something of this magnitude. She threw the van in park and then settled deeper into her seat.

"Arliss speaks highly of you," she said. "He says you're the best boss he's ever even heard of."

"That's good to hear," Phillips said, wary, waiting for the other shoe to drop.

"He doesn't know I'm calling."

"I gathered that," Phillips said.

"Chief . . . should I call you Chief?"

"Jill is better."

"Okay, Jill," Mim said. "Please call me Mim. I'm talking to you because Arliss trusts you. And if he trusts you, then I trust you."

"Do you need me to have him call you when he phones in?" Phillips said. "He doesn't have cell reception where he's at now, but he has a satellite phone."

"No," Mim said. "Please no. The last thing I want to do is bother him at work. I want to talk to *you*. I'm calling because . . . Well, I'm worried about him. I need to know if there's anything I can do for him. He seems so . . . I don't know . . ."

"Ready to explode?"

"Yes!" Mim said, exhaling with relief that the chief understood. "Exactly. I don't want to get him in trouble."

"You're not," Phillips said. "I'm worried about him too. The problem is, I'm his boss, and his new boss at that. He's not likely to confide much in me. Not until we know each other a little better. I know he thinks the world of you and your family, though. He would never have left Florida otherwise."

"He loves the kids," Mim said. She knew how Arliss

felt about her in the past—or she'd figured it out, shortly after she and Ethan were married. But he'd been married four times since then.

"Has something happened?"

"Not at all," Mim said. "To be honest, he's been this way for years. It's nothing new. I'm just able to see it more clearly now." She closed her eyes, pausing for a moment to screw up her courage. Jill Phillips seemed to know it was time for her to be quiet and listen. A rare trait in a boss, or any human being for that matter.

"I know it's a lot to ask," Mim said at length. "But, can you tell me what happened to him in Afghanistan?"

Silence.

"I'm overstepping," Mim said. "Asking you to betray a confidence."

"No," Phillips said. "It's not that. As a matter of fact, I've been wondering the same thing myself. And honestly, it's more your business than it is mine. You're his family. The U.S. Army doesn't provide that kind of information when someone gets out. There are no specifics in his record other than the fact that he was awarded a Silver Star."

"I knew about that," Mim said. "He doesn't talk about it, but I knew."

"There's a citation with it," Phillips said. "But it's vague. They do that if the action has to do with something classified."

"My husband thought it was some other event that was bothering him," Mim said. "Not related to the stuff that led to him getting the Silver Star. Their grandfather, the man who raised them, he thought so too."

"Grumpy?"

Mim smiled. "Yes. I got the impression Grumpy found

out something about what happened from one of the guys in Arliss's unit, but Grumpy passed away before he could tell Ethan."

Mim started to mention her conversation with Arliss at the Dome, but that seemed a violation of trust. It was a stupid notion. She was asking the chief to tell her Arliss's secrets. She should be willing to do the same thing in order to help him. Phillips spoke before Mim had to.

"Listen," the chief said, sighing as if she'd reached a major conclusion. "I've been going back and forth for the better part of three months about contacting one of Arliss's old US Army Ranger buddies—a guy named David Carnahan. He's a physician in Virginia now. For all I know, he's the same one who Grumpy got his information from."

Mim's hands gripped the steering wheel. She rocked back and forth in her seat. "You have his phone number?"

"I do," Phillips said. "But I have to tell you, there's a danger here you need to keep in mind. People who serve together can be awfully protective. There's a better than average chance Dr. Carnahan won't tell you anything, but will call Arliss and let him know you're digging around."

"I . . ."

"You worried I might do the same thing?"

"I kinda did," Mim said.

"I might have," Phillips said. "Had you been a flake."

"Dr. Carnahan's number?"

"Here you go," Phillips said, reading off the digits beginning with the 703 area code. "Arliss is fortunate to have you in his corner."

"And you too, Jill," Mim said, writing the number on her hand. "Tell me again what kind of doc Carnahan is. I'm a nurse. I know how to talk to doctors."

"A pediatric surgeon," Phillips said.

"But he wasn't a doctor in the army?"

"No," Phillips said. "A Ranger. So tread lightly. There's a good chance that if something terrible happened to Arliss, David Carnahan was smack dab in the middle of it with him."

"I've gotta do something," Mim said.

"I'm that way too," Phillips said. "A fixer."

Chapter 20

Vitus Paul's tracks stopped in the snow ten feet from the prone body. It was easy to see why.

Snow lent a peculiar intensity to blood, unmuted by the fog.

Pooling on the grimy asphalt of a city street or oozing onto the dirt floor of a mud hut, blood is placidly silent and more akin to used motor oil or spilled chocolate syrup than a vital life force. But smeared and sprayed with all the attendant gore against the crystalline white backdrop of snow, it becomes the visual equivalent of a scream.

Cutter and Ned Jasper approached slowly, the VPSO taking photos, Cutter looking at the ground for tracks and any other evidence that might have been left behind. They were still ten feet from the body when Lola came out to join them.

"Markham's good and pissed at you," she whispered to Cutter.

"At me?"

"I guess he's just pissed." Lola rubbed her hands together to warm them, staring at Rolf Hagen's body as she spoke. "And you happen to be in the way."

"Can't be helped," Cutter said. "I'll worry about that when I see what we've got here."

Lola stayed a half step behind, as if she didn't know where to put her feet. She was young as deputy marshals went, with less than four years on a job that focused primarily on protecting judges and hunting fugitives—not investigating homicides. Certainly, deputies saw more than their fair share of blood and gore—but not nearly as much as a rank-and-file patrol officer working the street. There were shootings, fights, and the occasional stabbing, but frozen bodies were far from the norm. Cold and snow had done a good job of keeping the body intact. It didn't happen that way in the south. Cutter had gone out with Grumpy a couple of times in his Florida Marine Patrol boat. A body in the swamp became unrecognizable in just a few hours. Forensic experts could approximate the time of death by measuring the size of the specific larvae types feeding on the corpse. There were no flies here, not yet anyway.

A couple of ravens *ker-lucked* in the nearby trees, hidden by the fog. The birds had found the body at first light, and done what scavengers do. Their drunken tracks staggered around the pink snow like tiny pitchforks. They'd paid special attention to the flesh around a massive head wound.

Ned Jasper stood frozen in place, staring down at the body. "I hate it when I know them," he whispered.

Cutter put a hand on his shoulder. "I understand. How do you say *raven* in Yup'ik?" Sometimes, thinking of something else for a moment gave the mind time for a needed reset.

The VPSO looked up at him, surprised by the question.

Cutter repeated himself. "Raven?"

"*Tulukaruq*," Jasper said, clicking the word from the back of his mouth. The sound was remarkably similar to the bird's call. "I heard white people call a group of 'em an unkindness." Jasper looked at the tracks around the head wound, shaking his head a little to clear it. "Unkindness sounds about right."

Out of the momentary stupor, he snapped a photo with his phone, then used his thumb and forefinger to zoom in on what was left of the face. "Hard to be sure with that damage to his head, but I'd say that's Rolf Hagen. He's got the right kind of beard."

Cutter understood all too well what the VPSO was going through. He'd seen a lot of people who'd met their end. Some of them, he'd ended himself—in the army and the Marshals Service. He didn't try to keep track, at least not consciously, but a record was made. He saw them all, like a fanned deck of playing cards. Some of the faces were partially obscured, but most, he saw all too well.

Lola took a photo of a blond spot in the logs, chipped away on the otherwise amber wood on the lodge wall above Rolf Hagen's body.

"You think that could be the bullet?"

"I do," Cutter said. "I'm sure the Troopers will want to be the ones to dig it out."

"If they make it out here," Ned said, half under his breath. He took a satellite phone out of his coat pocket, waited for a signal, then punched a number into the pad.

"Lieutenant Warr," he said. "It's Ned. We're out at the lodge. Rolf Hagen's dead all right. We haven't gone up to the body yet, but it looks like he's been shot. Any luck getting more people out to us?"

He stood and listened for a time, ankle deep in the snow, broad face screwed into a fearsome scowl of concentration. Jasper was a smart man, good at his job, if a little overwhelmed by the present situation.

"I thought that might happen," he said at length. "I guess I can stay, but this fog's camped out right on top of us. This crazy weather has temperatures going up temporarily. The body's lying in a low spot. If the snow melts, the whole area will be under six inches of muddy water. Good chance any evidence is gonna be washed away if we leave him in place until you get ABI out . . . Yeah. Hang on." Ned held the phone out to Cutter. "The L.T. wants to talk to you."

He checked to make sure he still had a signal, then put the phone to his ear. "Cutter."

Lola scanned the trees while he spoke.

"Any sign of the Meads?" Warr asked.

"Nothing good," Cutter said. "Do you think they'd be the kind of people to murder the handyman? An affair gone bad maybe, something like that?"

"I don't know." Warr groaned. "I only met them when they came through. Newlyweds, really. He was kind of flaky, but it seemed to me that she was squared away."

"Flaky?"

"Goofy," Warr said. "Never serious. Like a middle school kid. Still. This has the feel of a kidnapping."

"Search teams then?" Cutter asked. "There's been snow since the murder, but it's trackable."

"Aircraft are still on a weather hold," Warr said. He sounded harried, like he was spinning way too many plates at the same time. "I can't even get anyone from Alaska Bureau of Investigations into Bethel from Anchorage. I know it seems unthinkable not to respond, but I can't let my troopers take off if there's no way for them to land where they're going. I have two of my troopers standing by with the 185 as soon as they can lift off. If they can get to Stone Cross they'll work their way to you. Two more made an attempt by boat, but there's ice blocking the river between here and Kwethluk. They ended up going downriver and making it across to Napaskiak—which is on the same side as you—then started your way on ATVs. I just got a call to tell me they've already sunk one machine up past the axles in the mud."

Cutter scuffed at the snow, testing the frozen ground with the toe of his boot. "How long's this weather supposed to hang on?"

"That's the thing," Warr said. "There's a big cold front moving in off the Bering tonight or early tomorrow."

Great, Cutter thought, but he didn't say it. He was still relatively new to Alaska, but he'd watched *Deadliest Catch* enough to know that the Bering Sea was well-known as the birthplace for hellacious weather.

"A winter storm?"

"You could say that," Warr said. "Think hurricane but with snow instead of rain. It will blow this fog out, but the whiteout conditions won't help our mission. The ice on the river will just get worse. Our flight window is going to be limited if we get one at all."

Cutter turned in place, phone to his ear, scanning as he listened. He couldn't shake the feeling that there was someone out there, watching. The air hovered just above freezing. Intermittent snowmelt dripped steadily off the metal roof into a growing puddle at the back corner of the lodge. The fog distorted sounds, making it difficult to tell where they were coming from. Deeper tones, like croaking ravens, the grinding hiss of ice in the river, and the constant dripping, seemed to come from every direction.

The ravens *ker-lucked* again, drawing his attention to the tree line. Considering the layout of the buildings and how they'd block certain shots, there was a good chance the bullet that killed Rolf Hagen had come from out there.

"Ned is right," Cutter said. "We're melting for the time being, which will put the area around the body under a couple inches of water by nightfall."

"Then freeze when the storm comes in," Warr said. "I know your responsibility to the judge makes going after the Meads impossible . . ."

The lieutenant paused, as if waiting for an argument. Cutter's gut churned at the prospect of inaction, but Warr was right. As much as he wanted to head for the woods, he couldn't leave the judge to Lola with an active threat in the village.

"It's a big ask," Warr continued. "But how would you feel about collecting what evidence you can before it washes away?"

"Bluntly speaking," Cutter said, "I'm a hell of a man hunter. But I wouldn't be anyone's first choice as a crime scene investigator. That said, I've assisted on more than one homicide investigation. We can help Ned take photos, get you some measurements, and comb the snow for any evidence, including tracks."

"That would be much appreciated," Warr said. "Get the body and anything else in plain sight. I'll have a team out there as soon as humanly possible. At least by tomorrow morning. Right now I've got a suicide in Nunam Iqua, a moose hunter up the Andreafsky River who's two days overdue, and the body recovery Earl was supposed to go get today in Nightmute."

"Kind of a perfect storm," Cutter said.

The lieutenant gave an exhausted sigh. "Nope. Just an average day in C Detachment—nothing sixty good troopers couldn't handle. Trouble is, we have to make do with twenty-seven."

"We'll help however we can."

"All I can ask," Warr said. "Anything jump out at you at first glance? Something I can tell my brass other than we're not responding to a homicide and kidnapping?"

Cutter eyed the body. "Looks like Hagen was shot from the trees."

"That doesn't rule the Meads out," Warr said. "But it makes them less likely. Jasper will stay out with the crime scene until we get a trooper out there."

"Due respect, Lieutenant," Cutter said. "He's unarmed. At the very least, we have a murder and a couple of fugitives. They could be the killers, but I tend to agree that this feels like an abduction."

"I hear you." Another phone rang on Warr's end. "Listen," he said. "I have a call from the captain I need to take. If you don't mind, give me a call back before you leave."

Cutter handed the satellite phone back to Ned. "Looks like he wants you to stay and guard the crime scene."

"He told me," Ned said. "Honestly, I'm fine with that. But I'm thinking it's going to be a while before they get anyone out here. That leaves Stone Cross with no VPSO." He shrugged. "It is what it is, I guess."

"It's your business," Lola said, "but somebody shot that guy over there in the head. You think it's a good idea to stay out here by yourself?"

Ned smirked. "No," he said, lowering his voice. "Vitus is staying with me. He just doesn't know it yet."

Ned tramped down to the boat to retrieve a body bag while Cutter and Lola took photos and measurements, noting how far the body was from the lodge wall and the direction Rolf Hagen had been facing before he was killed.

Cutter squatted next to the body. "There's some solace in the way he fell."

Lola gulped. The corner of her lip curled, like she might get sick at any moment. "I can't see any solace in having your brains blown out."

"See how his boots are slightly crossed at the ankles?" Cutter pointed toward the river with an open hand. "If you look at the track impressions under the snow, he was walking this way."

"Then why is he facing the trees?"

Cutter gestured to the wound. "Bullet hit him here, where the collar of his coat touches his skull. He didn't have time to know he'd been shot. His body collapsed instantly, corkscrewing as it went down."

Lola gave a tiny nod, back to her robust self now that she focused on science instead of the gore. "That accounts for the crossed legs."

"Yep," Cutter said. He studied the sole of each rubber boot, then checked the loose rubber tops. More than once he'd found an ankle gun on a dead body.

"How long do you think he's been here?"

"That's a tough call." Cutter nudged Hagen's outstretched arm with his knuckle. "Rigor is still present," he said. "That usually starts to relax after fifty hours or so, but in these temps, when the body doesn't start to break down for a while, it could hang on for twice that, or even longer. Aften Brooks said she hasn't been able to reach the Meads since the afternoon of the day before yesterday. If the killing happened right after that . . ."

Lola checked her watch. "A little less than forty-eight

hours. That's a long time to be kidnapped." She looked up at the log wall. "What do you want to do about that?"

Cutter stood with a groan, and went to examine the hole where the bullet had burrowed into the wood.

"Sloppy," Lola said. "Leaving evidence behind that way."

"I'm not sure I've ever seen a tidy murder," Cutter said. "Except in the movies." He stooped a little, putting the entry point at eye level. "Hagen's lying on top of a half bottle of R&R whiskey. He's not wearing socks with his boots, which suggests he slipped them on in a hurry. All that, combined with his flannel jammies pants, leads me to believe this happened at night." He tapped the log beside the bullet hole. "That means the shooter likely didn't see this. If we leave it unattended, he or she could come back, and it could very well disappear while we're gone, and we'd lose a valuable piece of evidence." He glanced at the tree line, then back at the bullet hole. "Go in the lodge and see if you can find something to use as a pointer stick. A dowel, an arrow, something like that."

Lola returned at the same time Ned got back with an ungainly black body bag rolled under one arm.

"Sorry, boss." Lola held up a wooden spoon. "No arrows or dowels. But this has a long handle."

"That'll do," Cutter said. He took the spoon and carefully placed the end into the bullet hole. As he suspected, the straight handle pointed toward a dark spot in the tree line. "We'll need to check out that area over there," he said. "After we're done here."

Ned nodded. "Might be less snow under the trees. Maybe we'll find some tracks—"

A strained shout from Judge Markham interrupted him. Cutter and Lola were moving the moment they heard it.

Chapter 21

Cutter and the others rounded the corner of the lodge in three strides, nearly running headlong into Birdie, who was on her way to get them.

Markham shouted again.

"I wish people wouldn't be so loud," Birdie said under her breath. "Stupid to yell out here. Wrecks my concentration."

The judge and Vitus Paul stood looking down at the snow next to a small storage shed just south of the main lodge. Both men had their hands in their pockets as if they didn't know what to do with them.

"What is it?" Cutter asked as Birdie turned to follow him.

Markham looked up, flushed with cold and excitement. "Ms. Pingayak found more blood. Is it possible that the victim was wounded here and then died over there?"

Cutter shook his head. "No, sir. Too much head trauma. That one died on the spot."

"Maybe it's from one of the Meads, then?" Lola offered.

Cutter bent to get a better look. Several drops of spattered blood formed a rough fan shape, pink under the dusting of snow. There wasn't enough blood for a substantial gaping wound, more likely a concussive blow to the mouth or nose. Both parts of the body were prone to bleed when hit even slightly.

Cutter gestured with an open hand to a spot a few feet on the opposite side of the blood spatter. "If you all could do me a favor and shine the flashlights from your cell phones across the ground, low so I can pick up some definition."

Vitus Paul gave a nod of approval, as if that's what he would have done.

Lola continued watching for threats, while Markham and the others did as directed. The low-angle lights allowed Cutter to pick up a telltale depression in the snow, roughly the shape of a prone body. Closer examination revealed two slightly deeper divots, where someone had fallen to their knees. Cutter lay down on his side, eye level with the ground.

He thought out loud as he worked. "Let's say the blood came from someone who was hit in the head—"

"You mean shot?" Markham said.

Birdie gave him a side-eye then quickly returned to Cutter. "Not enough blood."

"More likely struck with something," Cutter said, his cheek pressed to the snow. "Hard enough to drive them to their knees . . ." He motioned for Birdie to move her light a little, to above the place where he suspected the body would have pitched forward when it fell. It took a full two minutes of gentle probing in the snow before he found what he was looking for—a thin disc of bloodied ice about three inches across. He rolled up on his side long enough to retrieve the old Barlow pocketknife from his pocket, then used the tip of the blade to gently pry up the edge of the ice. Vitus turned up his nose in disgust. Birdie bent at the waist, leaning forward to get a better look.

"What is that thing?" Judge Markham asked.

"If I had to guess," Cutter said, "frozen spit." He laid the opaque disc in Lola's gloved hand and got to his feet. "And a broken tooth."

Vitus gave a solemn shake of his head. "Mr. or Mrs. Mead . . ."

"Looks like it," Cutter said. "And since Rolf Hagen went down over there, that means either the shooter closed the distance . . . or, there are at least two people involved."

"Two people missing," Lola mused. "It would take more than one to carry them away."

"Or one of the Meads is also a kidnapper," the judge said. "Nothing people do surprises me anymore."

"I hear that, Judge," Lola said. "I hear that . . ."

"One thing is certain," Cutter said. "At least one of the Meads was struck violently enough to break a tooth. Judging from the frozen saliva in one spot, the blow was enough to knock them unconscious so they could be taken to a second location." He shot a glance at Ned Jasper. "And when there are two separate crime scenes, the second is almost always a homicide."

"That puts them gone for two days," Lola whispered. "Not good."

Ned took an evidence baggie from his jacket and held it open so Lola could drop in the frozen disk to retain its DNA before it melted, along with the tooth.

Birdie stared at the bloody ice as if hypnotized. Her head suddenly snapped up and she looked toward the river, as if she'd heard something through the fog. "Okay," she said, sounding like the principal that she was. "It's twenty minutes to five. If you want to get back to Stone Cross tonight, we gotta be on the boat in no more than one hour. Less is better."

Markham gave a soft smile. He surely meant well, but his words came like a condescending pat on the shoulder. "Homicide investigations take time, Ms. Pingayak."

"I'm sure they do," Birdie said. "But the river doesn't give a shit . . . Your Honor. Either you finish up in an hour, or this turns into one of those Agatha Christie–type deals where we're all stuck here together playing gin rummy and trying to figure out which one of us is the killer—maybe until the ice gets thick enough for someone to come get us on snow machines."

"You guys should go ahead and wrap it up," Ned said. "Me and Vitus are gonna stay here anyway."

"Isn't somebody going after the Meads?" Birdie asked, looking directly at Cutter.

He gritted his teeth. Thinking through all the possible outcomes. It felt so very wrong not to leave now, to go after them at this moment. The storm would blow in and cover any remaining tracks, and likely make travel impossible.

Lola spoke next, while Cutter lay down again to study the ground where he'd found the tooth.

"There's this scenario question we always hear about in the Marshals Service," she said. "You're working the back of a residence, assigned to guard this mob witness with a serious threat on his life. A little girl runs up to your post crying her face off and saying her kid brother is drowning in the pool a few houses down. She begs you to come save him. You call for backup, but the instructor tells you the radios are down. The scenario is a no win. There's no way to know if it's a trick or not without abandoning your post. If you stay at your post like they tell you, the kid drowns. You go check on the kid, the mob comes and whacks your witness."

"I'd fail that scenario," Birdie said.

"Ah," Markham said. "Reality isn't a scenario, Deputy . . ."

"True enough, Your Honor," Cutter said, rolling back to his feet. "This reality is even more stark. We don't know if there's enough of a trail to take us to the Meads, or if they'd be alive when we got to them. But I'm certain there's a woman back in Stone Cross who wants to see you dead." He looked up at Jasper. "It's up to you and the lieutenant, of course, but I'm not comfortable leaving you here. There's too great a chance Rolf Hagen's killer will come back."

"I know," Jasper said, resigned to it.

Cutter gave a curt nod, coming to a decision. "Warr seems like the type to trust the boots on the ground. I'll give him a call. Nobody should stay here under these circumstances."

Vitus slumped in relief. "I wouldn't mind not staying out here all night. I saw some big tracks downriver. A mile or so back when I was riding in."

"What do you mean by big?" Cutter asked.

Ned closed his eyes and groaned. "Let me guess: Aru-lutaq?"

"I think it was," Vitus said.

"The Hairy Man," Birdie said. "It's like the bigfoot."

"Worth checking out the tracks," Cutter said.

He'd seen weather morph human tracks into all sorts of odd shapes and designs. The ground didn't lie—but some-times she fibbed. You had to listen to the entire story.

Chapter 22

Sarah Mead's shoulders felt as if they'd been wrenched off her body. Her hips were on fire from the pressure of the hard bed. As she was on her side, her head lolled, straining the muscles in her neck. She'd lapsed in and out of consciousness ever since glimpsing the toes of David's boots. She would wake up in a sort of painful oblivion and then the memories came flooding back. Bitter, gut-wrenching sobs wracked her body until she couldn't breathe. Overwhelmed and in shock, she'd pass out to repeat the process over and over. Awake again, she tried to blink away the agony of betrayal, worse even than the physical pain of her shattered teeth and injured jaw.

There were two of them. She'd been able to suss out that much, even blind and deaf. She could smell David's body wash, but there was someone else too, someone more musky, like he needed to put on deodorant. This made no sense. How could her husband be involved? Why had they taken her? And why were they now keeping her alive? Her family had no money to speak of. David knew that. Why hadn't he just killed her if he wanted her dead?

Her mind on fire, she rolled over, wobbling on her

bound hands at the small of her back, bucking her hips to thrash like a beached fish. She screamed, past caring.

"Daawiid!"

Something slammed into her thigh. A barked command followed, too muffled to understand.

Stunned but not deterred by the blow, she screamed again, louder now, like a child having a tantrum, completely undone. At least she was getting a reaction. Maybe they would just kill her and this would be over.

"Daawwiid!"

A shadow loomed over the top of her, nose to nose. She could smell the sickening sweetness of chewing tobacco on rancid breath.

"Hey!" A cruel hand grabbed her by the jaw and squeezed.

She froze, despite the unbearable pain. "Shut your mouth," he said, in a gravel hiss brimming with savagery and hate. "Or I'll nail it shut."

The hand held her this way for what seemed like forever, thumb and fingers cruelly gripping her jaw, grinding the inside of her cheeks against her teeth. Her body went limp, her mind reeling. Blackness crept in from the edges of her consciousness, but for some reason, she didn't pass out.

A second voice boomed, somewhere in the distance. The cruel hand relaxed, slowly, reluctantly, finally letting her slip away.

She scrambled backward, but the log walls trapped her on the narrow bed. She barely had time to catch her breath before a shadow fell over her face again. "Relax," a voice said, this one deeper, more precise. It wasn't David, nor was it the tobacco chewer.

She shuddered, wincing at the pain even this small

movement caused her damaged teeth. Her head lolled, too heavy for her neck. There were three of them? Why? What was happening to her? She broke into uncontrollable sobs.

"Stop," the deep voice said. "You'll break a rib."

A hand pressed on her shoulder, almost gently, then coaxed her to the end of the bed and helped her to her feet. She felt pressure against her wrists, tried to pull away out of instinct, but strong hands held her in place. A moment later, her arms suddenly fell to her sides, free. Fiery pins and needles surged into her hands with the renewed circulation.

"Come," the deep voice said, leading her sideways by the arm.

"Whaaa?"

She bumped into something to her left, reached out, felt a shoulder of someone seated there. A groan, then a whimper. "Sarah . . ."

It was David. She ripped away the hood with numb fingers, blinking, even in the dim lamplight of whatever hellhole she was in. Her husband was tied to a chair at the foot of her narrow bed. A thread of bloody saliva dripped from the corner of his broken lips, hanging down to the lap of his soiled shorts. One eye was swollen completely shut. The other bloodshot and dazed, as if he couldn't focus.

Sarah turned to find two of the biggest men she'd ever seen. Both wore faded jeans and old flannel shirts, like lumberjacks, or hunters—or someone pretending to be lumberjacks or hunters. The darker of the two seemed to focus all his anger and hate out of one surviving eye. The place where the other eye should have been was a mass of white scars against a weathered face. His hair, black like his thick beard, was slicked straight back over a high forehead. Large hands held some type of club or whip. Sarah guessed him to be in his fifties, but the years had not been kind to him. The nearer and larger man had a disinterested face covered with red stubble. His thinning red hair was pulled back in a stubby ponytail. This one was wearing David's boots.

"You should sit down before you fall down," the redhead said.

Sarah looked at David, then back up at the two men. She should have fallen to her knees and comforted him, but she still couldn't help but think this was all somehow his fault.

"Sarah," he said again, a whispered groan. He knew she was there, but seemed to look past instead of at her. "I'm so sorry."

His shirt was torn and open, revealing burns the size of quarters on his chest. A trickle of blood ran out his ear. Sarah put a hand on his shoulder, carefully so as not to cause him any more pain. It was the best she could do for now, while she processed all of this. His body slumped at her touch.

They were in a small cabin, maybe sixteen by sixteen feet. It was cramped for the four of them, dark, and stiflingly hot from a blazing fire in the woodstove. Other than the fire, the only light came from a candle lantern and a small window on the wall opposite her rough bed. To her left, beyond David, was a set of bunk beds, each with a rumpled sleeping bag.

She looked at the man, hand still on David. "Who . . . aahhr . . . you?"

"Doesn't matter," the dark man said. When he spoke, the dark beard opened to display white teeth. Every word was a snarl.

"Whaaa . . . ?" Sarah couldn't get her jaw to cooperate.

She clenched her eyes, trying to force away the pain, then tried again, sobbing, wincing, then sobbing some more through her slurred and drooling words. "Whaaa do yoou . . . ?"

The one with the red beard touched his own face. "I'm sorry about your jaw," he said. "Things were happening kind of fast. You came out of nowhere. After that, I couldn't leave you—"

Sarah wanted to pull her hair out. If this guy was sorry about nearly killing her, then why was he holding her prisoner?

"Whaaa . . . ?" she said again.

"What do we want?" The dark one finished her sentence.

She managed a meager nod, despite the fact that it made her head feel as if it might topple off and land on the floor at any moment.

"Answers," the dark one said. "That's what I want."

Red Ponytail stood directly in front of her. He ran a finger down her jawline, flowing with her when she tried to pull away. He needn't have worried. There was nowhere for her to go.

"I should have set this when you were still unconscious," he said.

"Whaaaa?"

"Your jaw," he said. "It's not broken. Just knocked out of kilter. Promise not to bite me, and I'll set it for you."

Thumb in her mouth, he grabbed her by the chin like a hooked fish, pulling her jaw sharply downward and toward him. Sarah resolved to bite off every finger the man had, but the pain was so great she passed out the moment the jaw snapped into place with an audible crack.

Chapter 23

Lieutenant Warr agreed it was too dangerous to leave Ned Jasper at the lodge with no backup coming on the near horizon. With time ticking down until Birdie Pingayak's "drop-dead" departure time, Cutter gave the lieutenant a thumbnail brief of his plans, then made a quick visit to the tree line while the others got Rolf Hagen loaded into a body bag and stowed on the boat. Cutter hoped to cut some sort of sign, to find a direction of travel for the shooter or shooters. The least he could do was point the troopers in the right direction when they arrived to find the missing couple. Whoever the killers were, they'd kept to well-used trails around the lodge, deeply rutted paths that guests had used to explore the woods all summer long. There was a stand of white birch to the southeast. Leafless and skeletal without their leaves, many of the trunks provided a home for a gnarly chocolate-colored growth called Chaga, the supposed superfood fungus that gave the lodge its name. Thick willows and alders grew around the perimeter of the grounds, the bark nibbled by rabbits and scraped by moose and caribou antlers. Numerous animal tracks crisscrossed the snow. There were trails everywhere, but Cutter found nothing new belonging to a human.

He felt confident that he could have found something,

given time and an ever-increasing search pattern, but Birdie Pingayak's whistle cut him short. He chuckled at the fact that she didn't yell, even when she was worried about getting iced in with a dead body. Cutter took one final look around at the duff and snow of the forest floor, and resigned himself to the fact that he'd have to leave the tracking to the troopers.

Birdie's open aluminum boat was rated for seven people. Counting Rolf Hagen's body, Vitus Paul, and the five who'd come upriver to the lodge, it was at max capacity on the return trip. Birdie gave the rubber ball on the fuel line a couple of pumps to make sure the engine had gas, and then pulled the starter rope. The fifty-horse Tohatsu caught the first time, burbling the brown water at the stern. Birdie leaned backward a hair to see that the engine was peeing, or pumping water through the system to keep it cool. She gave Lola and Ned a thumbs-up, and they pushed the bow away from the bank before jumping in with everyone else. Vitus rode up front with them, leaving the middle seat to Cutter and the judge again. Rolf Hagen lay sideways, gunnel to gunnel, just forward of Birdie. They'd propped the foot of his body bag up on the extra fuel can to make him fit.

Birdie adjusted the choke so the outboard ran more smoothly, then backed into the current. She pushed the tiller away from her, swinging the bow to the south.

"It should be a faster ride home," she said, "now that we're going with the flow. You guys up front watch for big ice and logs again. Okay?" She settled in on her seat, bright brown eyes flitting back and forth from bank to bank, as far as she could see in the fog. The lines of her tattoo highlighted the reverent smile on her lips. She was at home on this river, no matter the circumstances.

* * *

The tall silhouette of Aften Brooks pacing back and forth in her wool Sherpa hat materialized in the fog as Birdie nosed her boat toward the mud bank. Judge Markham slumped against the bench, head down, deep in thought. Cutter's anxiety level had gone up by degrees the nearer they got to Stone Cross. He also had time to come to grips with the fact that the investigation into Rolf Hagen's death and the disappearance of the Meads was a matter for the Alaska State Troopers. As difficult as it was, his primary focus had to be protecting the judge. Thankfully, Markham had fallen into a funk, making him less social than usual. He assured Cutter that he planned to make only a short appearance at the potluck before retiring to his room for the night.

Birdie came in at an angle, throwing the outboard into reverse when they neared the shore, slowing their approach. Water churned at the back of the boat. The aluminum bottom scraped gravel. Broadside to the current now, the stern swung sideways, and the little boat settled into an eddy of slower water so she faced slightly upstream.

Lola climbed out first, taking a position that faced the village proper even as her boots hit the water. The fog provided cover to any would-be shooters, but it also made targeting the judge more difficult. Cutter had asked Ned not to announce their arrival over the VHF, hopefully making it less likely that Daisy Aguthluk or anyone else would be waiting. He was surprised to see Aften and told her so. Surprises were rarely a good thing in the world of dignitary protection.

"How did you know when we were coming in?"

Aften grabbed the bow line and looped it around the piece of drill pipe to secure the boat. "I didn't," she said. "Not for sure at least. But I know Birdie, and she's smart enough to get home before dark in shitty weather." Like most people who weren't guilty of anything, Aften Brooks didn't waste time defending herself. Instead, she took a step toward Ned. "What about Sarah?"

The VPSO crinkled his nose, saying no without having to utter the actual words.

"Is it true?" she whispered. "Rolf's dead?"

"I'm afraid so," Jasper said.

"Did you find . . ." Aften's voice trailed off. "I mean, did it look like Sarah was hurt?"

"I'm really sorry," Jasper said. "I shouldn't talk about the investigation. We have to turn everything over to the troopers." He set his dry-bag on the bank along with the hunting rifle and returned to the boat to retrieve Rolf Hagen's body.

Aften began to pace again. "But she's missing. What if she's hurt? Somebody killed Rolf, so—"

Birdie put a hand on her shoulder. "They've thought of all that. I promise. We have to let them do their job. Where's Jolene?"

Aften closed her eyes and gave a helpless sigh. "At the school. Everybody is."

"What about Daisy Aguthluk?" Judge Markham asked.

"Daisy?" Aften shrugged, caught off guard that the judge would know the woman's name. "Yeah . . . I'm sure she's at the potluck too."

"Good," Markham said. He threw the duffel over his shoulder. "I want to talk to her."

Cutter looked back the way they'd just come. Ice chattered and hissed as it floated past in the darkness. It killed him to leave things undone. Something was going on out there, something bad. He sloshed into the river, ready to help Lola and Ned, who were in the boat again maneuvering the body bag into position. Even in the slower current of the eddy, Cutter could feel the frigid water shoving his calves. He leaned across the rail to get a good grip on the nylon straps. Rolf Hagen weighed well over two hundred pounds and even with rigor mortis, lifting him out of the boat was an ungainly task.

"Glad you're playing the details of this close to the vest," Cutter said to the VPSO as they worked. "You might consider letting it slip that we found a bullet. Don't mention that we already took it as evidence, just that we saw it in the logs."

"Good idea," Jasper said. "If the shooter is somebody in town, he'll want to go back and retrieve it before the troopers get here. Maybe we'll see 'em go."

Lola wedged herself against the side of the boat, ready to helplift the body bag. She looked up and gave Cutter a nod of approval. "Wow, boss," she said. "You're not just a badass. You're a sneaky badass."

Cutter convinced Markham to get his gear stowed in the Family and Consumer Science classroom, where he'd be sleeping, before he tried to speak with the woman who wanted to kill him. This gave Ned and Lola time to find Daisy Aguthluk and make reasonably sure she didn't happen to be holding a butcher knife when the judge approached her.

Cutter dropped his own gear in the library, which was next to Markham's room. He locked the door with the key

Birdie had given him, and then waited in the hall under some hand-carved wooden Yup'ik masks.

The potluck was going full swing in the gym down the carpeted hallway. Anyone coming into the school through the main entry had to turn left, just two doors down from where Cutter stood, in order to reach the gym. Some were still arriving, others were going the other way, probably stepping outside to smoke. Most smiled politely at Cutter, not quite looking him in the eye when they said hello or offered the Yup'ik greeting, "*Waqaa.*"

The din of hundreds of chatting voices spilled into the hall each time the gym doors opened, along with the tantalizing odors of smoked fish, freshly baked bread, and other things Cutter couldn't quite identify.

Markham came out wearing the same clothes he'd had on to go upriver—an open-collared shirt and jeans. Focused on the gym, he looked drawn and solemn instead of his usual bombastic, bow-tied self.

"We believed we were doing what was best," he said.

"I'm sure," Cutter said.

"The bush is a dangerous place," Markham said, as if trying to convince himself. "Especially for someone with physical or mental problems . . ."

Cutter nodded without interrupting.

"Medical personnel are the experts at this sort of thing, you know. We had to rely on their knowledge. We still do. Attorneys, law enforcement, judges, we do not make our decisions in a vacuum. We depend on the eyes and ears of the people who are out in the . . ." His voice trailed off. "I'm assuming your partner is already in the gymnasium?"

"Yes, Your Honor," Cutter said. "I don't suppose I could convince you to—"

"You could not," Markham said, and started down the hall.

Cutter located Lola right away, even in a sea of other people with jet-black hair. She stood at the far end of the gym, next to a table with two stainless-steel coffee urns and an orange insulated water jug. Her jacket was un-zipped, allowing quick and easy access to her pistol. Her hands hung loose and relaxed at her sides. She spoke with a Native woman wearing jeans and a blue fleece jacket over her *kuspuk*. Cutter couldn't see the woman's face, but he was sure it was Daisy Aguthluk. Ned Jasper stood qui-etly to one side.

Lola nodded politely, listening to what Aguthluk was saying. She glanced up when Cutter was still halfway across the gym. Her arm stayed down by her side, but she lifted her hand slightly, warning them not to approach. Cutter reached to touch the judge by the elbow, but he shrugged it off and plowed ahead like a moth to a flame.

Aguthluk caught the look in Lola's eyes and turned, arms folded staunchly across her chest. She was in her late fifties, maybe even sixty, which added another layer of dif-ficulty to the mix. If she did decide to take violent action, the headline would be DEPUTY MARSHALS SLAM ELDERLY NATIVE WOMAN IN SCHOOL GYMNASIUM BRAWL. Hell, there would be videos on YouTube as soon as it happened.

Lola took a half step forward, blading her body so she could pounce if Aguthluk moved for a weapon under her fleece. Cutter felt the white-hot rush of adrenaline down his arms. He took a deep, cleansing breath to keep his movements fluid, and then crowded in close so he was just a few inches from the judge.

If there was ever a time to get underfoot, this was it.

Markham cleared his throat, sounding authoritative as ever. He looked the woman dead in the eye.

"Mrs. Aguthluk," he said, still walking.

Her face was pinched, eyes narrowed, mouth a tight line.

The judge stopped just five feet away. All his usual bluster had bled out of him. Standing before this squat Native woman who had very likely been the person who threatened to carve out his beating heart, he seemed to wilt, not from fear, but from shame.

Aguthluk gave him a slight dip of her head. "Yes?"

"I am Anthony Markham," he said. "I owe you and your family an apology."

Chapter 24

Morgan Kilgore heard the gunshot about the time that he set the girl's crooked jaw. She was a big girl, apparently able to handle a lot. He hoped so, because this little dance was far from over. It wasn't her fault she married a spineless punk who'd left Rick's son to die in the mountains. But she was up to her neck in it now, especially since Kilgore had to leave her alone in the cabin with his partner. Rick Halcomb wasn't the gentlest of souls, not by a long shot. Even odds whether she'd still be alive when he got back. That would be a waste. Shameless, really. But like Kilgore's dad always said, *Sometimes, it just bees that way*.

Kilgore couldn't let the opportunity of a gunshot pass, even if his leaving did drop the girl in the grease.

A gunshot meant hunters, and hunters meant food—not just the meat they brought down, but the supplies they packed in with them on the hunt. Morgan Kilgore was particularly interested in coffee. Like plundering guerillas living off the land, he planned to hunt down the hunters and get him some, even if it was that instant mud stuff. He and Rick had never planned on the river freezing up, not in October, which meant they'd run out of important supplies the day before. They were supposed to get more, but that had yet to show up, and Kilgore's head felt like somebody was driving a spike through it.

He picked his way across the spongy ground, taking the only route possible by following an old game trail along a meandering river. If there was a hunter out here, the places he could walk or ride would be limited too, so Kilgore figured his chances were good they'd run into each other eventually. He didn't have to worry about snapping twigs or crunching leaves. The ground was too wet for that. Ice crystals laced the moss and feathery lichen. It was snowing now, and pockets of the stuff stuck here and there in the shadow of a rock or willow scrub. But nothing frozen enough to walk on. Every step made a slurpy, sucking sound, which, when he thought about it, was a good description of this whole escapade he'd gotten himself involved in.

He pulled his head deeper into the heavy wool coat, hoping to keep the falling snow off his neck. To make matters worse, the idiot at the sporting goods place had sold him gloves that were too thin for this shit. He'd heard the bush maxim that "cotton kills"—after it was too late to get anything other than cotton jeans. They were soaking wet now, would probably freeze solid around his legs if the temperature dropped much more before he got back to the cabin. That would be just his luck—the ground would stay mud but his pants would turn to jean-cicles. It didn't matter. His head was killing him and he was going to get him some coffee.

He'd heard voices earlier, like singing. The hunters couldn't be much farther ahead, through the willows. Kilgore slowed, which made him colder. Hopefully, one of the hunters would have a warm hat.

None of it was supposed to go down this way. Kilgore

had been happy to leave town for a while. An interdiction unit for the Arizona Highway Patrol had popped a couple guys in the club with enough fentanyl to kill half of Phoenix. Hell of a deal, really. All because of a blown tire. It was good to be out of Arizona until the dust settled. Kilgore had thought he might as well be in Alaska helping out one of his guys. Rick had been a hot mess for the last year anyway, as soon as he found out his son was dead. He'd done nothing but mope around the clubhouse talking about how he was gonna find out the truth. He planned to roast some kids' heads on a spit because they let his boy die in the mountains—which sounded eminently reasonable to Morgan Kilgore. He didn't have any kids that he knew of, but that kind of spinelessness couldn't be left in the gene pool.

When Rick's wife told him one of the kids in question was going to work at a remote lodge, it had seemed like the perfect setup. Boat up the river, snatch the kid, heat him up until he told his story—sometimes that took a while—and then get the hell out of Dodge. Easy peasy— except it had all turned to shit. Nothing was ever easy in this business. Guns jammed, knife blades broke, and bike tires blew out at the most inopportune times—like when you were carrying around bottles of fentanyl.

Kilgore was no woodsman, but he didn't worry about finding his way back to the cabin, even in the dark and snow. He had a GPS for that. No, the bigger worry was freezing his ass off. If that girl was still alive when he got back, she could warm him up. Kilgore knew he didn't look as mean as Rick. Having two eyes instead of one helped with that. The girl trusted him, which was stupid, but not surprising. It happened all the time, girls trusting him—until they got to know him. That always changed things.

He was dressed for fall—the way October was supposed to be, not this winter blizzard shit. A ball cap kept the snow off his head, but his ears felt like they were about to break off. They should have taken some more stuff from the lodge—at least some coffee, and maybe some gloves and a good hat, but the stupid Viking guy had gotten in the way while they were grabbing the Mead kid. Then the girl had stumbled in out of nowhere. Lucky for Kilgore, David Mead wore the same size boots—even if the dumbass had drawn little smiley faces on the toes like some kind of third grader. Killing him would be a service really.

Kilgore moved slowly toward the direction of the gunshot, keeping his flashlight off so no one would see him coming. He cursed under his breath each time a branch slapped him in the face or he slipped in the muck. This whole thing was one big soup sandwich. With the change in the weather, Rick was supposed to be working on a way for them to get out, but he was berserk with grief. Everyone mixed up in this thing was off, including Morgan Kilgore for bringing his ass to Alaska in the first place.

As bad as he needed coffee, he couldn't quite get his mind off the girl. That piece of split wood had nearly taken her head off, which was a shame. She'd have been a hell of a lot easier to look at without fluid dripping out her ear. Rick had wanted to leave her where she fell. Even if she would have come to, she would have just drifted off to sleep again and died from exposure. There were worse ways to die than just drifting off to sleep. It would have been a mercy.

But they had her, Kilgore had reasoned. Might as well

hang on to her for a bit, see where it led. Hell, she wasn't going to eat much with her jaw like that. Kilgore brushed a ginormous flake of snow out of his eyes, picturing the girl's face without the swollen jaw, and hoping Rick didn't fly off the handle and finish her off while Kilgore was out getting supplies. Rick Halcomb was unpredictable. He did his own thing, always had. But he was a hell of a useful guy to have with you in a fight, or if someone needed heating up. This was his plan, and Kilgore would help him see it through, but he sure hoped Rick didn't kill the girl while he was gone.

The Mead kid was a different story. Kilgore kind of hoped he just keeled over from fear. It might deprive poor Rick of a little revenge, but at least this would be over. Hell, Rick hadn't even started in on him for real yet and he'd already pissed himself. Rick Halcomb was a master at inflicting pain. When he decided to get serious, you begged for him to go ahead and kill you.

Mead was still in the bargaining stage, begging, trying to make a deal. It was pitiful and only served to make Rick angrier. So far the kid hadn't offered up his wife, but Kilgore was certain that would come next. This kid seemed the type to run over his own mother if he thought it might save his life. People did crazy shit to wiggle their way out of the inevitable. There was no telling what Mead would do to try and save himself. One thing Kilgore knew for sure is that the kid wasn't going to get out of this little party alive.

The singing was louder now, along with the gurgle of a flowing stream. The noises came from the other side of some gnarly evergreen trees that looked like something out of a Dr. Seuss book. Another few steps and Kilgore could make out a fire through the branches. Sixty, maybe seventy feet away. Kilgore stopped, one foot hovering in the air. There was only one guy, a skinny Eskimo kid, maybe nineteen or twenty years old, with a wool hat pulled down over his ears. He was singing the "eye of a tiger" chorus part of that Katy Perry song "Roar," over and over to himself while he squatted in front of the fire in his long underwear and rubber boots. Steam rose from a pair of army surplus wool pants draped over a clump of willow scrub on the opposite side of the fire.

A dead caribou lay on the tundra in front of the singing Eskimo's ATV, about ten feet from the fire. A bolt action rifle leaned against antlers.

Crouching, Kilgore crept a few steps closer, pulling aside a wet alder branch so he could see. From the looks of things, the animal had fallen in the water after it was shot. The hunter had waded out to tie a rope on it, then used the ATV to pull it out. He'd taken the time to gut his catch—the liver lay on a piece of tarp beside the hunter along with his knife—but was evidently waiting for his clothes to dry before butchering the rest of the animal. A quick scan revealed a large rubberized duffel strapped to the rack of the ATV as well as a trailer with a hard plastic lid. Kilgore smiled. Oh yeah, he'd have coffee somewhere in there.

Red Kilgore shivered and slid the pistol out of his jacket pocket. First, he would grab this poor kid's hat—and then the coffee. That would warm him up. Hell, he'd drink what the kid had on the fire and then brew himself another pot right here—soon as he did what he had to do.

Chapter 25

While not exactly friendly, Daisy Aguthluk didn't snatch up any of the nearby cake knives and go for Judge Markham's heart. Instead, she stood with her hands folded in front of her, listening while the judge asked her not to forgive the state of Alaska or the federal government, but him personally. To his credit, he offered only regret without a single excuse.

The Yup'ik woman stood stoically for a time when he was finished, staring straight ahead, as if she were looking through instead of at the judge. Her chest rose and fell. She closed her eyes and her entire body shuddered. Then, she waved a hand at the food laid out on the long table.

"I made boiled tomcod," she said. "You should eat some."

Daisy Aguthluk didn't seem the type to try and murder a man who'd just come clean about a terrible injustice. Still, Cutter nodded for Lola to stay close. Jasper remained with them too. Markham's clerk, already holding a plate of food, started to approach, but the judge shooed him away.

A quiet cough behind Cutter amid the echoing din of the open gym caused him to turn. He found Birdie Pingayak holding a Styrofoam cup of something that looked like pink marshmallow fluff.

She held the cup out in front of her. "You look like a man who's about to get back on the trail without eating."

"Thinking on it," Cutter admitted. "I'm used to working through logistical problems, but this sitting on my hands . . ."

"Fog's still too thick," she said. "We're all trapped."

"Agatha Christie scenario." Cutter gave her a rare smile. "Just like you predicted."

Grumpy would have said she had flinty eyes. Beautiful to look at, but plenty sharp enough to slice to the bone if she looked at you wrong. Cutter thought such eyes would come in handy for a principal.

He scanned the faces in the crowd. Kids of all ages hung around the fringes of the gym, like youth everywhere, mildly stupefied that their parents were talking with their teachers. In a sparsely inhabited area like this, there was a better than average chance that someone here in Stone Cross was Rolf Hagen's killer, or was somehow involved.

He shot a glance at Birdie, then back to the people lined up at the tables, filling paper plates with food. "There's a good chance someone here has blood on their hands."

"I imagine so," Birdie mused. "Both literally and figuratively. I'd bet a forensic examination would show that most of the men and all of the women in Stone Cross have dried blood under our fingernails. Virtually everyone here has a rifle, and we use them regularly—like you go to the grocery store."

"I'll keep that in mind," Cutter said. "Tell me more about Rolf Hagen's girlfriend. You said she has a disgruntled ex."

"James Johnny." Birdie nodded. "Far as I know, he hasn't come back from hunting yet. I don't think he'd kill

Rolf even if he was worked up over Marlene, but even if he did, then why would he kidnap the Meads? If he was going to kill the witnesses, he'd have left them to lie there with Rolf. Don't you think?"

"That is the more likely scenario if he did it," Cutter said. "There's a chance we're looking at this wrong. Maybe Rolf was the witness and the Meads were the intended victims."

"Or the murderers," Bridie said.

"Don't forget about the tooth," Cutter said.

"So maybe only one of the Meads is the killer," Birdie said.

"You think David Mead shot Rolf Hagen, then bashed in his wife's teeth and carried her off?"

"Could be," Birdie said. "Or it could be the other way. David is . . . *qumli* . . . kind of an idiot. If I was married to him, I'd be tempted to knock out his teeth."

"You seriously believe that's a possibility?"

"Sarah's tough," Birdie said. "But I don't think she's the type to kill Rolf."

"So who then?" Cutter mused, half to himself. He looked around the gym again. "I've never met a principal who didn't have a list of likely suspects for everything that goes down in his or her bailiwick. You know everyone in town, probably know some of their secrets too."

Birdie pursed her lips, like she'd just eaten something that tasted bad. "We all got secrets," she said. "Even you, I suppose. Dangerous to go poking around in 'em."

Cutter shrugged. "That can't be helped. Think about it. What does your gut tell you?"

Birdie sucked on her bottom teeth, looking around the gym like she expected to see someone in particular.

"I guess the killer could be James," she said. "He's the obvious choice considering Hagen was sweet on his girlfriend—What do they call it? Occam's Razor. But there's a chance it . . ." Her voice trailed off as she continued to scan the gym.

Cutter waited a beat for her to finish. When she didn't, he asked, "Is everything all right?"

"Sorry," Birdie said, snapping out of her daze. "Been a long day, that's all. There's a chance it could also be one of the teachers. I caught Mr. Richards surfing some porn sites on his school computer a couple weeks ago. You'd think he'd know better because I make it clear that I get a printout every month from district IT. Judging from the sites he visited, he's got a thing for 'sturdy' women. Sarah Mead could certainly be described as sturdy. Maybe he has a type."

"Maybe," Cutter said. "Surprised you didn't fire him."

"I should have," Birdie said. "But he was crying so hard he blew snot all over my office. Sobbing about how it was just so lonely out here and promising me it wouldn't happen again. Frankly, I don't care how many sturdy rumps he looks at online so long as they're adult sturdy rumps and he looks at them at home on his personal computer. It's not easy to get teachers who want to live in these conditions. Most of them are incredible, but we get more than our share of misfits too."

"So Abe Richards is a misfit who likes sturdy women." Cutter couldn't blame him for that, though he preferred the sturdy women he associated with to be flesh and blood rather than pixilated. "Who else?"

"Donna Taylor mushes dogs out toward the lodge most nights. She's subbing for Mr. Gordon's class while he's out getting surgery. He's supposed to run a three-hundred-mile race in a few months in Bethel, so he asked her to keep his dogs in good shape while he's gone. I used to mush with my dad when I was younger so I was going to help him, but I really don't have time, so this is better. Anyway, there's not enough snow for a sled right now, but she hitches the team up to an ATV and runs them a couple of hours each night when the ground freezes up."

"So she has opportunity," Cutter said. "How about motive?"

"I don't know her very well," Birdie said. "She's only been here a little over a month . . ."

"Don't overthink it," Cutter said. "Just go with your gut. You mentioned her because she's odd?"

Birdie laughed. "Most people out here are odd in one way or another. I know I am. Ms. Taylor's got something going, there's no doubt about that. Doesn't everybody? No, I mentioned her because she was out with the dogs last night. That's all."

"Anyone else?"

Birdie's face darkened, like she needed to spit. "Vitus Paul isn't exactly a saint."

"The one who found the body?" Cutter said, taken aback. "Doesn't he work for you?"

"He does," she said. "Oh, he's all right . . . I guess." Birdie lowered her voice, eyes flitting around the gym again. "It's his cousin who's a piece of shit. We should probably talk to him."

"What's his name?"

Birdie looked at her shoes, then up at Cutter. "Never mind. He's just a guy I don't want around Jolene. He probably doesn't have anything to do with this."

"Is that why you keep eyeing the doors?" Cutter asked. "Is some guy giving you problems?"

Birdie took a deep breath. "You could say that."

"Has he threatened your daughter?" A passing woman glanced at his frown and almost dropped her plate of food.

"As far as I know he hasn't spoken to her," Birdie said. "I don't think he'd hurt her, but he's behaved viciously toward me."

Cutter's hackles went up. "Physically?"

She nodded. The lines on her chin quivered.

"Is he here at the potluck?"

Birdie blew out a long breath, throwing her head back, eyes closed, like she was upset with her own behavior. "I shouldn't have brought him up."

"What's his name?"

"I . . ."

"Don't worry about getting somebody in trouble," Cutter said. "I'll speak to him if you think there's any chance he might be involved in Rolf's murder. It doesn't mean I'll arrest him."

"Believe me." Birdie's chin quivered. The muscles along her jaw clenched now. "If he threatens me again I'd just as soon you beat the shit out of him."

"That's kind of what I do," Cutter said.

"I gathered that," Birdie said.

"So what's his name?"

"Sascha Green."

"Sascha Green?" Cutter repeated.

"You know him?"

Cutter nodded. "I'm familiar with the name."

"How?"

"Doesn't matter," Cutter said. "Tell me about Green's connection to the Meads or Rolf Hagen?"

"His hunting camp is about halfway between here and the lodge," Birdie said. "He's originally from Stone Cross, but lives downriver now, closer to Bethel. I saw him in the village yesterday. I'm sure he's trying to intimidate me."

"I'm glad you told me," Cutter said. "You think he's capable of killing Rolf?"

Birdie's eyes flashed. "You said go with my gut, and my gut says he's worth looking at."

"Then we'll look at him," Cutter said. "I'm not ready to mark anyone off the list. You point me toward everyone you think might be involved. In the meantime, Jasper's spreading the word that we left the bullet that killed Hagen buried in the log wall at the lodge. It won't do us any good if Vitus is our killer since he knows the truth, but if anyone else goes out there later, they merit a little more attention."

"Smart," Birdie said, staring into the crowd again.

"I'll talk to Sascha Green," Cutter said. "You have my word."

"What if he's not in the village?"

"You have my word."

"I believe you," she said. "And I understand you have to look at everyone who might be involved with the murder."

"Anyone else come to mind?" Cutter asked, following her gaze around the gym.

A new batch of home brew or not, he suspected most everyone in the village would make an appearance at the potluck for the free food.

Large metal bowls and trays brimming with pasta and potato salads occupied the center of three long folding tables, each surrounded with dishes of boiled caribou, sliced moose roast, duck soup, assorted fish, and meat dried like jerky until it was black. Judging from the people of both sexes sitting on the bleachers by themselves with plates piled high, there were obviously plenty of folks who didn't care for any conversation. Everyone here had their quirks, but none more than any other that Cutter could see. He looked for loners, people who paid undue attention to him or Lola—or Judge Markham. That didn't narrow it down much. Along with the visiting attorneys, they were all novelties, inviting more than the occasional stare.

The look on Birdie's face suddenly softened.

"What?" Cutter said, following her gaze across the gym. Lola stood holding a plate, having a lively chat with Jolene Pingayak. The teenage Yup'ik girl wore a hoodie and red basketball warmups. Black hair hung straight and loose around slender shoulders. Even from a distance it was easy to see she had Birdie's nose and chin—minus the tattoo. She was taller than her mother, almost as tall as Lola. The deputy faced the judge, glancing up at him every few seconds, but still listened with rapt attention to the teenager.

"This is incredible," Birdie whispered. "I haven't seen my daughter laugh like that in . . . I can't remember when. Your partner must have magical powers."

"Who, Lola?" Cutter said, nodding slowly like a proud father. "Don't tell her I said so, but she's got a gift with people." He chuckled. "She puts up with me. That says a lot."

Birdie turned to face him. "This must be hard on both of you. The troopers have a job. You have a job. Sometimes those jobs overlap. Sometimes one gets in the way of the other."

"Sounds simpler than it really is," Cutter said.

"I don't think it's all that complicated."

"Maybe," Cutter said. "I have to admit it goes against

my grain to walk away from a trail when there's a killer on the other end of it. Standing around at a party when someone's been taken . . ." He exhaled sharply, rubbing a rough hand across his face. "You know, it baffles me that we are able to put a man on the moon, but we can't get a couple of Alaska State Troopers to Stone Cross."

Birdie gave a knowing smile, like the indulgent parent of a child who didn't quite understand the way of things.

"Sometimes we may as well be on the moon." She gestured toward the coffee urns. "See that long table? That's where our village health aide saved her dad's life after he accidentally got shot during a moose hunt. His nephew brought him back here and laid him out right there. The health aide stood over him for three hours pinching off the blood vessel in his armpit while we waited for the fog to lift enough that someone could airlift him back to Bethel. The river was open then, but a boat ride would have killed him. She's done quite a few emergency surgeries with the doc guiding her through it over the VHF. Oh, and did I mention she's nineteen years old. One of my former students."

"I'm new to Alaska," Cutter said. "But I'd lay odds that half the deputies I work with don't realize the depth of what it's like in the village."

"That goes for most everyone in Anchorage," she said. "And Juneau too, except for when they want our votes. Think about it. Since you arrived, we've had at least one case of domestic violence, a physical assault on a teacher, a murder, and a kidnapping. I'm willing to bet most of that won't get more than a few seconds of coverage in the Anchorage news—if that. We are accustomed to being afterthoughts."

"Just another day in Stone Cross?"

"Not quite like that," Birdie said. "But just another day in the bush. This is my home. Good, industrious people . . . Wonderful culture . . . And a really shitty dark side." The tattoo on her chin quivered. "Do you know Alaska leads the nation in violence toward women?"

Cutter sighed. "I'm afraid I do."

"Do you also know that Archie Stepanov is half Yup'ik and half Russian?"

"That, I did not know."

"You think it is the Yup'ik half or the Russian half that beats his girlfriend?"

Cutter shrugged. "I think it's the mean half."

"Good answer," Birdie said. She nodded at the Colt on his hip. "I didn't know anyone carried revolvers anymore."

Cutter chuckled, but he said nothing.

"It stands out, like you're not trying to hide that you're old school."

"I'm not sure I could hide that if I tried."

"Which you do not."

"Yep."

"I was wondering," Birdie said, moving a little closer. "Do you have any Native blood by chance? All this ancestry DNA stuff has people finding their red roots, if you know what I mean."

"Nope." Cutter put a knuckle to the blond hair on his forehead. "My forefathers were axe-men who settled in the British Isles, with some German, and a bit of Dane, I think."

"Hmm," Birdie said. "I ask because of the little leather bag on your belt. Not many white guys carry a medicine bag as a fashion accessory. Thought maybe you were a stealth Native."

"Nope," Cutter said. "Just some mementos from my grandfather."

She opened her mouth to say something, seemed to think better of it, and then went another direction. "Anyway, this fog's still greasy thick. Can't blame the pilots for not flying in it, especially at night. I have no doubt we would have gone after the Meads if not for the thing with the judge."

"We?"

"Absolutely." Birdie nodded. "I'm sure you're a capable mantracker where you come from, but it's different in the bush. That's why there's so many stories about spooky stuff out here. The Hairy Man keeps you out of the woods by yourself. My grandmother used to tell me stories about Long Nails—a horrible old hag who gallops on all fours through the tall grass by the water. You can hear her sharp toenails clicking across the ground when she's coming after you. If you don't think that kept me from venturing too near the water."

"I'll bet," Cutter said, resolving to keep that one from the twins or they would never go to bed.

"The stories serve a purpose," Birdie said. "The river, the ice, even the tundra itself can eat you up whole—and as you see, often as not, nobody can come lookin' for you."

Cutter gave a mock shudder. "I'm going to have bad dreams now that you told me about the galloping toenail lady."

"That's the point," Birdie said. "Scare the shit out of you so you stay safe. Anyway, if you're planning to run back out into the woods, you'll need something in your stomach to keep you warm." She pushed the cup toward him again.

Cutter took it, eyeing the frothy pink contents. "Looks like buttercream frosting without the cake."

"*Agutaq*," Birdie said. "Eskimo ice cream. Fat, berries, sugar, and boiled whitefish." She leaned in closer, confiding her secret recipe. "Some people use Crisco but I stick with caribou fat. More traditional."

"Caribou, sugar, and fish . . ." Cutter mused.

Birdie winked. "Don't forget the blueberries. Jolene and I picked them ourselves."

He took half a bite with the plastic spoon, his eye on a plate of fry bread just in case he needed a quick chaser to mask the taste. Birdie watched him closely, judging his reaction. The *agutaq* wasn't horrible, not really.

"It really is a little like buttercream frosting . . . except for the fish." He wasn't sure if he could even taste the fish, and found himself wishing he didn't even know it was there.

"You should eat it all," Birdie said. "Especially if we plan to go out. My mom used to make it for my dad when he'd go out with his dogs."

"You keep saying we. Aren't you worried about Jolene since you saw this Sascha Green yesterday?"

"To be honest," Birdie said, "it scares me almost to the point of paralysis, him creeping around like this. I'm sure that's why he does it." She looked at the bleachers again. "But, your partner will be here. She looks like she could handle herself in a pinch."

"Lola will have her eyes on the judge." Cutter's cell phone chirped. It was Warr. "And so will I." The phone chirped again.

"You better get that," Birdie said, giving him a resigned smile. She heaved a heavy sigh, then began to look around the gym as she spoke, no doubt still watching for Sascha

Green. "But wait and see, you are going out there to save Sarah Mead."

Cutter's thumb hovered over the phone, ready to answer it before it went to voicemail. "You seem sure of yourself."

"I am." Birdie turned to look straight at him. "It's kind of what you do."

Chapter 26

Mim sat on her bed in one of Ethan's old T-shirts and a pair of gym shorts, staring at the phone. The twins were watching a movie in the living room. Constance was on her way home from the tutoring session. This was a perfect time to call Dr. Carnahan, at least for Mim. She didn't know how he would feel about it. It was almost nine thirty in Virginia. Surgeons got up early, so they went to bed early. Still, if Carnahan had kids, well, this could be the right time.

She punched in the number before she changed her mind and chewed on her bottom lip while she waited for it to ring.

A woman picked up, a little harried. A child screamed in the background.

"Hello."

Mim put on her professional, this-is-going-to-hurt-but-it's-necessary nurse's voice. "Mim Cutter here. May I speak with Dr. Carnahan?"

"David! It's for you!"

Mim heard bathwater splashing. A child's giggles. Then a man came on the line.

"This is Dr. Carnahan."

Mim got directly to the point, introducing herself as Arliss Cutter's sister-in-law.

"Is he okay?" Carnahan asked. "Has something happened?"

"No, no," Mim said. "He's safe. But I wouldn't exactly say he was okay."

Carnahan groaned. "You can never be sure, of course, but I don't believe Arliss would hurt himself."

Mim kept her voice low, controlled, like nurses had to do when they spoke with doctors. "You're certain?"

"If the sarge was going to hurt himself, he would have done it a long time ago."

"Doctor," Mim said, "I realize you don't know me, but I really am worried about him. He's been such a help to me and my kids. I want to do something for him. Can you tell me, was there some event, some trigger that happened when y'all were overseas?"

The bathwater and baby noises faded and Mim heard a door click shut.

"You're Ethan's widow," Carnahan said.

"That's right."

"I've heard a lot about you," Carnahan said. "I haven't talked to Arliss in . . . gosh, it's been nearly a year. Funny, but we always pick up again like we've never lost track. How's he sleeping? Does he wake up sweating? Nightmares?"

"I . . . I don't know about that."

"I'm sorry," Carnahan said. He affected a more clinical tone. "I thought the two of you . . . Never mind. What is it specifically that has you worried?"

"I don't know," Mim said. "I guess it's just that he has such a short fuse. It's like he's ready to blow up at any little thing."

"I see," Carnahan said. "I suppose we're all a little bit that way after . . ."

Mim waited for him to continue, but prodded when he did not. "After what?"

"Listen," Carnahan said. "I'm really not comfortable talking about this with you."

The words felt like they flayed Mim's skin. She didn't have the energy to beg, or the right. She began to sob. "I . . . I'm so sorry to bother you . . ." She lowered the phone, ready to end the call, when she heard Carnahan's voice.

"Wait! I'm the one who should be sorry."

Her thumb stayed over the button, fearful now that she might hear something she didn't want to know.

"Are you still there?" Carnahan asked, meeker now.

"I am," Mim said.

"I apologize. You called wanting to help one of my buddies and I bite your head off. That's not me."

"It's okay . . ."

"No," Carnahan said. "It's not . . . I have to admit, Arliss talked about you enough that I feel like I know you. I'm going to tell you something, Mim Cutter, that I have only told my wife and my pastor. That's it. I'm not sure Arliss has ever told anyone, well, maybe his last wife before she passed away, but I'm not even sure about her."

"Okay," Mim said.

"Did Arliss ever tell you what he did in the army?"

"He was in the Seventy-Fifth Ranger Battalion," she said. "I know that much."

"Seventy-Fifth Ranger Regiment," Carnahan corrected. "Third Battalion. He and I went through training at the same time—crawled, walked, and ran together—and bled. Did most of our orientation courses at the same time. We both ended up as part of a recon team in Nangarhar Province. Cutter was senior to me so he was NCOIC—sorry—the noncommissioned officer in charge. He never wanted to be the boss, but he was, and that time it screwed him." Carnahan's voice grew soft, distant, like he was seeing the place he told her about. "Seven of us were sent out to recon a little stretch of road in the Kunar River valley. That part of eastern Afghanistan is pretty, you know. Bucolic. Green. Not like the desert or mud huts you see in photos of the shithole country. Anyway, the mission was simple. A local mullah had some information on an HVT . . . a high value target in the Haqqani network that we wanted. You need to understand that Osama bin Laden started with the Haqqanis. They recruited a lot of foreign fighters—the same SOBs that killed our guys at Tora Bora in 2001—not that far from where we were doing our recon. Anyway, our job was to snatch this mullah and find out what he knew about the Haqqani HVT. We knew he wouldn't come in willingly, but intelligence said he'd talk if he was captured. The brass stressed that the mullah was as important as anyone we'd ever gone after because of the information he was carrying around in his skull. Lives depended on us successfully grabbing him. Tell someone like Cutter that lives will be lost if he fails . . . You know how seriously he takes that kind of thing."

"I can only imagine," Mim gasped, enthralled with the curtain being pulled back on her brother-in-law. Her friend.

"The seven of us set up at zero-dark-thirty," the doctor continued. "We were in little hides in the walls of this coulee leading down to the river near a big wooden suspension bridge, about a kilometer outside this tiny village. There was a well, maybe forty meters below us—close.

The mullah had to come past and we planned to grab him at the bridge. So, we watched, and we waited. We thought of home, and wondered what the hell we were all doing there, for about four hours. A little after daybreak, the prettiest little girl came walking down the road from the village, carrying two water jugs nearly as big as she was. I guess she was maybe eight or nine. All by herself, which was rare from our experience.

"Those Afghans have been at war for . . . well, forever, just about. When they weren't trying to kill each other, then they were busy fighting the Persians, the British, the Russians, or us. As a result, they can be a moody bunch. Even the kids. Especially the women. You read Kipling?"

"The Jungle Book?"

"Same guy, different sentiment. We used to recite a little poem . . . *When you're wounded and left on Afghanistan's plains, and the women come out to cut up what remains . . .*" Carnahan's voice trailed off. He sniffed again, then came back still sounding as if he were about to break down.

"So . . . as bad as things were over there, in the middle of that horrible war, this little girl comes out of the village singing her heart out, strolling along with her water jugs like she didn't have a care in the world. It took a bit for a child to walk a kilometer on those little legs, and we had her in our sights for a long time. All seven of us were missing our moms and our kid sisters and our girlfriends or wives. We felt like we got to know this sweet little kid by the time she reached the well, forty meters below us. We found out later that her name was Manoosh, but one of our guys started calling her Sunny because she'd been coming out of the east when we first saw her. She was such a bright little thing, the name fit her to a T. What I'm trying to tell you is that seven battle-hardened US Army Rangers, all of us in our twenties, thought of this child as our kid sister by the time she got to the well. Do you understand what I mean?"

"I . . . I think so," Mim whispered. Her chest filled with dread, heavy against her lungs.

Carnahan paused for almost a minute. Mim could hear him breathing deeply. Sniffing. Composing himself. His voice was tight and strained when he continued.

"The mullah we were after always traveled in a convoy of two Toyota pickups. Nothing the seven of us couldn't handle. But for some reason, on this day he traveled with three pickups. He sent an advance team of three Chechen fighters out ahead in the third, checking the route to make sure the bridge was safe. The drones said our guy was about ten miles back with his customary two pickups." Carnahan's voice pinched tighter with every word until it trailed to a whisper. "The Chechens, they checked the bridge for the mullah, but then they went back to the well for Sunny . . . She must have been scared out of her mind, but she didn't even try to run. Every one of us, including Cutter, ached to save that little girl, but Cutter ordered us to hold . . . The Chechen bastards threw her body into the well after they were done . . . and we, the good guys, we watched it happen."

Mim gasped, tears rolling down her cheeks, for the little girl, for Carnahan—for Cutter.

"Dear God . . ."

"Yeah," Carnahan said. "God just sat back and watched it all go down that day. Just like all the rest of us." He no longer tried to conceal his sobs. "Every one of us had been told that grabbing this mullah would save American lives. We all knew that making any move to protect that little child would ruin the mission. The advance team wouldn't give the all-clear over the radio. The mullah would spook and slip away with his important information. The hell of it is, absent orders, not a single one of us would have interceded. We were too well trained . . . too disciplined. But then we each would have had to carry around the guilt. Cutter fell on that grenade for us when he ordered us all to hold. That put the weight of it all on his shoulders. He's the one that ordered us not to help. He's the one who made us let those bastards rape and murder a nine-year-old girl. The rest of us got to hang on to the lie that we would have done something different. We would have saved her." Carnahan swallowed hard. "I owe my sanity to that man."

"I'm so sorry," Mim whispered, not knowing what else to say.

Carnahan gave a disgusted laugh. "We nabbed the mullah—and he didn't give us shit. The whole damned thing was a waste. Such a tragic waste . . ."

"I can't even—"

"Can I tell you something about Arliss Cutter?" Carnahan went on. "The Chechens went into the village right before the other two pickups came through with the mullah. We got the mullah and his surviving stooges sent out on a chopper, then we took Sunny's body back to her village. I will never forget the agony on her father's face. I am a father now, and I don't think I could bear it. Hell, I almost couldn't then."

"Those men," Mim heard herself say. "The ones who did that to her?"

"There were no Chechens in the village when we left," Carnahan said. "I'll leave it at that. All seven of us got out not long after that deployment. None of us will ever really atone for our inaction by the Kunar River that day, but we all try, every day. I used the GI bill to finish college and then went on to med school, hoping to save as many kids as I can. One of the other guys has raised at least ten foster kids. Three are firefighters. One is a cop in Dallas. And then there's Cutter."

"I . . . I thought there must have been something," Mim said. "But I had no idea . . ."

"From that day, from that moment, I don't think Arliss Cutter has ever let bad behavior against someone else slide. If he sees somewhere he needs to step in, he steps in. No waiting. No thinking about the consequences. He makes it his mission to worry about the little guy. It's kind of heroic really, but it'll probably get him fired someday." Carnahan paused. "There are worse things to live with than getting canned for doing the right thing."

"Thank you for telling me," Mim said.

"Yeah," Carnahan said. "Arliss won't be happy."

"He won't know."

Carnahan sighed. "You're kidding, right? The guy's spooky. Fact is, he probably knows already."

Chapter 27

Cutter didn't bother turning away to take the call from Warr. Birdie was right. If he did anything on the river, there was a better than average chance she would be with him. No point in shutting her out of the conversations with the Troopers.

"I hope you called to tell me you're on the way," Cutter said.

Lieutenant Warr paused, a nonverbal squirm. "Afraid not. Temperatures are dropping out west though. We should see some clearing in a few hours."

"Still no luck with a chopper?"

"Lake Clark Pass would be tricky in this weather even during daylight hours. Pilots say it's a flat no-go at night. I guess the fog screws with their night vision and infrared devices or something. Did you have a chance to look at the bullet you dug out of the logs?"

"It's from a rifle," Cutter said. "At first glance, I'd say a .45 caliber, but there's something about it I haven't been able to put my finger on. Maybe a .45-70 or a .458 Lott. Your lab will be able to tell better once they put some calipers on it."

He watched as Birdie moved to the end of the table and

said something to Aften Brooks, who turned immediately and left the gym.

"Lieutenant Warr," Cutter said. "I want you to know, I understand you're doing all you can to get someone out here. No judgment on this end."

"I appreciate it," Warr said. "I don't know you from Adam, Deputy Cutter, but I have to imagine it guts you to sit there on that judge when someone is in trouble."

Cutter clenched his jaw. *You have no idea*, he thought. He said, "Thanks." He shot a glance at Birdie, who was still at the other end of the tables talking to someone he suspected was Aften Brooks's husband. "Listen, how well do you know Birdie Pingayak?"

"By reputation, mostly," Warr said. "I can tell you she's a rock star. Crappy past though."

"How's that?"

"Sexually assaulted when she was fourteen. She was hurt bad . . . you know, beyond the obvious trauma of being raped. Guy did a number on her with a knife. She still had the juice to stab him in the face. Anyhow, I guess the attacker's family had some juice too. They convinced an overzealous prosecutor to charge Birdie with aggravated assault."

"Hang on," Cutter said, watching Birdie. Talking about her behind her back turned his stomach. "Aggravated assault? So she didn't kill him?"

"Nope," Warr said. "Fortunately for her, the grand jury came back with a no-bill on her charge. She ended up pregnant as a result of the attack. Kept the baby. And, despite all that, she finished high school, then left the little girl with grandma while she got her degree at UAF. Completed grad school online while she was teaching full time at Stone Cross. She's been the principal there for . . . three years, I think."

"Man," Cutter heard himself whisper. He was more than a little in awe. Birdie glanced at him from the other end of the gym, unaware, grinning pleasantly. He forced a tight smile in return. His voice was low, husky. "Let me guess. The guy who attacked her. Was his name Sascha Green?"

"You already heard the story?"

"Not this part," Cutter said. "Go ahead."

"Sascha did eleven years in Spring Creek Correctional."

"Birdie mentioned the name, said he might be good for a kidnapping," Cutter said. "She didn't tell me the rest though. I can't believe he's not still in prison."

"I know what you mean," Warr said. "He lives in a village between Bethel and Stone Cross. I'm sure Birdie runs into him from time to time on the river."

"I understand he has some kind of hunting camp between here and the lodge."

"So he's officially a suspect?"

"I guess that's up to you," Cutter said. "But he's on my list."

"Watch yourself if you do cross paths," Warr said. "The courts, in their infinite wisdom, decided that this violent convicted felon should be allowed to keep his guns for subsistence hunting."

"Pistols too?" Cutter asked. "Or just long guns?"

"Just his rifles," Warr said. "But which would you rather be shot with?"

"That's mighty big of the courts," Cutter said.

"Preach, brother," Warr said.

Cutter glanced up to see Aften return to the gym carrying something small. She tapped Birdie on the shoulder as she went by and they both walked together toward Cutter.

"Can you hang on a minute, Lieutenant?" Cutter said. "Looks like they found a set of calipers. I may have some new information for you momentarily."

Cutter motioned to Jasper, who still had the bullet in his vest pocket. Cutter, Birdie, Aften, and the VPSO all stepped into the hallway, out of view of the potluck crowd. Lola excused herself from Jolene, and stood at the door so she could see what was happening and still keep an eye on the judge.

"Point four-two-three inches," Cutter said, measuring the milled piece of copper alloy between the jaws of the calipers twice to be sure. The bullet's impact against the heavy logs had deformed its blunted nose, but apart from the grooves it got on its trip down the rifle barrel, the base looked pristine. Cutter brought it closer to his eye for a better look. He described what he saw over the phone for Lieutenant Warr's benefit. "It's a solid. I'd guess around four hundred grains. Maybe heavier. Definitely meant for dangerous game. Bear hunter, maybe?"

"Could be," Warr said.

Birdie shook her head. "There's big bears farther upriver, more toward the interior, but that's an awful lot of gun for this low on the Kuskokwim. Makes me think we should be looking at a white guy. We're meat hunters. Biggest thing anyone uses around here is a .30-06. Most go even smaller than that. A lot of .243s and .270s—plenty good for the head shots we take."

Lola took the bullet and lifted it up and down in her palm, feeling its heft. "Takes a lot of powder to push something this hefty. I'm guessing a cartridge like this is pretty expensive."

"Close to two hundred bucks for twenty rounds," Cutter said.

"Two hundred dollars a box?" Birdie gasped. "It's definitely a white guy."

Lola handed back the bullet. "I've never heard of a .423 caliber."

"It's likely a .404 Jeffery," Cutter said.

"You said .423."

"Odd, I know, but the .404 Jeffery uses a .423 caliber bullet. It's a popular Africa cartridge, meant for big, dangerous stuff like Cape buffalo."

"Something like that would certainly work on a grizzly," Warr said.

Aften Brooks whispered, "Or Rolf Hagen."

Cutter turned to Birdie. "Would Sascha have a rifle this big?"

"Not unless he stole it. Any of his guns wouldn't cost as much as a box of these bullets." She squinted slightly, nose wrinkled. "I can't think of anyone I know who would spend ten dollars a shot to catch a caribou."

Chapter 28

The potluck wound down by seven thirty. A dozen young men hung around hoping to play basketball, but Birdie told them they needed to leave the school to their guests. By eight, the voices of the last few attendees were just echoes in the fog as they drifted home. Birdie disappeared to her office, leaving a crew of high school boys and girls stacking the chairs and tables to work off some kind of detention. The visiting attorneys, including Markham's law clerk, stood and chatted under the far backboard. Markham had the locker room showers to himself with Cutter in the gym to watch the only door. Lola sat on the top row of the bleachers with Jolene Pingayak, their backs to the big Timber Wolf mural on the cinder-block wall. Jolene leaned forward, elbows on her knees, head turned toward Lola Teariki, who had rolled up the sleeve of her polo shirt to show the girl something, probably her Polynesian tattoo or her extremely cut deltoid, knowing Lola's penchant for talking about exercise.

Cutter sat in a folding chair outside the locker room entrance, back to the wall, using an earpiece and dangling mic to make a static-filled call to say good night to his nephews—and Mim. He had his Barlow pocketknife out, carving on a piece of cottonwood root that was very close to becoming a small wolf—or maybe a coyote. Cutter was never sure what a piece of wood would yield until the carving began to emerge from the wood.

Talking things over with Mim while he carved helped him get his thoughts in order. She seemed even more subdued than usual tonight, but assured him that everything was fine.

"So," she said after he'd given her a thumbnail sketch of the day. "Do you still believe there's a threat to the judge's life?"

"Probably not." Cutter blew wood dust away from what was becoming the animal's face. "But at this point, Markham could stub his toe and it would be the Marshals Service to get the blame since we have the de facto protection detail up."

"That sucks," Mim said.

"Big-time."

"How are you going to go after the people who murdered that poor man and still watch the judge?"

"I can't," Cutter said. "That's just it."

"What would Grumpy do?"

Pocketknife in one hand, cottonwood root in the other, Cutter rubbed the back of an arm across his forehead and then glanced up at the locker room entrance to be certain Markham wasn't coming out. The judge was nowhere to be seen, but Cutter lowered his voice anyway. "Grumpy would tell the judge to watch his own tail end and then he'd go look for that killer."

"What about the couple who's been kidnapped?"

"Find one, find the other."

"I guess that's true," Mim said. "I know your propensity to run into the fire. You're not going to leave the judge, are you?"

"Probably not." Cutter leaned back in his chair, stretching. He looked at his watch, suddenly feeling guilty. "Sorry to keep you up so late gabbing with me. I know you have an early shift tomorrow."

Mim gave a forlorn laugh. "Like I ever sleep."

"You should try."

"Arliss . . ." She paused.

He could hear her breathing, even above the static.

"Yeah?"

"Don't get fired."

"Okay . . ."

"Or transferred."

Cutter chuckled softly. "You bet," he said, thinking she knew him all too well.

"Frankly, I am surprised," Judge Markham said ten minutes later at the door to the Family and Consumer Science room where he would spend the night. Dressed in a white V-neck T-shirt and absent his trademark bow tie, he seemed a shade more down-to-earth. Birdie had put him here because it had a private restroom. It was a courtesy befitting a judicial bladder—which, all deputy marshals knew, had to pee more frequently than the normal bladders of common folk. Cutter found himself glad though, since the FACS room was next to the library, and the attached restroom meant Markham wouldn't have to venture into the hall during the night.

Cutter braced himself so he could remain civil no matter what the judge came up with. "Surprised, Judge? How's that?"

"I'm not an idiot," Markham said. "You don't enjoy protecting me any more than I enjoy having your protection.

You would much rather be out there hunting whoever murdered that man at the lodge. You want to be out looking for that couple. It baffles me that you aren't."

"That's an Alaska State Troopers problem," Cutter said.

"Pfft," Markham scoffed. "It's society's problem. At this precise moment, you are the man in this society with the expertise to pursue the killer and, Lord willing, rescue the Meads." He leaned a hand against the door frame, gesturing toward his chest with his shaving kit. The leather bag probably cost more than all the luggage Cutter owned put together. "I know all the jokes about federal judges. Good hell, man, we tell them to each other. Do you know what the difference is between me and you?"

"I think I have some idea," Cutter said.

"I don't believe you do," Markham said, thumb to his chest. "The difference is that I do not look down on you."

The judge may as well have thumped Cutter on the nose with the shaving kit.

"Your Honor—"

"I merely dislike being followed too closely by anyone," Markham said. "It makes me feel weak. I can't speak for anyone else on the bench, but I know full well that when I issue an order, it's the marshals who put the muscle behind what I say. I make judgments; you make certain those judgments are enforced. It's a good system—and, by the way, it is that system which you are protecting, not me. I do not care if you like me. I stopped worrying about what people think of me or my decisions many years ago."

Cutter thought about that for a moment. "You know, Judge," he said, "I have protected cabinet members who were absent any hint of a moral compass, and foreign ministers from countries known to harbor terrorists. I've driven the armored limousine with some shmuck diplomat who entertained a prostitute in the back seat while his wife rode in the car behind us in the motorcade. What I'm saying, Your Honor, is that I have protected a hell of a lot of people I did not like." Cutter grinned. "But you, sir, are not one of those people."

Markham let the shaving bag fall to his side. "You don't do that very often, do you?"

"Do what?"

"Smile."

"I guess not."

"Neither do I," Markham said. "They mean more when they're rare. Now, go do whatever it is you need to do. I'm in for the night."

Chapter 29

Lola followed Birdie Pingayak's directions to the cabin where Donna Taylor was staying at the edge of the village. With the judge tucked away, Cutter had decided they should look at a few people of interest in the village. That was fine. Sleep was overrated anyhow, Lola thought. A walk would be good exercise. Even if someone in the village was part of the mess out at Chaga Lodge, they were likely working with others. Lola mulled the possibilities. There was always a chance that this was one of those "Butcher Baker" things. That had happened before Lola's time, before she was born even, but everyone in Alaska law enforcement knew about Robert Hansen. The serial killer had kidnapped Anchorage prostitutes throughout the 1970s and early 80s, and then flown them out to his remote cabin where he raped them a while and then let them go so he could hunt them like animals. If it was something like that, then maybe nobody in town was involved. They were dealing with an entirely different animal. The Meads might already be dead, or they could be out there running for their lives from some madman with a rifle. The thought of it made her look behind her a little more than usual.

The Meads had been taken away from the lodge for a

reason. Someone could be hunting them, but the more likely reason was . . . well, just about anything else. In any case, it didn't hurt to check out the likely bad actors here in Stone Cross. One of them might lead the way back to his or her buddies.

Lola had a powerful flashlight, but she left it in her pocket. Instead, she slogged through the darkness using her peripheral vision and a sort of echolocation from the sucking slurp of her boots against the mud in order to stay on the trail. The inky blackness creeped her out a little, but she liked the on-edge feeling. The village was already remote enough. If she got in trouble out here, where no one could hear her, she'd have to figure a way out of it on her own—a feeling she liked even better.

There were no street signs, and the houses she passed— the ones she could see through the fog—all looked alike, but the musty odor of two dozen wet dogs and their associated crap made the place easy enough to find. She followed the smell past three junked snow machines that had been made into a fort, and beyond a dense thicket of willows and alders. It took a lot of food to feed so many working dogs, and the telltale odor of a full rack of dried fish was soon added to the moist air.

The wet snow had stopped and temperatures hovered somewhere around thirty-two. That was downright balmy by Alaska standards, but moist fog crawled inside every layer of Lola's clothing, sapping the heat from her body. Even her stomach shivered. Her grandfather's people were Cook Island Maori, seafaring souls accustomed to co-conuts and warm South Pacific breezes. He'd married a hardy blonde who'd run away from her Nebraska farm to see what the rest of the world had to offer. Lola's thick black hair, high cheekbones, and bronze skin made her look more like her Polynesian ancestors, but at times like these she wished she could channel a little of her Nebraskan grandmother's Nordic blood. Maybe even a little of her body fat for insulation . . . No, that was just crazy.

Instructors at the academy did their level best to prepare baby deputy marshals for life on the street—running, shooting, interviewing, driving, more running—but freezing to death in ankle deep mud while on the lookout for rabid foxes was never mentioned once in Lola's training. These Alaska moments made her wonder if she'd ever be able to adjust to the rest of the Marshals Service. Her Basic Deputy classmates had almost four years on the job now, and each of her classmates' experiences were as varied as the ninety-four districts in which they served. Those assigned to sub-offices got their feet wet hunting fugitives straight after graduation. The ones who landed in bigger districts, especially those along the southwest border, or, God forbid, DC Superior Court, got to be besties with the inside of a courtroom for days, weeks, and months on end. She had heard from fellow deputies that they stowed their side-arms in a lockbox when they got to work, spent all day escorting prisoners in three-piece suits (handcuffs, waist chains, and leg-irons) back and forth from the cellblock to court, and then didn't arm up again until they left for the evening jail run.

Lola didn't mind hooking and hauling prisoners, or sitting in court once in a while. It helped her learn about people. She was a student of human nature—you had to be in this business. The sad sacks caught between the millstones of their own behavior and the unyielding weight of government justice lost any pretense or façade. Learning what made people tick helped Lola hunt them. Many law enforcement officers only saw bits and pieces of an outlaw's personality. A prisoner might curse and swagger at his arresting officer or put on a meek face in front of the jury. But alone in the cell, facing the prospect of years in prison, bravado got flushed down the stainless-steel sink-and-toilet combo. For some reason, federal sentences always came down in months—*You shall be confined to the custody of the Federal Bureau of Prisons for a period of three hundred sixty months* instead of saying straight out, *thirty years*. The lawyers explained it all beforehand, but the poor bastards always stood there in front of the judge, first with a look of bewildered relief because they heard *months* instead of *years*. Months didn't seem so bad, even if there were hundreds of them. And then they got back to the USMS cells and did the math. One guy, a man in his early fifties who'd just been sentenced for child exploitation, finally figured out how to divide by twelve and realized that three hundred months meant twenty-five years. "There's no federal parole," he'd whispered, like all the air was leaking out of him. "I am going to die in prison . . ." "Things change all the time," Lola had said, tossing the guy a flimsy lifeline, not because she felt sorry for him. He was a piece of human trash. But because she wanted him to behave on the ride back to the jail.

Lola picked her way through sparse willows, edging close enough she could see the outline of the cabin.

She loved this stuff, but hoped to be promoted someday, or at the very least, try something different in the Service. Some specialty position like witness security inspector or a sex offender investigations coordinator. The problem with all that was Cutter. She'd never say it to him out loud, but he was such an outstanding boss that any move away from the district felt like a demotion. At least he was a good boss so long as he didn't beat the shit out of someone and get her jammed up with OPR—the Office of Professional Responsibility. Not that the guys he smacked didn't deserve smacking. They did. But Cutter had a reputation, which tended to make misuse-of-force cases extremely palatable to attorneys.

The man flat did not care. He was an enigma, like he didn't need the job.

Ninety-eight percent of the time he was all Southern manners and yes-ma'ams. But that other two percent . . . Heaven help the poor soul on the receiving end of Arliss Cutter's wrath. Something had apparently happened to him during a deployment with the army. He never talked about it. But whatever it was, it took away his ability to suffer a bully, even for a millisecond. Spit on him, you'd certainly get thrown to the ground and handcuffed. Spit on someone else—especially someone he saw as needing his protection—and you were going to get your ass whipped. No questions, no reprieves, no warning. He hardly ever smiled anyway, but his frowns were enough to loosen the bowels of anyone who got in his way. His anger focused like the light of a thousand suns, withering everything in its path. Lola liked that.

He'd never so much as raised his voice to her—and she'd screwed up plenty of times—but she'd seen him nearly take the head off a guy who spoke rudely to the clerk at a little stop-and-rob where they were gassing up the G-ride. Arliss Cutter didn't mollycoddle her, didn't hold her hand during the tough stuff, but she was dead-level certain that he always had her back. A good boss gave you room to move, to make decisions, to stomp your own snakes—and she was damned good at stomping, even out here in this sloppy mess.

Cutter had gone to watch the shop teacher, who apparently spent his off time frequenting websites that featured sturdy women with big asses. Lola tensed her drum-tight glutes. She wasn't a small woman, but probably wasn't big enough for that kind of website. She thought about it for a second, then resolved to do more lunges to make sure. That guy was one surveillance she was happy to skip.

Lola was still fifty yards away when twenty-four Alaska sled dogs announced her presence with a riot of barks and whines. Chains rattled, wooden houses thumped and thudded as the dogs jumped on top. Lola stopped, then stepped slowly sideways, attempting to fade into a stand of willows. The notion of bumping into a rabid fox crossed her mind, but the porch light flicked on, giving her something else to think about. The door opened slowly and Mrs. Taylor stepped out, causing the dog yard to go completely crazy.

It was difficult to tell for sure in the fog, but it looked like Taylor was dressed in long johns and house slippers. Staying-in-by-the-fire clothes. That was good.

For one terrifying moment, Lola was worried Taylor might have one of the dogs in the house, off the leash. If that happened she was screwed. She remained motionless, fog and darkness her only concealment. No growling guard dog bounded out. Donna Taylor stood with one hand on the doorknob and leaned against the frame. It seemed as if the woman was looking right at her, but Lola chalked the feeling up to nerves. Bad guys always seemed to stare straight at your hiding spot. The truth was, most people didn't give a second thought to anyone else in the world. It was usually only longtime criminals and meth heads who thought they were being followed. Lola took a couple of deep combat breaths to steady herself. Taylor definitely knew something had excited the dogs. She was a tall woman, sturdy looking—Lola stifled a chuckle, wondering what the pervy shop teacher thought about that. Blond hair was pulled back haphazardly with a wide elastic band, like she'd been interrupted in the process of washing her face before bed. She turned her head slowly, trying to see what had spooked her dogs, but she'd just come from a room with all the lights on. There was an open woodstove behind her, blazing away, which meant she had probably been staring into the fire. Her night vision would be toast.

Lola remained motionless anyway, except for the shivering. Hopefully, her chattering teeth sounded much louder in her head than they really were.

A cold wind freshened from the west. It wasn't much, just a gentle back-of-the-throat puff, like the gods breathing fog against a glass. The temperature was dropping. Lola could feel it pinch her nose. She shivered from excitement now. Wind and falling temps meant the fog would lift and the troopers could start looking for the Meads. Maybe they could get the judge out of here and help with the hunt.

Taylor reached inside and grabbed a puffy down jacket. Draping it over her shoulders, she stood at the door and stared into the night, singing something that Lola couldn't quite make out. A lullaby maybe? It would take half an hour for Taylor's eyes to fully adjust to the darkness, especially if she'd been staring into the fire, but every second that ticked by made Lola feel more exposed.

After five full minutes, Taylor gave a final yell at the dogs, and then turned to go inside. Lola checked her watch. Nine thirty was late for someone who faced down elementary school kids all day and then mushed dogs several nights a week. Taylor was dressed in fuzzy slippers and jammies—well, thermals she probably used as jammies. She'd stoked up the fire in the stove and was in the middle of washing her face for bed.

"You're not going anywhere," Lola whispered.

James Johnny, the guy who was jealous of Rolf Hagen's choice of girlfriends, lived on the road out toward the airport. Lola would go there next to see if he'd returned from hunting. Or link up with Cutter if he'd come up with anything good on the shop teacher.

The slurp of her muddy boots brought another eruption of yelps and barks from the dogs—the rural equivalent of a knock at the apartment door. It didn't matter. By now, Taylor must have thought she had a moose or a bear stomping around outside. The wind had picked up enough to rustle the smallest willows, sending a fresh chill down Lola's spine. Her Maori relatives on Rarotonga told stories of spirits, restless warriors who marched in the mountains and fog at night. As a little girl, she'd giggled when her grandfather told her about a ghost pig that haunted the area near Black Rock—until it was time for bed. For some reason, ghost pigs weren't so funny when the lights were off. She wondered if Yup'ik people believed in ghosts. It was hard not to on nights like this, with fog and darkness so thick it felt like you had to swim through it.

Lola broke out her flashlight as soon as she made it beyond the willows, well away from the boisterous dog yard and Donna Taylor's cabin. The beam was incredibly bright, six hundred lumens or something, but it did little good to light her way now, reflecting back to her like a broken light saber in the white vapor. But it made her feel better, and with any luck, it would help her catch the approach of any rabid foxes. Her hand dropped to the butt of her pistol and she picked up her pace, nearly losing a boot to the sucking mud.

Rabid foxes . . . Thc Action Service indeed.

Chapter 30

Birdie Pingayak slid the yellow margarine tub containing leftover *agutaq* onto the top shelf of her refrigerator, between a mayonnaise jar half full of seal oil and a clear baggie of smoked salmon strips that she intended to eat for lunch the next day. She'd been too twisted up inside to eat much of anything at the potluck, especially after she'd seen Jolene talking to the lady deputy. Lola Teariki had actually made her daughter laugh. What was up with that? Birdie got herself a glass of water from the tap—which, miraculously, was working today. She thought about boiling it, but decided her stomach bugs were accustomed to their little friends in the village water by now. She leaned against the counter, arching her back, catlike, while she looked around her living room. It was a good house, fairly new. Like most houses in the village, it had a crapload of framed photos covering the walls.

Jolene was six years old before she'd asked why there were no photos of her father. *Tony's mom had pictures of her dad and her dad was dead. Robert's dad caught a lot of caribou. Melissa's mom hated her dad. Did her mom hate her dad too? Was her dad dead? Was her dad off hunting caribou? Did she even have a dad?*

There was no good answer. Birdie wasn't about to let

Jolene's DNA donor near her, let alone put his photo on the wall of her house. He was dead, to her at least. If he was ever foolish enough to come to the door, he'd be dead to everyone.

Before Birdie's time, the principal at Stone Cross school lived in the big three-bedroom unit at the south end of district housing. That boss's proximity to everyone else had cramped teacher parties, which these guys badly needed because they were away from all their families and friends. It wasn't exactly a downside as far as the district head-shed was concerned. Birdie grew up in Stone Cross, so she already had a house when she was hired as a teacher. It was a nice place, warm, sealed against western Alaska's notorious weather with Tyvek wrap, but it was small. Then this place had become available, with cold-resistant siding that was a pretty robin's-egg blue instead of the wind-scoured plywood like so many of the other houses in Stone Cross. One of the elders on the village council had it built after making a ton of money off the contract to upgrade the road leading out to the airport. He'd died shortly after and Birdie was able to scoop it up.

It was less than ten years old, with the cluttered look of a grandma's house with far too many mementos—nothing like her office, which she preferred to keep sparse. Like most people in Stone Cross, Birdie was brought up Russian Orthodox. Icons of the Virgin Mary and other assorted saints hung on the woodgrain panel in the corner of the living room. Photographs of Jolene in her soccer uniforms for every year since she was five ran the length of the couch. There was a Jolene-performing-traditional dances section, Jolene as a baby, Jolene fishing, and Jolene's beautiful chubby face, almost swallowed by the fur ruff of her parka as she sat on her grandfather's dogsled. Portraits of

Birdie's parents and both sets of grandparents watched over the house from the dining nook. Her mom and dad were smiling, looking happy to be in photos together. Both had their share of issues, especially when a new batch of home brew made the rounds, but Birdie had no doubt that they loved each other. In the center of the wall above the dining table, in a place of honor that was visible from virtually anywhere in the room, hung a black and white eight-by-ten photograph of Birdie's great-grandmother.

The black and white photo was taken a few years after World War II, when Bertha Sovok Flannigan was already an old woman. She sat flat on the floor with her legs stretched straight out in front of her while she sewed the sole on the freshly chewed skin of a mukluk. A long piece of sinew thread hung from a needle in her hand. Her hair was parted in the middle, braided on each side. Dark Asian eyes were set over prominent cheekbones on a wind-burned face that looked as though it might have been carved from polished mahogany. She looked directly at the camera, smiling so hard her eyes almost disappeared in her cheeks. The tattooed lines below her chin were faded with age, but still visible. According to the back of the original photograph, it had been taken by Birdie's great-grandfather, Horace Flannigan, a school administrator assigned to Wainwright—Ulguniq in the old times—by Alaska Native Services. It was the only photograph Birdie had of her great-grandmother. She loved it most of all because her Protestant great-grandfather had been un-ashamed of his tattooed Eskimo wife. Bertha's smile said it all, really. You didn't smile like that unless you loved the guy taking the photo.

Birdie took another drink of water and closed her eyes. The potluck had gone by much more quickly than she had hoped. This Deputy Cutter fellow was interesting. She'd hoped to find out what he planned to do about the murder if the Troopers couldn't make it in for a few days—as she suspected was going to happen.

They were marooned a lot this time of year, before it decided to be winter.

Her high school basketball team made up a chant about it when they got stuck in Shungnak up on the Kobuk River for three days one winter. They made up a chant about it that got them all detention. *Bad ice, no dice. Bad sky, can't fly. Planes stuck . . . you're shit outta luck.*

She wanted desperately to tell Cutter more about Sascha Green, but even giving voice to the name made her physically ill. Kidnapping was right up his alley. He'd kidnapped her, all right. He would have killed her too if she hadn't stabbed him in the neck with a kitchen knife.

Suddenly hungry, she got the leftover *agutaq* out of the fridge. It took some searching to find a clean spoon. Jolene hadn't done the dishes in two days, but that was not the hill Birdie wanted to die on at the moment. She rinsed a teaspoon from the sink and took a bite of the frothy pink stuff. The sugar came from the AC store, but Birdie had caught the caribou, picked the berries, and netted the whitefish. She rolled the berries around with her tongue, popping them as the fat and sugar melted in her mouth. Her belly warmed immediately. Energy rushed to her muscles. A single bite made her full, but she ate another spoonful before going to bed. She'd sleep better. As good as she ever did anyway.

The *agutaq* went back in the fridge by the seal oil. The glass and spoon went into the sink, along with the other dishes that would have to be done tomorrow.

Jolene's bedroom door was open—an unpopular rule

that Birdie strictly enforced. She'd already showered, and was now dressed in running shorts and a loose T-shirt, sitting on her bed with her knees drawn up to her chest. A Paris Saint-Germain poster was tacked to the wall behind her, along with several ribbons from soccer camps she'd attended in Anchorage. She looked up, actually said hello, and then went back to whoever she was texting.

Birdie paused at the door—*hovering*, Jolene called it. How could something so beautiful come from such an ugly encounter?

Jolene glanced up. "Good potluck, Mom."

Flustered at the civil tone from her normally icy offspring, Birdie struggled to think of something worthwhile to say.

"It was." She wracked her brain and came up empty. "I'm going to have a shower."

"'Kay."

Jolene returned to her text.

Unwilling to squander the moment, Birdie banged her head nonchalantly against the door frame. "You and that lady marshal seemed to be having a nice conversation."

"You mean Lola?" Jolene said, looking down to pick a piece of lint off her toe. "She's badass."

Birdie felt the *agutaq* churn in her belly.

"Is that so?"

"Yep."

"Anything interesting?"

"Some."

"She seems like a tough one."

"She is." Jolene looked up again, but only with her eyes. "Have a good shower, Mom."

The moment was over before it started, but Birdie was around fifteen-year-olds every day, enough to know her daughter wasn't an anomaly. Teenagers were snarky. That was the way of things. Birdie had been a handful when she was that age—until that day with Sascha Green. After that, she'd become a real problem.

She said good night to Jolene and got a nod back. Status quo.

Birdie shut the door to her own bedroom—no rules there—and stepped on the toe of each of her socks to pull them off, kicking them into the hamper in the corner. Her khaki slacks were clean enough to get another day's wear—a miracle considering the mud outside—so she hung them over the back of a wooden chair beside her bed. It was all relative anyway. If everyone was muddy, then the acceptable level of mud went up. It was like being drunk. Birdie had spent her freshman year of college slightly less intoxicated than her friends, so no one had noticed.

Her shoulder ached more than usual today and she winced when she pulled the polo shirt over her head. It always hurt when she lifted her arm that way, especially when a big storm was blowing in off the Bering. Her hand hurt too, worse than her shoulder. She had scars there, deep ones, and another behind her ear in her hairline. The worst one—the worst physical scar anyway—ran from her left buttock to the side of her knee. That one had nearly killed her. It had earned her a flight to the Alaska Native Medical Center in Anchorage, eleven days in the hospital, forty-two stitches, and gallons of antibiotics.

Sascha had done a number on her. He'd hurt her, bad, and in countless ways, but he hadn't been the one to take her virginity. Sadly, that job had been done the month before she turned thirteen. She'd always looked older than she was and told herself that the boy was just a high school jock taking things too far. He had not hurt her, or at least he wasn't cruel about it when he did. She still saw him almost every day around the village. He'd grown up to be the local agent for one of the bush airlines. Later, she'd come to realize that he had some level of fetal alcohol syndrome. It didn't excuse what he'd done. She was twelve and he was sixteen, but his mental state made it easier for her not to fixate. Now, if he came near Jolene, Birdie would lure him out to the tundra and gut him on the ice. That went without saying. But he hadn't. And she didn't hate him. Much.

Though her virginity was no longer up for grabs, Sascha had still managed to rob her of health and youth. She reserved the bulk of her hate for him. He'd separated her collarbone during the attack and almost sixteen years later it still crunched and popped if she moved her arm just so. One of her shoulders was all wonky, sloping downward a hair lower than normal and making it impossible to keep bra straps and swimsuits in place. The unevenness was an unforeseen consequence that, while not horrible in and of itself, reminded her daily of the violence of the event.

She thought about it each day, some days more than others.

Some days, it was all she could think about.

Chapter 31

Word had gotten around about the new batch of home brew before fifteen-year-old Birdie even left school that day. Her parents never hurt her when they got drunk, but they screamed way too much for people who loved each other like they did. She decided it would be more peaceful to watch television at her uncle's house after she fed her dad's sled dogs, instead of going home and listening to a screaming match. Her uncle had satellite TV, with one of those little dishes that he had to point almost straight down at the ground to get a signal this far north. Her auntie had passed on, and her uncle worked late cleaning the city offices, so Birdie had the house to herself—with no yelling.

Sascha must have seen her go in. He came to the back door and knocked softly, like a friend would knock, not like a monster at all. Birdie remembered clearly the conversation Alex Trebek was having with a contestant from Cedar Rapids when she got up off the couch to answer. She opened the door, thinking it might be Patricia Chiklak coming over to watch *Jeopardy!* with her. Sascha didn't say a word. He didn't make a sound. Instead, he just stood there, looking at her and breathing fast, like some weirdo. She tried to slam the door, but that broke the spell and he bounded inside the house. He caught her immediately and slammed his fist into her belly before she could scream. Then he turned calmly to shut and lock the door, like he had it all planned out. Birdie could do nothing but sink to her knees, trying in vain to get a breath of air.

No sooner had the dead bolt clicked home than he grabbed her by the hair and dragged her toward the living room. She twisted and kicked, but the linoleum floor was too slick to get any footing. Screaming when her lungs started working, she clawed at his hands, but nothing would scare him off. At fifteen Birdie weighed less than a hundred pounds. He was twenty-six, strong, determined, and crazy drunk on home brew. For whatever reason, he was incredibly angry, hitting her as much as he groped her breasts, as if Birdie was the cause of everything bad that had ever happened in his life.

The troopers came to the school to talk about this stuff all the time. She remembered they'd told all the kids in her class to fight back, to scream and yell and bite, to do anything to get away. She had done all that, but it didn't matter. Alex Trebek kept talking, her uncle stayed at the school. Nobody heard. Sascha was just too big and too drunk. Much of it was a blur, like a bad car wreck that went on and on and on. She remembered pulling away, him grabbing her again and dragging her toward the couch. How that patch of hair had just pulled out of her scalp in one big clump and how he'd stood there holding it in his fist and laughing hysterically. She'd tried to run, making it to the kitchen before he caught her. She was all screamed out by then, unable to utter anything but whimpering baby sounds, barely able to breathe. This only made him madder. Her uncle's house was small and she landed hard against the edge of the Formica table when he threw her.

It was the table where her uncle played dominoes with her parents, and told stories, and ate dried fish dipped in seal oil. That's when her collarbone snapped. Sascha loomed over her, grinding her face against a piece of bloody cardboard where her uncle had been cleaning ducks that morning before work. The carcasses were still on the table in a metal bowl and she'd pulled the whole thing off when Sascha dragged her to the floor. She remembered the searing pain, being covered in blood and meat slime, the smell of the butchered ducks on the slick floor beside her. Sascha hit her again with his fist, eyes red, black hair pasted to his forehead with sweat. Pinned against the floor, she couldn't go anywhere. He'd connected with the side of her head that time, and everything went black. It wasn't like the movies though. She was only out for a minute, long enough for him to tear away her shorts and do what he needed to do to feel like he dominated her—and to make Jolene. He was still laughing when she regained consciousness, making fun of her because she wasn't a virgin. He said that the troopers wouldn't even get him in trouble because it wasn't rape if the girl was a slut already.

She'd found her voice at that, and screamed up at him, trying to scramble backwards like a crab. His hand shot to her mouth, plugging the scream. Pressing down with the weight of his body, he subdued her against the linoleum floor while the fingers of his free hand wrapped around her throat. All the while he laughed, grunting, chuckling, against her half-naked bucks and squirms. He was bigger. He was stronger. He could do whatever he wanted.

A cold realization gushed like ice water through her limbs.

He had won. There was nothing left to do but kill her.

The knife her uncle had used to butcher the ducks that

morning had fallen on the floor during the struggle and now lay on the floor next to the carcasses. It was a small thing, serrated, like something you'd have next to your plate if you were eating a moose roast—not something you'd use to fend off a rapist. But it was all Birdie had.

Her fingers brushed the blade as she flailed. Somehow, through the fog of panic and fear, she realized what it was. Grabbing blindly, she screamed again, driving the little blade over and over again into Sascha's neck and face. He must have thought she'd merely hit him at first, but his eyes went wide when he brought his hand back and saw the blood. She managed to stab him two more times in the neck and shoulder before he wrested the knife away. He'd tried to stab her too, but blood was slick and they were covered in it, making her impossible to hold now. He lashed out as she squirmed away, slicing her deep across the thigh before collapsing on the floor.

Birdie didn't remember much after that, she'd lost a great deal of blood too, but she remembered the pain, and Sascha's face, swathed in gore, as he lay there on her uncle's floor with the knife clenched in his fist, beside a pile of butchered ducks.

Now, sixteen years later, Birdie sat on the edge of her bed and ran her fingers over her uneven collarbone, touched the scars on her hand and thigh. Her friend had come over to watch *Jeopardy!* like they'd planned, and found them both on the floor unconscious. Sascha had lived somehow, despite his wounds. He was, Birdie suspected, too evil to die without the chance to observe the hell he'd put her through. She was surprised she'd been able to say his name to Cutter, though he was an obvious suspect. It was something she rarely spoke out loud, certainly not to Jolene.

Birdie's friends who were divorced, the smart ones anyway, took great pains to say good things about the fathers of their children. But Sascha wasn't Jolene's father. He wasn't her dad. He was the rapist who got Birdie pregnant. There was not one thing good to say about him, but she didn't speak ill of him either. That kind of talk would only bring down Jolene's self-esteem—and that was low enough already. Kids with low self-esteem ran the risk of following Sylvia Red Fox's path, dying alone on the loading dock with a packing strap around her neck.

Birdie shuddered, then fell against her pillow. No sleep tonight. She stared up at the light fixture on the ceiling. It was cracked, and filled with dust and the bodies of a dozen dead bugs. There was one way this might all work out. Deputy Cutter might very well have come along at just the right time. She felt bad for Rolf Hagen, but in some perverse way, she hoped Sascha had been the one to murder him and kidnap Sarah Mead. Prison had done nothing but give him time to feed that fantasy that he owned her. That was why he was hanging around now. It had to be. He'd go crazy jealous if he knew that Birdie and Arliss were friends. Birdie smiled, feeling relaxed for the first time in days. Sascha would fight if confronted. He was too vain not to, too impulsive. And when he fought, she had no doubt that Cutter would end him.

Chapter 32

Cutter and Lola walked through the doors of the school at a quarter past midnight, wet and chilled. Donna Taylor, Abe Richards, and Daisy Aguthluk looked to be tucked in for the night. James Johnny had yet to return to Stone Cross from his hunting trip. Temperatures were dropping, but according to Lieutenant Warr, the fog remained too thick for air travel. He was still at the office, spending the night there, he said, readying what few pieces he had so he could move them around the chess board the moment the fog lifted but before the front blew in off the Bering Sea. Troopers with the Alaska Bureau of Investigations in Anchorage were working up packages on the names Birdie had given Cutter. Full backgrounds would be available anytime. He'd call back when they were.

Judge Markham's room was dark when they passed; the small piece of tape Cutter had left on the lower edge of the door was still there. No one had been in or out.

"Does this place seem haunted to you?" Lola said, glancing up and down the dark hall while Cutter used the key Birdie had given him to unlock the library. Lola didn't exactly appear to be scared, just interested, like someone noting the color of the carpet. "Because I heard it's haunted. A young girl who died here years ago is supposed to appear once in a while. You know, she just stands there and watches you . . ."

"As long as she doesn't have long toenails," Cutter said.

Lola frowned. "What?"

"Nothing," Cutter said, easing open the door. "Just a story Birdie told me."

Everyone else in the school was likely asleep, so he took care to be quiet, though all the other doors in the hall were shut and there was probably no need.

Lola shrugged since he didn't engage with her ghost stories, and disappeared into the small book room off the library where she'd stowed her bags. Cutter laid out his air mattress and sleeping bag near the back wall between the stacks. The shelves were close enough that he could reach across with outstretched hands and touch books with the fingers of each hand. It wasn't long before he had a reasonably comfortable nest beside a dusty Time Life set about seafarers. He fought the temptation to pull a volume and read, knowing he needed sleep more than a primer on windjammers or steamships. His brother, Ethan, would have gotten a kick out of this.

On his knees, Cutter took off his Colt and set it on the right side of his mattress next to a small Streamlight, both within easy reach from his sleeping bag. The Glock 27 would stay in the holster on the belt of the Fjällräven pants, which would eventually go beside the rolled fleece jacket he'd use for a pillow. It was like camping in a fort made of books. Flanked by shelves, he'd put the foot of his sleeping bag toward the library door. On the far side of the stack with the Time Life books to his right, a row of windows ran the length of the wall. He walked around the shelving and raised the mini-blinds a few inches, cranking the brass handle a couple of turns. The open window gave some ventilation, but there was more to it than that. Contrary to his present demeanor, Arliss had been timid as a boy, scared of the dark, nervous and jittery about what evil might be lurking outside. Grumpy hadn't made light of the fears, but challenged young Arliss to sleep with the window open every night—to make anything out there more afraid of him than he was of it. Doors were one thing, Grumpy explained, but windows were only suggestions of security. They kept drunks from wandering in and provided an early warning if a bad guy did want to intrude, but, when you got right down to it, a thin piece of glass provided little more protection than a blanket fort. True security, Grumpy explained, lay with the individual. Ironically, the hard truth of his grandfather's words made Arliss feel safer. Rain or shine, he'd slept with the window open since he was eight.

Window cracked, he'd just sat back on his bedroll to untie his boots when Lola called from around the chest-high shelves.

"You decent?"

Cutter pulled off a boot. "I'm still dressed," he said. "Wouldn't say decent."

"You joke," Lola said, mimicking the schoolgirls they'd seen earlier in the hall. She'd changed into a pair of gray sweatpants and a loose navy-blue T-shirt with the Marshals Service star silkscreened in gray on the chest. Her hair was down, slightly frizzed, thick and full around her shoulders. It looked heavy, like it should make her head tilt. The smile faded. "You okay, boss?"

"I'm fine," Cutter said, wondering where she was going with this. "You should get some sleep. The judge is an early riser."

Lola sat down and leaned against the bookshelves,

knees to her chest, chin on her knees, obviously planning to stay a while. She was limber enough, but it made Cutter's back hurt to watch her sit that way.

"You need something?" he asked.

She shook her head, deep in thought. "Not really."

Cutter worried a little that someone might have seen this cute Polynesian drip down behind the shelves where he'd made his bed. Four marriages had given him a bit of a reputation in the Service. He started to say something about it, but realized any mention of it would only make things weirder. He took off the other boot and set both at the foot of his air mattress, laces arranged so they wouldn't get in the way if he had to put them on in a hurry, a habit that seemed particularly appropriate under the circumstances. "Good job with Birdie's daughter, by the way."

"She's a great kid," Lola said. "Nice job with her mother."

"I'm not sure what that means."

"Sure you are," Lola said. "She could use a nice guy for a friend, even if he doesn't smile much."

"I'm not looking for romance," Cutter said.

Lola batted her eyes, chin still on her chest. "I know you're not, boss," she said. "That's what makes you so hot."

"Lola."

"Not to me," she said. "I mean, not that I don't think you're hot, but you're my boss. That would be . . . I don't know . . . problematic. I'm saying that women are naturally attracted to guys who don't try too hard. You don't try at all, which makes you . . . unobtainium. That stuff's even more valuable than diamonds."

Cutter leaned back on his sleeping bag, throwing an arm over his eyes. "Sleep fast, Lola." He yawned, the day catching up with him. "You can dream about applying for Special Operations Group."

"I could," she said. "But I was thinking . . . I wouldn't mind if you started teaching me how to track." Her Kiwi accent came on much stronger when she was tired—which she obviously was since she made *track* sound more like *trek*.

Cutter moved his arm slightly, peeking out with one eye. He gave her the smallest of nods, like Grumpy would have given him if he was proud about something.

"I could do that," Cutter said.

"Sweet." Lola stood and gave him a finger-gun thumbs up. "Night, boss."

"Night, kiddo."

Cutter woke to the snapping flutter of mini-blinds banging against the window—like a rattlesnake on steroids. He wasn't the jumpy sort, grabbing blindly for a pistol in the dark, but he did check to make certain the gun was where he'd left it. The wind shook the blinds again, bringing him fully awake. The storm from the Bering must have arrived. He rubbed a hand across his face, thought how he needed to shave, and then pushed the button to illuminate his G-Shock: 3:07. With any luck, AST SWAT would have found a weather window and were on their way. Cutter would still be antsy that he couldn't get out there himself, but at least someone would be looking for the Meads—and Rolf Hagen's killer.

He went to shut the window, hoping the racket hadn't woken Lola in the office. His cell was ringing by the time he got back around the stacks. It was Lieutenant Warr.

"Sorry to call you in the middle of the night," the trooper said.

"I was up," Cutter said. He rubbed his eyes with a thumb and forefinger, then stretched, feeling his back pop and snap. He was getting a little old to sleep on a library floor.

"How's the weather out there?" Warr asked.

Cutter walked back around to the window and peeked out between the mini-blinds. "Hard to tell in the dark, but it's blowing like hell. Getting colder. Looks like we've had a few inches of snow."

"We can deal with that." Warr sounded preoccupied, like he was reading and talking at the same time. "Listen, our intel shop ran those names you gave me. James Johnny and Abe Richards are unremarkable so far. But I did get something interesting on Donna Taylor. Turns out, her name isn't Taylor, not anymore at least. That was her maiden name. She's got two arrests for assault with a firearm out of Washington State, no convictions though. They don't show up unless you run her by her married name, which is Halcomb."

"That is interesting," Cutter said. "Any details on the assaults?"

"Used a rifle both times," Warr said. "Put one guy in the hospital. Looks like she's got a temper. Charges were dropped for some reason. I don't know all the Washington State codes."

"Who's her husband?"

"A thug named Richard Halcomb," Warr said. "Goes by Rick. A real piece of work, that one. Affiliated with an outlaw biker gang that runs between Arizona and Washington. Criminal history shows a half dozen arrests for auto theft, assault, and MICS." Each state had their own jargon and acronyms that incoming federal agents had to learn in order to communicate. In Alaska, MICS—pronounced "micks"—was misconduct involving a controlled substance. More than half the state fugitive cases the task force worked were MICS related.

Cutter yawned, mulling over the new information, finding a place for it among his various theories of the case. "That's a hell of a background for a third grade teacher."

"It gets even more so," Warr said. "Rick Halcomb just finished doing a nickel in Walla Walla for manslaughter—which looks like it was originally a second-degree murder that got pled down. You'd know him when you see him. He's got a big scar running across his face where his left eye used to be. He and Donna split the sheets about the time he went into Walla Walla. Judging from vehicle registration and driver's license dates, Donna Halcomb moved to Alaska with her son, Reese, a year after the divorce."

"Okay," Cutter said, waiting for the lieutenant to make a connection but wanting to show he was still listening.

"Reese Halcomb died two years ago while he was out hiking in Hatcher Pass with two friends—Conner Brady and—"

"David Mead." Cutter finished the sentence.

"That would be correct."

"Suspicious circumstances?"

"It happened in late September," Warr said. "One of those snotty, cold rains that moved in before they knew it. There was already some snow on the ground at that elevation. Medical examiner ruled the cause of death was exposure, but she also noted several areas of blunt-force trauma to the Halcomb kid's head. One of the wounds was significant enough it could have been life threatening if the cold hadn't killed him first."

"That gives mom and dad both motive," Cutter said.

"And neither appear to have any problem shooting people."

"Hypothermic and stumbling in rocky terrain," Cutter said. "The boy could have fallen."

"The ME's report says the same thing. His body was found at the base of a talus slope, one drainage over from where the other boys said they were. Mead and Brady told the troopers that they'd decided to go for help when Reese hurt his ankle. They swore he was alive and coherent when they saw him last." Warr cleared his throat. "Both boys are athletes, so there's a question about why they didn't just carry the Halcomb boy out."

"They just left him alone—"

"That's exactly what they did," Warr said. "Lucky for them, Rick was still in prison. Donna Halcomb made some threats at the time, but everyone wrote off her behavior to grief. The trooper's notes say she always had a suspicion the boys had been drinking, and that some underage girls were present on the hike. A convenience store clerk in Palmer saw two females who looked like they were in high school with the boys earlier in the day, before they went hiking. Never did get any ID on the girls though. And the boys stuck to the story that it was just the three of them. There was also the problem of six missing hours in their timeline. Seems like Mead and Brady didn't report Halcomb missing until well after they were back within cell range. It looked to the trooper who first made contact like they'd both showered, even had something to eat before they called."

"They were giving the alcohol time to get out of their

systems," Cutter mused. "And dropping off the girls. Probably took some convincing to keep them quiet."

"Seems likely," Warr said.

The library door rattled as someone turned the lock, then creaked open.

"Hang on a second," Cutter said, lowering his voice. "Sounds like I have a visitor." He picked up the Colt.

Birdie Pingayak's voice came from around the corner. It was quiet but firm, the kind of voice that had bad news.

"Marshal Cutter? I'm sorry to bother you . . ."

Cutter stood and peered over the top of the shelf, keeping his gun low and out of sight. Birdie was in the shadows, illuminated by the green glow of the exit sign above the door. Thick beaver fur mittens dangled from a braided cord yoke around the neck of her parka. Snow melted off a wolverine ruff thrown back from her face.

Lola heard the commotion and was already up, standing at the book-room door in black wool long johns, pistol in hand. She slumped a little when she saw it was Pingayak, and turned, scratching her butt with her free hand as she disappeared back into the book room.

Cutter slipped on his pants and then waved Birdie over. He held up the phone so she could see it in the scant light of the exit sign. "Troopers," he said.

She nodded, folding her hands in front of her.

"Ms. Pingayak just came in," Cutter said.

Warr gave a low groan. "Am I on speaker?"

"No, but hang on a second." Cutter held the phone away from his ear and cocked his head, looking at Birdie. Jolene waited at the library door, dressed in sweats and a heavy parka. Cutter braced when he saw her. He shot a look at Birdie. "Did Sascha come around?"

She shuddered, but waved the idea away. "No, nothing like that. I just didn't want to leave her home alone, in case."

"Okay," Cutter said. "This is Lieutenant Warr. Just one minute."

"Oh, sure," Birdie said.

"Everything all right?" Warr asked when Cutter put the phone back to his ear.

"I think so," Cutter said.

"I'm sure she's not going to be happy to lose a teacher," Warr said. "Think you could do me a favor and pick up Donna Halcomb or Taylor or whatever she's going by at the moment? I don't want her slipping off before we get a trooper there to talk to her. Earl should be able to fly back to Bethel from Nightmute inside the hour. Until then, I have four troops gearing up to head your way in the 185 the second we get any kind of a window."

"I'll check in on her," Cutter said.

"You watch herself," Warr said. "Don't forget, she's got a history of being quick on the trigger."

"Always." Cutter nodded at Birdie. "Let me check with Ms. Pingayak before we hang up. Now I'm putting you on speaker." He lowered the phone and held it flat in his palm between them. "What's up?"

"Not sure if this means anything," Birdie said. "But Donna Taylor is hooking up her dogs to go out."

"Are you kidding me?" Warr loosed a string of expletives. "At three in the morning?"

"She runs them for Mr. Gordon," Birdie said. "Could be she just wants to do a quick circuit and get back before time for school. Anyways, I figured I should let you know."

"Does she have a rifle?" Warr asked.

Birdie's eyebrows shot up, then she realized Warr couldn't see her. "Sure. Everyone does."

Cutter looked out the window at the falling snow. It was coming harder now and the spots that had been mud were now covered with a blanket of white. "I'll go stop her."

"Oh, she's not going anywhere," Birdie said. "I already called Ned Jasper. He'll beat us there."

"Ned's going to Donna Taylor's right now?" Warr's voice carried more than a little panic. "Well, shit . . . Sorry, Birdie . . ."

The Yup'ik woman shuffled back and forth on her feet, stunned at the reception her news had garnered. "He said he was. Why? What's happened?"

"I'll call you back," Cutter said, already putting on his gun.

Chapter 33

Cutter rode on the back of Birdie's ATV. Her 7mm-08 rifle was in a hard plastic scabbard mounted by the rear fender. She assured him the magazine held three rounds but there was nothing in the chamber. Good information to know if Donna Taylor decided to shoot it out. He loved the Colt and he held a grudging affection for the Glock, but the relatively small 7mm-08 would reach out better than a handgun.

Cutter didn't quite know what to do with his hands as they rode. The frozen ruts and new snow decided for him and he had to wrap his arms around Birdie's waist to keep from getting bucked off the ATV. Her heavy parka smoothed out her form, and made it a little less awkward. She'd thrown the thick hood back so she'd be able to hear over the wind and growling engine. Taylor's house was less than a five-minute ride from the school and Cutter brought her up to speed on the way.

Birdie half turned when he was finished. "If she's gone, you know we gotta go with Ned to find her."

With so many unknowns in play, Cutter had asked Lola to stay at the school with the judge. Now he wished she'd come along so he could talk this over with her. Donna

Taylor was now the prime suspect in a murder and kid-napping. It was unthinkable to let her get away. She was also the best chance to lead them to Sarah and David Mead.

Cutter leaned in closer, catching the slight ammonia odor of the fur parka and, thankfully, the more pleasant coconut of Birdie's shampoo. "I wish I could," he said. "But we can't be a hundred percent sure Daisy Aguthluk is the one who made the threat against Markham."

Birdie turned in her seat again. Tears, caused by the cold and stress, streamed from her eyes. Her nose and cheeks shone pink in the reflection of the headlight off the snow.

"Well, I'm sure of it," she said. "Daisy told everybody what she wanted to do to him—you know, hold his beating heart in her hand, that type of deal."

"Wait a minute." Cutter forced himself not to squeeze tighter with his arms. He spoke directly into her ear. "You knew Daisy mailed a threatening letter to a federal judge and you didn't report it?"

"Everybody in Stone Cross knew," she shouted over her shoulder.

"Birdie," Cutter said, exasperated. "That's the reason Lola and I came out here."

"See," she said. "It's lucky nobody mentioned it then. You would have arrested her and left. We needed you here to help us out."

"I can't believe this," Cutter said. "We didn't know about Aguthluk until we landed and Markham got off the plane. What if she would have followed through with her threat?"

Birdie scoffed. "She wouldn't have. She's angry and hurt, but she's still just a sweet old lady."

"Did Jasper know?"

"Don't go getting pissed at Ned," Birdie said, cranking the handlebars to dodge a large pothole. "He's new in the village. He didn't know about Daisy until just before you arrived—and he told you. Anyway, he's the law—*tegusta*—just like you. The only difference is, the people he takes away come back."

Birdie switched off her headlight when she saw the VPSO's Arctic Cat ATV parked alongside the road next to a stand of snowcovered willows. Boot tracks led toward the cabin through otherwise virgin snow, so he hadn't been there long. The dogs were going crazy with yelps and barks.

"Park here," Cutter said. They were closer to the house now, so he dropped his voice. "We're going to have to talk about Daisy Aguthluk later. Misprision of a felony is a serious crime. You know that."

"You ever hear the story about the guy who shot the eider duck up on the North Slope?"

"Yeah," Cutter said, still fuming. "Ewing told it to everybody on the flight when we were coming out here."

Birdie gave a well-there-you-go shrug. "This is that type of deal," she whispered, sliding her rifle out of the scabbard on her ATV. "Guess you can go ahead and arrest everybody in the village for protecting a sweet old auntie, or you could admit to yourself that the judge is safe as he's ever going to be, and we can go find the Meads." She stopped and turned to face him, only her face visible in the circle of fur around her parka hood. "Look, I'm not a cop. I didn't see a threat, so I didn't want to get Daisy in trouble."

Cutter raised a hand, listening to the dogs. There was no point in arguing now. "Wait here. I'm going to find Ned." He started to say something about being careful with the rifle, but decided against it.

A half moon showed through the clouds on the new

snow around the cabin, bathing the area in purple blue. Dogs jumped on and off their plywood houses, howling, straining at their chains when Cutter approached.

"She's already gone," Birdie whispered, following close behind Cutter.

"What part of *wait* don't you understand?"

"The part that says you got no right to tell me what to do."

Cutter sighed. His right hand rested on the butt of the Colt Python as he played his flashlight across the yard with his left. The light swept across something near the cabin door that made Cutter swing it back. His Colt cleared the holster the moment he realized it was Ned Jasper lying on his face.

Birdie saw it too and rushed forward, boots crunching in the snow.

Cutter's light crossed a fresh track, wide and flat. The dogsled. The trampled snow out front and boot prints beside the track showed clearly that Ned had come upon Donna Taylor while she was hitching dogs to her sled. The trail ran past Ned's body and into the tree line to the northeast.

Taylor was gone, but she hadn't been gone long.

Holstering the revolver, Cutter ran to Ned's side, dropping to his knees. A line of blood-soaked snow trailed behind the VPSO for nearly twenty feet, where he'd been trying to drag himself toward the safety of the cabin.

Birdie knelt beside them, shrugging off the cord yoke that held her mittens around her neck. She lay her rifle on top of the beaver fur to protect it from the damp. Frantically, she dug the snow away from Jasper's face so his mouth and nose were clear, then pressed her fingers along his neck.

"I got a pulse," she said.

"Entry wound here," Cutter said, pointing to the small hole above the knee in the back of Jasper's uniform pants. He handed her the flashlight. "Hold this up for me so I can see if there's an exit wound."

Ned groaned at Cutter's touch. His eyelids fluttered, but did not open.

Birdie took the light with one hand and kept her fingers on Jasper's neck, as if to reassure herself that he was indeed still alive.

"Ned!" Cutter said, gently but firmly. "Stay with me, buddy. We're with you now."

Ned Jasper was a large man, at least two-seventy and pushing six feet tall. Cutter rolled him on his side, using his own knee to prop him in place. The exit wound wasn't difficult to find. Blood soaked the VPSO's brown uniform slacks, pooling in the snow beneath where he'd fallen. A quick scan revealed a golf-ball size hole approximately six inches above his left knee, slightly toward the inside of his thigh. Cutter rolled the wounded man all the way onto his back, then used his pocketknife to slice away the pant leg, exposing the wound.

Blood arced out with each beat of Jasper's heart.

"Artery!" Birdie gasped.

"The shot must have nicked the femoral," Cutter said. Snapping his fingers to get Birdie to give him the flashlight, he pointed to the junction where Jasper's thigh met his pelvis and then to the wound itself. "Push there," he said. "And here. The heel of your hand in each spot. Lean in. Put all your weight into it."

Jasper moaned at the sudden pressure. His eyes fluttered open, glancing down at his crotch. "Well, Birdie," he said sleepily. "I didn't know you felt that way . . ."

"Hey, Ned," Cutter said. "How you doing there, bud?"

"The bitch shot me!" Jasper said, suddenly angry, then sedate again, breathless. "Sorry, Birdie, but this pisses me off."

"Save your energy, Ned," Birdie said.

"I can't believe she shot me . . ."

Cutter held the light between his teeth and reached into his back pocket for a coiled length of bright orange cord. Far too many peacetime protectors suffered from it-will-never-happen-to-me syndrome. Cutter had watched enough people bleed out in Afghanistan that he always carried some kind of tourniquet in his pocket or bag—even if only for self-care. This one was called a RATS, Rapid Application Tourniquet System—essentially a flat elastic bungee cord with a metal clasp on one end.

"Okay, my friend," Cutter said, his words garbled by the light in his teeth. "This is gonna hurt some, but I have to put it high and tight."

"Do it," Jasper said, coughing a little. "High or die, right?"

"Nobody's gonna die," Birdie said.

"Except the bitch who shot me . . ."

Looping the RATS around Jasper's thigh, Cutter pushed it up well past the wound, so the bright orange band nestled against Birdie's hand as she maintained pressure. The cord was long enough he was able to take a second wrap, pulling it tight as he went, and tucking the end into the metal clip.

He checked the wound, flashlight in a blood-stained hand.

"We've slowed the bleeding for now," he said. "But we need to get you out of the snow." Cutter shrugged off his coat and rolled it into a ball. Ned winced when he stuffed it under his leg.

"Pulse is awful fast," Birdie whispered, looking grimly at Cutter. Jasper's body was struggling to make up for blood loss.

Cutter fished the cell phone out of his pocket, punching in a speed-dial number with his blood-covered thumb. He looked up at Birdie while he waited for the call to connect. "Health aide," he said.

She understood and got her own cell phone.

Lola picked up right away.

Cutter gave her a ten-second brief, then said, "Wake up the judge, Ewing, Paisley, everyone and get them out here to help."

In addition to the village health aide, Birdie activated the emergency telephone tree. It took less than ten minutes for Melvin Red Fox to arrive on the first ATV, pulling his plywood trailer. A second headlight rounded the line of willows a half minute later as Daisy Aguthluk rode up with her twenty-year-old daughter, who happened to be the village health aide. Lola and the others followed moments later with Judge Markham. Aften and Bobby Brooks rode in behind them. The machines formed a large circle around Ned Jasper, like musk oxen protecting their young, providing enough light to get him on a backboard.

A frigid wind had pushed the fog away, filling it with snow.

"Let's get him loaded in the trailer," Melvin said, raising his voice just enough to be heard over the barking dogs.

"Wait," Cutter said. "Is there oxygen at the clinic?"

Daisy's daughter held up a bag. "I got oxygen, and an IV. Only thing at the clinic is a bed and phone to call the doc."

Snow was coming down fast now—big, popcorn-size flakes, driven at an angle by the arriving storm. The temperature had fallen over ten degrees in the last few minutes.

"We have a bed here." Cutter pointed toward the cabin. "Let's get him warm and stable before we move him that far."

"He's right," Birdie said. "Here is better."

Cutter shot a glance at Lola. "Jolene's not with you?"

"I sent her to pick something up," Birdie said.

Four men, including Judge Markham, grabbed the backboard and lifted together. Jasper gritted his teeth as they shuffled him quickly into the house. Cutter went ahead, putting a boot to the locked door. It was heavy timber, but there wasn't much to the lock and it gave way with a single kick. He stepped inside to clear a path, pulling the single bed away from the wall so the men could walk up both sides and more easily lower the heavy backboard without too much discomfort to Jasper.

Lola posted outside the door, keeping an eye on the trail. If Donna Taylor had any sense at all, she had to know she'd burned her return the moment she shot Jasper. But Cutter knew all too well that people did strange things under pressure. Birdie remained outside as well, presumably calling to check on her daughter.

Judge Markham stoked the stove while Aften Brooks turned on all the lights. Daisy Aguthluk's daughter got an IV started in Jasper and was already on the phone with the doctor in Bethel. Cutter did a cursory search of the cabin. The one-room cabin was roughly sixteen feet square, with a plywood counter in the back corner serving as a kitchen. There was running water in the sink, and electricity. The toilet was through a door that led to a small addition off the same corner. It was cluttered but clean, decorated like a sporting goods store during inventory. Bamboo fishing rods hung on pegs in the log wall above a workbench with a fly-tying vise. Pallets of dry dog food, partially covered with a striped Pendleton wool blanket, took up much of the south wall. A couple of rifles leaned against the one corner. A Remington 870 pump shotgun hung over the door. Insulated bib overalls, too big to belong to Donna Taylor, were draped across a rack beside the stove. A mound of multicolored fleece dog booties sat on a plastic storage tote in the corner next to an unopened bulk bag of wool socks from Costco. Several harnesses in varying states of repair lay stacked on the floor along with several neatly coiled ropes and cables that Cutter assumed to be lines for a sled. The whole place smelled faintly of wood smoke and wet dog, which Cutter found oddly comforting despite the circumstances.

There was little inside the cabin that said Donna Taylor had ever even been there. She'd apparently been living out of a suitcase and a Rubbermaid storage tote. The lid was off the tote, with some underwear and a digital camera set on the floor as if she'd been looking for something.

The judge stood beside Cutter, watching him search. "You don't expect she'll come back for any of this, do you?"

"No, sir," Cutter said, thumbing through a notebook that was by the bed, hoping to find contact numbers, addresses, anything to help him locate Donna Taylor if she made it out of the bush. "I have no idea what her escape plan is, or if she even has one." He gave Markham a quick thumbnail of Taylor's connection to the Meads, including her violent record and her husband, Rick Halcomb.

"How did such a horrible woman ever get hired as a teacher?" Markham said, mostly to himself. He squatted down to grab something behind the plastic tote, then held it up for Cutter to see. "What do you make of this? Some kind of bracelet?"

Cutter had seen one before. A band of a dozen or so black plastic-like cords lying together, untwisted, each a little smaller in diameter than a pencil lead. Two knots of twisted copper on either side of the bracelet were used to adjust its size. He held the open circle between his fingers and gave a light squeeze, testing its springiness.

"Elephant hair," he said.

"From a real elephant?" Aften Brooks asked.

"Looks like it," Cutter said. "Fits the scenario. The .404 Jeffery cartridge that killed Rolf is over a hundred years old, but it's still used by game management folks in Africa."

Daisy Aguthluk gave a somber nod from where she stood assisting her daughter with Jasper's IV. "I've seen Ms. Taylor wear that bracelet before."

"Been to Africa, have you?" Markham said to Cutter.

"Nope," Cutter said. "I just read a lot of Capstick and Ruark when I was growing up."

Ned Jasper suddenly became more lucid, squinting at Cutter through the bright cabin lights. "What are you doin' here?"

"Gathering evidence for the troopers," Cutter said, keeping his voice low and calm for Jasper's benefit. "You just rest."

Jasper gave an emphatic shake of his head. His voice was tight with pain, like he was trying to talk and hold his breath at the same time.

"She shot me, Marshal. You gotta go after her. Find the Meads."

Cutter checked his watch, then moved nearer to the bed so Ned didn't feel he had to work so hard to be heard.

"The troopers will get here in less than an hour."

He didn't say it out loud, but that was assuming the troopers' aircraft was able to make it out at all with the tiny window of marginal weather before the full brunt of the Bering Sea storm hit with a vengeance.

Jasper tried to push himself up on his elbows, then fell back against the pillow. "Too long. You got a few minutes before snow's going to cover any tracks. My pack's out on my Honda. It's got all the gear you need. Food too. I see a good pair of bibs on the wall over there and you can wear my parka." He coughed, then spoke through clenched teeth. "You gotta go right now."

Cutter gave Jasper a pat on the knee and stepped outside to think. Markham followed tight on his heels. Both men stood in silence for a moment, heads bowed against the storm. In the bright headlights of two parked ATVs, Birdie Pingayak led a dog to a picketed gang-line where seven others already stood in harness. Behind her, in the yard, other dogs yipped and squealed like a barrel of squeaky toys, hoping to be chosen next. The hood of Birdie's parka was pushed back on her shoulders, exposing the top of her head and half her face. A stiff wind blew strands of black hair across her cheek. She snapped in the dog and stood up straight, arching her back from the effort of hitching up this many dogs so quickly. Rifle slung diagonally over her back, she took a moment to stare into the night at the trail left by Donna's team—which was rapidly disappearing under a heavy snow—and then went to get another dog.

Jasper was right, and Birdie Pingayak knew it. They needed to go now.

Chapter 34

The large door that comprised most of the eastern wall of the Alaska State Troopers hangar stood raised and open to the weather when Lieutenant Warr led Doctor Marta Dubois inside. Four men stood under the wings of a blue and white Cessna 185 that bore the golden bear badge of the Alaska State Troopers. The pilot, an affable guy named Huston, was a trooper himself, which made what Warr was about to do a little bit easier.

The YK Delta was an unforgiving place in any season. Coldweather gear was cumbersome but vital, so the packs were nearly as big as the men. They made last-minute checks to gear and stowed black padded Cordura gun cases containing their M4 carbines.

The Caravan's little brother, the 185, was a taildragger, with two balloon-like tundra tires up front under the cockpit and a single wheel under the tail. There were seat belts for six passengers, but weight restrictions made it a decent four-person airplane. Even then, with the survival gear required on the airplane at all times, along with all the equipment specific to this mission, Trooper Huston had to be judicious with how much fuel he took on. Fortunately, Stone Cross was a short hop away, so he was able to fill up the aircraft with people and bags, and still take on plenty of fuel for a roundtrip before he went over gross weight.

Warr was not a pilot. Even in the Marines he'd never seen the allure of flight, except to get from point A to point B. He let "the surly bonds of earth" keep a firm hold on him every chance he got, thank you very much. Sure, planes were a necessity here in C Detachment where roads, such as they were, ended at the edge of town. Sometimes, though, the aircraft section seemed more trouble than it was worth.

As the boss trying to move pieces around the map every time the shit hit the fan, it seemed to him like the aviators told him *no* a lot more than *good to go*. A get-it-done guy with a Devil Dog mentality, Warr took a while to learn to trust his AST pilots when they told him it just didn't matter who was hurt or sick or lost. A lucky pilot might find a hole in the clouds and be able to land safely—or what was left of him might end up in a hole in the ground. The axiom that *There are old pilots and bold pilots, but no old, bold pilots*, proved all too true in the Alaska bush.

But for now, they had a weather window. According to Trooper Huston, the trip to Stone Cross was "only slightly suicidal."

Eager to go, the troopers made ready to wedge themselves in the cramped aircraft. Each of them was dressed for a long slog in the arctic weather, with heavy boots, and insulated snowboarding bibs with loops to accommodate their pistol belts. Their layered parka systems allowed them a full range of motion in the event they had to go hands-on with someone, or sit for hours behind the scope of a rifle. All of them had enough experience to know that when a plane went down, there was a good chance that the only gear they might have was the gear they had on their persons—and they equipped themselves accordingly. Two of the men were bush veterans and wore seal and sea otter fur hats that had been made by local Native women. The newer pair wore wool balaclavas they could pull down over their faces against the rapidly falling temperatures.

"Earl called," Warr said, when the trooper pilot looked up from the left cockpit door. The 185's high wing threw him into the shadows. "He can't get the Caravan out of Nightmute. Too much danger of icing."

"Figured," Trooper Huston said. "That thing turns into a two-million-dollar lawn dart when the wings ice up."

"You're not worried about ice?" Doctor Dubois said, smiling nervously and looking like she was drowning in her giant parka.

"I am always worried about ice, Doctor," Huston said. "That said, I've got a system that bleeds deicer on the leading edge of the wing and the prop if it becomes a problem. Honestly, though, I plan to be on the ground in a wink."

"I see," Dubois said.

Huston and the other troopers eyed the doctor warily. All of them knew her from the YK Regional Emergency Department. They also knew Mrs. Warr was not the type to look kindly on the L.T. cruising around Bethel with a pretty physician unless there was a reason.

Warr saw the question in their faces, and gave them the reason.

"Trooper Fisk, the doc needs your seat. You'll stay here until Huston gets back to pick us up."

Fisk, a burly twenty-six-year-old who'd played college football for Ohio State, stepped away from the airplane, swallowing his disappointment. The kid had been a star down at the academy in Sitka, but he was the newest set of boots in the Bethel post, so he drew the short straw.

"Joe," Warr said to the pilot, "drop the other two off to assist the marshals. If the doc says Jasper can be moved, take out the seats and bring him and the doc straight back. You can pick up Fisk and me on that trip."

"Roger that," Trooper Huston said. He nodded to the other troopers, who helped them push the Cessna out of the hangar into blowing snow. The runway was visible, so that was something. Doctor Dubois walked out after them, looking awfully small in her oversized parka and heavy Sorel winter boots.

Warr gave the pilot a thumbs-up. "They've got ATVs at the airport lighting the strip."

"Roger that, L.T.," Huston said. "I'll call with a sit-rep as soon as we're on the ground."

Trooper Fisk moved his pack nearer the hangar door and set his rifle case beside it.

"You're coming too, Lieutenant?" the young trooper asked. "Want me to help you grab your gear?"

"I got it," Warr said. "You go ahead and shut the hangar door before we freeze some of Earl's sensitive equipment."

"Mind if I ask a stupid question, L.T.?" Fisk said, moving toward the black button that would close the east wall door.

"That's how we learn," Warr said.

Fisk paused at the door switch. It would be impossible to hear over the squealing gears once he hit the button and the door began to come down.

"If the marshals are going out after this woman to try and find the Meads, they must be taking the VPSO snow machines. I'm sure they have some extras in the village, but Robinson and Wallisch will be on those. What are we gonna use when we get there?"

"We'll have to adapt," Warr said. "That's the AST way. Didn't they teach you that at Sitka? And anyway, the marshals aren't on snow machines. They're using dogs."

"Dogs?" Fisk scoffed. "Are you kidding?"

"Wish I was."

"Do the marshals even know how to run dogs?" Fisk asked. "Because I don't know how to run dogs."

"Birdie Pingayak knows how," Warr said. "And I got a feeling this Cutter character is a fast learner."

Chapter 35

Less than half an hour from the time Donna Taylor shot Ned Jasper and fled north through the willows, Birdie had eleven yipping Alaska huskies ready to go. Each dog was hitched to a long cable gang-line via a tug-line that ran from the rearmost point of a webbed harness that went around the animal's chest and front legs. Except for the leader, each dog was also secured to the gang-line by a shorter length of rope attached to its collar. This neckline kept the excited dogs pulling parallel to each gang-line, working together. Absent a sled, the tail-end of the cable was, for the time being, attached to a stake driven into the ground. The dogs reared up on their hind legs like excited horses, pawing at the air, straining against their harnesses, yelping and yipping, eager to run. Birdie explained to Cutter as she worked that she was using Digger and Hawke as wheel dogs, the two that would be hitched directly forward of the sled. Though known to be hardheaded as a box of rocks, these were two of Gordon's toughest, strongest remaining dogs. As wheel dogs, they would bear the largest load during a turn.

She chose one of Gordon's older dogs as the single leader—a rangy, amber-eyed male named Smudge. At just over fifty pounds, the dog's brooding manner and agouti coloring gave him the look of a small wolf. Smudge was tried and true, Birdie said, but the main reason she'd picked him was because Donna Taylor had taken Smoke, Smudge's litter mate. Gordon habitually ran the two dogs together as leaders, so it stood to reason that Smudge would be on a seek-and-find mission for his companion the moment they took to the trail.

Jolene arrived on her ATV before the last dog's tug-line was hitched, pulling a ten-foot dogsled with a flat toboggan bottom and spots for two drivers to stand. The dogs went crazy at the sight of the sled, jumping in place, arching their backs into the harnesses.

The sled was called a double-trainer. It had an arched wood handlebar situated about a third of the way back, behind a short basket for gear or a tired dog. There was a second handlebar three feet farther to the rear on the runners for another musher. Birdie explained that her father had used this sled when he'd let her come along with him to train his team. The main musher, which would be Birdie on this trip, stood at the forward bar nearest the dogs. The driver and passenger positions each had spring-loaded brakes they could step on to slow the dogs if needed. Birdie had a spiked length of rubber snow-machine track she could deploy when going downhill—or any other time she wanted to add a little more drag. There was also a metal anchor called a snow hook, with two curved claws she could set as an emergency brake when they stopped, if she wanted to step away from the sled.

Judge Markham stood to one side watching the procedure unfold, arms crossed, shoulders hunched. The storm blew steadily now, not in gusts, but like a fan blowing out of a deep freeze. Snow didn't so much fall as shoot in sideways from the west, scouring exposed skin, drifting against anything that stood still.

"Have you ever mushed before?" Markham asked, loud enough to be heard over the wind and yodel-yelping dogs.

Cutter pretended he didn't hear, busying himself instead with strapping Ned Jasper's pack of emergency gear beside Birdie's dry-bag in the small basket area at the front of the sled. He'd brought the insulated bibs from inside the cabin, but decided to pack them instead of putting them on, for the time being. Temperatures were still in the teens for the moment, but they were apt to keep falling as the storm blew through. Cutter had no doubt he'd be jogging as much as he rode on the sled, and he expected the merino wool long johns and Fjällräven pants would keep him warm enough, while still allowing him access to his weapons. Ned had graciously loaned him his scoped .270 rifle. The smaller Winchester cartridge was certainly no match in size for the gun that had killed Rolf Hagen—a beefy .404 Jeffery—but Cutter wasn't hunting Cape buffalo. If it came down to a gunfight, the .270 Winchester had superior reach, and plenty of power for the dangerous game he was after. Lola would keep her M4, and follow with the troopers once she had the judge on the plane back to Bethel.

"Okay," Birdie said. She threw her parka hood back so she could be heard. The guard hairs of the rich chocolate-brown wolverine ruff enveloped her roundish face like an Alaska postcard. Snowflakes landed on her lashes and stuck there like tiny fluffs of feather down. She put a hand on Cutter's arm to make sure he knew she was saying something important. "Eleven dogs give us lots and lots of power. The ground is frozen, snow's not too deep. It's gonna seem like we're flying. I've watched Donna run the dogs. She's tentative, so we might catch her quick." Birdie sniffed from the cold, then rested a beaver mitten on the rear handlebar. "Hang on tight. Really easy to tump over on a corner if we're not careful. You're gonna do what I do. Lean when I lean, kick when I kick. Don't forget to yell if you fall off. Commands are simple. Gee, haw, hike, whoa." She handed him a headlamp, like the one she already wore around her forehead. She kept hers off for now so she didn't blind him as she made these last preparations to hit the trail.

"But you'll be giving the commands," Cutter said, strapping the light over his wool hat. He wasn't the nervous sort, but this was completely foreign to someone who'd spent most of his life in Florida.

Birdie grinned. "Of course. But I won't have to do much. The dogs want to go. They're gonna feel our energy."

At that moment, the wheel dogs, Digger and Hawke, turned and glared over their shoulders, as if to say, *What are you idiots waiting for?*

Cutter looked at the dogs, then at Birdie. "You think they know we're chasing someone?"

"These are race dogs," Birdie said, a gleam in her brown eyes like she was as ready to go as the dogs. "I guarantee they do. Besides, Smudge is gonna go hunt for his sister. The rest of them will follow his lead."

Judge Markham stepped closer, his questions no longer rhetorical. "Are you sure it wouldn't be wiser to take snow machines?"

Birdie dabbed the moisture off her nose with the back of a mitten, then shook her head. The movement was almost lost in the huge parka ruff. She raised her voice to be heard over the moaning wind. "Snow machines are too loud. Donna would hear us coming a mile away." She checked her rifle, then patted the handlebar again, signaling to Cutter that it was time to go.

"We gotta run silent," she said, "so we gotta run dogs."

It made no logical sense, but the traditional tattoo on Birdie Pingayak's chin made Cutter feel like he was in more capable hands, as if she were an incarnation of one of her ancient Yup'ik forebearers who knew the old ways that would keep them alive—someone who whispered to sled dogs. The here and now made that notion more of a reality, considering Cutter's view. Three feet in front of him on the sled runners was a Native woman clad in a traditional fur parka and caribou skin mukluks, rifle slung crosswise over her back.

Birdie half turned, pressing the fur hood aside to give Cutter a quick glance. She checked that he was where she'd told him to be, then pulled the metal claw anchor from the snow. Lifting her foot off the brake, she smooched at the dogs, raising her voice above the moaning wind.

"Let's go, Smudge. Hike! Hike!"

The dogs leapt against their harnesses, breaking the runners loose from the snow. Her left foot on a runner, Birdie kicked with her right, like skating. Cutter followed suit, helping the dogs as the sled began to pick up speed. The team gave a few last yelps and squeals, then increased their pace, settling into a quiet rhythm before they'd reached the spot where Donna Taylor's tracks cut into the willows. Birdie and Cutter stood with both feet on the runners, knees slightly bent, kicking for balance now and then and when the dogs needed an extra boost up an incline or through a drift. The only sounds were the hiss of runners over frozen ground, and the whistle of wind through the willow scrub. Birdie and the dogs were in their natural element. Considering the other dangers ahead of them, so was Cutter.

He chuckled, despite the situation. They didn't talk about this in the academy.

Using sled dogs for important missions wasn't exactly unheard of in Alaska. Rangers in Denali National Park still relied on teams of Alaska huskies to work the back-country where motorized vehicles were restricted. Every year, dozens of mushers raced in shorter races like the Kuskokwim 300 in Bethel, as well as grueling races like the thousand-mile Yukon Quest between Whitehorse and Fairbanks. The world-famous Iditarod is 1,049 miles, inspired by the Nome serum run in 1925.

Growing up in sunny Florida, where your jacket got traded in for an honest to goodness coat if the thermometer got anywhere close to sixty degrees, the fifty-below temperatures of the serum run had been unfathomable to Arliss when he was a boy. He'd devoured any book or magazine article about adventure, hot or cold. The Nome serum run was his perfect story. Heroic and difficult.

In 1925, Nome was hit with a deadly outbreak of diphtheria during one of the worst blizzards in history, with temperatures dropping below minus fifty and windchill a mind-numbing eighty below zero. Airplanes were relatively new in 1925, and in Alaska, only used in the summer months. Flying the flu serum to Nome in that weather was deemed too risky for the finite supply of serum. The idea that men and dogs would brave frostbite and death to relay vital serum through six hundred miles of remote wilderness in blizzard conditions seemed to nine-year-old Arliss Cutter like the purest form of adventure.

And now, he was here, standing on the runners of a dogsled, hunting for a killer, or, more likely, killers. It wasn't a serum run, but it was an adventure, and despite the grisly circumstances, Cutter was enjoying himself. He might have even smiled had his face not been so cold.

Chapter 36

"**S**he should be here by now," the dark one called Rick said, staring into the stove with his only eye. "What do you think is keeping her?"

The horrific winds outside felt as if they were about to blow away the log walls. Sarah sat on her rude bed and wished they would go ahead and do it. She would have preferred the bitter cold to a warm cabin with the man with one wild eye.

They'd left her hands untied the last time they'd taken her outside to pee. She was almost as tall as the one with the red ponytail—she'd heard Rick call him Morgan—but she certainly didn't look like much of a threat. Her badly swollen jaw and shattered teeth made it impossible to close her mouth all the way. This left her with a constant line of drool that she had to dab away every few seconds with the sleeve of her fleece. She lost all track of time, but she'd been there long enough that her sleeve was soaked with her own spit and blood from her badly chapped skin. She sat with her back against the log wall, legs out in front of her. David was still tied to a rough wooden chair in the corner, his head lolling back and forth like he was constantly falling asleep and then snapping back awake. Rick had marched him outside a couple of times, and she'd been surprised and relieved when she didn't hear a shot. Sarah didn't think she was in love with him anymore. They were obviously in this mess because of something he'd done. Still, he was a human being, and he was her husband. He needed comfort, but they wouldn't allow her to touch him. She tried to make do with whispered words of encouragement, but Rick had beat him so hard she wasn't sure he could hear, or if he could, if he was still coherent enough to know what was going on.

Morgan seemed to be the nicer of the two, if you could call someone nice who kept you tied up until your hands almost fell off and then stood by while someone beat your husband's face to a bloody pulp. He'd warned Rick that he should cool it, that he was never going to find out what he wanted to know if David died. Sarah got the impression that they had already asked a lot of questions while she was unconscious. She was too scared to ask what the questions were. Rick didn't go into detail now. He just screamed the same thing over and over: "What happened?" or "Tell me the truth!" or some variation of the two. It was about to drive her insane.

She'd felt sure Rick would kill her when Morgan had gone. Her mind was already feverish with terror and shock. She told herself that Morgan was leaving because he was too kind to be there when One-Eyed Rick murdered her. She'd cowered in the corner of her hard bed for hours, expecting to be stabbed, or strangled, or hacked to death at any moment. One-Eyed Rick seemed the type to do his killing face-to-face.

As it turned out, the one-eyed man hardly said a word to her. His slaps to David had become more restrained, as if he didn't quite trust himself not to take the prisoner's head off. He went to the window often, wiping away the condensation with a nasty red shop rag he kept on a nail there. He paced a lot, like a wild thing in a cage. The cabin was small, and he was rarely out of striking distance if he'd wanted to hit either David or Sarah. Once, he caught her looking at the big rifle he kept in the corner next to the door.

"Bad idea," he'd growled. "That thing kills on both ends."

She'd looked away, terrified that any response would only set him off.

"You want to know what happened to my eye?" Rick touched the scar where his eyeball used to be with a thumb and forefinger as if he were trying to open it wide.

Her tongue shot nervously across her swollen lips.

"It offended me," Rick said, as if the notion was so easy to understand. "It offended me, so I plucked it out. That's what the Bible says to do. Your husband offends me . . ."

Morgan finally returned with some coffee and a new hat, throwing open the door to make a grand entrance with the raging storm behind him. She'd sobbed in relief when he came in. That was stupid. She was no better off. This one would give her no more than a sad smile when he shot her in the head. And maybe he wouldn't enjoy it quite as much as One-Eyed Rick.

At least she could move her jaw now. Her broken teeth still throbbed anytime air got to them, and the pulsing flame in her brain was the worst agony she'd ever had to endure. Surely Morgan wouldn't have helped and set her jaw if he planned to kill her anyway. There was something in his face, like David's cruel streak, only so much worse. He was only feigning kindness to control her.

"Sorry," Morgan said, sliding a metal cup of coffee across the bed toward her. "There was milk but no sugar."

Rick glared at her. "Don't even think about throwing the coffee in his face."

Something inside Sarah clicked, and she laughed maniacally, wincing as she leaned forward to take the coffee. She'd had enough.

"It's like you're reading my mind, you ignorant, one-eyed ape."

Morgan opened his mouth to speak, then stopped, smiling softly instead like he wanted to shield her from something bad. But she already knew. She'd never been more certain of anything in her life.

They were going to kill her. She could not fathom a single reason why, but there was no way around the truth of it. She was going to die because of something in her witless husband's past. The idea that David Mead—a guy who drew smiley faces on the toes of his boots—had anything of value locked away in his brain was beyond laughable. But he had to know something, something he'd kept hidden from her. Not even a week after they'd arrived at Chaga she'd realized she hardly knew the man. And now this. Had he been involved in drugs? Or some robbery where the money was lost? The information was important enough that these men had killed Rolf Hagen when he got in the way. Sarah suspected they would eventually use the threat of torturing her to convince David to cooperate. If threats didn't work, they'd rape her in front of David, or just beat her slowly to death. One-Eyed Rick would enjoy that. Yes. That was it, she was a weapon to use against David. That was the only possible reason to keep her alive.

The mood in the cabin had changed over the last few hours, ever since Morgan returned. It was dark outside, and it felt incredibly late, but instead of sleeping, the men had grown more active. They'd snorted something earlier, to keep them awake no doubt, and they were now bouncing off the log walls. One-Eyed Rick still swabbed the window with his rag every time he paced by, but the falling temperatures were quickly turning the condensation to a layer of greasy ice. Morgan stoked the fire, and put on more coffee. He went so far as to give a few sips to David. They'd given Sarah softened crackers a few times—it was all she could manage with her jaw and teeth. But this was the first time she'd seen them offer David anything. Morgan even dabbed away some of the blood on his face, as if to make him more presentable.

Sarah ran her tongue over broken teeth, bringing a spark of intense pain to the back of her eye. She was getting used to the pain. If anything, it brought more clarity.

Whatever they were going to do, it was going to happen soon.

Soon.

She certainly hoped so.

Chapter 37

"Whoa!" Birdie shouted over the storm. "Whoa, Smudge." The dogs slowed, grudgingly at first, the snaps on their lines jingling as the sled hissed to a halt. Birdie stepped on the brake, raising her left hand in the universal sign to stop. Cutter assumed she was making a fist, but it was impossible to tell in the oversize beaver mitten. He followed her example and stepped on the brake at his station as well.

They'd broken through the trees and willows onto open tundra. The sailor in Cutter guessed the wind at forty knots or better. It hammered the dogs, forcing them to lean into it when they stopped. Headlamp beams illuminated a faint trail ahead left by Donna Taylor's team. Cutter had learned in the last hour that sled dogs tended to defecate as they ran instead of waiting for a break. Eight dogs left a considerable amount of sign for Birdie's team to follow, but even that was quickly being eroded by the scouring snow.

Birdie set the snow hook and gave it a stomp with her mukluk. Cutter scanned for threats. The beam of his headlamp caught nothing but a moving curtain of white snow, white ground, and white sky.

He moved closer to Birdie, shouting above the blow.

The bone-numbing cold gripped his lungs, making him sound like he was out of breath.

"Why did we stop?"

She pointed overhead.

Digger, the wheel dog, barked, upset at the interruption in his run. Smudge threw back his head and gave a long, frustrated howl.

Then Cutter heard the drone of a distant airplane.

"I bet it's the troopers," Birdie yelled. A smile perked the corners of her lips. "They must have made it out of Bethel."

Cutter held on to the bowed handlebar of the sled to stay on his feet. Birdie's heavy parka acted like a sail, catching the wind and shoving her across the slick ground like a hockey puck. She was much lighter than Cutter and had to work extra hard to keep from blowing over.

"Afraid they're not going to be any help to us," he said.

Birdie nodded, standing close enough that her parka hood cut the wind for Cutter too, making it so neither of them had to shout. "I know we can't wait for them, but maybe they could still catch us on snow machines . . ."

The engine noise grew louder as the plane overflew them, hidden somewhere in the clouds.

"They're heading due south," Cutter said. "Probably weren't able to land in Stone Cross. I'm no pilot, but I can't imagine anyone would want to hang around in this mess for long, just waiting for a hole in the weather."

"You think they're going back to Bethel," Birdie said, resigned. Their foreheads were almost touching now.

"I imagine they'll make another attempt to land, but it doesn't look good."

"So it's just us?"

"Just us," Cutter said.

Birdie took a step back, yelling again as she pulled the snow hook and whistled up the dogs.

"I guess we better hurry then."

A scant half mile ahead, Donna Taylor Halcomb had her hands full untangling her dogs from a wreck. The Gordian knot of cables, lines, and snarling dogs would have been daunting in good weather. The blizzard made it impossible. Had she not needed these dogs so badly, she would have just walked away and let them get out of their own mess. She'd just dragged a reluctant dog back to his side of the gang-line when she heard the airplane.

The wreck had nearly killed them all. The thought of that made her heart stutter. Maybe it had killed them and she just didn't know it yet. She'd lost control when she hit a patch of overflow—where water had risen above ice that had already formed. This nameless tributary was much narrower than the Kuskokwim and only a few feet deep. It had already frozen solid enough for travel. In fact, she'd been using the edges of the meandering little river as a highway for the past week, going back and forth from Stone Cross to the cabin where her ex-husband was hiding out with Red Kilgore—and David Mead, the man who had murdered her only son.

Fortunately, the ice beneath the overflow was still relatively solid. Unfortunately, four inches of water left that ice greasy-slick. An unseasoned musher, Donna had lost track of her progress in the blizzard, and hadn't realized how far along the trail she actually was. She'd taken the team in too fast, hitting the ice in the middle of her turn. The swing dogs, which kept the team in line with the leader, lost traction an instant before the sled careened into the water. Panicking, Donna stomped the brake. Useless. The carbine spikes did nothing but throw up a rooster tail of slush that soaked the front of her bibs.

Even worse than useless.

The team went right and the sled continued left. Donna was thrown clear as it whipped around, an arcing pendulum at the end of a knot of tangled dogs. She took the brunt of the fall on her right hip and shoulder, careening to a soaking-wet stop nearly ten feet from the dogs. While not waterproof, most of her clothing was wool or synthetic. It didn't exactly keep her comfortable when it was wet, but she didn't think she would freeze to death if she could get this team untangled without getting her face bitten off.

She estimated she had less than an hour to go until she reached the cabin. She would have been there already, but an earlier patch of open water—one she'd seen—had forced her to make a detour up to another crossing that cost her over a mile. Now she had to deal with the wreck caused by her own carelessness.

"Come on, Smoke," Donna said to one of her leads. "We are so close, girl." She tried to sound earnest, like she cared, but dogs could see through a lie. Gordon had told her that. *If you don't want to run, they won't want to run. If you're excited, they'll be excited.*

The lead dog whimpered, soaked to the bone, hunched up like she was in pain. She lifted a foreleg, then yelped when Donna touched her shoulder. One of the swing dogs must have slammed into her trying to escape the oncoming sled when they hit the ice. Gordon had told her that too. It was easy for an inexperienced musher to make the dogs afraid of being run over by the sled. Her stupidity had done just that.

Shit happened. Donna didn't hate the dogs, but she didn't love them either, not like Gordon did anyway. They were part of his family. To Donna, they were a means to an end, a method of conveyance. She loved them no more than she loved her pickup truck. If she were honest with herself, she loved that Toyota far more than any bunch of mangy dogs. The truck she'd take to the shop if it broke down. This was the end of the road for Smoke. The rest of the team would get her to the cabin and then she didn't care what happened to them.

Stone Cross was a write-off since that idiot VPSO had gotten in her way. In hindsight, she should never have shot him. The fool didn't even carry a pistol. He was still a cop though, so there was that. There was no going back from this, not to the village, not anywhere. It didn't matter, as long as the kid who had watched her son die confessed his crimes. He would tell her the truth. Rick would make sure of that.

And now there was a damned plane. No one would be out here in this except the troopers. They'd probably already found Ned Jasper's body. She hadn't seen any witnesses when she'd shot, but Jasper was dead in front of where she'd been staying, and she'd fled the scene with the dogs. Even the troopers were smart enough to put those clues together. That noise above her would be them now, out searching for their killer. There was a small unmarked runway half a mile from the old cabin. She'd planned to get picked up there—after they did what they had to do.

She doubted that would happen now. The troopers would land there and arrest everyone . . . or try to. Rick had already assured her he wasn't going back to jail.

The noise of the airplane faded quickly, swallowed up

by the gale as she untangled the last dog and stretched seven of them out on the gang line. She left Smoke un-hitched, not bothering to remove her harness. The dog could follow along or freeze, that was up to her. The troopers would eventually find a hole in the weather, and then it was only a matter of time before they zeroed in with their search. Donna couldn't let that happen before she got what she came for. She stomped her foot, shooing the cowering Smoke out of her way as she retrieved the claw snow hook, and then stepped on the runners. Tail down, the former lead dog skulked toward her, shivering, not understanding what was going on. She squinted into the storm, amber eyes crusted with ice and snow.

Donna whistled, getting the team's attention. Smoke's ears came up, hopeful. The arctic blast was already turning her wet fur into a coat of solid ice.

"Hike! Hike!" Donna shouted, ignoring the cowering animal. She couldn't wait around and play nursemaid. She needed to get to the cabin. It was time to end this thing.

Chapter 38

Lola Teariki resigned herself to the fact that the troopers were not coming to Stone Cross, no time soon anyway. Markham, his law clerk, and Ewing were all in the library drinking instant coffee Ewing had scrounged from the teachers' break room. It was the first useful thing she'd seen the man do on this trip.

He'd found sugar, but no creamer, so Jolene had gone to get some from the other end of the school, in a storage closet off the gym where she said her mom kept popcorn, syrups for the slushy machine, and other sundries she used for school fund-raisers. Lola had promised to watch over Jolene since Sascha was lurking around the village, and it made her a little sick to her stomach to let the girl out of her sight. She'd already started a timer on her phone, resolving to go and check if Jolene wasn't back in six minutes.

One of the great things about Cutter was that he trusted her to handle things in his absence. One of the crappy things about Cutter was that he trusted her so much it gave her plenty of room to screw up. When it came to Judge Markham, there was no way she was going to make everyone happy.

Lola no longer believed Daisy Aguthluk was a direct threat. Still, as Cutter pointed out, once the Marshals

Service went up on a protection detail, they got blamed for every hangnail or sunburn that happened to the pro- tectee. It was their responsibility to protect their charges not only from harm but from embarrassment as well. If Daisy Aguthluk or anyone else so much as threw a pie, a tub of seal oil, or whatever the hell they threw out here— the marshals had failed in their mission.

Lola had hoped to get Markham on the return trip to Bethel along with Ned Jasper—but the troopers weren't able to land. The judge was packed, grudgingly sitting on his bag now in front of one of the book stacks. Nobody liked to be told they were too fragile to hang around—least of all someone with a level-ten ego like the judge. Still, Lola felt sorry for him. She'd been sent to the rear of plenty of warrant services as a baby deputy—and it sucked. Markham held his ceramic mug in both hands, hunched over slightly, staring into the coffee as if it could tell him his future. Lola had seen her dad do just that many times when she was growing up. He called it *brooding with his brew*.

She looked at her phone. Three minutes gone. How long did it take to unlock a door and grab a handful of creamer packets?

This standing around was about to make her climb the walls. She'd wanted to stay and help with Ned Jasper's medical care, but the judge had a tendency to offer non- stop advice. Some of it was even good. In the end, Lola decided the cabin was too small for everyone and took the judge back to the school before he got on Daisy Aguth- luk's last nerve and she made good on her threatening letter. Aguthluk, her daughter, and Tina Paisley were still there, along with Melvin Red Fox and a stoic Mrs. Jasper. Ned was stable, but in dire need of a surgeon in order to save his leg. There were a lot of arguments about the use of tourniquets—tissue damage and limb loss—but the truth was simple. If Cutter hadn't applied the RATS when he did, Jasper wouldn't be alive long enough to argue about any of them.

Lola checked her phone again. Two minutes left. *Stuff that*, she thought. "I'm going to go check on Jolene," she said on the way out the door.

"Stir sticks if you find them!" she heard Ewing say, demonstrating his priorities.

Lola reached the gym in half a minute, groaning inside when she found the storage room door wide-open—and no Jolene. She stopped and listened. Whispered voices came from somewhere, but it was difficult to tell in the echoing gym. There were two exits other than the double doors from the interior hall. One was at the northeast corner under the scoreboard, the other, hidden from view, was at the far end of the bleachers. The voices had to be coming from there.

Lola inched sideways a half step at a time, bringing the area behind the bleachers slowly into view. Cutting the pie, they called it. If she did it right, she would see danger before it saw her.

She caught a glimpse of black hair—the back of Jolene's head. She was just standing there talking to someone in the shadows and didn't appear to be under duress. Lola continued to move, bringing Sascha Green into view. He looked older than she'd expected, tall but slightly stooped, a considerable amount of gray at the temples of his short, military-style haircut. Prison could do that to you.

"Hey!" Lola barked. She'd inherited her father's command voice and it carried easily across the gym. At half-court now, she was still over fifty feet away from the doors.

Sascha's head snapped up at the intrusion, his face a twisted mixture of surprise and disdain. He took one look at Lola and bolted, flipping her off over his shoulder as he hit the doors.

Lola sprinted to catch him, reaching the doors before the hydraulic closer pulled them shut. She pulled Jolene behind her, then leaned out slightly, pistol in her hand. "Sascha Green!" she shouted over the storm, fighting the wind for control of the door. Driven snow stung her face. "I know you're hiding out there in the dark. Next time I see you, you're going to jail."

She pulled the door closed and turned to Jolene, brushing a loose strand of hair out of her eyes.

"Are you all right?"

"I'm fine," the girl snapped, scowling. "He only wants to talk to me. I don't understand why everyone is so cruel to him. I'm his daughter."

"It's not my place to explain that to you."

"I've heard the stories," Jolene said. "He and my mom made a mistake, but he's the only one who had to pay for—"

"Hang on," Lola said. "You think your mom made some kind of *mistake* with Sascha Green?"

Jolene crossed her arms. "There are two sides to every story."

"No offense," Lola said, "but that is bullshit. I had a teacher once who used to say 'No matter how thin you slice the cheese, there are always two sides.' That, my friend, is also bullshit. Sometimes what you have is thinly sliced cheese—and a victim. Look, Jolene, you don't know me, and I don't know you. But you appear to be a bright young woman, no matter the crappy circumstances that brought you into this world. I'm not going to go into all the details of the awful things that happened to your mom.

It's a matter of court record though. You might want to look it up one day. It's horrible, but it'll give you some context about your mom's actions."

"Sascha told me he paid for his crimes," Jolene whispered.

Lola put a hand on her shoulder. "Life's not long enough to pay for what that guy did to your mom."

"He said she led him on, flirted with him and it got out of hand."

Lola closed her eyes, groaning softly inside. No, it wasn't her place, but she charged forward anyway.

"Rape isn't about sex," she said. "It's about control, anger, showing a woman who's boss."

"But . . . he's still my father . . ."

"How old are you?"

"Fifteen."

"I see you got a few love bites on your neck. Have you and your special guy . . . you know . . . ?"

Jolene blushed, eyes locked on her shoes. "I haven't had sex, if that's what you're asking. A lot of my friends have, but my mom hardly lets me out of her sight."

"Good for her," Lola said. "Not for nothin', but a hickey that's been planned is just a guy planting his brand on you. You'll find the best ones come as a surprise when you look in the mirror the next morning . . . But it's not my place to tell you that."

"You tell a lot for it not being your place."

"That's what my mom always says," Lola chuckled. "Keeps me in hot water all the time. Anyway, back to sex. You're fifteen, so you're old enough that you know all about it, right?"

"Well, yeah," Jolene stammered. "Of course I do."

Lola gave a sad shake of her head. "No. You don't. You

only imagine that you do. I thought I knew it all until the first time. Even then, I only learned enough to know that I didn't know a damned thing."

"Okaaaay," Jolene said, wagging her head like the teenager that she was, agreeing with Lola just to end this excruciating conversation.

"But you do know the nitty gritty, the ins and outs, so to speak, of how it all works?"

"Oh, my gosh," Jolene said, adamant now. "I told you I do."

Lola looked at her, clicking her front teeth together the way her favorite auntie did when she was thinking. At length she said, "I know you don't like me very much—"

"That's not true," Jolene gasped, shaking her head. "You're the first person who's even talked to me about what happened. The first person to be honest."

"Well, here's my honest opinion then. Somehow, the genetics gods made sure you ended up with your mother's attitudes about right and wrong. You are obviously nothing like Sascha Green. He is an egg. He's rotten. You should get rid of any idea that he's your dad."

"What else could he be?"

"You like soup?"

Jolene laughed out loud. "You're the weirdest person I've ever met."

"I'm serious," Lola said. "Do you like soup?"

"Yes," Jolene said, wagging her head again. "I like soup."

"It takes water to make soup, right?"

"Okay."

"The water is a necessary ingredient, but it isn't the soup. The carrots, onions, potatoes, pasta, rice, green beans, meat, whatever you put in it, those are what makes it soup. Not the water." Lola put her hand on the girl's shoulder again. "Look, Jolene, your mother got you as a result of some extremely shitty minutes of anger and violence. And you know what? She deserved a blessing like you, because she didn't do anything wrong. None of it was her fault. Zero percent. Anyone would be proud to have you for a daughter. She's happy to be your mom. I can tell. Excuse me for being so blunt, but Sascha Green will never be your father. He provided nothing but the water. Your mom made the soup."

Jolene drew a deep breath. "That is blunt."

"And the truth."

"Are you really going to put him in jail?"

"Yes, I am," Lola said.

"For talking to me?"

"No," Lola said. "For—"

Judge Markham opened the double doors at the other end of the gym.

"Everything all right?"

Jolene sniffed back a tear, composing herself.

"Thank you," she said under her breath.

Lola gave her a wink, then waved at the judge. "We're good, Your Honor. Jolene and I were just discussing the mysteries of making soup."

Chapter 39

Arliss Cutter had spent a grand total of ninety minutes on a dogsled during his entire life, and even he could tell when Smudge's demeanor changed. The lead dog slowed at first, turning his head side to side as he ran, as if he recognized some smell.

"We're getting close," Birdie yelled over her shoulder.

Smudge slowed even more, forcing the rest of the team to slow down as well or pile up behind him. Birdie tapped the brake to keep the sled from running up on Digger and Hawke. Visibility was better than it had been with the fog, but that wasn't saying much. Cutter could see maybe fifty feet with the headlamp, but reflected snowflakes made it look like they were making the jump to hyperspace, obscuring what he could see, and making him see things that weren't there. There was nothing ahead but tundra—and nothing was a difficult thing to see.

"He smells something," Cutter shouted, before Smudge veered off the trail and trotted a few more steps.

"Smart dog," Birdie said. "He knows the deeper snow will slow us down and keep the sled from smacking into him."

She set the snow hook and unslung her rifle.

Cutter brought his rifle around as well.

The tracks left behind by Donna Taylor's sled were still visible in the snow, going almost due north now. If she was out there somewhere, she must have circled back because Smudge was staring intently to the east.

Instead of angling into the wind as they normally did when they stopped, the other ten dogs turned toward the darkness to follow Smudge's stare.

"Could be a moose," Birdie said. "Or maybe wolves."

Rifle in hand, Cutter trudged through the gale past the team so he could study the trail at something slower than ten miles an hour. He took shallow breaths, giving his lungs a chance to warm the frigid air.

Unimpeded by windbreaks, the storm quickly eroded the twin lines left by Donna's sled runners down to almost nothing. But here and there, in the lee of a tussock or tiny mound of lichen, the tracks were relatively protected. Much more comfortable in the estuaries and glades of his boyhood home, Cutter didn't have a great deal of experience with snow. But he was a quick study, and knew that when the stuff was disturbed it went through a sort of metamorphosis, often hardening like cement. Survival instructors pointed this out when they piled fluffy snow into a mound, and then waited a short time until it became firm enough to dig out a shelter.

Pressure from the weight of Donna's sled compacted the snow and melted it into a micro-thin layer of water. That's what made the sled glide so well. With temperatures hovering around zero now, that water had quickly frozen into a glaze of ice. The disturbed snow at the side of the tracks remained soft, like an uncompacted snowball. It hadn't had time to morph, to set up.

Donna Taylor was minutes in front of them, maybe

seconds. It was difficult to tell when they couldn't see more than fifty meters.

Cutter wheeled and made his way back to the sled, the wind now blasting his right shoulder. They were sitting ducks out here in the open. The lack of visibility offered some protection, but Donna had to suspect she'd be followed after shooting the VPSO.

He lifted the rifle over his head, waving his free arm to get Birdie's attention. She'd been staring into the darkness beside the dogs. He gestured up the trail with his mitten.

"We need to go!" he shouted.

Birdie kicked through a foot of snow to get to Smudge and drag him back to the trail. The rest of the team grudgingly followed.

Cutter was waiting for her at the back of the sled.

"What's up there?" he asked, taking his spot on the runners.

Birdie pointed north then waved her mitten from east to west. "There's a band of spruce less than a mile in front of us. It's maybe a quarter mile wide. Beyond that it's just more braided rivers and open tundra for a good ten miles."

"She's close then," Cutter said.

"Very close."

"Okay, guys!" Birdie said, whistling up the dogs. "Let's go."

The dogs threw themselves into their tug-lines and the sled began to pick up speed.

"Let's go!" Birdie said again. "Good dogs. Good Smu—"

She went quiet, leaning forward over her handlebar to get a better view. Cutter saw it too.

A lone dog caked in snow and ice limped out of the darkness, head down, tail tucked. Smudge went crazy, arching at the end of his tug-line, trying to escape and go greet his sister.

"It's Smoke!" Cutter said, stomping on his footbrake. He didn't have to look to know Birdie would do the same.

She set the snow hook and they stumbled off the trail to the injured dog.

"That bitch just left this dog to die!" Birdie said. "Still in harness."

Cutter unzipped his parka and scooped the shivering dog in his arms. He had on a lot of layers, but was hopefully sharing some of his body heat. The dog whined and looked up at his eyes. He'd never been one to attribute human traits and emotions to animals. To believe, for instance, that this dog was thanking him was absurd—but she sure looked grateful to be inside his coat.

Birdie moved close, pulling her own parka open so the two of them made a nest for Smoke, out of the wind. It was like dancing, with a dog between them.

"The poor thing is soaking wet," Birdie said, not bothering to hide her contempt for Donna Taylor. "She's been in water. If we hadn't come along she would have frozen to death."

"She may still," Cutter said.

Birdie nodded. "Glad to see your propensity to save wounded things extends to dogs."

"Of course." Cutter got the bibs out of the basket, wrapping Smoke inside the thick material. "We have to put her in the sled and keep moving."

"I know," Birdie said. "You stopped though. A lot of men I know would have just gone on by."

Cutter was struck by a sudden thought as he made the little dog as comfortable as possible. "She's covered with more ice than snow. You think she fell in the river?"

"I do," Birdie said. "Probably some overflow up ahead. Easy place to get into a jam if you're not careful."

She took her position on the runners and retrieved the snow hook.

"If she went into overflow," Birdie said, "there's probably bad spots all along the river. If we press her, then there's a good chance we'll catch her before she gets to the trees."

"Press her then," Cutter yelled.

A familiar tickle crept down the back of his neck, not unlike the feeling he got when he was about to kick down a door with a fugitive on the other side. Smudge picked up the pace, hurling himself and the rest of the team into the teeth of the storm. They were closing in. The dogs could feel it too.

Chapter 40

"**I**'m going after her," One-Eyed Rick said, using his fingernails to scrape away the frost from the tiny window. "I'll take care of these two first, then I'm leaving." He looked up at his friend, turning his head farther than normal so his one eye would come into play. "Unless you want to do it."

Morgan Kilgore looked up from where he was reading the back of a pilot-bread box he'd gotten from wherever he got the coffee and his new hat. He held up the dark blue box. "These things are tasty for just water and flour."

Sarah pushed her back flat against logs, getting as far as possible from these two insane men. Rick had been glaring at her with his single eye for the past half hour. All the while, Morgan did nothing but make idiotic observations about trivial things—a redbacked vole that kept poking its little head out from under the eaves over the stove, the way the pitch and timbre of the wind sounded like a bad orchestra, and now the stupid Sailor Boy crackers.

She couldn't take this inane banter anymore. Knowing she was about to die imparted a certain freedom that she'd never felt before.

She sneered at One-Eyed Rick. "You're so tough." The

pain in her jaw and teeth still gave her trouble when forming some words but she was infinitely more understandable now. "Beating a man who is half unconscious. What do you expect him to tell you when you don't give him a chance to talk? No one has asked me a single question."

Still at the window, Rick wheeled, giving her a squinty glare before stomping to the woodpile next to the stove. He picked up the camp axe by the bit and pointed at her with the handle. "You should shut your mouth," he said. "I'll get to you in a minute."

Spewing curses, he split a piece of wood that seemed too large for the stove and then buried the hatchet into one of the logs in the pile.

Morgan dropped the pilot-bread box on the table and got to his feet with a groan. "Don't worry so much, brother," he said. "Donna said she would be here, so she'll be here. She probably just had a bit of trouble slipping away from the village."

"Maybe so," the one-eyed man said. "But what if something's happened? It's blowing like hell out there. Could be the troopers figured out who she is. Or maybe she broke her leg. You don't think I should go check on her?"

"It would just piss her off," Morgan said. "You know how mad she'll be if the boy dies before she gets a few minutes to talk to him."

Rick squatted in front of the open stove door holding the length of wood he'd split, staring at the flames. His eye was red from the drugs and lack of sleep. He rubbed his face with his free hand and then began to bounce his fist off his own forehead. "This didn't go like I pictured it," he said. "I thought it would . . . I don't know, give me some answers, make me feel better about Reese."

Sarah threw back her head and screamed. "Will someone tell me what I'm doing here? Who is Reese?"

Rick crammed the piece of wood in the stove, disturbing the fire and sending up a shower of sparks. He ignored Sarah altogether, but his hulking shoulders heaved with emotion.

Morgan looked at her and raised a hand, as if to warn her off. It did no good.

"Who is he?" she asked again. "You're going to kill me anyway. You may have already killed my husband. I have a right to know why we're here."

"Reese was his son," Morgan said.

"And you think David hurt him?"

Rick wheeled, snatching up the axe, and stood so he brandished it above her. His voice was low, viperous.

"Your precious husband let my boy die. I want to know how it happened."

Sarah was too exhausted to be terrified anymore. Pain and futility flatlined all her emotions. What should have been white-hot anger had dulled to a mechanical frustration directed at these two men. Unclouded by panic or fear, her mind began to form the sparks of a plan. It was likely to get her killed—but doing nothing was worse.

"Does it occur to you that David might have told me whatever it is you want to know?"

Rick reared back, holding the axe higher, as if he were about to swing it. He paused for a moment, considering what she said, and then scoffed. "Not a chance. This guy doesn't have the balls to tell the truth about anything." He gave David an openhanded smack of contempt to the side of his head. "He's too much of a coward."

Sarah slammed her hands down flat on the bed. "Stop it! Stop hitting him!" She snapped her fingers when Rick turned away. "Here, jackass! Here. Focus on me. You're going to kill us whenever this Donna gets here, because you think my husband hurt your child." She shook her head, crying now, not begging, merely pointing out the idiocy of the situation. "I have done nothing wrong. I'm someone's child, and you plan to kill me. Should my parents come after you when this is over? Maybe scoop up one of your other children in the process and kill them too?"

"Yeah, well." Rick sneered. "Reese was my only kid."

"What does all this accomplish?"

Rick shrugged. "I'm going to hell, but my boy will get a little justice. That's what it accomplishes. It's your sorry luck you married this spineless worm. I guess life's a bitch."

"And you're a bastard," Sarah hissed. "A weak and pitiful bastard." She leaned forward, daring him to do something. "You know what I think? I think you probably never paid any attention to your son anyway. You were too busy out scoring drugs or killing other people's kids. That's why you're so broken. So twisted up in the brainpan. The guilt of being such a shitty father when he was alive—"

Rick roared, his one eye opening wide. He came up on his back foot to put power into the axe. Morgan rushed him, catching the big man's arm mid-swing.

"Knock it off!" Morgan snapped. "Both of you." He gave Rick a withering glare as he took the axe out of the man's hand and tossed it to the corner. "Can't you see that she's just trying to make you mad? She knows what's happening here. She wants you to kill her quickly so you can't use her as leverage to get David to talk. Take a breath, my friend. Calm your ass down. Donna will be here any minute and you can finish what you came here to do. This girl is broken. She isn't going anywhere."

Sarah stared into Rick's eye. Mocking him. Men like this fed on fear. Letting him know she wasn't scared starved him of what he needed. It made him weak. Morgan Kilgore gave her one of his soft smiles—but she saw through it. He wasn't saving her life. He was just saving her for later.

She rolled her lip into a snarl, showing broken teeth, and then spit a slurry of blood and mucus on Rick's crotch.

His hand came around in a powerful haymaker, connecting with the side of her head. Her already injured brain fairly exploded with molten pain—but she'd been hit before and knew it was coming. She rolled with the blow, landing on her side, her face pressed against the old blanket that smelled like motor oil. Her right hand broke her fall, clutching the edge of the bed, a mere three feet from the axe.

It was just where she wanted to be.

Chapter 41

Donna Taylor heard the first bark behind her during a momentary lull in the storm. It was a shrill, chattering sound, like chalk squeaking on a blackboard. She screamed for her dogs to pick up the pace, kicking repeatedly alongside the runner to help move the sled along. She wondered if it was a wolf. They were out here. She'd never heard a wolf bark like that. Maybe Smoke was able to keep up. These dogs were tough.

Donna hunched low over the handlebar to cut the wind. Every inch of her body was cold. Parts of her she didn't know she had, ached. Even her mind—no, especially her mind—was on fire. Cold, foggy, and on fire at the same time. She felt as though she'd jumped aboard a runaway train, and she was powerless to stop it, unable to get off. Wherever it was going, she was going there too. She was so ready for this to be over—one way or another.

Still following the river, she was ever on the lookout for overflow after her previous screwup. There were dangers everywhere, hidden under the snow, but this was the fastest route to the cabin. The dogs knew the way, so it was even faster. She hadn't been out since the night they'd taken David and Sarah Mead. The girl had been unconscious then. It was a big mistake not to leave her where she fell.

They'd left the big Norwegian after Rick blasted him with the Africa gun, but there was no saving him.

The troopers might take a while to get organized looking for a missing man. They'd surely go on the hunt for a murderer, but they'd pull out all stops to save a kidnapped woman.

Even crazy with grief, Donna should have known better. They'd discussed killing the girl at the cabin while she was still unconscious. Rick said it would be easy. He'd just put a hand over her mouth and she'd never wake up. Easy peasy. Morgan Kilgore had suggested they keep her alive in case they needed her for leverage on her husband. Donna had thought that a good idea at the time, but now she wasn't so sure. Kilgore wasn't going soft. It was the opposite, really. Killing came easy to her husband, but Morgan Kilgore was like a cat. He liked to play with his food.

The barking came again. Her heart sank when she realized it was a dog team. She was less than an hour from the cabin. The truth she'd wanted, needed, so desperately for two years now was within reach. She was so close to finding out what had happened to her boy—not the lies the newspapers told.

And now someone was actually chasing her with dogs? Seriously? She'd known the troopers would eventually come when they found the VPSO's body. But they would be on snow machines or ATVs. She would have heard the engines. Maybe it was some of Ned Jasper's friends. No, he was new to the village, *and* he was a cop—not well-loved enough for anyone to risk frostbite and death to hunt his killer. The marshals didn't seem likely. They were more worried about their precious federal judge than the goings-on in the bush. This made no sense at all.

The barking grew closer now, close enough to hear over

the storm. She thought she heard a shout, but couldn't be sure. She tried to look over her shoulder, but the cumbersome parka would have made it difficult in perfect conditions. Her hood had gotten wet when she wrecked and was frozen into a football-shaped tunnel of cloth that extended six inches out from her face. In order to see directly behind her, she would have to turn a complete 180 degrees.

The river straightened out ahead, narrowing to just fifty feet or so from bank to bank, making the water run faster, slower to freeze. The week before that had meant an area of thin ice. Donna had hugged the back then, in the shade of a high bank where the ice was already thick enough to support the weight of the dogs. She hit it mid-river this time, caught unaware when she looked back and forth after trying to see over her shoulder.

Collectively, the dogs weighed somewhere around four hundred pounds, but their weight was spread out over the surface. They made it across with no problem. The sled was an entirely different story. The ice under the runners cracked like a rifle shot, sending out a web of long fissures the instant Donna crossed it. She slammed forward against the handlebar as the brush bow plunged through a soft spot. Terrified, the dogs kept pulling, miraculously getting the front end back up on solid ice, but the lip of the basket stuck on the edge, anchoring the team in place as surely as the snow hook. Donna screamed, chided, and threatened, begging the dogs to pull. The sled hung there over the gaping hole for an agonizing second before a ten-foot section of ice shattered, all but vaporizing beneath Donna Taylor. The rear of the sled fell like a stone, sending Donna's stomach into her throat and her feet into the river.

The frigid water closed around her, flooding her heavy clothing, dragging her downward with the unstoppable force of the current. She gasped reflexively, inhaling deeply of the frigid air and almost as much freezing water. Coughing and cursing, she fought to keep her head above the surface. The current pressed her hard against the downriver edge of the hole, threatening to suck her under, but for the moment wedging her in place, just below her shoulder blades. The ice was only a few inches thick, and rotten, crumpling away each time she struggled to reposition herself. The dogs looked back from the far side of the gaping chasm, scared and confused, trapped. The arched piece of hard plastic that formed the brush bow was jammed against the ice, held in place there so the sled lay at an angle with the back of the runners digging into the gravel river bed. Donna's legs dangled over nothingness, unable to touch the bottom. She considered using the sled like a ramp to climb out. The handlebar was underwater, down by her waist. She still held on to it, using it for support, but each time she tried to pull herself forward, or bring a foot around, the entire sled shuddered. She could feel the vibrations as the runners plowed along the gravel bottom, losing precious inches—and degrees of the angle that kept the sled lodged against the ice. Much more and it would slip completely under, dragging the dogs and her along with it.

Where her initial response at hitting the frigid water had been to inhale in shock, Donna now found it difficult to draw enough air into her lungs to scream at the dogs. She tried urging them forward, wondering if they heard her, or even if they did, if they'd have enough juice to pull the sled away. Maybe, if she let go—which would happen soon enough. Her clothing had already soaked up enough water to double her weight. Any movement threatened to break the ice behind her. Doing anything would kill her. Doing nothing would kill her.

She worked herself up for another scream, hoping the troopers or whoever had the dog team behind her might hear. She managed no more than a pitiful gurgle. Maybe there was no one there anyway. Her mind was just playing tricks on her. She laughed out loud, wedged there against the ice over a merciless black torrent of frigid water. Anyone who saw her might think she was going crazy— but that had happened a long time ago.

Six inches of ice crumbled away behind her, causing her to drop deeper as the river drove her backward, only to pin her against the ice again. The water reached high on her chest now. Only her fingertips touched the handlebar. If she lost it she'd be sucked under.

Unless . . .

An idea wormed its way into her freezing brain and warmed there long enough she could get her head wrapped around the gist of it. Panic killed most people when they fell through the ice. At least that's what she'd read, but that was when they fell in a lake and the rushing water itself wasn't trying to beat you to death. Still, if she could calm down, and moved slowly, she might be able to turn around, to work with the current to get her chest out of the water and up on top. Her gear was gone, the cabin too far away, so she'd probably still freeze to death, but that wouldn't be as bad as drowning in the dark as she bobbed along trapped under the ice.

She rolled sideways, kicking as best she could in the heavy clothing while applying the tiniest bit of pressure to the handlebar to assist her movements without dislodging the sled. She tried twice, but it was no use. The hydraulic force held her fast. It was simply too strong, but the attempted movement did free the rifle sling—and gave her another idea.

Carefully, moving sloth-like from fear and cold, she pulled off her right mitten with her teeth, then reached with a shaking hand to unsnap the top swivel of the rifle sling at her shoulder. Her fingers were dead nubs at the end of a dead hand. They seemed to belong to someone else. She almost dropped the gun four times in the process, but miraculously, she was able to bring it around in front of her. The hole was relatively narrow, just wider than the sled. She set the gun across the ice, the barrel on one side, the butt on the other, forming a crossbar she could hang on to. The ice wasn't strong enough to pull herself up, but she found she could now let go of the sled handle without getting swept away. It was only a momentary stay of execution, but momentary was better than the alternative.

Her dogs heard the other team before she did. They went crazy, yelping and jumping against their lines. The movement dislodged the sled and it began to slip farther into the water, dragging the team backward.

"Serves you right!" Donna sputtered, her sodden arms draped over the rifle. The grip of the cold water was slowly squeezing the life out of her. "I hope you all drown!"

And then the beam of a headlamp cut the night, illuminating the falling snow and the terrified dogs. Low voices whispered behind the light, then a second sled slithered out onto the ice without any dogs attached. A parka-clad figure lay facedown in the basket, reaching forward over the brush bow with mittened hands.

Donna shuddered, at once flooded with relief and fear.

It was Birdie Pingayak. Out of all the people in Stone Cross, she was the closest to the VPSO. She was also the bravest. Of course it would be her.

* * *

Cutter stood as far back on the runners of the double-trainer as he could, skating gently to push it and Birdie with it onto the thinning ice. The howling wind made it impossible to hear the tiny fractures spider-webbing across the surface, but he knew they were there. Birdie had unhooked her own team and left them on the bank along with Smoke, anchored with the snow hook. She lay on her belly now, distributing her weight along the entire sled. Donna called out, but instead of helping her, the little Eskimo woman reached across and unsnapped the gang-line from the sled.

"Are you kidding me?" Donna screamed. "Birdie! Forget the dogs and pull me out of here!"

Freed from certain death, Donna's trapped team made a mad dash for the bank, allowing the sled to slip beneath the surface and tumble downriver under the ice.

"Birdie!" Donna began to sob. Pleading now, her voice wobbly with cold. Black water seemed to boil around her, hissing against the ice. "I can't hold on—"

Cutter shifted the sled, taking it dangerously close to the edge.

Birdie gave a shrill whistle. She'd angled her headlamp slightly away so it wasn't blinding the other woman. "Donna! Look at me."

Side-arming, she threw a piece of yellow line, laying it expertly across Donna Taylor's shoulder.

"Tie this around the rifle and we'll pull you out."

Donna lifted her hand to grab the rope, but slammed it back in place. "I can't," she said, panting, eyes wide. She tried to speak, took on a mouthful of water, then spit it out, sputtering and coughing. "It's . . . It's . . . pulling me under. I'll go down if I let go. Please . . ."

Birdie inched out farther so her torso hung over the brush bow well beyond the front of the basket.

The ice snapped in earnest now, clearly audible over the wind, as the angle of Birdie's lean focused more weight on a smaller portion of the runners.

"That's far enough," Cutter yelled. "Donna, the ice will break if she comes any closer. You have got to grab the rope."

Donna shook her head. "You just want me to die."

Birdie pulled the rope back, hand over hand, tied a quick loop, and then tossed it again. She was throwing into the wind and it took her three attempts to get it back in place across Donna's shoulder. "Here," she said. "All you have to do is get an arm through the loop. But you have to let go of the gun."

"I never . . . planned . . . to hurt the girl," Donna said, shaking her head. "It's just that . . . My son . . . I have to know . . ."

"Where did you take the girl?" Cutter asked, seeing how this was going to end.

"Cabin," Donna said. "Half . . . a h . . . h . . . half mile north . . . They expected . . . me . . . hours ago . . . killed her . . . by now."

Donna's arm slipped off the rifle. She flailed. Her chin dropped beneath the surface, then she caught herself on the gun, barely keeping her head above water.

"Donna," Birdie pleaded. "Take the rope!"

"I . . . I . . . can't . . ." Her voice was breathy, like she was falling asleep.

"You said they," Cutter said. "Who has the girl?"

"Husband," Donna said. She turned her head directly toward Cutter, staring hard, trying to make him out behind the glare of his headlamp. She'd stopped shaking now. A bad sign.

"My sweet little boy," she said, her words hissing out of her. Both arms slipped off the rifle, and the water quietly swallowed her up.

Smudge barked once, standing on the bank looking down at the river. Cutter turned his headlamp on the little wolf-dog. No, animals didn't have human characteristics, but this one didn't seem too awfully sad that Donna Taylor was out of his life for good.

Birdie was still facedown, hand on the rope, staring transfixed at the spot where Donna vanished. Cutter whistled to get her attention.

"I'm pulling you in."

Birdie wriggled backward on her belly, farther to the rear of the basket.

"Be careful," she said, grunting. "I can hear the ice snapping under me."

Cutter kept most of his weight on the runners, skating backward inch by inch toward the bank where the dogs were waiting.

"We're almost there," he said, pivoting the sled slightly.

"I trust you," Birdie said, a moment before the ice gave way and they both plunged into the icy water.

Chapter 42

Cutter's feet slammed into the gravel riverbed. He fell backward from the momentum of the sudden three-foot drop, landing on the seat of his pants, clutching the back station of the sled as black water rushed in around him, slamming violently against his back, trying to push him downriver, under the ice. His chest and head were above water, and he still had a grip on the sled's rearmost upright stanchion, but the sled and Birdie had both disappeared beneath the surface.

Scrambling, Cutter grabbed a sled runner with his other hand. Then he leaned toward the bank and pulled, using his legs to press with every ounce of strength. For a moment, it seemed the sled was hopelessly stuck, but little by little it began to swing in the current. Cutter was able to take a half step backward, getting better purchase with his boot in the gravel. Then, hand over hand, he drew the heavy sled toward him under the water. Seconds later Birdie's head broke the surface. She dragged herself forward while Cutter pulled the sled, until she was close enough he could reach out and grab her parka ruff. Filled with water, the clothing acted as an anchor, effectively doubling her weight and threatening to tear her from his grasp.

Cutter let go of the sled, feeling it slip away with the

current as he got both hands around the parka and towed a gasping Birdie Pingayak into the icy shallows. She sputtered and coughed, clambering up alongside him in the shallows as they splashed and stumbled their way through and over rotten ice until they reached the actual bank.

"Took you long enough," she said, laughing like a crazy woman as she fell back in the snow. Her headlamp was still working and fired a beam skyward, straight up into the storm. Snowflakes swirled above her in the white light.

"The sled's gone," Cutter said, not even sure if Birdie could hear him. Without the sled, they had no food or dry clothes. Without food and dry clothes, they would be dead in hours, maybe even minutes. "I'm game to hear some of your Native wisdom about how to survive this."

Birdie rolled over and pushed herself up on all fours. Groaning, she took Cutter's hand and used him to get to her feet.

"The meaner you are the longer you last," she said. "How about that for Native wisdom?"

Her teeth were beginning to chatter, but she was still joking and seemed no worse off than Cutter after having been underwater for the better part of a minute.

"Come on," she said. "Help me let the dogs go."

Cutter plodded after her. At least the dogs would find their way home.

"You got good wool drawers on, right?" Birdie asked, slipping harnesses off each dog and freeing them as she spoke.

"I do," he said.

"Good. You should be okay for a few minutes." She pointed downriver, the direction they'd come from. The hair on her parka was beginning to freeze. "We crossed some ATV tracks about two hundred yards back. Caribou hide out in the thickets during storms like this. James

Johnny is probably trying to catch one there. His camps aren't much, but he'll have some food. Maybe some emergency blankets. He might even have a fire going."

Cutter stepped in close. His own teeth chattered now. He felt as though even his belly was shivering. "Let's just go to the cabin."

Birdie shook her head. "I don't trust the river. Snow's too deep if we go cross-country. We'd have to post-hole all the way—and that would kill us. Even if we don't freeze to death, we'll be in no shape to fight. James's camp is on the other trail. We can make it from there, but we'll need to borrow his Honda."

Smudge and five of the other dogs, including Smoke, Digger, and Hawke, stayed with Cutter and Birdie as they trudged south along the riverbank through bitter wind and blowing snow. The rest of them disappeared into the night. Just as Birdie said, they crossed an ATV track less than two hundred meters back. Leading the way, Birdie pointed, then turned to the east without speaking a word. She was a picture out of time, a sturdy Eskimo woman, her back to the blizzard, surrounded by a half dozen Alaska huskies.

It took too much energy to try and talk so Cutter sang songs in his mind to keep it active. He thought of Mim and the kids. This would be one of those stories like Grumpy had. His stories were always too big to believe, but somehow you believed them anyway, because they were true. When you'd lived a life like Grumpy Cutter, you didn't have to make stuff up. Cutter wondered if the boys would believe him. *I was chasing a murderer through the Alaska wilderness and had to walk through snow up to my knees back to camp after falling through the ice with my dog team* . . . It sounded bizarre even thinking about it. But things like this happened. People froze to death in the bush—bad guys and good. The tundra didn't care.

The twins would eat it up. Constance would roll her eyes and call him a dumbass—*ass* was her pet word nowadays. Mim would give him that cloudy, suspicious look like he was being too frivolous with his own safety—which was probably true most every waking moment of his life.

Grumpy would have had something to say about this. Grumpy Man-Rule number . . .

Cutter stumbled on a hidden clump of willows, face-planting in two feet of wind-driven snow. He caught himself on both hands, risking a sprain. Stupid. Just let yourself fall. He brushed himself off and floundered to his feet. Both arms and hands still worked, no worse for wear except that he looked like a sugar cookie and was freezing to death. He kicked his way forward, picking up the pace so he didn't lose sight of Birdie. She was a fast walker, as if pushing through snow up to her knees while wearing sopping wet clothes in subzero temperatures was an everyday occurrence for her. She was the personification of Grumpy Man-Rule number . . . What was it again? Cutter's mind was a wall of frozen fog. This rule was important, so it was up there at the top somewhere. Rule number one—Watch your heading. Rule number two . . . That was it! Cutter pounded his forehead with the flat of his frozen mitten.

Grumpy Rule number two—*Fight on*!

Head down, he almost ran over Birdie when she stopped in the trail.

"Not good," she said, so cold now her arms and shoulders jerked and bounced as if a puppeteer were pulling randomly on her strings. She turned so her light fell on a parked ATV and trailer with knobby balloon tires. Beyond the four-wheeler, the dark form of a body lay half hidden in the snow.

The dogs rushed forward to investigate, no doubt hoping to find something to eat at the smell of a camp. They bypassed the body to sniff at the carcass of a dead bull caribou in front of the ATV. Cutter and Birdie stumbled forward side by side.

The hole in James Johnny's neck left no room for doubt that he was dead.

Birdie stood in the wind and prodded the bull with the toe of her mukluk. "He must have caught it right before he was killed. Looks like he was gutting it when they got him. This meat might be enough to save us . . ."

Johnny had rigged a tarp on the lee side of the ATV trailer to use as a windbreak. He was probably planning to cook a bit of his catch before heading home, Birdie observed. Cutter noted how the Natives he'd met all said they caught things instead of killing them. Where a white hunter would say he *killed* a caribou or *caught* a fish. To an Eskimo, the act was *catching* in both instances. For some reason, Cutter found he liked the Native way more.

Birdie turned mechanically, forgetting about the caribou, and went straight to work, searching the small trailer until she found a dozen pieces of scrap two-by-four lumber Johnny had brought along to use as firewood. Cutter helped her unload it and piled half of it on the spot where he'd had a previous fire, protected by the tarp windbreak. Birdie doused it liberally with gasoline from a spare fuel jug James Johnny had bungeed to the rack of his ATV. Cutter tried his Zippo lighter, but it was soaked. Birdie reached down the front of her shirt and drew out a leather cord, at the end of which was a small plastic match case. She gave him a stupid grin and said something he couldn't quite hear about being prepared. It took her several failed attempts with ungainly, half-frozen hands, but she was finally able to touch off the gasoline.

Cutter almost cried as the warmth from the flames began to seep into his clothing. He was still wet and cold and uncomfortable, but he was alive—and on his way to getting warm if not dry.

Soon, Cutter and Birdie had stripped down to their underwear and were both squatting out of the wind facing the fire, with their wet coats and pants hanging over the trailer behind them. Cutter had found a box of granola bars in the trailer. They were each already on their second. Birdie had hacked out a length of backstrap from the caribou and it was now sizzling on a length of willow next to the fire. Steam rose from their wet woolies. Orange firelight flickered off their faces and hands. The dogs had wolfed down the half frozen offal from the caribou gut pile and were now all gathered round, lying on their bellies in the snow, noses toward the warmth.

"He must have been planning to head back tonight," Birdie said, throwing a granola bar wrapper into the flames. Smudge lifted his head at the movement, hoping for a scrap of food, and then relaxed when he didn't get one, nestling in beside a very tired but now-dry Smoke. "Probably caught this bull and decided to quarter it and bring it right home, otherwise he'd have set up a better camp." She shook her head. "This wood's not gonna last us long. There's a sleeping bag in the trailer and another tarp. We can make a burrito if we have to, maybe coax the dogs to stay next to us for warmth."

"We could," Cutter said. "How far is the cabin?"

"Maybe a mile," Birdie said, nodding in thought. "It

would be warmer in there than a sleeping bag burrito in the snow."

"No doubt," Cutter said. "But Donna mentioned there was someone else with her husband. They're not likely to move out without a fight. If we'd met them half an hour ago, I'm not sure I would have been capable of holding a gun, much less pulling the trigger."

Birdie used her knife to cut off a piece of very rare but hot caribou loin from the willow skewer. She ate a bite and offered the rest to Cutter. His eyes fluttered involuntarily as he chewed the savory meat. She gave him an approving nod.

"Good, huh?"

"I think caribou cooked over two-by-four lumber scraps might be my new favorite food," Cutter said.

"It is good," Birdie said, gingerly cutting off a steaming chunk and tossing it to Smudge. She cut another and handed it to Cutter. "But what we need is fat to keep us warm." Her eyebrows shot up and she smiled. "Wait here," she said. She took her knife and the headlamp to crouch over the caribou's head. Smudge followed her. She was less than six feet from where Cutter waited so he could see perfectly when she used her knife to pry out one of the caribou's eyes, and then, using the blade of her knife as a spoon, dug around in the socket, coming up with a dollop of white flesh almost as large as a golf ball. A further search got her almost as much again in smaller portions from the same side. This she set on a clean spot of snow while she repeated the process with the other socket. A few moments later, she returned with two handfuls of gleaming white fat from behind the caribou's eyeballs.

Realizing he wasn't getting any of this prize, the husky resumed his place by the fire, snarling to move one of the other dogs so he was closest to Birdie.

She held one hand toward Cutter while she began to nibble at the contents of the other.

"Eat this," she said. "It'll warm you up as good as the fire."

"And I thought the *agutaq* was unique," Cutter said, turning up his nose. "I'm gonna be just fine with the backstrap."

"No," Birdie said. "You're not. Your body needs fat out here in the cold. A lot of fat. Especially after what we just went through—and what we are about to. If we had time I could crack the leg bones and we could dig the marrow out with a stick. It's good stuff on pilot bread." She took another bite of the eye fat. "I used to beg for this part when I was a kid. Jolene loves it. Try it. Tastes like—"

"Chicken?" Cutter joked, holding the greasy blob up to his nose. Surprisingly, it had no odor.

"No," Birdie scoffed. "I was going to say bread dough."

Intrigued at that, Cutter took a small bite. She was right. The damned stuff did taste like bread dough. It had the same texture too. Cutter swallowed it all like medicine, feeling warmth radiate through his body as the rich fat hit his belly.

Birdie threw the last four pieces of lumber on the fire. Hands and legs open to the flames again, arms resting on her knees, she looked over at him and smiled. Her chin tattoo shimmered in the firelight with a coating of fresh grease.

"I've known you for what, eighteen hours now?"

Cutter nodded sleepily. "Has it only been that long?"

"You got to Stone Cross yesterday at the middle of fifth period," she said. "Lots of stuff happened in that short time. I'm sorry I never told you about Daisy when you first got here."

"Forget about that," Cutter said, meaning it. Aguthluk's threatening letter seemed trivial compared to everything else that had happened. "You saw things through your lens, I saw them through mine."

"So neither of us were wrong?"

"I guess not." Cutter winked. "But I was a little bit more right."

Birdie duck-walked sideways like a baseball catcher adjusting her position. She sidled up close until she was shoulder to shoulder and hip to hip with Cutter and then, out of nowhere, she leaned in so her nose and lips pressed against his cheek. Surprised, he didn't move away, even when she lingered there for a few seconds before sitting back up.

"*Kunik,*" she said.

"*Kunik,*" Cutter repeated, having no idea what he was saying. The cold had made him loopy, and for all he knew he'd just accepted a marriage proposal.

"People think that an Eskimo kiss is only rubbing noses," she said. "But it's more than that. It is a way to greet our family and loved ones when our noses and cheeks are often the only thing exposed during the winter."

"I like it," Cutter said, nodding slowly at the fire. He didn't address the fact that she'd just lumped him in with her loved ones. They were both running on fumes. People sometimes got too honest when they were exhausted. Cutter decided to change the subject. "You know what we need besides fat?"

Birdie turned to look at him. Smudge raised his head again as if he wanted to know too.

"We need a plan," he said. "I think I might have one if you trust me."

"Remember when I said the meanest survive the longest out here?" Birdie began to draw in the muddy snow with her willow twig.

"I do," Cutter said. Her doodling in the dirt put him in

the mood to whittle, but there was no time. The fire was getting smaller by the minute. There was no question that they'd had to stop. It wouldn't do anyone any good if they froze to death, but he was already feeling the urgency of getting back on the trail.

"Years ago," Birdie said, "some sociologists did a study at some villages up north of here. Their evidence was anecdotal, 'cause it'd be hard to quantify meanness, but these guys theorized that the ones who got in the most fights, got in trouble with the law the most, they were most likely to survive extreme hardships like weather. A couple years ago, I had a couple of elementary school students get caught in a blizzard when they were out lookin' for their grandfather. That little brother and sister survived three nights in subzero temperatures beside their overturned snow machine, living on nothing but some jelly beans and a Hershey bar—and I gotta tell you, those two kids were in my office all the time. They had to be the two worst-behaved students in the school—always in fights, always breaking the rules . . ."

"Fight on," Cutter said.

"What?"

"Something my grandfather used to say."

Birdie pointed at him with her drawing stick, punctuating each word. "Nine and eleven," she said. "That's how old they were. Three nights . . ." Birdie pushed off her knees with both hands to stand. "I'm gonna have to get mean to put on that wet parka." She hefted the still sodden fur and groaned in disgust. "You said you had a plan as long as I trusted you."

"Do you?" Cutter asked.

She shrugged on the coat and picked up her rifle.

"I trust you to be mean," she said. "You seem pretty good at that."

Chapter 43

Lola Teariki nearly jumped out of her skin when Jolene's cell phone rang. Jolene leaned over a library table, resting her head on her hands. She sat up on the second ring and gave a long, feline yawn. If the noise startled her, she didn't act like it.

They were still in the library with Markham and the lawyers, waiting on pins and needles for Cutter to check in on the satellite phone. Lola had already fielded two calls from the chief. Jill Phillips was good about giving the fugitive task force a wide latitude when they were working, but she was quick to put on her mother-hen hat when things got sticky. Chasing killers in forty-knot winds and twenty-below temperatures certainly qualified. There was a hell of a lot of stuff that could kill you out here— even if you were Arliss Cutter. This storm could rage for days—stranding them here with no backup and leaving Cutter . . . Well, there was no way to know what Cutter was doing right now. For all she knew, he was sitting by a warm fire, carving some piece of wood while he told Birdie Pingayak about his grandpa's rules for good behavior.

Lola hadn't been able to tell the chief much of anything, which sucked because Jill Phillips was the kind of person you wanted to please. She was hoping this call was from Jolene's mom, telling them all was good.

It wasn't.

Jolene spoke to the caller in Yup'ik for a moment, then whispered, "It's Daisy," before passing the phone to Lola.

Lola's heart sank. "Is Ned all right?"

"He's good," Aguthluk said. "Good as can be expected anyways. Melvin Red Fox had to go to the airport to see about helping with the Troopers plane. We could use another set of hands over here."

"Of course," Lola said, relieved to have something to do. "We'll be right—"

Aguthluk ended the call, apparently not one to chat after her message was delivered.

"Looks like we're going to lend a hand at the cabin," Lola said. She looked at Markham, hoping she wouldn't have to remind him that the two of them were all but joined at the hip.

He raised his coffee mug as if to toast. "Lead on, Deputy."

Ewing and Markham's law clerk stayed at the school, agreeing to pull the next shift watching over Ned Jasper at the cabin if the troopers couldn't land like they hoped.

"You think Donna Taylor is going to come back?" Jolene asked as they walked down the hall.

"Not likely," Lola said. "She probably believes she killed Ned Jasper. We'll be careful though."

The scream of the blizzard hit Lola full in the face the moment she pushed open the front door, careful to keep a tight grip so it wasn't ripped out of her hands. The wind burned her face, feeling like it might flay skin if given too much of an opportunity. She adjusted her rifle on the single-point sling so the weapon was parked comfortably behind her sidearm, over her right kidney with the barrel pointed down. She could access it quickly, but it remained out of the way for the multitude of other tasks she might need to accomplish that didn't call for a long gun.

It was almost eight in the morning, but it wouldn't be light for at least another two hours. Most of the houses were dark, and the raging storm only added to the inky shadows. Their route to the cabin took them past teacher housing, a dark set of small duplexes set in a square with a center courtyard. Every teacher had been up all night, either helping Birdie, helping watch after Ned Jasper, or standing by with their ATVs and snow machines to light the runway for the troopers' aircraft if it was ever able to catch a break in the weather. The snow-covered roads and walkways around the housing area were dark and sinister, reminding Lola of the low-income projects where she'd worked a fugitive roundup in Baltimore her second year in the Marshals Service. She chuckled to herself that these bush teachers had their own "hood." There were no Crips or Bloods out here, no MS-13, but she was glad to have her rifle nonetheless.

Markham and Jolene walked a few feet in front, heads bowed into the squalling wind and snow. Lola felt better if she could keep them both in sight, especially in this mess. She turned around to check her back-trail, and nearly ran into Markham, who'd stopped directly in front of her.

"Scram!" the judge said, bringing a derisive laugh from Sascha Green.

"Scram?" Green sneered. "Is that the way they talk in the big village?"

To her credit, Jolene stepped back. Lola used her left

hand to position the girl beside her, but far enough away that there was plenty of space to move.

"Get out of here, then," Markham said, using the disdainful judge's voice he often used from the bench. "You understand that?"

Sascha's right hand was behind his back, out of view, prompting Lola to raise her rifle and aim it at his forehead. "Just because you're a judge," Sascha said, "don't give you the right to tell me where to be."

"Sascha, do not move!" Lola barked. "Judge, get down!" She had a clear shot, but didn't want to shoot over Markham's shoulder if she didn't have to.

Instead of dropping, Markham took a step forward, flicking his hand at Green as if shooing away an insect.

Sascha saw his opening and rushed in, putting the judge in between himself and the long gun. Lola cursed, stepping sideways, unable to see Sascha's hands or get a clear shot in the melee.

Sascha ran straight into the judge, no doubt intent on running him down and using him as a human shield to get to Lola. At fifty-seven, Markham surprised her with his agility. He sprang to the side, catching a grazing elbow to the jaw that sent him to his knees, but not before giving the younger man a brutal openhanded slap to the right ear.

"Listen to me, Anthony!" Lola was yelling now, rifle still up with one hand, the other waving the judge back and keeping track of Jolene. She used Markham's given name, hoping the breach in decorum would piss him off enough to pay attention. "Get your ass behind me!" Without waiting for the judge to comply, she zeroed in on Green again. "Sascha, you are under arrest. I said do not move!"

She could see both his hands now—empty. Shooting him became a little more problematic, though she still feared for the judge's safety. She changed her tack, keeping her voice loud, but pointed and sure, anything but shrill.

"Sascha, I want you to listen to me. Very slowly raise your hands."

He sneered, flipping her off. "It's just you and the old man. You're not going to arrest me. I just want to talk to my daughter."

"Hands," Lola said. "Slowly."

"Not happening, bitch," Green snapped. "I'm not lettin' some gash arrest me . . ."

Cheek welded to her rifle and still aimed in, Lola's eyes flicked momentarily to the judge. Having him here as a witness might be a good thing . . . or not. She grimaced. "Honestly, Sascha, part of me is glad you feel that way. It's good Jolene gets to see how you talk to women."

"Hey, hey." Sascha raised both hands, not in surrender, but to get Jolene's attention. "I only called her that because she's a cop, sweetheart. She's trying to keep us apart."

"Yeah," Lola said. "I'm sure Jolene's getting that loud and clear. You'd be a real gentleman if I wasn't a cop. You know what I think? I think it embarrasses the hell out of you that Birdie nearly killed you that day. I mean, you were a grown man and she was what, just fifteen—the same age as Jolene. You could barely live with that. You had to listen to female corrections officers, and now a female deputy marshal is about to throw your ass back in jail."

A low growl, like a wolf caught in a trap, grew from Sascha Green's chest. He snarled, charging blindly, straight for Lola.

There are exceptions, but most law enforcement officers don't want to risk a full-blown brawl. There are too many variables—wild elbows and knees that come out of nowhere from people who could not usually fight their way out of a wet paper bag. The popularity of mixed martial arts had everyone and their brother thinking they could go three rounds in the octagon. The truth was, in a venue where there were no rules, even the winner—the one who came out alive—could get maimed in a hurry. A blown knee could mean the end of a career. A misplaced foot might cause an unplanned meeting between face and concrete. Dojos and octagons were exciting, but by law, they had not seen many realistic fights since the days of the samurai.

Lola Teariki was one of those exceptions. She'd grown up with three brothers. She was *tuakana*, the eldest, but her brothers were big boys who'd turned into big Maori men. She'd taught them all to wrestle, and as they got older, refused to let them ignore her during their impromptu battles in the backyard. All of them, including Lola, were taller than their Japanese mother. And they all relished a good scrap, fed off it, really. Oddly, the Marshals Service didn't require a psychological exam, and Lola often found herself wondering how she would have answered questions about fighting if she'd ever bothered to apply anywhere else. The bad guys weren't civilized. It didn't seem like too big of a stretch to think sometimes you might need a shark to catch a shark. The truth was, if there was violence, she didn't want to miss it.

She did not, however, draw out a fight unnecessarily.

Sascha Green was taller than her, probably a little stronger too. She had no doubt that he would kill her if she gave him the opportunity.

Lola swept her rifle back on the sling the moment Green ducked his head to rush her, parking the gun over her kidney again. She grabbed the expandable baton from her belt and flicked it open with a snap of her wrist, extending the rigid metal sections to a full twenty-one inches.

She stepped to her left at the last second, moving off the line of attack like a bullfighter. Green rushed past, exposing his calf and getting a snap from Lola's steel baton. She let the blow die there a split second for maximum effect, then hammered him again before he could recover, following up to his forearm when he turned. Dropping his right arm at the blow, he came around with a wicked left that glanced off the point of her shoulder and crashed into the side of her neck, making her bite her tongue. Green was blind with rage and pain, making the strike a Hail Mary, thrown wildly at the wind, but it connected and proved devastating.

Stunned, Lola dropped the expandable baton. Getting hit in the brachial nerves was a hell of a lot like grabbing a handful of electric fence, and she was lucky to keep her feet. Exhaling hard, she spat a mouthful of blood, feeling it get torn away in the wind. Sascha was on her again in an instant. She raised both arms, warding off blow after blow meant to knock her out. Sascha grabbed her by both shoulders, attempting to drive a knee into her groin. She managed to twist sideways, taking the knee on her thigh, and getting the sinking feeling that it had done some real damage.

Jolene screamed for him to stop. The judge rushed in again, landing at least one more good punch before Green knocked him back with an elbow to the nose. Markham fell back on his knees, still conscious enough to spew curses into the blizzard. Lola used the few moments to shake off the pain in her neck and hip. She needed to finish this quickly or risk getting her ass kicked—at which point Sascha Green would likely kill her, judge or no judge, Jolene or no Jolene. That much was clear in his eyes.

He turned toward her, chest heaving inside his open parka. His lips drew back in a vile sneer, revealing bloody teeth. Someone had connected.

Thick black hair blowing like a curtain across her face, Lola bent slightly forward at the waist, shoulders rounded, hands loose and low. She'd been described as beautiful many times; men hit on her often when she went out with friends. But those same Polynesian eyes and prominent cheekbones above full lips could be terrifying if twisted into her warring haka face. She'd once made one of her nieces break into tears. Lola wanted Sascha Green to believe her to be a weak thing—not a woman who relished battle.

She did her best to keep her face relaxed, fighting the natural urge to open her eyes wide in challenge and sneer at the evil creature in front of her. She wanted him to rush in, thinking he'd won. Then, she'd arrest him if she could. If not, she'd beat him to death—judge or no judge. Jolene or no Jolene.

He charged in again, a little farther out than suited her. He grazed her belly with a sloppy right as she turned to let him go by. The blow would hurt later, but she barely felt it now. Green slid on the ice, waving his arms to keep from falling. Lola moved directly in front of him now, presenting the tantalizing target of a woman who didn't know what she was doing. He'd no sooner stopped flapping his arms than he rushed her again, but this time he was over the same patch of ice he'd just slipped on.

Lola took quick advantage, planting her back foot on

solid ground while she drove her right knee into a startled Green's groin three times before he could arrest his forward momentum. He screamed, doubling over in agony, and when he did, Lola Teariki's knee was there to meet his face. Her hands came down at the same time her leg came up, catching Sascha's parka hood on both sides and slamming it down to meet her knee. Downward momentum arrested, his teeth cracked together like a pistol shot. His head snapped up and his feet flew out from under him, depositing him flat on his back in a snowdrift. His skull missed the edge of a concrete walk by mere inches. *Pity*, Lola thought, her aggression still pumping from the heat of battle.

"Deputy!" Markham shouted, obviously sensing that she was about to do something she couldn't take back.

Lola shook her head, then stooped to grab Sascha by the wrist, staying out of his reach just in case he wasn't as hurt as he made out to be. She extended his arm and gave his hand a hard twist toward the pinkie finger, forcing him to turn over onto his belly.

Once she had control, she stepped over Green's outstretched arm, retaining control while she walked around his body to place her knee firmly in the small of his back.

"Give me your other hand." She increased the pressure on his wrist until he complied and she could ratchet on the handcuffs. She coughed, spitting more blood in the snow. It had been a while since she'd taken a hit like that. It didn't exactly make her smile—but it was exhilarating nonetheless. "Sascha Green," she said. "You are under arrest for urinating in a national park within three hundred feet of an authorized outhouse."

He turned his head, face covered in snow, and looked up at her as if she were crazy.

Behind her, Markham laughed out loud.

Green thrashed his legs, but she lifted up on his arms, putting pressure on his shoulders until he stopped. "Knock it off!"

"What the hell are you talking about?"

"I'm not finished." Knee still against his back, Lola pulled the windblown hair out of her face with her free hand and continued. "You are also being charged with violation of a domestic violence court order, assault on a federal judge, assaulting a federal law enforcement officer—and for calling me a gash."

Now Jolene laughed, which Green appeared to take harder than the knee to his face. He was near tears when he lifted his head out of the snow again.

"That's not a crime."

Judge Markham stood over the prisoner, ignoring his own bloody nose.

"It is today," he said.

Chapter 44

Sarah began to think of her plan as her only possible hope—and even that was thin. She had enough sense not to focus on the little details. That would only slow her down.

She stayed put at the foot of the bed. Rick's fist had put her there, so neither of the men appeared to give a second thought to the fact that she was near the axe. David had become more animated since they'd lightened up on his beatings, and spent a lot of time dazed and blinking as he looked around the room trying to get his bearings. Sarah wondered if he remembered why he was here. He recognized her, and kept apologizing through the bloody mask of tears and saliva and snot that covered his face.

Morgan Kilgore looked at her differently now, hungrily, like there was no point in pretending anymore. That's what people like him did. They drew you in close with a bit of warm soup and soft crackers, and then, when it suited their purposes, they tore you apart.

Sarah spent a good deal of time testing the grip in her hands. The cords they'd used to tie her had damaged some nerves. She was sure of that. Just days before she'd been capable of splitting a pile of spruce logs as high as her waist before lunchtime. Her back and shoulders and forearms knew and understood hard work. There was no way to know how much they'd forgotten until she tried to pick up something heavy—like the axe. Until then, she bunched the corner of her stinking blanket into a tight ball, squeezing and releasing, testing her grip as best she could. It was painful at first, even making the roots of her teeth throb, but she pushed through it. She was likely to have more than a few broken teeth on the other side of this.

Her poor grip was only the first of many problems. The axe was like a single-shot rifle. Even if she killed one of them, she'd need time to reload and swing at the other—who would be stunned by the attack, but probably not enough to stay in one place long enough for her to hit him too. She'd gotten her axe stuck in a piece of wood enough times to know it took time to pull it free, not to mention more grip strength.

She found herself wondering about targets. A blow to Rick's head would certainly kill him, though maybe not right away. And the skull was hollow. Would the blade lodge in there too tight for her to retrieve? That would leave her a sitting duck for Morgan, who would probably just take out his pistol and shoot her while she tried to wrench the axe out of Rick Halcomb's brain. Soft tissue would be better—like a young willow branch—but you needed a sharp axe for that, and this one didn't look like it had seen a stone in a while. Morgan was squatting next to the open stove again, staring at it like it was TV or something. His neck tilted to one side slightly, offering a tempting target. If it was sharp enough, maybe she could just take off his entire head . . . She pictured it—or what she imagined it would be like. Surely cutting off someone's head wouldn't be liberating, but in her mind, it was all of that and more.

She glanced sideways now, measuring the distance to the axe. She looked at Rick, who stood glued to the frosted window, then Morgan. Maybe she should kill Morgan first. They wouldn't expect that. The high side of that, she thought coldly, was that Rick would just kill her if she wasn't able to get him too. Morgan would eventually kill her if he was left alive, but not for a while. He had other plans. She could see it now in his eyes every time he looked at her. He was probably imagining them now. Drawing out his pleasure by pondering on what he would do, while he looked at the fire.

Sarah gave an involuntary nod, sending more pain down her neck. She squeezed the blanket tighter in her fist. No, she would take Morgan first. Dying was far from the worst thing there was. All she had to do was look at David to know the truth of that.

Another gust of wind hit hard, feeling like it was about to tear the roof off. A flurry of sparks blew out the open door of the stove. It happened every time the wind gusted, and Morgan stomped out any embers that hit the floor. Rick glanced over his shoulder, almost caught her looking at the axe. Then both men resumed their vigils of fire and ice.

Another gust rattled the window.

Sarah released the corner of the blanket, using the palm of her hand to smooth it flat against the bunk.

Rick scratched more frost off the glass.

"I think she's here," he said, leaning close enough to touch the windowpane with his nose.

A dog yipped outside, setting Sarah on edge. Donna was coming. She had to move now.

Sarah rolled off the bed as soon as both men's attention was focused on the door. Morgan was still squatting by the fire, groaning, putting both hands on his knees to stand the way he always did. Brimming with relief and excitement, Rick put a hand on the doorknob, ready to go greet his wife.

He was closer. She'd have to hit him first.

Sarah swung the little axe with everything she had at the same moment he turned to give some last bit of instruction. The blade hit him just below the nose, stopping his words as it cut downward, bisecting his chin and then opening his windpipe from top to bottom before severing his jugular.

Her legs were wooden from sitting for so long, and she stumbled, carried away with the ferocity of the swing, burying the blade in the side of the wooden bed.

Rick Halcomb slumped to his knees, croaking in dismay, hand clutching his throat. Sarah turned away as he fell, struggling to free the axe.

Morgan Kilgore was on her in an instant.

"You little shit!"

He grabbed her by the hair and heaved her backward, away from the axe. Flailing, she slipped on the growing puddle of Rick's blood and fell face-first against the logs. Morgan left the axe where it was, hopelessly lodged in the wood, and turned to check on Rick. He cradled the dying man's head in his lap, looking up every few seconds at Sarah to make sure she didn't move. It was impossible to stanch the massive flow of blood. The axe had done its job too well. Rick Halcomb could not have survived if he'd fallen directly onto an emergency room table.

Morgan stood, wiping blood-covered hands on his shirt. "That man was my friend," he spat, seething with rage. "You worthless little whore, I'm—"

He stopped midsentence as more barking erupted outside. A contemptuous smile spread across his face. "That will be Donna," he whispered. He threw on his coat and hat, and dragged Sarah to her feet.

"Come on," he said, dragging her toward the door. "I'm going to help her with the dogs. You can explain how you just split Rick's face in half."

Sarah pedaled backward with her bare feet on the rough plank floor, attempting to pull away. He only pulled harder, nearly tearing her arm out of the socket.

"My shoes . . . What about a coat?"

"Forget 'em," Morgan said, flinging open the door to the raging blizzard. "We won't be—"

A white dog came out of the curtain of snow, free from any lines or sled. Another dog, darker, and colored like a small wolf, came next. Both were tentative, investigating.

"Something's not right." He pulled Sarah in front of him, like a shield, then reached inside the door, coming out with Rick's big rifle. "Donna!"

Squinting against the wind, Sarah thought she saw someone in the trees to her right. Morgan saw it too and turned to look.

"Donna!" he called again. "You all right?"

A bright light suddenly cut through the blowing snow directly ahead, casting long shadows among the trees. The growl of an oncoming ATV rumbled over the wail of the storm.

Morgan Kilgore came up on his toes like he'd just been shocked. His whole body stiffened. "This isn't right," he said again, a hoarse whisper now. He looked to the right, where they'd seen movement before, then ahead at the oncoming light. He was deciding what to do.

Sarah Mead gave him a nudge.

Chapter 45

Cutter watched from the back of the ATV as a man dragged a barefoot woman out of the house. She wore no coat or gloves. Birdie had thrown a couple of meat scraps at the door, causing the dogs to rush in snarling for food, luring the man outside. There was only one of them, which was not what Cutter had expected—but he'd learned long ago not to expect any particular scenario too often. It was much better to roll with the punches.

The man looked back and forth, called for Donna over the wind, and then reached around the doorjamb to come out with a rifle.

The woman suddenly threw her feet out from under her, falling out of the man's grasp and into the snow. Instead of reaching down to gain control of her, the man took one look at the approaching headlight and fled pell-mell into the trees.

The woman just sat there in the snow, dazed, looking out at nothing. Cutter relaxed a hair when no one else came out to secure her. He circled around, keeping the cabin between himself and the place where the man had disappeared.

One glance inside the cabin told him what had happened. Sarah Mead said the man's name was Morgan

Kilgore and he'd been on the verge of raping and killing her when they'd arrived. Birdie held her rifle close, and told Cutter to go.

And he did.

Tracking a man in the snow is simple. Following that man in the dark when he is armed is tricky business, especially since Cutter was teetering on the razor's edge of hypothermia. He felt and looked like Jack Nicholson in the last scene of *The Shining*, certain there were icicles hanging off his forehead. He moved quickly, his hand a frozen claw around Ned Jasper's .270 rifle. There was a round in the chamber, and three more in the magazine. If that wasn't enough, he'd resort to his pistols. The blowing snow helped to give Cutter some concealment, but Kilgore could easily just lie down in the snow and wait for him. Cold seeped deeper into Cutter's bones with every step, and he couldn't help but think he'd freeze to death before anyone had a chance to shoot him. For some reason, the thought of cheating Kilgore out of the opportunity made him laugh into the howling wind.

After he'd trudged through calf-deep snow for fifteen minutes, the trees began to thin. Kilgore was moving back to his right in a big arc, circling back the way he'd come. It was likely an unconscious move, common in people who ran without thinking. People who were lost often walked in circles, thinking all the while that they were walking out of their predicament. Cutter found a spot where Kilgore had indeed lain in wait in the snow. The imprint of his prone body told an easy-to-read story to someone who knew what to look for: splayed legs, elbows offset to reveal that he was behind a rifle rather than looking through a pair of binoculars. Thankfully, the bitter cold had forced the outlaw to keep moving instead of sitting still.

Cutter closed the distance about the time Kilgore realized he'd traveled in a big circle. He came out of the willows a hundred meters from the cabin, with Cutter another fifty meters behind him.

Cutter gave a shrill whistle to get his attention, postholing now through knee-deep snow.

The big .404 boomed as Kilgore spun and fired a snap shot. The round went wide, missing Cutter by a dozen yards. Still, the adrenaline of being downrange to gunfire gave his chilly bones a much-needed rush of warmth.

Cutter paused long enough to aim. Putting the crosshairs of Ned Jasper's scope on the gray spot that was Morgan Kilgore's chest. The shot kicked up snow at Kilgore's feet, sending him running again, this time for the safety of the cabin.

Cutter groaned, the cold coming back full force now as exhaustion chased away the effects of adrenaline. Kilgore had likely figured out it was just him out here. And now, with Kilgore running away, a shot was more problematic— if Cutter was even able to hit his target with his hands shaking so badly from the cold. He turned the scope power all the way down to 3X, the lowest setting, giving him less magnification but allowing a wider field of view and letting in more light.

Kilgore probably doubted anyone would shoot him in the back, but he didn't know Arliss Cutter. Cutter sat down crosslegged in the snow so he could steady his shivering body. There was no way Kilgore was getting back to the cabin with that rifle. Cutter welded his cheek to the cold stock of the rifle, aligning the crosshairs in the scant light, before releasing half a breath. Another miss. Kilgore was less than thirty yards from the cabin now, floundering in the deep snow.

Cutter chambered another round, and looked through the scope again. Both his shots had been low. This time, he aimed at the back of Morgan Kilgore's head.

Kilgore pitched forward at the shot, screaming and thrashing. Cutter chambered his last round and slogged forward, his rifle at low ready.

"Hands!" he yelled when he was twenty yards away. He could see the rifle barrel sticking up in the snow, but Kilgore could still easily have a pistol. "I said let me see your hands!" The rifle barrel jerked and twitched with his shivering muscles.

"You shot my leg off!" Kilgore yowled. "That's police brutality. You're not supposed to aim to wound."

"Oh, I meant to kill you," Cutter said, teeth chattering, his voice wobbly with cold. "But I'm c-c-cold, so my aim is a l-l-little off-f-f."

Chapter 46

Cutter used his belt as a makeshift tourniquet to tie off the rifle wound, then half dragged, half carried a subdued Morgan Kilgore back to the cabin. Shaking so bad he could hardly hold his head still, Cutter shucked off the frozen parka and got Birdie to help him replace the belt with a slightly better piece of cord. It was, in fact, the same cord that Kilgore and Halcomb had used to tie Sarah Mead's hands.

They'd tried to bring the dogs in the cabin, but all of them had stood with their noses to the door, waiting to be let back out, where they promptly buried themselves under drifts of snow. The woodstove was cranked up so high that it was just too hot for them inside.

Cutter wanted to crawl inside the stove, but instead spent a few minutes searching his prisoner and the area around the bunk where they laid him out. He'd seen too many good soldiers and law enforcement officers killed or hurt by people who looked near death.

Birdie and Sarah had already untied David and laid him out on the bed, nursing his wounds—which were major and many. His face was a bloody mess, but the serious wounds were internal. It seemed Rick Halcomb had gone after each organ one at a time, even going so far as to tie the poor kid backward to the chair to hammer his kidneys with repeated blows, getting tired on one before starting in on the other. Halcomb had taken his time, methodically moving to a new bunch of nerves when he'd overloaded any one spot. The brutality of the beating left a normally stoic Birdie near tears and Cutter sick to his stomach. Sarah, who'd witnessed much of the torture, appeared numb. A blessing, Cutter thought. It would all come crashing down around her soon enough.

Cutter doubted the kid would have lasted another hour in that chair, let alone another day. But with the lion's share of the damage internal, there was nothing to be done beyond making him comfortable until they could get him to a hospital. Cutter had seen people die from head trauma half as bad as David Mead's looked. If he lived, it was even money as to whether he'd have permanent brain damage or not.

Sarah had broken into tears when she thought she'd been rescued. Her tormentors were dead or in custody, but she and her husband were a far cry from being out of danger. It was a strange reality, with all the advances of the twenty-first century, that they all now had to sit tight in the same cabin where the Meads had spent the last three days in captivity. The radio and satellite phone had gone through the ice with the sled. Kilgore had a cell phone, which was worthless this far out. He told them Donna carried a satellite phone to communicate with the air service that was supposed to pick them up, but they hadn't used radios for fear that troopers or other people in the area would pick up the transmissions.

Birdie and Cutter had used much of the spare fuel for the ATV to get the fire going after they'd fallen through the ice. It wouldn't make it a quarter of the way back to the village. The lodge was closer, but not by much. Sending someone there would just put them in the same situation, but separated from the others.

The cabin protected them from the weather, but it was also a crime scene that needed to be preserved. Cutter covered Richard Halcomb's body with an old blanket, knowing the troopers would want to photograph it as it had originally fallen. The gaping wound in the man's face was a testament to Sarah Mead's tenacity and bravery. The axe was evidence too, but Cutter elected to pull it out of the bed frame before the troopers arrived. Survival took precedence over evidentiary value. They needed it to split wood so it would fit into the stove.

Birdie and Sarah spoke in whispers, Kilgore groaned on his bed. Cutter sat in a wooden chair beside the stove, using his grandfather's Barlow pocketknife to work on his carving while he thought.

The sheer helplessness made Cutter want to put his fist through a wall. They'd come all this way, braving the ice and mud and tears and blood, only to have to sit and watch David Mead die. The kid's kidneys would just shut down if he didn't get help beyond a school principal and an ex-soldier with a pocketknife and a plan. Sarah was ambulatory, but she was in more danger than she realized. Her broken teeth made anything but broth and soft crackers impossible to eat—and even then, she threw up most of what she took in. She was badly dehydrated and she needed nourishment now more than ever. A severely swollen jaw led Cutter to believe she probably had an abscess, something that had killed countless people throughout history and could prove deadly in her weakened condition.

They would be found, eventually, but David had hours, not days. Kilgore would go next, then Sarah, if the storm raged on more than two days. Birdie didn't say it to anyone but Cutter, but she'd seen these blizzards last the better part of a week.

At some point, the blizzard would let up and a search party would come out. Kilgore would certainly lose his leg if he didn't get to a doctor before too long, but that couldn't be helped. The first medical treatment available was going to David Mead—triage by how much you deserved it.

Three hours in, Birdie decided she was tired of nibbling on pilot bread.

Kilgore dozed on the bottom bunk, probably lapsing into shock. Birdie shook him awake and gestured to the door.

"Where's the caribou shoulder you took from the meat house? You got it hanging outside somewhere?"

Kilgore coughed, eyes heavy now. "What caribou shoulder?"

Cutter looked up from his carving. "The meat house at the lodge where you kidnapped the Meads."

"I don't know what you're talking about."

"Nice try," Birdie said. "We caught you here with them—"

Kilgore swallowed hard, grunting as he came up on one elbow. "I'm not denying I was at the lodge. Hell, I'll even admit to giving the girl a whack in the head after Rick shot that big guy with that humongous rifle of his. But I'm telling you we didn't take any caribou shoulder. Why would I lie about that?"

Birdie motioned Cutter to the door. "The Meads need some soup," she whispered, nodding toward the ATV outside. "I was hoping I could find some meat I didn't have to chop with the same axe that killed that guy on the floor."

She'd insisted on cutting off another backstrap and a large chunk of back fat from James Jimmy's caribou before they left the campsite. It was now an icy block tied to the back of the fourwheeler.

"I'll go get it," Cutter said, dreading another second in that biting wind. He wondered if hypothermia was like heat stroke—when you got it once, you were more prone to the effects of it a second time.

Birdie put a hand on his arm, her voice still hushed. "If they didn't take the shoulder when they kidnapped the Meads, then who took it?"

Cutter rubbed his eyes with the heels of his hands. This was on the low end of the scale of mysteries he had the energy to solve. "Birdie—"

"Remember those tracks Vitus Paul told us about?" She gave a little I-told-you-so nod. "Maybe that was the Hairy Man and he took the shoulder."

Cutter chuckled, exhausted. "Maybe it was that old lady with the long toenails."

"Now you're just being crazy." Birdie grinned. "You gotta admit it's weird, though."

"I'm sure there's a more plausible explanation," he said, going out the door. Though when he watched the storm whip through the shadowed forest beyond the ATV, he half expected to see the Hairy Man.

Ten minutes later, Birdie had a caribou soup heating in a dented pot on top of the woodstove. She found salt and pepper in Halcomb and Kilgore's meager larder, along with a couple of ramen noodle mixes, which she added to the broth along with a good quarter of the backstrap and a handful of creamy white fat. There was some hair in it too, but Birdie said that was not out of the norm in bush soup.

Cutter didn't care. He was so hungry he would have eaten more eyeball fat.

Cutter went back to carving on his wolf-dog cottonwood root while he waited for the soup to boil. Birdie sat at the little table preparing the rest of the backstrap for later use, in case they ended up being here for more than a few days.

She looked up suddenly, her knife in one hand, a chunk of bloody caribou in the other.

"What about that thing in the meat house?"

Across the room beside her husband, Sarah Mead gave an audible shudder. "Are you talking about that design on the concrete?"

"Yeah." Birdie glared at Kilgore again. "The blood circle. What was that all about, anyway? Something to throw us off the trail? Make us think it was a cult or something."

Kilgore tried to roll onto his side, but much of his lower leg stayed in place on the mattress, putting it at an unnatural angle and bringing a grimace to the man's face. "You're talking out your ass, lady," he said through gritted teeth. "I got no earthly idea about any blood circle."

"I might," Cutter said, looking up from his carving.

He found a piece of twine about a foot long and tied it to the bloodiest piece of caribou from Birdie's pile. Even Kilgore craned his head to watch as Cutter suspended meat at the end of the twine over a relatively clean portion of the table, about a foot from Birdie's face.

"The meat shed had screened windows," he said.

"Right," Sarah said. "To allow for air flow."

Cutter nodded to the caribou pendulum and winked at Birdie. "Blow on it. Softly, but enough to make it move."

She leaned across the table and blew a puff of air on the swinging chunk of meat. A drop of blood plopped to the table. Cutter held the end of the string steady in the same spot, while the meat swung slowly ahead of Birdie's breath, spinning and unspinning, as it made slow arcs. Drop after drop of bright red blood fell to the table, creating an almost perfect design of concentric dots and circles.

"It was the wind," Birdie said, wide-eyed, obviously impressed. She took the chunk of meat and returned it to her pile. "So you know what caused the blood circle. But what happened to the meat?"

"Sorry." Cutter grinned. "I got nothin'."

Birdie wiped her hands on an old rag that was hanging on a peg by the window, then pointed at the carving with her chin.

"Looks sorta like Smudge," she said.

Cutter held the piece of cottonwood out at arm's length. "You think?"

"Is that what you were going for?"

He stuffed the carving back in his pocket and gave a halfhearted shrug. "I go for whatever the wood gives me."

"You sure you're not Yup'ik?"

Cutter folded the little Barlow.

"This belonged to my grandfather," he said, pushing the knife toward her. "I'd like you to have it."

"I . . . I couldn't."

"It's something we do," Cutter said, "give something of value to our family and loved ones—like your nose kisses."

"*Kunik*," Birdie said. She took the pocketknife and touched it to her nose. "Thank you."

"Thank *you*," Cutter said. "I'm carrying around a few secrets of my own. Getting to know you taught me that people can get past some truly horrible events—"

"Ha," Birdie scoffed. "I'm not past anything."

"But you're moving in that direction." He winked at her again, like Grumpy would have. "You're fighting on . . ."

The storm didn't calm enough to see the sky until a little after noon. Birdie fed the woodstove a steady diet of green spruce boughs along with the dry wood, giving any trooper pilots plenty of smoke to home in on with their search.

Five and a half hours after they'd arrived at the cabin, Cutter heard a plane fly overhead. An hour later the *brap* of snow machine engines echoed through the trees. Three Alaska State Troopers and one very worried Polynesian deputy US Marshal approached the house slowly on foot, bringing their machines in only when Cutter went outside and waved, letting them know it was safe.

Lola stayed behind with Cutter and Birdie while the troopers used sleds to transport both the Meads and Morgan Kilgore to an airstrip a quarter mile away for pickup.

Cutter was glad to hear that the judge had gone back to Bethel on the return flight with Ned Jasper and a traveling doctor.

"Jolene?" Birdie asked, twisting the dirty red cloth in her hands.

"She's great," Lola said. "Sascha Green won't be giving you any more trouble for at least ten years, probably a lot longer since he qualifies for career criminal status now. He's had his three strikes, so he could very well go away for good."

Lola recounted the arrest like she was calling play-by-play at a ball game. Birdie Pingayak hung on every word.

Chapter 47

Lieutenant Warr allowed Birdie and her daughter to accompany the deputies and remaining attorneys on the troopers' Caravan back to Bethel. They arrived in time to catch the evening Alaska Airlines flight back to Anchorage. There would be statements to be given, but those could wait until the following day, when everyone had had a hot shower and a good meal.

Aften Brooks was at the airport too, having gotten permission from Birdie to miss a couple days of school so she could fly to Anchorage and visit Sarah Mead in the hospital.

Judge Markham shook hands with Lieutenant Warr at the airport before going through security, thanking him for the most interesting trip he'd had in . . . well, ever. The arbitration was rescheduled for mid-January so as not to interfere with Eastern Orthodox Christmas. Lola about spewed Diet Coke out her nose when the judge promised Jolene that he was going to request Deputies Teariki and Cutter as his security team on his next visit.

Birdie and Cutter had said most of their goodbyes at the cabin, both knowing things would be moving a million miles an hour once they returned to civilization.

She waved as Cutter and Lola were ushered past security and out a side door, since they were both armed. Jolene stood close, hand on Birdie's shoulder, the way she used to do before she'd grown too cool to hang out with her mom.

"Lola told me all about Sascha," Jolene said out of the blue.

Birdie swallowed hard. "I'm so sorry," she managed to say.

Jolene scoffed. "You got nothing to be sorry for, Mom. She didn't tell me exactly what happened. Just that it was really bad, and it wasn't your fault."

Birdie released a slow breath, bracing herself. "Do you *want* to know what happened?"

"I can guess," Jolene said. "I mean, I'm here, right. And I remember seeing all the scars when you took me swimming at that hotel in Fairbanks when I was little."

"I can tell you if you want," Birdie said.

"Tell me if *you* want," Jolene said. "Someday. I'm sorry it happened to you. But I'm glad you're my mom."

"Me too," Birdie said. "Me too."

"Lola also talked to me about sex."

Birdie laughed at the suddenness of that. "She did, did she?

"She had to, so I'd understand what happened with Sascha. I mean, I already know the basics—"

"You do?"

"Mom! Of course I do. You've told me the basics. The point is, you don't have to worry about Sascha. Lola told me he's just the liquid you used to make my soup."

"That sounds like an interesting conversation."

"It really was." Jolene chuckled. "She's like talking to a big sister or something. You know she's Maori? They're the ones who do that haka war dance I showed you on YouTube. She asked me about your tattoo."

"Why?"

Jolene shrugged. "Just interested, I guess. She has a Maori tattoo on her shoulder. It's a really cool design of a shark. She had it cut in on the island her family comes from—the old way. Said it hurt 'like a bitch.' I told her your *tavlugun* was stitched in with a needle and thread. She said you were badass."

"Is that right?" Birdie said. Her face flushed.

"I told her I was thinking of getting one like yours, skin-stitched on my chin—like you and Great-Grandma."

Everything Birdie thought to say sounded hollow, silly, trite. She wanted to scoop up her little girl, to laugh out loud. Instead, she stood quietly, stoically, in the terminal and watched out the window as Cutter and Lola walked across the tarmac toward the Alaska Airlines jet.

Jolene gave her a soft nudge with an elbow. "You are, you know, Mom."

Birdie looked over at her. "I am what?"

"A badass," Jolene said, smiling softly.

Tears welling in her eyes, Birdie Pingayak pressed her forehead and nose against her daughter's cheek and breathed.

Epilogue

Two days after Cutter and the others returned from Bethel, Anchorage Police Canine Zeus was buried on a small plot of land belonging to Theron Jensen's father in Chugiak, a few miles north of Anchorage proper. The procession of marked police cruisers and other law enforcement vehicles was a half mile long.

Mim brought the kids and met Cutter there, standing beside him as the rest of the procession parked and the officers made their way to the mound of dark earth in a field otherwise white with new snow.

Chief Phillips had come as well, and stood with Lola Teariki a few rows back in the crowd of almost two hundred people. Both Jensen and Zeus were extremely well loved and everyone there had had some kind of interaction with the team, working a canine track on a runner, searching a building, or just saying hello at the station.

"I'm glad you came, Chief," Lola whispered.

"Sad deal," Phillips said. "I'll deny it if you tell anyone, but I'm damned glad Cutter wasn't too gentle when he took down that son of a bitch Twig Ripley."

"Twig fought him," Lola said. "Cutter used the force necessary to—"

"I told you I am glad," Phillips said. She gave a somber

nod. "Your report on Sascha Green was interesting. Sounds like you're no stranger to using the appropriate amount of force yourself."

"He punched the judge," Lola said.

"You thought Green was nothing but a CVB warrant. You didn't do a background workup before you went out there, did you?"

"No," Lola admitted. "But I called back from Stone Cross and had Nancy run him for me when we started hearing his name. I won't make that mistake again."

"Good." Phillips nodded thoughtfully. "He's a fighter. It was good you knew that when you were ready to arrest him."

"I'm kinda glad he fought," Lola admitted.

"I understand," the chief said. "Just remember, you can convince virtually anyone they need to fight you if you look at 'em just right. The trick is using that power judiciously."

"Gotcha," Lola said. "Speaking of the judge, I never did hear what happened between the judge's secretary and Cutter that pissed the judge off so much."

"Gayle?" Phillips smiled. "You'll have to ask Arliss about that. Or the judge. You can ask him if you want."

"Markham's a good guy," Lola said. "But I think I'll pass on that."

Cutter had a nephew on each hand, Michael on his right, Matthew on his left. They were both quiet, looking as though they might break into tears at any moment. Losing a dog was part of growing up, but Cutter wondered if the memorial was too much, this close to the death of their father. Mim had insisted they attend together.

An honor guard of four officers in dark blue Anchorage PD class A uniforms carried the small wooden casket to the grave and laid it gently across the support ropes. The chief of APD said a few words, as did the mayor, and the Eagle River woman who had donated the money to the department to sponsor Zeus's training and upkeep. A piper from a local pipe-and-drum corps played "Amazing Grace." Associated with police funerals, the song always brought a tear to Cutter's eye—and he was not the only one.

When the song was finished, a few officers walked up and placed challenge coins or other mementos on top of the casket to honor the fallen police dog. Cutter gave a small cottonwood carving of a dog to Task Force Officer Nancy Alvarez, who passed it to her boyfriend. Officer Theron Jensen nodded in gratitude, and then placed the wooden figure on top of his partner's casket with the other items. The chief then stepped forward and set a handheld police radio upright at the foot of the casket.

Even the wind seemed to fall quiet as a female dispatcher's voice crackled loud and clear over the radio.

"*K9 Zeus.*"

Silence.

"Anchorage Police Dispatch calling K9 Zeus."

More silence.

The dispatcher's voice trembled now as she tried in vain to hold it together.

"K9 Zeus, no response. K9 Zeus is out of service. God speed, dear friend. You are gone, but not forgotten."

The twins were bawling by the time the end-of-watch call was over.

"I'm so sorry," Cutter whispered, wiping away a tear.

Mim spoke between her own sobs. "If you don't cry

when your friend's dog dies, then you're not much of a man."

"I never heard that Grumpy Rule," Cutter said.

"It's a Mim Man-Rule . . . Check that, a Mim Human-Being Rule."

A rare smile spread across Cutter's face. "I just love you, Mim," he said, hoping it sounded nonchalant, brother-in-law-like.

She reached to touch his arm. "I just love *you*, Arliss Cutter—and don't you forget it."

Grumpy Cutter's Cowboy Chili Pie

2 pounds ground beef
1 onion, diced
3 cloves garlic, minced
1 tablespoon oil
2 tablespoons flour
2 tablespoons chili powder
2 teaspoons dried oregano
1 teaspoon ground cumin
1 7-ounce can diced green chilies
1 28-ounce can diced tomatoes with juice
2 to 3 cups grated cheddar cheese
Salt and pepper to taste

For the corn dumplings:
1 8½-ounze package corn muffin mix
2 eggs
⅓ cup sour cream
1 12-ounce can whole kernel corn, drained

Cook beef, onion, and garlic in oil on top of stove, in a cast iron or other oven-safe frying pan, until meat is done. Drain off excess fat.

Preheat oven to 375° F. Combine flour, chili powder, oregano, and cumin, then sprinkle over meat. Stir, cooking mixture over medium heat for one minute

Mix in green chilies and tomatoes with juice. Cover with shredded cheese and set aside.

Mix eggs and sour cream into corn muffin mix until dry ingredients are moistened. Fold in drained corn.

Space rounced spoonfuls of corn dumpling mixture evenly on top of cheese. Bake in oven 20 to 30 minutes—until corn dumplings are browned and mixture is bubbling

Remove from oven and let stand 10 minutes.

Acknowledgments

Writers are like mollusks. We strain the world around us for stories and characters that we can use later to flesh out the tales we want to tell. Over the last two decades in Alaska, I've had the opportunity to know and work alongside astounding law enforcement officers from Anchorage Police Department, Alaska State Troopers (including AST pilots), Village Public Safety Officers, my own agency, the United States Marshals Service, and a host of other agencies that have a footprint in The Great Land. The characters in *Stone Cross*, while not based on any one individual, are certainly inspired by many of these stellar people. The bad guys, and the fights, too, are inspired by people I've arrested, and the violence that happens in rural Alaska virtually every day.

The forty-ninth state makes a wonderful if somewhat fickle character. There is a callousness that goes with the cold and wideopen spaces that lends itself to adventure—and terror. Out of necessity, I've touched on some of the darker issues facing rural Alaska. The problems are real—but so are the wonderful people and rich cultures. Some of the happiest moments of my life have been spent huddled around a stove, driving a river boat, or riding snow machines with friends in the Alaska bush.

Over the years, my dear friend Brian Krosschell (a talented rural teacher) has guided me to villages on the Kuskokwim, Yukon, and Kobuk rivers. His wife, Lila, welcomed me into their home, feeding me seal oil, tomcod, and muktuk, among other traditional foods. My friend Perry Barr took me up and down the river when we were both still wearing badges—inviting me to his fish camp on our off time and sharing his smoked salmon strips, which are like gold. James Hoelsher and his family hosted me in their village countless times, and then invited me into their home, giving me salmon, homemade agutaq, and friendship.

The folks at Northern Knives in Anchorage don't just help with the Jericho Quinn books. Their shop provides a place where I can sit among friends and talk—about blades, or whatever.

As always, my friend and martial arts instructor, Jujitsu Master Ty Cunningham, provided wise counsel and comment when it came to fight scenes and conflict in general.

Robin Rue, with Writers House, is the best literary agent I've ever even heard of. My editor at Kensington, Gary Goldstein, took the time away from his busy schedule to come visit me in Alaska and see what all the fuss was about. A real "author's editor," he's a good guy to have in my corner.

The teachers who serve in the remote villages of the Alaska bush are an adventurous lot. I've spent many nights in a sleeping bag rolled out on a library or classroom floor, often sharing a cup of cocoa or tea with these bush teachers while I listened to their stories late into the evening. My hat is off to them for what they do. It's too difficult to be only about the money. I asked a young teacher once if he thought it took something special to be a teacher in the bush. He smiled and said, "I think it takes something special to be a teacher."

He's right. My wife, Vicky, is a teacher. Without her guidance and encouragement, I'm sure I would have stopped writing a long time ago.

Connect with

Visit us online at
KensingtonBooks.com
to read more from your favorite authors, see books
by series, view reading group guides, and more.

for sneak peeks, chances to win books and prize packs,
and to share your thoughts with other readers.

facebook.com/kensingtonpublishing
twitter.com/kensingtonbooks

Tell us what you think!

To share your thoughts, submit a review,
or sign up for our eNewsletters, please visit:
KensingtonBooks.com/TellUs.